the
Italian
Vineyard

BOOKS BY ANITA CHAPMAN

The Florence Letter
The Tuscan Diary

The Venice Secret

ANITA CHAPMAN

the Italian Vineyard

bookouture

Published by Bookouture in 2025

An imprint of Storyfire Ltd.
Carmelite House
50 Victoria Embankment
London EC4Y 0DZ

www.bookouture.com

The authorised representative in the EEA is Hachette Ireland
8 Castlecourt Centre
Dublin 15 D15 XTP3
Ireland
(email: info@hbgi.ie)

Copyright © Anita Chapman, 2025

Anita Chapman has asserted her right to be identified as the author of this work.

All rights reserved. No part of this publication may be reproduced, stored in any retrieval system, or transmitted, in any form or by any means, electronic, mechanical, photocopying, recording or otherwise, without the prior written permission of the publishers.

ISBN: 978-1-80550-002-5
eBook ISBN: 978-1-80550-001-8

This book is a work of fiction. Names, characters, businesses, organizations, places and events other than those clearly in the public domain, are either the product of the author's imagination or are used fictitiously. Any resemblance to actual persons, living or dead, events or locales is entirely coincidental.

For my readers

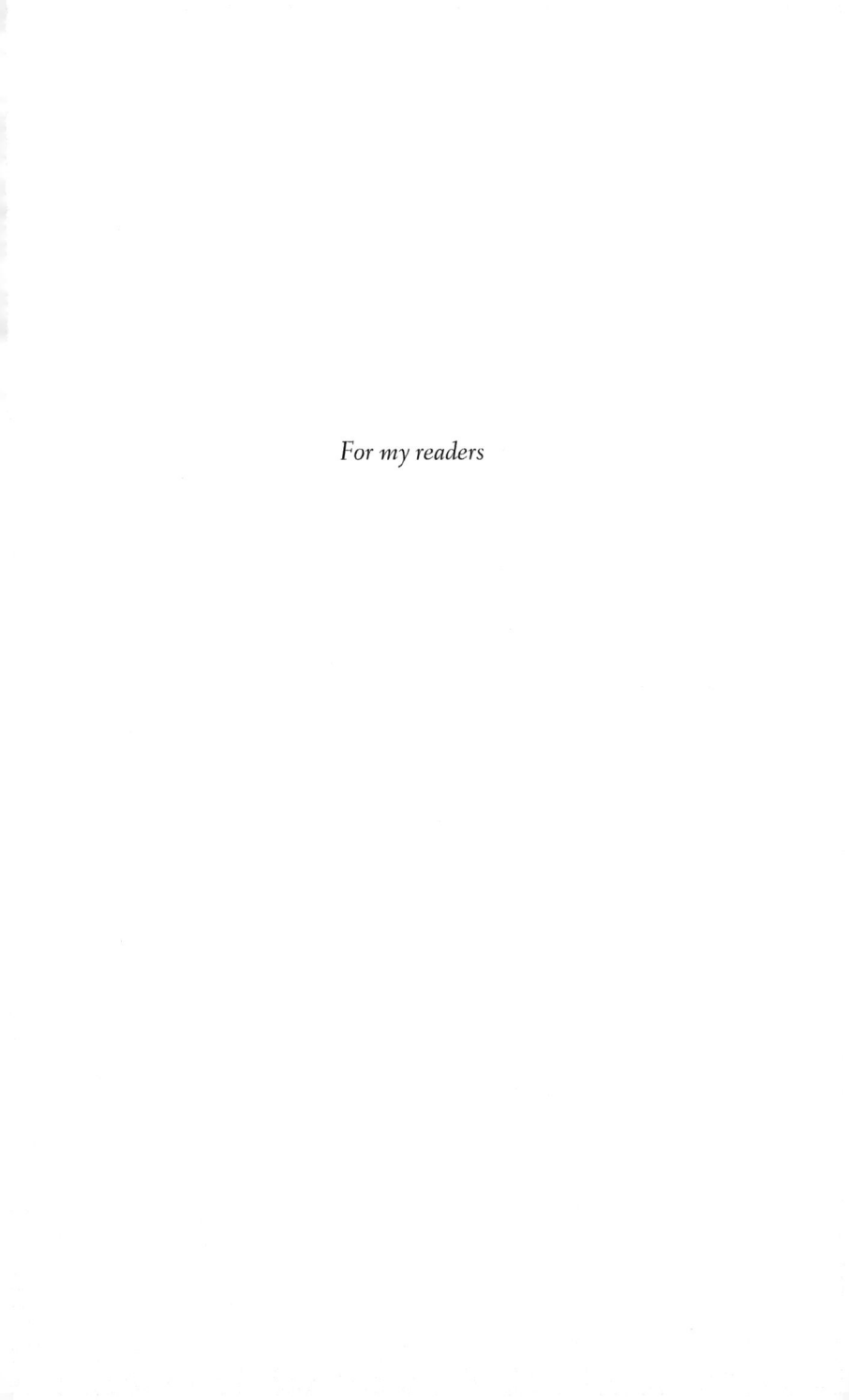

PROLOGUE

~~~~

A VINEYARD NEAR VERONA, AUGUST 1939

The woman pushed open the shutters and was blessed with the most breathtaking view – one she'd fallen in love with at first sight, since arriving from England only days before. Beyond the terrazza and the tall, slender cypress trees were neat rows of vines – oh so many of them – leading down to the valley where the early-morning mist hung in the air. The grapes picked from those vines produced the most sumptuous wine she'd ever had the pleasure to sip from a glass – with notes of chocolate, cinnamon and cherries. And in the distance was her beloved Verona – the birthplace of *Romeo and Juliet* and the city that had stolen her heart. She stood at the French doors, her white cotton nightdress billowing gently in the breeze, and made out the River Adige and the bridges providing a crossing from one side to the other. The river twisted and wound its way amongst the medieval buildings, church spires rising into the deep-blue sky. She drew in her breath as she realised how lucky she was to have experienced this paradise – a magical place that had brought her back to life after rather a tumultuous time. For this Italian vineyard had given her immense joy in a matter of days.

A smile passed her lips as her eyes fell upon the wooden box on the dressing table with its white marble top swirled with grey. She'd placed it there the night before, somewhat inebriated from all the wine tasting, and fatigued after a long but delightful dinner. They'd indulged in bowls of freshly made tagliatelle with a rich butter sauce and slices of white truffle – hunted by pigs in the nearby woods – and the pasta was followed by the tenderest of steaks that melted in the mouth. And then ice cream, churned from milk taken from goats on the neighbouring farm, drizzled with honey from the hives in the kitchen garden, and scattered with walnuts.

What on earth was she to do with something so precious? She picked up the box, made from the finest oak, and ran a hand over the words branded on the top, dipping a finger into the indentations – *Vineria di San Martino* – in brown cursive letters. Underneath was a simple drawing of Villa Romeo, the eighteenth-century residence of her hosts. And then she undid the clasp and slowly lifted the lid. There it was, nestled in a bed of straw – a bottle of her favourite of all the wines sampled on the vineyard – Amarone 1936, an exceptional year for the Veneto region of Italy. A rich and full-bodied red wine, it had been matured for three years in eighteenth-century oak barrels, and only recently bottled. Coveted by many, only a handful of these boxes remained in the cellar, but the hostess wanted her to take one home as a keepsake – to remind her of the place she'd fallen in love with. She could drink the wine upon her return, of course, or she could store it in a cool place, and on its side so the cork did not dry out. With each year the wine would continue to mature, tasting richer and richer on the tip of the tongue. How long should one leave it for? The hostess had suggested she open it to celebrate a special occasion, with someone she cared about deeply.

The woman hadn't yet decided what she would do with this thoughtful souvenir. But she would certainly ensure it was transported safely back to England. And then she would store the box as advised until that opportunity to celebrate arose. She would not open this bottle without considering carefully when was the absolute best time to savour this fine wine – a gift to cherish.

CHAPTER 1

KATE

COPELEY PARK, SURREY HILLS, OCTOBER 2015

As I passed through the black and gold gates, I was struck by the sight of beech trees lining the main drive, in all their autumn glory, the leaves shining like gold coins in the late-afternoon sun. I hadn't been back for a while and a mix of emotions consumed me all at once. Joy as I took in the beautiful scene that lay before me, recalling childhood memories of running across never-ending fields on long summer days, and building dens in the woods. But sadness also wrapped itself around me like a musty moth-eaten blanket, because being here wasn't the same with Mum gone. Tears pricked my eyes, and I blinked them back. Now was not the time to be crying. I swallowed, and looked back at the beech trees, and the resplendent carpet of leaves beneath, and then at the North Downs beyond.

Inhaling, I fought to push the melancholy thoughts from my mind, and as the drive twisted round I was distracted by the main house, painted in lemon yellow, as it came into view. As majestic as ever, it belonged in a Jane Austen novel. The house at Copeley Park, my childhood home, had been built in the eighteenth century by the third Duke of Dorking after he returned from a grand tour to Italy with paintings and statues and busts of Greek gods. On one occasion he'd taken his head gardener, and they'd brought back vine cuttings.

White pillars stood at the front of the house, with steps leading to the front door. All around were rows of vines, as far as the eye could see, and in the distance the Gothic tower rose into the sky, dominating the landscape. For the estate had many eighteenth-century features, including a man-made grotto and a temple dedicated to Bacchus, the Roman god of wine. Copeley Park boasted one of a handful of vineyards in the Surrey Hills, and produced award-winning Copeley wine.

Before reaching the arch next to Porters' Lodge, I turned down the single-track lane leading to Keeper's Cottage, where my great-grandmother, Granny Charlotte, lived. I always dreaded driving along this lane as the hedgerows were several feet high and aggravated my claustrophobia – there was barely enough room for two cars to comfortably pass each other. I reached a T-junction where a sign pointed to Rosemary Cottage in one direction, and to Keeper's Cottage in the other. I took a right, and was relieved when Granny's cottage appeared after the next bend. Although I'd done my best to stay in touch with her over the past year, I hadn't been to the main house since Christmas, when Dad had introduced us to his French fiancée, Emilie. They'd met skiing at Val-d'Isère and I'd been horrified to discover that she was fifteen years his junior, only five years older than me.

Since receiving Granny's letter a few days earlier, asking me to visit at my earliest convenience, I'd been feeling guilty about not seeing her since the spring. Well into her nineties now, she wasn't getting any younger. She did still have her marbles though, and attempted the newspaper crossword every day.

And she would take her golden Labrador, Monty, out for short walks sometimes. I wasn't sure why she'd summoned me – perhaps she knew her time was almost up and wanted to see me before it was too late. The encounter was likely to leave me in pieces. I pulled into the drive and got out of the car, the aroma of wood smoke coming from one of the chimneys familiar and instantly comforting. It smelt like home.

Keeper's Cottage belonged on a chocolate box with its Georgian sash windows and duck-egg shutters. The door, standing at the centre, was painted in duck egg to match, and it came complete with a porch, the tiles covered in emerald moss. I lifted the latch on the gate, and it squeaked as I pushed it open. Closing it behind me, I walked up the path, and passed through the front garden – the grass on the lawn was luscious from a recent bout of rain. A few roses still bloomed on bushes in the flowerbeds. I leant forward and inhaled the sweet scent of one that was fully open with large red velvety petals. Nature had a habit of encouraging me to get lost in the moment and being here brought a sense of peace and calm that I'd forgotten about.

I rapped the brass knocker and waited. Having lived in London for several years, the near silence of the countryside was more noticeable to me than ever – all I could hear was the wistful sound of a robin singing in a nearby tree, the persistent barking of a dog on Manor Farm, and the swishing of the river that ran along the back garden.

Granny's carer, Jane – who was a kind of modern-day lady's maid, PA and companion all rolled into one – opened the door with a smile.

'Do come in, Kate,' she said, and I stepped over the threshold.

Jane led me down the hall, past paintings of country scenes and framed black-and-white photographs of Granny in her heyday. She'd been a glamorous woman with a svelte figure and high cheekbones, and looked like a Hollywood star from one of those old movies. I passed through a door at the end, into the drawing room. And there she was, sitting in her favourite armchair beside the fire, logs crackling in the hearth. Monty lay on the rug, fast asleep, and couldn't have looked more content. Granny wore a pastel-blue dress to match her eyes. A cream pashmina, no doubt woven from cashmere, was draped around her shoulders. Her outfit was accessorised with a string of pearls and matching drop earrings. She liked to dress up for visitors, for her wardrobe was crammed with carefully selected clothes collected over the decades.

'Hello, Granny,' I said, bending down to kiss her on the cheek. She was so small and slight, even smaller than me – for I was petite – and seemed so fragile she might break. I was instantly hit by a waft of the amber scent she liked to wear.

'Dear Kate, it is so good to see you. Jane, bring us some tea, will you please?'

'Certainly,' Jane said.

I took the armchair opposite Granny.

'I was sad to hear about you and Spencer,' she said.

I hadn't seen her since our split in the summer, three months previously. I was embarrassed about the whole episode, and worried she was disappointed in me for only sticking out my marriage for two years.

'Yes, it's a shame, but we both agreed we weren't meant to be.'

'Well, one must make the most of one's life and spending it with the wrong person isn't a good use of one's time. I do admire you for being so brave, Kate.'

'Thank you, Granny,' I said, breathing a sigh of relief. Her approval meant so much to me.

'I'm sure you'll find someone more suitable before long. Have you met the new head gardener yet?' she said.

'No, I haven't been here much since Christmas.'

'Ah yes, you must sort out all that nonsense with your

father. But, more importantly, you should meet this young man. He lives at Rosemary Cottage. I've met him when walking Monty, and he seems like a decent chap – handsome and charming he is too. I can introduce you, if you like...'

Granny playing the role of matchmaker brought a smile to my face. I shook my head.

'I'm not sure that would be the best idea at the moment, but thanks for the offer.'

'Why ever not?'

'Because... I don't exactly feel like meeting anyone new right now.'

'No doubt you'd have plenty in common. He's around your age and could be a friend for you, if nothing else.'

I racked my brains, trying to come up with a way to change the subject – making new friends wasn't something I felt like doing. I'd only have to explain about my break-up and everything else that had happened in recent years. So when Jane came through the door, I was relieved. She carried a tray with teapot, jug of milk and blue cups and saucers with flower patterns on them. Granny gestured for me to do the pouring, and so I filled two cups, and set them on the coffee table between us.

She leant forwards, placing her wrinkled fingers around the handle of her cup, and looked at me over her glasses.

'Now for the reason you're here – I want to give you something rather special.'

Ooh, what could it be?

'That sounds exciting. What is it?'

'Jane informed me that it's your thirtieth birthday tomorrow.'

I wasn't looking forward to my big birthday and had nothing arranged. It was on a Monday – not really the best day to celebrate. I'd planned to get stuck into some client work until the day was over and I didn't have to think about the milestone any more.

Nodding, I said, 'Yes, it is.'

'Well, I have a unique gift to mark this significant birthday.'

She picked up a handbell and shook it. Jane came in, holding a narrow wooden box, and passed it to me.

'Go on. Open it, then,' Granny said.

The box appeared to be quite old and made from oak. The words 'Vineria di San Martino' were branded on the top in a beautiful chocolate-brown font, the letters 'V', 'S' and 'M' swirling and curvaceous. I undid the latch and slowly lifted the lid. Inside lay a bottle of red wine, nestled in a bed of straw. I put a hand to my mouth when I saw that the label said: *Amarone 1936*. I knew enough about wine to be certain that this bottle was probably worth a small fortune. That was, as long as it hadn't turned rancid.

'Wow, this is wonderful. Thank you... where did you get it from?'

'That bottle of wine is very dear to me. It comes from a vineyard in Verona that I visited just before the war.'

'Oh, Granny,' I said, my voice croaking. I couldn't help being touched by her generous gesture. She was choosing to give this bottle, which must have sentimental value, to me.

'Where have you been keeping this?'

'The truth is, I'd forgotten all about it until recently when I asked Jane to go down to the cellar and have a bit of a clear-out. I didn't want to leave your father with all my belongings when I kick the bucket... and she stumbled upon this box, in the drawer of an old dresser. And when she showed it to me, I instantly thought of how it would make a delightful gift for you.'

'This bottle of wine is indeed something to treasure, Granny.'

'If you get the chance, perhaps you could visit the vineyard where it came from – relive some of my memories for me. I could pay for you to go if you wanted?'

'What, really, Granny?'

She nodded.

This was very generous, but I wasn't sure if I had time to go away, especially with all the client work I had on.

'That's lovely of you, thank you, but things are so busy at the moment.'

'There's always time if you are willing enough to find it. Why don't you think about it? Who knows, it could bring you luck in love too – Verona is the city of *Romeo and Juliet*, after all.' She winked at me, and I rolled my eyes with a smile. She really needed to give the idea of me meeting someone new a rest.

I lifted the bottle out of the box and turned it over to look at the label on the back – there were a few words in Italian. But then I saw something else in the box – a piece of paper peeking out from the bed of straw. Was this a note or something?

'Granny...'

'Yes, dear?'

'What's this?'

'What's what?'

I picked up the piece of paper, folded in two, and opened it.

'I think it's a note from someone.'

Her face scrunched up, and she seemed anxious about my discovery.

'Oh! Really? I had no idea that was there. What does it say?'

My dearest Charlotte,

I hope that we can share this bottle of wine to celebrate my return, as we agreed. But if by some chance I don't come back, I urge you to drink it anyway, and to think of me, and the wonderful memories we made together in Verona.

Love always,

B

Who on earth was 'B'? A friend? A relative? A... lover? My great-grandfather had been called Winston. Did Granny not go to Verona with him? And if not, who was this mysterious 'B' she went there with...?

CHAPTER 2

LADY CHARLOTTE

COPELEY PARK, MARCH 1939

It was an odd feeling, waking up in my new abode. I'd only ever known life at Rodene Hall in Cheshire with Mama, Papa and my two younger sisters, Mary and Grace. And then, it all came back to me. My wedding day, at St John's Church in the Surrey village of Copeley. Walking down the aisle with our families, friends and acquaintances filling the pews, all eyes on me, the bride – as the organist launched into 'The Arrival of the Queen of Sheba' – carrying a bouquet of yellow roses, violets and salmon-pink sweet peas. It was overwhelming being the centre of attention, and I desperately wanted the sham of a wedding ceremony to be over and done with. Winston wore a gloomy look on his face as I stepped towards him, my arm threaded through Papa's. My future husband couldn't have looked less thrilled as I walked down the aisle, and the feeling was sadly mutual. When I reached the altar, he attempted a smile, the corners of his lips slightly upturned, and his beady brown eyes displayed no affection towards me whatsoever. I reciprocated, doubting he could make out much through the veil covering my face.

We stood side by side before the vicar, and said our vows in turn, my chest tightening as I repeated the words, 'love, honour and obey'. I didn't wish to do any of those things with this man I barely knew, and who was almost twice my age – for I was only nineteen years old. I said, 'I do', and removed my engagement ring so that Winston could slide the gold band encrusted with diamonds onto my finger. I put the sapphire engagement ring that had belonged to his grandmother in front of it. I didn't give Winston a wedding band in return – the signet ring on his pinky finger, bearing the Clarkson family crest, mattered to him more than any symbol of our union. He then lifted my veil, in a clumsy fashion, and leant forward to press his lips to mine. I found myself repulsed by his moustache, as bushy as a squirrel's tail, as it brushed my face. And worse than that was the vile odour of alcohol and tobacco on his breath. Not a jot of electricity passed between us. A dull ache rested in the pit of my stomach throughout the whole service for I wished that Rupert – Papa's protégé at the railway company he owned – was standing there in Winston's place. How I'd pleaded with Papa to allow me to marry him – for he was handsome, and we'd grown up together in the same village. But when the offer of marriage had come from Winston's father, the Duke of Dorking, after lunch at a London club, Papa had been delighted to accept on my behalf. For it had always been his ambition – while working his way up from clerk to the owner of a railway company – to enter the aristocracy. Papa wanted his descendants to have titles – that had been his intention all along. He was nouveau riche and often looked down upon by dukes and marquises and earls – although they socialised with him because of his vast wealth and Mama's ability to throw spectacular parties at Rodene Hall – and he'd worked hard to provide his daughters with what he saw as a promising future.

There was a knock at the door, and my lady's maid, Gwen, entered, carrying a tray.

'Good morning, milady,' she said, with a smile as she emphasised the word 'milady'. For I had woken up with the newly acquired title of countess.

Gwen, who was originally from a mining village in Wales, had come with me from Rodene Hall. Despite being aware of my concerns about the marriage, she was doing her best to go along with it all. Most women would be overjoyed to wake up as a countess, and to have entered such a world of privilege. I knew that I ought to be grateful, but instead disappointment gnawed at my insides. All I could see was an unappealing life stretching before me. I didn't want any of this, but it was too late now. Should I have been firmer with Papa? If I'd persisted with my pleading, maybe he would have listened. But at least Gwen was here, for I'd be lost without her gentle nature and ability to listen lifting me up on gloomy days. Besides, she had impeccable taste when it came to selecting my clothes. The girl was a veritable gem, and I wouldn't be able to manage without her.

'Good morning, Gwen,' I said.

She placed the tray on my lap, and went to open the curtains, revealing a stupendous view of the lake behind the house, and the Gothic tower in the distance. Exploring my new eighteenth-century surroundings was something to look forward to, at least, but this life seemed too much for a girl like me. I didn't see myself as a countess.

'Did you sleep well?' Gwen said.

'My sleep was rather broken, which is understandable considering the circumstances. How is your new room?'

'It's lovely, milady. I feel rather spoilt, I do.'

On the tray was a plate of scrambled eggs and toast, and a pot of tea along with a jug of milk and a bowl of sugar.

'What will you be doing this morning?' she said.

I hadn't thought that far ahead, but needed to give her some guidance so that she could choose my attire.

'I suppose I shall begin the day in the library,' I said.

Gwen opened the wardrobe and then went over to the Georgian chest of drawers with its marble top and animal feet – brought back from a grand tour by one of Winston's ancestors, no doubt – gathering a dress, undergarments, footwear and jewellery as she went. She placed the clothes on a chair and put the shoes underneath, and a necklace and earrings on the dressing table.

'Will that be all, milady?' she said.

'Yes, thank you, Gwen.'

I wasn't sure if I'd ever get used to being called 'milady'.

She left the room, closing the door quietly behind her, and then I was all alone. I tucked into my breakfast, studying the lake through the window and the rolling hills of the North Downs beyond. It was a view to be savoured, and I knew that I should count myself lucky to be in the position I now found myself in. A countess indeed, residing at one of the most impressive eighteenth-century homes in the country. But my husband was a drunk – this was a well-known fact – and a womaniser, and a voracious gambler. Before the gift of my generous dowry from Papa, he'd been on the cusp of bankruptcy and about to lose Copeley Park, the estate his father had purchased for him when he married his first wife. She was now deceased, as was his second wife, and I hoped that this marriage would not be the end of me.

My family money had rescued Winston from near destitution, although he'd had other offers. The fathers of my competitors were an American entrepreneur and a cotton mill owner. I'd been selected over their daughters, apparently because I was easier on the eye, and, more importantly, Papa was the wealthiest. And that was why I was sitting in a four-poster bed in this house with the view of a lake designed by Capability Brown.

Although I loved my father with all my heart, I couldn't help resenting him for what he'd done to my life. What did a countess do all day? Although I'd been educated by a governess and at school, and I enjoyed reading novels and writing in my diary, I was a woman who needed to spend time outdoors. My grandmother had lived with my family for many years, after my grandfather died. She was fond of gardening and had taught me everything she knew. We'd planted vegetables in the kitchen garden, and she'd shown me how to take cuttings and grow plants from seeds in the greenhouse.

Perhaps I could spend some time in the gardens here at Copeley Park, although Winston would disapprove of me being on my knees, my hands covered in mud – it was no place for a countess, he'd already told me during one of our encounters before the wedding. 'We employ gardeners to do all that,' he'd said. I had so hoped that Papa would have paid for me to go to university and study botany – my dream since I was a little girl. I had wanted to be the first woman in my family to obtain a degree. Marianne North, the Victorian botanist, was my inspiration, and I'd devoured her autobiography, *Recollections of a Happy Life*, longing to live as she had. She'd travelled far and wide, painting exotic flora – I liked to sketch flowers and plants in my diary when so inclined, although I knew this was hardly the same. But Papa had pooh-poohed my idea of going to university when I put it to him. He saw me as a woman who was merely capable of being a wife, and the bearer of my husband's heirs. Winston had two daughters from his late wives. The first wife had died from diphtheria, and the second during childbirth. Both girls lived with their grandparents now, which at least spared me from also fulfilling the role of wicked stepmother. Imagine if I'd been obliged to perform that role as well – it didn't bear thinking about. Winston was desperate for a son and heir, and time was running out. My destiny was to be summoned to his bedroom over and over again until I carried his child inside of me. He'd invited me to consummate the marriage the night before, and I'd undertaken my duty as his wife before he promptly fell asleep, snoring loudly. I tiptoed back to my own room, relieved the ordeal was over. Until the next time.

As I spread butter onto my toast, I began to feel slightly breathless with fury at the situation I found myself in. It simply wasn't fair that I'd had to give up my dream of studying botany. And then it occurred to me that being married shouldn't mean I had to give up gardening. Surely Winston couldn't stop me from following my passion? I always found it soothing to push my hands into the dirt when life became too much – time would stand still and those thoughts I didn't wish to have would dissipate. Instead, my mind would become occupied with whatever mundane task I was undertaking – whether it was pulling up weeds, pushing seeds into the soil, pricking out or pruning. Emboldened by these thoughts, I reached over my nightstand to press the servants' bell. Within minutes, Gwen came through the door.

'Yes, milady?'

'Gwen, would you be so kind as to find me a pair of breeches and a shirt instead of the clothes you've laid out? I have decided to do a spot of gardening.'

CHAPTER 3

KATE

'What does the note say?' Granny said, her eyes widening.

I read it out to her, and she gasped, clutching her chest.

'Who is "B"?' I asked. 'Where were they returning from? And what were you doing in Verona with them?'

She inhaled, her upper lip quivering, and her hand started to shake.

'I had no idea this note existed,' she said. Her face had gone very pale. 'All this time it's been there, and I didn't know anything about it.' She seemed so vulnerable, and I felt responsible for this sudden change in her. Seeing her like this was so upsetting. I got up and went over to her and placed a hand on her arm.

'Granny, are you all right?'

'Go and fetch Jane, will you, dear?' she said, her voice breaking. 'I can't remember when I last took my pills.'

I found Jane, who was unloading the dishwasher in the kitchen.

'Granny is asking for you. She seems quite off colour.' I explained about the note, and how she seemed to be in shock.

'Let's take a look,' Jane said, calmly. She took a blood pressure monitor out of a drawer and followed me back into the drawing room. She fitted it around Granny's arm, and squeezed the pump, inflating the cuff – it seemed to take forever – until it hissed and she was able to take a reading.

'Ah yes, I need to get your granny a couple of pills. I hope you don't mind, Kate, but I think it would be a good idea if you leave so she can get some rest.'

'Is everything okay?'

'Yes, she'll be fine. But it seems that bottle of wine has caused enough excitement for today.'

'Will you message me later, and let me know how she is?'

'Of course.'

I leant down and kissed Granny on the cheek.

'I hope you feel better. Thank you for the wine. I'm sorry if that note has upset you in any way.'

She reached out and put her hand on mine, squeezing it weakly.

'Don't worry, Kate, it's just a bolt out of the blue, that's all. I'll be right as rain.'

After saying goodbye, I put the wine box in the boot of my car and made my way back along the narrow lane. It had been a surprise to be given such a meaningful gift. But I hoped Granny would be all right, and that Jane would text later to put my mind at rest. She had seemed sure that the pills would work once they'd had a chance to kick in. The note was an interesting find, and I still wondered who this 'B' was. I could ask Granny again, but worried about causing a similar reaction. Perhaps I should do my own digging. Dad might know who it was, if I could bring myself to drop in and see him. That certainly wasn't going to happen today, though. All I wanted to do was get home.

It was a bumpy ride along the narrow lane – who knew when it had last been resurfaced? Couldn't Dad at least fill in the potholes? There were so many, and most of them were deep enough to cause serious damage. I slowed down, doing my best to navigate the car around them, although this required some concentration. And I was tired. The sun setting was a nice distraction, the clouds tinged with pink, but the light was fading fast. Before long, it would be dark, and I couldn't wait to reach the main gates. Rain pattered the windscreen, making visibility even more difficult. I switched on the wipers, leaning forward to see where I was going. As I turned a corner while trying to drive around a pothole that looked dangerously deep, a muddy old Land Rover came speeding towards me. I swerved out of its way and there was a clank and a thump as my car hit the pothole I'd been trying to avoid.

'Ahhh, for goodness' sake!' I shouted.

The front tyre on the passenger side barely stood a chance of surviving that ordeal. With my heart racing, I put my head in my hands, blazing with fury at whoever had been driving that fast around the corner in such a narrow lane. Who on earth could be approaching Granny's cottage with so much enthusiasm?

Closing my eyes, I inhaled through my nose to steady my breath, the squeaking wipers mocking me as they swiped from left to right and back again. I switched off the ignition to shut them up. I really didn't feel like stepping out of the car in the rain to assess the damage. My stomach sank as it dawned on me that my breakdown cover had expired. Spencer had been supposed to renew it in the autumn, but he hadn't got round to it. This task was on my never-ending to-do list. Even if I could get my car to a garage, there wouldn't be anyone there until the next morning. I'd need to get a taxi to the station and return the next day. Rain hammered the windscreen, and light flashed across the blue-black sky, then thunder cracked in the distance. I was wearing a jacket without a hood and was bound to get drenched.

A tap on the car window interrupted my thoughts, making me jump out of my skin. Looking up, I saw a man with a torch in his hand, staring directly at me, as the rain poured down on him. His eyes were scrunched up in concern. Wait, was this the man responsible for the situation I now found myself in? Well, I had a few things to say to him. I turned on the ignition and pressed the button for the car window. It whirred open.

'Hi there,' he said, gently.

His hair was soaking wet from the rain, and he wore an olive-green Copeley Park fleece – ah, so he worked here. It was impossible not to notice that he was quite nice-looking, but I pushed this thought to the back of my mind. He'd put me in a right fix with his reckless driving and I could do without this hassle on a Sunday evening, especially after seeing Granny so upset. I needed to get home and make something to eat, and to mentally prepare for work as well as my big birthday the next morning.

Still in shock, and thrown by his distracting good looks, I was momentarily lost for words. But he needed a good telling-off.

'Nice driving,' was all I could come up with, but I threw in an eye-roll for good measure.

'I'm really sorry,' he said. 'There isn't usually anyone else on this road – which is *no* excuse. I just wasn't expecting to see you.'

'You're right – it is absolutely no excuse,' I said, tersely.

He nodded and sighed.

'I know.'

'My tyre is almost certainly flat.'

'Well... I can check that for you, if you like?'

Shrugging, I closed the window, as rain was now coming into the car. I was acting like a moody teenager but couldn't help myself. Holding up his hands, he stepped backwards, not seeming to care about the rain now coming down thick and fast. He went to the front of the car, disappearing from view as he bent down, and I took the opportunity to check my phone.

There was a message from Jane to say that Granny was much better already and not to worry. What a relief. I wouldn't press her any further about the identity of 'B' just yet – maybe I could find out for myself.

The man came back and tapped on the window. I opened it again a little.

'Yeah, sorry to tell you, the tyre is as flat as a pancake.'

Shaking my head, I said, 'What am I supposed to do now?'

'I can get my jack and change it, if you want, assuming you have a spare with you?'

I hesitated. 'Really? Yes, I do – it's in the boot.'

'I live at Rosemary Cottage, at the end of this road.' Hold on, was this the new head gardener Granny had mentioned? 'Why don't I drive you there, and you can wait in the warm? I'll even make you a nice cup of tea.'

A cup of tea would certainly be welcome, and maybe it would help me to calm down.

'Okay, thanks that would be good. Although I hope you'll be driving more carefully...'

He scratched his forehead. 'Of course. Come on then, I can't stand in this rain for much longer.'

He went over to his Land Rover, and I got out of my car and followed. I opened the door on the passenger side and stepped up into the seat. Starting the engine, he said, 'I'm Ben Grant, by the way, head gardener here at Copeley Park. Officially, I'm head winemaker too, but everyone refers to me as the head gardener.'

So, this *was* the man who Granny had been talking about. She'd been so keen for us to meet, it was almost as if she'd engineered the whole thing.

CHAPTER 4

LADY CHARLOTTE

After breakfast, I put on a pair of breeches and a white shirt and studied myself in the looking glass while Gwen styled my hair into a low bun.

She carefully placed a straw hat on my head.

'The sun is out this morning, milady, and you ought to protect the skin on your face.'

The dear girl always thought of everything, and I was grateful. I thanked her, and she scurried off, back to the servants' quarters, where she would darn stockings, press blouses, remove stains and sew on buttons, amongst other things. I would be quite lost without her.

I left my room and descended the vast staircase, passing portraits of the Clarkson family going back to the era of Charles I, the men wearing wigs, as well as serious looks on their countenances. The portraits were no doubt painted by renowned artists, and a symbol of the heritage of an aristocratic family. Papa had commissioned portraits of him and Mama, and of my sisters and me. Despite vast sums of money accumulated during his career as chairman of the Cheshire Railway, status in society was what Papa coveted for his descendants. He lived in hope that the King would give him a title for his contribution to society – he was well acquainted with George VI, who had an interest in the railway network. He'd often visit Rodene Hall with Queen Elizabeth, and she'd always bring a thoughtful gift such as a Fabergé animal to add to our collection in the glass case in the library. Mama would always be thrilled. My parents were part of a group of aristocrats known as the Hatchley Set. Papa's gentleman acquaintances would bring their wives, and even mistresses, to Rodene Hall on occasion – often at the same time – and would go hunting, shooting and fishing while the women drank tea and made small talk. Mama would host elaborate dinners, and she'd even hired a French chef especially, in order to impress these distinguished guests. Winston's father, the Duke of Dorking, was part of this set, and this was how my marriage had come about.

In the grand hall, the butler, Mr Skinner, stood by the front door. As I approached, he opened it with a gloved hand, and gave me a nod.

'Good morning, milady.'

'Good morning, Skinner,' I said, stepping outside.

I planned to find a spot in the vast gardens, and push my hands into the soil until each and every one of my fingernails was dirty underneath. I had no idea exactly what I was going to do – I would find somewhere and decide there and then. Surely there would be a task for me to undertake.

I'd been introduced to all of the servants the previous evening, after the wedding reception. They'd lined up outside the front of the house as Winston and I arrived in a Rolls-Royce, decorated with white ribbon in a criss-cross pattern. Exhausted by what had been a long and emotionally charged day, I had still managed to raise a smile in the manner of my newly acquired countess title. I'd greeted them one by one as the housekeeper, Mrs Parsons, a buxom woman with an apron tied around her waist, made the introductions. The women curtsied, and the men bowed – and it was staggering that these people should think that I was so important. Then Mrs Parsons had taken me inside and showed me to my room.

I took a right at the bottom of the steps, hoping to find a quiet spot in order to escape the reality of my new life. For I was concerned about my future. How would I ever be content as Winston's spouse? As I walked past swathes of bright-yellow daffodils on the front lawn, their heads pointing in all directions, I saw a wall, built from red bricks. The kitchen garden was bound to be on the other side. The thought of such a discovery thrilled me, and I considered which vegetables would be in season – new potatoes, spring onions, broad beans – the garden would be abundant. I opened the cast-iron gate and passed through to the other side, closing it behind me. There before me was a beautiful walled garden – an oasis in a desert. It was so peaceful, the air filled with a chorus of delightful birdsong from nearby trees. A long greenhouse dominated one side, and a shed stood opposite. At the far end was a quaint cottage with smoke wafting from the chimney.

As I walked, I studied the beds – the borders were filled with spring flowers such as tulips and hyacinths, and those in the centre were labelled with writing on wooden sticks. And then I saw rows of broad beans, and there were many weeds amongst them – well, I would just have to do something about that. I got down on my knees and started to wiggle the weeds, in order to pull them out of the ground. They came easily, for the earth was soft due to a recent bout of rain. I hummed to myself, already beginning to relax. As I worked my way along the row, my back started to ache, but I carried on regardless. The soil made its way under my fingernails, and I studied them, satisfied. This was indeed inappropriate behaviour for a countess, but I was a woman who liked to get her hands dirty. No one could stop me from nurturing my passion. How was it fair to be deprived of doing something that was good for one's soul? My father had rescued the Clarkson family from the threat of bankruptcy, after all. I was chuckling to myself at the thought of the dour look on Winston's face if he could see me now when a male voice came from above. It gave me quite a fright, and I started.

'What on earth do you think you're doing?'

Looking up, I saw a handsome man standing there, wearing a shirt with the sleeves rolled up, a waistcoat and trousers tucked into knee-high boots. His hair was blond, and his face was covered with a thick beard. This was the head gardener – I remembered him from the servant line-up. His exasperated expression told me he disapproved of me squatting amongst his broad beans, even though I was doing him a great service.

'What does it look like I'm doing? Weeding, of course.'

He glared at me with big green eyes from under the brim of his cap.

'But who *are* you?'

Ah, he didn't have any idea who I was. This made sense. When Mrs Parsons had introduced him to me the night before – although I couldn't recall his name – I would have looked entirely different with my hair down, and in my wedding dress. Now my hair was styled into a low bun under my straw hat, and I was sporting breeches and a shirt. Did I really need to reveal my identity? Perhaps he thought I was an impoverished villager who'd sneaked in through the gate to steal his vegetables. No, I needed to come clean and then he'd soon change his tone, although it pleased me that he was being more forthright than the other servants at Copeley Park.

I stood up and brushed the soil off my breeches.

Proffering my right hand, I looked him in the eye, and said, 'Clearly you don't remember me from last night, but that's understandable. I'm Lady Charlotte, the new Countess of Waverley. My hand is covered in dirt, but I'm sure a man like you is used to that.'

He bit his lip and appeared to be blushing. I couldn't help feeling sorry for him – the poor man was probably wondering if he was about to get the sack. He'd only been protecting the garden, and so he should be. I could be anyone, after all.

He doffed his cap, then shook my hand, firmly. His hands were large, for he was a big man with broad shoulders and muscular legs – strong and capable-looking, rather fitting for his role, which would have required a great deal of physical work. His fingernails had mud underneath them, and of course I approved.

'I do apologise, your ladyship. I didn't recognise you.'

'Yes, well, I am dressed in different attire from yesterday. It doesn't matter. Just do something for me, will you?'

He stroked his beard and nodded. I lowered my voice.

'Don't tell anyone about this. I hope you won't object to me partaking in a spot of gardening when I feel so inclined? It brings me a little joy, you see.'

'Of course not, milady. Gardening does tend to soothe the soul – I completely understand.'

'Very good. Now, if you don't mind, I'll finish this row before returning to the house for elevenses?'

'I'll leave you to carry on then.' He placed his cap back on his head as he walked away, glancing over his shoulder as he did so. He probably couldn't believe that he'd just come across a countess in his vegetable patch.

I called after him. 'And what, may I ask, is your name?'

He stopped and turned round to face me. 'I'm Albert Hicks, head gardener here at Copeley Park.'

'Delighted to meet you, Albert.'

He gave me a nod, before heading for the cottage at the far end – presumably his home – and I watched him open a door and go inside. Considering that I'd married Winston the previous day, I had enjoyed interacting with the head gardener far more than was appropriate. But how I wanted to come to this peaceful walled garden, bursting with birdsong, every morning, and get lost amongst the beds. Would Winston mind terribly if I did that? Well, it wasn't up to him, was it? I was the lady of the house, and surely I was free to do what I wanted with my time.

As I followed the path back to the gate, I replayed the encounter with Albert in my head. A head gardener indeed. He must know all there was to know about plants and flowers and trees. How I longed to ask him questions about the gardens. Would he show me around, if I asked him? Of course he would. He'd be obliged to fulfil my request. I pictured *that* face, and those large green eyes as they'd studied me. He was closer to my age than Winston, who was almost as old as Papa. Why couldn't I have a husband who I found attractive, a man who I wanted to pass the time with? A man whom I actually loved? Papa's wealth had put me in a situation where I was married to a man whom I did not even like, never mind love.

As I approached the front door, an unsettling feeling came over me. My breeches were covered in mud at the knees, and going through this door would be a risk. I didn't want to come into contact with Winston, but I could hardly use the servants' entrance. I took off my straw hat, and then removed the pins from my bun, allowing my hair to fall to my shoulders, giving it a shake as I did so. I went up the steps leading to the front door, but, as I was about to place my hand on the knob, Skinner opened it. Standing beside him was the earl's mother, Lady Victoria Clarkson, the Duchess of Dorking, a cigarette holder in her hand. Winston had informed me that she was staying on the estate, at Keeper's Cottage – a place she was fond of. It was just my luck to bump into her. A look of horror crossed her face.

'What do we have here?' she said.

She was dressed up to the nines as women of her ilk always

were, the skirt of her dress falling to her ankles. The sleeves were long and the neckline high. A corset pulled everything in at the waist. Her skin was pale, and her grey-white hair was piled upon her head.

'Good morning, your grace,' I said.

She took a puff of her cigarette and exhaled.

'Where have you been dressed like that?'

'Well—'

'My dear, you are in dire need of a lady's maid more suited to your new position as my son's wife. I know just the person.'

'What do you mean?'

'I heard on the grapevine that Madame Dupont from Paris is looking for a new position. She knows all there is to know about fashion. The woman will be an asset to you.'

'But I already have a lady's maid,' I protested.

'My dear, I regret to inform you that she is not up to the job.'

'I can't just send her back to Wales.'

The duchess sighed as she took a parasol from Skinner and held it above her head.

'Therein lies the problem. You need a lady's maid from France, not Wales. The Welsh hardly know the meaning of the word chic.'

'But I couldn't manage without Gwen, and besides it wouldn't be fair to dismiss her, especially after persuading her to come here from Rodene Hall.'

'I'm sure you can find her a different position in the house.'

Gwen wasn't just a lady's maid. She was also a confidante and someone whom I could trust.

'Perhaps we can discuss this matter further.'

'What else is there to discuss, Charlotte?'

Was my new mother-in-law to dictate how I lived my life? I hadn't agreed to this. Surely, being the woman who had enabled my husband to keep Copeley Park, I had more clout?

She started to walk down the steps, and I entered the grand

hall. When I reached the staircase, I rested my hand on the banister and turned round, thinking that I should go after the duchess and plead my case. But Skinner had closed the door behind her, and it seemed the moment had passed. What would I do now?

CHAPTER 5

KATE

Ben edged slowly along the lane. The rain was still coming down so heavily that it was hard to see much through the windscreen, even with the wipers going at full throttle.

'And what's your name?' he said.

'I'm Kate.'

I didn't add that my father was his boss, although Ben probably wondered what I was doing here at Copeley Park. He might assume I'd been on a vineyard tour and taken a wrong turn on the way home. Were they even running tours at the moment? I couldn't remember, but knew they were seasonal. As he drove, I remembered that Granny's bottle of wine was in my car boot. Should I be leaving it there, seeing as it could be valuable? But then who was likely to walk past and break into my car, here on the estate, especially in the dark and on such a wet and gloomy evening?

'Kate, short for Catherine?'

'Yes, but Catherine with a "C", not a "K".'

I automatically found myself telling people this when we met, as it could be annoying when my name was spelt wrong. He wasn't bringing out my fun side tonight.

'Ah, okay.' I looked across to see that his lips were slightly upturned, as if he found me amusing. 'A name fit for a princess. I'll remember that if I ever need to write it down.'

We reached the T-junction. Ben took a left and continued for a minute or so until we reached Rosemary Cottage, built in the same style as Keeper's Cottage where Granny lived, but smaller. It still looked just as charming from the outside. He parked, and I followed him through a gate and up the path. The front door wasn't locked, strangely, and he pushed it open.

As if reading my thoughts, he said, 'I never lock the door, you don't need to round here. Besides, I don't have anything worth nicking.'

Ben led me into a hall, and I took off my coat and hung it on the stand. The floor was cluttered with an array of muddy boots and wellies. He opened a door to a living room, where a fire glowed in the hearth. The cottage was more rustic than Granny's, with mismatched furniture and paint peeling off the walls. But these flaws were part of its charm. He picked up a log from a basket and squatted down to place it carefully onto the fire.

Using a poker to get the flames going, he said, 'Right, let's make you that cup of tea, and then I'll find my jack and sort your tyre out.'

'Thanks,' I said.

He gestured for me to take the brown leather armchair in front of the hearth.

'Why don't you have a sit-down.'

He went through a door, and I heard him turn on a tap. The chair was comfortable, and I sank into it. My view was of a bay window – it was now pitch black outside, the curtains not yet closed for the evening. The cottage was so quiet, apart from the sound of Ben clattering things in the kitchen. I could picture myself passing the time there, without the need for any form of entertainment. This was a place to 'just be' in. I'd forgotten what life was like when you had a real fireplace as the focal point of a room rather than a television with a big screen. Looking around, there was no sign of a TV, just musty old but tasteful furniture, and a few lamps.

Ben reappeared with a mug of tea and placed it on a side table next to my chair. He went round the room, clicking on the lamps, and then he turned off the main light overhead, creating a more cosy ambience. I thanked him for the tea, and he looked down at me with kind eyes. I couldn't help noticing that they were an interesting shade of blue, on the slightly misty side.

'Do you have the key for your car?'

I reached into the pocket of my jeans and gave it to him, our hands brushing.

'Make yourself at home, Kate. I'll be back in a bit.'

He left the room, and I heard him close the front door firmly behind him. I looked up at prints of eighteenth-century features from the estate – the temple of Bacchus, the Gothic tower – hung on the crimson walls. A shelf was filled with books about country life, gardening and winemaking, and there were classic novels such as *Jane Eyre*, *Rebecca* and *The Great Gatsby*. We clearly shared a love of reading, and I liked that. The flat I was living in couldn't compare with this old cottage. How many head gardeners had lived here, going all the way back to the eighteenth century? My place was lovely – an open-plan Victorian conversion with high ceilings – but it had modern fixtures and fittings, and was devoid of character with no period features. The walls were whitewashed, and the furniture was modern in style and beige or grey, and the fireplaces had been filled in. To think that I'd grown up in this world I now found myself in. Why had I discarded it so readily? Perhaps a home like this would suit me.

Rain pounded the window, and I sipped my tea, thinking of

poor Ben stuck out there in the dark, getting soaked through while trying to see what on earth he was doing. Should I have offered to help him, or at least hold a torch? He seemed like a capable type though, and wouldn't he have asked if he'd needed assistance? No doubt he'd return dishevelled and desperate for a shower and change of clothes. I guessed that then I'd leave him to it and go on my way.

But oddly, I found myself wanting to come back to this cottage, to spend more time here. The flat where I lived in Southfields was on the main road and there was always the sound of traffic and people talking as they walked along the pavement, often shouting late at night after leaving the pub. I couldn't help hoping there might be some reason I'd need to return. Ben was being friendly towards me, but that could be because he was responsible for my flat tyre, and I doubted he'd want to see me again. And I wasn't sure if I actually wanted to see *him* – I just found myself inexplicably drawn to the cottage. All these years that Rosemary Cottage had been on Dad's estate, with head gardeners living there, and I'd never once been inside. How I wished that I could live somewhere like this – perhaps I did belong in the countryside, after all. Granny had said the bottle of wine might bring me luck – maybe she'd somehow set wheels in motion that would make me re-evaluate my life.

Ben came back around half an hour later. He threw me a smile.

'Are you okay, Kate?' he said.

Nodding, I said, 'Yes, it's nice here by the fire.'

He removed his coat and a baseball cap he'd been wearing, and hung them on the stand in the hall.

'So, we have a slight problem...'

I sensed that, for some reason, he hadn't managed to change the tyre.

'What's wrong?'

'Your spare has a puncture in it as well.'

This was proving to be one big pain in the arse of a day. I sighed. Spencer had found the car for me online the previous year, and he'd collected it from a village near Sheffield. Foolishly, I'd presumed the spare tyre in the boot would not be a dud.

'I don't believe it.'

'All the garages will be shut at this time on a Sunday, but I can go to Guildford in the morning and get another tyre, if you like?'

'That would be lovely of you, thanks. Are you sure you have the time though?'

'Of course, it's the least I can do.'

'Well, that's great. But I do need to find a way back to my flat tonight in the meantime.'

'Where do you live?'

'Southfields. I can get the train to Wimbledon and then the tube.'

'I'll drop you at the station.'

'Don't worry, I can get an Uber.'

'Getting an Uber out here could take ages.'

I knew this, of course, but was being polite with my mild protestation.

'I'd offer to drive you all the way, but with Sunday night traffic public transport would probably be quicker.'

He really was trying his best to compensate for landing me in this situation.

'I'd appreciate a lift to the station, thank you.'

I took out my phone and checked the train app. 'There's a train in ten minutes. Is it okay if we leave now? We should just make it.'

'Sure, let's go.'

For some reason, I didn't feel ready to leave though – our

encounter had impacted me in some way, despite the circumstances, and I'd enjoyed our interactions. Sunday was usually a lonely day as my flatmate, Sophie, would go hiking with her boyfriend, Charlie. There was something about Ben Grant and his charming cottage, and I found myself almost pleased that I'd have to return the next day, and on my big birthday too.

CHAPTER 6

LADY CHARLOTTE

One evening, not long after we were married, there was a dinner party at our house. Winston asked to see me in the library before the guests arrived. I wore a royal-blue dress made from satin, selected by Gwen to match my eyes. It was a beautiful dress, and it swished as I moved. My shoes with a low heel and handbag were both cream-coloured, and my hair was styled into a French pleat. Gwen added a pearl necklace and matching drop earrings as finishing touches. When I studied myself in the looking glass, I couldn't help feeling pleased with what my dear lady's maid had done for my appearance. If only I were attending a dinner party with my own friends.

Winston was already seated when I entered the room, in an armchair in front of the fire. In one hand he held a crystal glass containing what appeared to be a generous measure of brandy, and, in the other, a cigarette rested between his fingers. He made a show of looking at his watch.

'There you are at last, Charlotte – you are late.'

I was perfectly aware of this, and it was intentional – the less time I spent with him before the guests arrived, the better.

'Oh, am I?'

He took a drag of his cigarette, tipped his head to the side and exhaled a cloud of smoke. I did my best not to breathe in the foul odour.

He gave me a sharp nod to suggest I sit opposite him, and, as I did so, Skinner came over to adjust the screen in front of the fire – it was not proper for ladies to look too flushed. I asked him to bring me a gin and tonic on the rocks with a slice of lemon.

'My mother has informed me that you are being difficult,' Winston said.

'What do you mean?'

Of course, I knew he was referring to my conversation with the duchess when I returned from the kitchen garden that day, but I was pleading ignorance in order to stall him.

'She feels that it's more appropriate for you to have a French lady's maid. That Welsh girl you brought with you is not sophisticated enough for a countess, my dear.'

It was bad enough being married to Winston without having to deal with his mother's meddling as well. I drew in my breath.

'Yes, she mentioned that she knew of someone. But I wanted to talk to you about it. Gwen is a companion and confidante, as well as the person who takes care of my wardrobe.'

'Charlotte, you need to stop acting like a child. You are almost twenty years old.'

His condescending tone grated. He was talking to me as if he were my father, not my husband. But what could I expect with him being almost twice my age?

He went on. 'With your new title of countess, and as the lady of this house, you'll need to adapt to this new world you find yourself in.'

He was enjoying the benefits of my dowry, with his debts paid off and plenty more money sitting in the bank. The brandy he was drinking had been paid for by Papa, yet here he was talking down to me. This didn't seem fair, just because I was the daughter of a man who had been desperate to elevate the social status of his descendants.

'So, you agree with your mother?'

'Of course I do. Being exceptionally well bred, she knows about these things, my dear. Seeing as your relatives have less experience in these matters, we shall need to provide you with guidance on occasion.'

He was being bold talking about my family in this way. Neither of my parents were 'well bred', as he put it, at all. Papa was the son of a tailor who'd landed on his feet when his childless uncle gave him a job at his railway company. When his uncle was taken ill a few years later, he asked Papa to take over the business. Mama was the daughter of a schoolmaster – my dear late grandfather – who'd introduced me to the work of Dickens, Austen and Shakespeare amongst other literary greats. Through him, I'd discovered my favourite play of all, *Romeo and Juliet*, and I still had the copy he'd given to me.

Indignation simmered inside of me, but I did my best to suppress my rising fury. How dare Winston imply my parents were less important than his, just because they hadn't been born with titles. Papa had only been in his early thirties when he bought Rodene Hall in Cheshire, a stately home going back to the Tudor era. The Clarkson family hadn't managed to hold on to all of their inherited money, passed down through generations. They'd been forced into sinking low enough to find a woman whose father could pay off their son's debts.

How I wanted to defend my family, and explain how inspiring Papa had always been, rising up from humble roots and making something of himself. But the Clarksons would always view my family as beneath them. Despite all my father had done for them, I didn't seem to have any influence. I'd had the title of countess bestowed on me, and I was supposed to be grateful. How could someone like myself be capable of fulfilling such a role? But it was too late – I was tied to Winston forever.

The only consolation was that, because he was so much older than me, it was likely that I'd have a period of time alone later in life as a widow. With no one to fight my corner, my only option was to give up Gwen. Somehow, I'd have to find a way to get along with the French lady's maid that the duchess was so keen on. Even though Gwen had more than proven herself when dressing me that evening.

'I shall be disappointed to let Gwen go, but it seems I have no choice in the matter,' I said, quietly.

Skinner brought in my gin and tonic and placed it on the trestle table beside me. I thanked him, picked up the glass and took a sip. It was a generous measure of gin, and I put the glass down again. This was bound to be a long evening and maybe drinking all of it at once would enhance my mood. However, being sloshed would not present me in the best light. But before long, the guests would arrive for dinner, and I'd be hosting my first event as Winston's wife. His acquaintances were bound to be closer to his age, and therefore intimidating. Nerves engulfed me – how would I get through it? I picked up my glass and downed the rest of my drink.

'There we are then,' Winston said. 'Mother will make the necessary arrangements, and Mrs Parsons can find your current maid something to do.'

'Do you think that's entirely fair on Gwen?' I asked.

'Pffft. You do not need to concern yourself with the feelings of servants, my dear.'

But I cared about Gwen, who had become a friend to me over the past eighteen months or so at Rodene Hall. If she remained in the house, I could still ask her to come and see me sometimes, I supposed. I'd have to be satisfied with that until I could concoct a plan to get her back. Madame Dupont would no doubt inform the duchess about how I spent every minute of every day, and I didn't like the idea of that. It was almost as if my mother-in-law were placing a spy in my midst.

'Winston—'

'Look, Charlotte, the decision is made, do you hear me?'

He looked directly at me with his beady brown eyes. They were so cold and hard. I knew he did not love me or have any intention of trying to. Winston had taken his mother's side over mine, and I expected it would always be this way. Now here I was, accepting that a mere stranger was going to spend hours with me every day. It was a bitter pill to swallow.

I fiddled with my earring.

'Charlotte, are you going to answer me?'

'Yes, Winston,' I said, looking away.

'Then the matter is settled. Now, the guests will be arriving shortly, and I expect you'll do everything you can to be a delightful hostess?'

'You have my word.'

But downing the gin and tonic had already made my head a little woozy, and I wasn't sure if I was capable of keeping it.

CHAPTER 7

KATE

We put on our jackets in the hall and went outside to get into Ben's Land Rover. It was still pouring with rain. He started the engine, and we made our way back along the narrow lane. It was now so dark that the only lights came from Granny's cottage and the main house.

'So, what were you were doing at Copeley Park today? Were you on a vineyard tour?' Ben asked.

'I actually went to see my great-grandmother.'

'Who's that... wait, are you related to Lady Charlotte?'

'Yes.'

'So, hold on... you're my boss, Hugo's, daughter? How haven't I met you before?'

'Have you been working here long?'

'Around six months.'

'That would explain it. I haven't been here since the spring.'

'Why, when you only live in Southfields?'

I breathed in. Was I ready to tell him about my personal life? We'd only just met.

As if reading my mind, he said, 'Sorry if that was too much. You don't have to explain anything to me.'

'Thanks.'

But there was something about him that made me want to tell him everything about myself. He seemed like the kind of person who would lend a sympathetic ear and know exactly what to say if you confided in him. At the same time, Dad was his boss and I couldn't be disloyal, even though we hadn't talked much lately. This estate was my father's livelihood, and it wouldn't be ideal to have members of staff talking about him behind his back. And so, I needed to give Ben an edited version of why I hadn't been to Copeley Park recently.

'Work has been busy,' I said. 'And I've just had a lot going on in my life.' I didn't want him to know I'd been married, yet – it seemed like too much information that would lead to further questions I wasn't in the mood to answer.

'Ah I see... that's understandable then.'

We reached the main gates, and they automatically opened. He drove through to the other side.

'Oh yes,' Ben said. 'I meant to say, there was a box of wine in the back of your car. I had to move it to get to the spare tyre, and, well, I hope you don't mind, but I couldn't help looking at what was inside. A bottle of 1936 Amarone... wow, I'm impressed.'

'Granny gave it to me this afternoon.'

'I'm not sure you should be leaving such a valuable item in the back of your car.'

'Well, I wouldn't want to leave it on the train by accident, or drop it even.'

'Would you like me to get the bottle out of your boot on my way back and keep it until you return?'

I thought for a moment. Should I get the wine now and take it back to Granny's cottage? But then I'd miss my train, and anyway, I should leave her in peace after what had happened earlier. Surely I could trust Ben to look after it for me.

'That would be very kind, thanks.'

'What do you plan to do with it?'

'I haven't had chance to think about that yet.'

'Would you try and sell it?'

'Not unless I have to, as it seems to have sentimental value for Granny. I think she wanted to pass it on to me for luck, or something. There was a note with it, and I'd like to find out who wrote it.'

'Ooh, a mystery too. Doesn't your granny know who it's from?'

I explained about what had happened when I asked her, and that I needed to work out who 'B' was.

'Do you think there's some kind of story attached to it, a secret even?'

'There could be... Granny didn't seem to want me to know who this person was for some reason.'

'Hmm, intriguing.'

'I'll have to see if my dad can shed any light on it.'

'Well, it was lovely of her to give the wine to you.'

'It was a present for my thirtieth.'

'Ah I see... when's your big birthday, not today? Please tell me I haven't ruined your birthday?' He groaned.

'No, don't worry.' I laughed. 'It's tomorrow.'

'Do you have any exciting plans?'

'Nope. None of my friends would really want to go out on a Monday.'

'You could always do something next weekend?'

I hadn't got round to arranging anything, mainly because my friends needed several weeks' notice these days – it was often impossible to find a date that suited everyone.

'I could,' I said, noncommittally.

We went into Copeley, past all the shops, and the Dog and Duck, and St John's Church, and eventually arrived at the railway station. Ben pulled into the car park and switched off the engine. The inside lights came on, and he looked across and gave me a smile.

'Here you are then.'

'Thanks for the lift – and for the help.'

'No problem. I'm sorry for getting you into this mess.'

I shrugged. He seemed like a decent person, despite his irresponsible driving.

'These things happen.'

'I'll pop into Guildford tomorrow, first thing, and get you another tyre.'

'Shall I give you some money for that?'

'Well, let's wait and see how much it costs... but actually, thinking about it, this should be on me, seeing as I'm the reason you're having to get a new one in the first place.'

'Really? Are you sure?'

I was protesting quite pathetically but, seeing as this was all his fault, he should be paying. And perhaps he'd think twice about driving round that corner so fast next time.

He nodded. 'Yes, I am.' Then he passed me his phone and said, 'Give me your number and I'll text when your car is ready.'

I did as he said and handed the phone back to him.

Opening the car door, I said, 'I'll see you tomorrow, then. Thanks again, Ben.'

'Bye, Kate. I'll be in touch.'

I stepped down from the Land Rover, and watched him drive away, along the station approach, before disappearing from view.

CHAPTER 8

LADY CHARLOTTE

Skinner opened the door to the guests, and in came a man and a woman. Winston and I stood as they approached us. Everyone shook hands as Skinner introduced the vicar, Mr Bridges, who had officiated our wedding ceremony, and his wife. And then came another couple – I recognised the man from the newspapers as a prominent member of the British Union of Fascists. I'd read an interview in *The Times* the previous week where he'd said that he was acquainted with Adolf Hitler and had been to Germany many times to meet with members of the Nazi Party. I couldn't believe it. Behind him came Herr Ribbentrop, the German ambassador, who liked to do the rounds of country houses apparently, in an attempt to ingratiate himself with the aristocracy – and so many of them seemed to be taken in by him and his Nazi ideology. Papa had told me that members of the Hatchley Set mentioned him when visiting. This was a man who'd greeted our King with the Nazi salute and an uttering of, 'Heil Hitler' when they met, instead of bowing as was customary. Papa and the King had discussed the incident during one of his visits to Rodene Hall. He'd recounted the story to Mama, my sisters and me at dinner one evening. And here this despicable man was in my home – what on earth was he doing here at Copeley Park? And why was my husband associating himself with antisemites?

When the leader of the British Union of Fascists, Oswald Mosley himself, entered the room, I was not at all surprised. These people were bad eggs, and, by associating himself with them, my husband was showing his true colours. As more guests arrived, voices filled the air, and footmen hovered around them with coupes of champagne and plates of canapés. But these were not the kind of people I wished to acquaint myself with. And to think that Winston looked down on me and my family. Surely Papa, whose Jewish father had changed his surname from Focht to Ford when he came to Manchester from Poland in the early 1900s – wouldn't have agreed to our marriage if he'd been aware of Winston's association with these people? Did my husband share their views? Had he been to Germany and received hospitality from Nazis? – many members of the aristocracy had apparently done this. And he'd started the evening by backing his mother over me during our first disagreement. None of this boded well.

A little later, Skinner came into the library and announced that dinner was to be served. The guests, with some encouragement from the footmen, moved at a snail's pace into the dining room and took their positions at the long table. The walls were crimson, and they were crammed with paintings – so many of them – by eighteenth-century artists such as Joshua Reynolds and Thomas Gainsborough, and there was a portrait of the third Duke of Dorking, sitting in a red armchair, by Henry Raeburn. Skinner, after a discussion with Winston, no doubt, had placed name cards carefully around the table. I smiled to myself mischievously at the thought of rearranging these cards when no one was looking. Presumably guests who might have had past squabbles, or who were likely to have conflicting opinions, were placed at a safe distance from one another, as was customary.

Everyone sat next to a member of the opposite sex. As hostess, I was opposite Winston, who was at the head of the table all the way down the other end. Thankfully, this meant I didn't have to put up with his booming voice in my ear. To my right was the vicar, Mr Bridges, and to my left a local accountant, who I noted from his card was called Mr Weatherfield. Ribbentrop, Mosley and the other fascist were seated close to Winston. Next to him was Lady Penelope, his younger brother Jasper's wife. I noticed her touch his arm, giggling rather flirtatiously as he talked, and recalled that apparently he'd originally wanted to marry her. But her father was a penniless baron, and so she'd won the consolation prize of his brother instead. Jasper had been placed towards the centre of the table, and appeared to have a rather glum look on his face.

A footman approached and filled one of my glasses with Burgundy, and another footman placed a bread roll on my side plate with a pair of silver tongs. I reached for the butter dish in front of me and tore a corner off my roll, and spread butter onto it with the knife from my side plate. Papa may be nouveau riche, but I'd been raised to know my cutlery. Steaming bowls of soup were brought into the room and placed in front of us. The menu informed me that this was asparagus soup, and I imagined it had been made with produce from the kitchen garden. This made me think back to my encounter with Albert. He'd made his way into my mind on more than one occasion since that morning, and I found myself yearning for another encounter with him. Spooning soup into my mouth, I stifled a yawn as the accountant told me in great detail about the British tax system. He pointed out his wife on the opposite side of the table and then proceeded to tell me about each one of their four sons – where they were being educated, what their strengths were, and so on. I nodded along, saying, 'Oh really?' and 'How interesting' at appropriate intervals. All I wanted to do was to make it through the evening in order to go upstairs and sleep.

As the empty bowls were being cleared from the table, I overheard someone say something about 'those damn Jews'. And then I was horrified to see Winston laugh, along with the fascists surrounding him, and actually quite a few people at the table. As the daughter of a Jewish man, I could not allow this to happen in my home. By now, I'd had a couple of drinks, and my tongue was looser than it usually would be.

'Sorry,' I said, loudly.

Everyone stopped talking, and all heads turned in my direction. It was so quiet, one could hear a pin drop – and all of them staring at me with dour looks on their faces was quite overwhelming. My heart pounding, I wrung my hands under the table.

'What is it, dear?' Winston said, in a strained voice.

There was no going back now – I needed to say *something*. Should I just thank everyone for joining us this evening? No, I owed it to myself, and Papa, to speak my mind.

'Did I hear someone say, "damn Jews"?'

Still all the faces glared at me, unsmiling. More silence.

'I must have been mistaken. Do carry on. Sorry for the interruption.'

I should have gone further, but in the heat of the moment nerves had got the better of me. What I'd wanted to say was, 'Because if they did, I would just like to say that, as the daughter of a "damn Jew", who has provided you all with what you're consuming, I'd prefer for those words not to be uttered at this table, or indeed anywhere else in this house.'

Winston cleared his throat, and I was relieved – he was going to support me, surely, as a husband should?

'I do apologise for my wife. She's had far too much to drink, and we've only just finished the starter. Slow down, dear. Perhaps have a glass of water.'

Laughter ensued, and I was completely humiliated. My face warmed, and all I wanted was for the ground to open and swallow me up. How dare my husband, whose family had benefitted from the money of a 'damn Jew', belittle me in front of these vile people. I desperately wanted to leave the table, but how could I? I would be glued to my chair for another two courses.

The guests recommenced talking, and I tried to pull myself together, in order to make it through the remainder of the meal.

After we'd consumed the main course of trout, caught from the river that ran through the estate, and then a dessert of trifle, the gentlemen retired to the blue drawing room. They would no doubt drink brandy, and smoke cigars and talk about politics and possibly play cards for money. Winston was known to be a voracious gambler, and, even though his debts had been paid off, I doubted he'd give up the horrendous habit. He probably saw the prospect of playing cards with these wealthy men as an opportunity too good to miss. How long would it be before he'd squandered all the money received from Papa? And then what would he do? Cast me aside and find a fourth wife so he could take her family's money too? If I gave him a son, he wouldn't be able to cast me aside, would he? Though perhaps in some ways I wished he would.

The wives gathered in the library, and we made small talk about the things women tended to be occupied with – fashion, husbands, offspring. I found the discourse rather dull. They all seemed satisfied with their mundane lives – performing the role of exemplary wives and mothers, and hosting regular dinner parties like this one.

I wasn't cut out to be a hostess, and certainly not at a dinner where bigotry was acceptable, but now here I was living the life that had been chosen for me. The footmen served tea and coffee and petit fours, and digestifs for those who wanted them – I asked for a glass of brandy. The evening went on until the men were ready to go home, or upstairs if they were overnight guests – Jasper and Penelope were staying as their home was in Kent. The next day, some of the guests would go fly fishing in the river as this was a pastime Winston particularly enjoyed. As the vicar's wife, Mrs Bridges, told me about her grandson and what an excellent piano player he was, I nodded along, and smiled. I was only half listening, as a thought had entered my mind – I must go and ask Albert if I could do more gardening the very next morning. The mindless tasks of weeding and pruning and sowing seeds would help me endure this place.

Later, when Gwen helped me to prepare for bed, I'd ask her to deliver a message to Albert in the morning. I would request a meeting to discuss me helping out in the gardens. Perhaps he could give me a tour of the estate as well. This might be one of the last tasks she carried out for me, as I had an inkling that Madame Dupont would arrive at Copeley Park before long. It would be up to me to inform Gwen of her fate, but that could wait until the morning when I was sober and therefore able to broach the matter with a clear head. Then I'd stand a chance of delivering the unfortunate news as diplomatically as possible. Whatever happened, I needed her to remain at Copeley Park and continue to work for Mrs Parsons – who I hoped could find her a suitable role – then I'd still be able to enjoy Gwen's company every now and again. A consolation at least.

CHAPTER 9

KATE

When I got back to Southfields, my flatmate Sophie was sitting on the sofa, watching *Friends* on TV. I'd moved in after splitting up with Spencer three months earlier. Shortly after Mum died, when I was twenty-five, I'd met Spencer at work – he was older than me, divorced, and handsome, with women throwing themselves at him all the time. When he sent me an email one afternoon, with the subject heading, 'I Fancy You', inviting me out for dinner, I was blown away that he'd chosen me. He was a senior editor, and we'd been making eyes at each other in marketing meetings ever since I started working at Snowflake Press. On that first date, he'd taken me to a cool restaurant on Dean Street in Soho, and we drank champagne followed by a bottle of Châteauneuf-du-Pape. He ordered the tasting menu of five courses of fancy food, served in teeny-tiny portions. At the end of the evening he saw me into a black cab, and the next day he emailed first thing and invited me out again.

Our romance was a whirlwind, and when he proposed within months it didn't feel too soon because we were *so* in love. Or I thought we were. In hindsight, I'd been clinging on to him as a means of support after all I'd been through. After losing

Mum to a brain tumour – she'd been given weeks to live when finding out the news – I then found myself losing Dad to one girlfriend after another. He'd apparently been a playboy in his youth, as part of the London scene in the 1980s. Granny had told me how he'd loved women, and they loved him, for he was very handsome and attracted admiring glances wherever he went. He bought a flat in South Kensington and frequented restaurants and bars and nightclubs with pop stars and actors and actresses and models. His photograph would often appear in tabloid newspapers and magazines. The paparazzi followed him everywhere, always wanting to know who his latest catch was. And then he met Mum, a model called Allegra Banks. She was from the East End of London, and the daughter of a builder and a cleaner. Mum had been spotted on the concourse of Liverpool Street station by a model scout when she was nineteen years old. Before long, she was gracing the front cover of *Vogue* and other big magazines. She had elocution lessons, and no one would have known she was from the East End. Mum being working class had always meant she kept me grounded. She brought a wholesomeness to Copeley Park that it had been lacking, Granny had told me – and it was always so clear how much she and Dad loved each other.

And so, I'd felt a sudden need to start my own family to replace the one I'd lost after Mum died. Spencer and I tried to conceive, but it didn't happen. After a year of trying – the sex going from mind-blowing to being more of a chore based solely around when I was ovulating – we arranged to see a fertility doctor and decided to start IVF. It was a horrendous time with the hormone injections impacting my mood and giving me hot flushes. Our relationship went downhill quickly from there. We began to argue more often than not, and the initial joy I'd felt on that first night out in Soho had completely dissipated. My marketing role at Snowflake Press became too much to cope with, and I began to lose focus. After a conversation with my boss, I took some time off before making the decision to freelance instead.

For a year, my life revolved around trying to get pregnant. It was physically and mentally exhausting, and, after a period of us not getting on, Spencer booked a holiday in Corfu to coincide with our second wedding anniversary. The location was beautiful – our hotel room had an uninterrupted view of the sea, and I would sit on the balcony and watch the boats go by. We sunbathed on the sandy beach in a private cove and drank cocktails in the evenings. For a few days it was like when we'd first got together. We laughed and talked about the novels we were working on as well as the ones we'd like to write ourselves. If only we had the time. But on the last evening we found ourselves discussing why it wasn't like this at home any more. Our relationship had been impacted by the pressure on us for me to conceive. Spencer said we needed to agree an end date. It was all right for him as he had two children from his previous marriage – he didn't see them often but, still, he'd been lucky enough to experience being a parent. I wasn't ready to give up on us having a baby, but we weren't on the same page. I'd rushed into the marriage to avoid properly grieving for Mum – to take my mind off the horror of it all. When you took away the good times Spencer and I had during those early days – our moods enhanced by endless dinners with fine wine, the novelty factor blinding us to each other's flaws – we didn't have much in common, apart from our place of work.

On our last evening in Corfu, we were walking back to the room after dinner, and I blurted out that I didn't want to be married any more. I needed to do the right thing and let him go. Spencer didn't love me enough to keep trying. He didn't want to move out of the house we'd bought together in Barnes, so we agreed that he'd buy me out of my half and take on all the mortgage payments. He hadn't done any of this yet. I didn't mind him staying there, as I couldn't wait to get away from the place where I'd been so unhappy. When my university friend, Sophie, said she needed a new flatmate to pay rent so she could afford her mortgage, I'd jumped at the chance to move in.

'Hi, Sophie,' I said, coming through the front door.

She picked up the remote control and paused the TV. 'Hi there, you.'

'Can I get you a cup of tea? I'm just going to make one.'

'I'm good, thanks.'

She didn't seem to be in the best mood, but then again she hadn't been that cheerful lately. I had been wondering if this had anything to do with me, if I'd offended her in some way. Was she fed up because I wasn't cleaning the bathroom as frequently as I could, or because I'd left dirty pans on the side the previous day? She'd brought all this up before, and I knew that I wasn't the tidiest person.

I filled the kettle and prepared a mug, then grabbed a chocolate digestive out of the biscuit tin on the side. I went to sit down on the sofa next to her. The living room was vast, with big windows and two three-seater sofas facing each other. There was a ginormous TV mounted on the wall that her boyfriend, Charlie liked to watch rugby matches on, at full volume. Like Sophie, he worked for a law firm – they'd met at some conference and hung out in the same circles. He was nice enough, but he stayed over far more than he should, considering that I was paying rent and half of the bills. They never went to his place because it was miles away near the end of one of the tube lines. He shared what sounded like a chaotic and disorderly house with other young male professionals who seemed to live as though they were students.

'It's been such a weird and annoying day,' I said with a sigh, biting into the biscuit.

Frowning, she said, 'Why, what happened?'

I told her about Granny giving me the bottle of wine, and then getting upset when I found the note. And then I explained how I'd ended up in the pothole when swerving to avoid Ben, and how I'd had to leave my car at Copeley Park.

'Oh dear, that's good he's sorting the tyre out though.'

'Yeah, he seemed like a nice guy,' I said.

She looked at me, and opened her mouth to speak but then closed it again. I sensed she wanted to tell me something. Yes, I needed to clear up more often, and I'd promise to do better. Maybe I could offer to pay for a takeaway.

'What's wrong, Sophie?'

'Nothing.'

'Are you sure?'

'You've had a bad enough day already. I don't want to add to your problems.'

What she had to say seemed to be bigger than me not having washed up or scrubbed limescale off the tiles in the shower. Whatever it was didn't bode well for me.

'Okay, well, you *have* to tell me now,' I said.

She looked away and then back at me again.

'I feel really bad about this, Kate, but well' – she ran a hand through her hair – 'I'm selling the flat.'

So, I'd need to find somewhere else to live. That was all right as it usually took ages to sell a place. I'd have at least three months, maybe six.

'Okay, that's not the end of the world.'

'Oh what a relief, I've been so worried about telling you!'

'When will you put it on the market, maybe in the spring?'

'Erm, well that's the thing... Charlie has been offered a new job in New York – it's his dream role, the one he's wanted for years.'

'And he wants you to go with him?'

She nodded.

'Yes.'

'But that won't be for a few months, will it? And can you work there without a visa?'

'I've actually managed to get a transfer to my New York office too – I wasn't expecting to. I asked my boss at work, and they can use someone like me. It would be a two-year contract, starting...'

My gut lurched. Soon, I knew it.

'Sometime in January,' she finished, unable to meet my gaze.

Finding somewhere new to live was the last thing I needed. It would be time-consuming, and more expensive too seeing as I'd no longer get mates' rates.

'But surely it will take some time to sell?'

'My brother is buying it from me – his girlfriend is pregnant, and they need somewhere bigger.'

'Oh.'

She sighed.

'I feel just awful about this, Kate, but they need to move in here in January. You're welcome to stick around for a bit, but her baby is due in February, so she'll need to make your room into a nursery.'

I didn't know how to take all this in. Sophie wasn't being entirely fair, throwing me out with barely any notice, and with Christmas coming, which was bound to make flat-hunting more difficult. What was I supposed to do? I sipped my tea and said nothing.

'I'm sorry, Kate,' she said again.

Shrugging, I said, 'It's okay. Congrats on the new job, I'll miss you.'

'Thanks, I'm really excited about it,' she said, her eyes lighting up. 'But I'll miss you too.'

It was a huge opportunity for Sophie. Normally, I'd be excited for her, and really I wanted to be, but the thought of having to find a new place so quickly was a real worry.

'Can't you live at Copeley Park until you find somewhere?' she said.

'I can... but you know the situation, with Dad and his fiancée, Emilie. I don't feel at home there.'

'It's a big old house – surely you can find a way to avoid each other?'

It was indeed, and Sophie was right, but it wasn't just the thought of bumping into Emilie. Going back to Copeley Park tugged at my emotions – I'd found the best way to deal with Mum's death was to pretend it had never happened. This probably wasn't the healthiest way, but when I wasn't at home there was a possibility that she was still alive, and I just hadn't seen her for a while.

'It's not that easy really,' I said.

Sophie had listened to me talk for hours on the sofa late at night when I'd been upset, and I was grateful for that, but she was probably tired of listening to my woes. I imagined that it could be draining being around a person who was going through a difficult time. Although I had helped her through a few disastrous break-ups over the years.

She got up off the sofa. 'I have to go and get ready. Charlie's taking me out for dinner tonight to celebrate the move.'

'Oh right, well you go and have fun,' I said, trying my best to sound cheerful.

'Thanks, Kate,' she said.

Since she'd been going out with Charlie over the past year, our friendship had changed. With her previous boyfriends, she'd always had time for me, but with him it was different. When he stayed at ours, he took over the place, as if they owned it together. And even though I was paying rent, I often felt like an imposter when he was around. The situation had been dragging on, getting gradually worse ever since I'd moved in, and perhaps being forced to leave would mean I'd find somewhere better anyway.

. . .

Sophie went into her bedroom and closed the door behind her. I picked up the remote control and skimmed the TV guide for something uplifting, but nothing grabbed me. I curled up on the sofa, pulled the throw over me and rested my head on a cushion. Closing my eyes, I took a deep breath. Maybe I'd have to move back to Copeley Park, but could I bear to be in the same house as Dad and Emilie? I was still paying half the mortgage on the house in Barnes, which meant I didn't have enough money to rent a place of my own. Spencer really needed to take over my share. There was no way I could afford to rent anywhere so close to central London without shelling out more. And that would be sharing with strangers. But then it struck me – I didn't need to live so close to central London now that I was freelancing. Sleeping on it was all I could do, and maybe the answer would present itself when I least expected it.

CHAPTER 10

LADY CHARLOTTE

When I woke up the next morning, my head ached from consuming far too much brandy in the library. I'd encouraged the footmen to refill my glass to soften the blow of Winston's humiliation of me. Besides it helped me to endure one dull conversation after another. But then I sat upright in bed as the previous night's dream played itself back to me. Albert had been showing me around the gardens, talking me through the eighteenth-century features – the grotto, the temple of Bacchus, the Gothic tower – telling me the names of trees and plants. After that, we'd gone into the woods, where a sea of bluebells carpeted the ground. He'd taken my hand in his, and we'd fallen against a tree. And then he leant in to kiss me. Sadly, I'd woken up before his lips reached mine.

Where had this dream come from out of nowhere? My subconscious must be mistaken. It was impossible not to notice that Albert was a fine-looking man, and he had a sympathetic aura about him. But I would need to dismiss any idea of us having romantic relations. I smiled to myself at a vision of the duchess discovering the two of us in flagrante delicto somewhere on the estate. The thought didn't bear thinking about.

A knock came at my bedroom door and Gwen entered, carrying a tray.

'Good morning, milady,' she said, brightly.

I always found it reassuring to see the dear girl when waking up as her demeanour was usually cheery. It would be unsettling to have someone I didn't know entering my quarters each morning. What if I didn't warm to this Madame Dupont? Would I be given the option to exchange her for someone else on the duchess's approved list? That was unlikely. All I could do was hope for the best. Poor Gwen didn't know of her fate yet, and it was up to me to inform her. Now was the time.

'You seem to be in a buoyant mood this morning, Gwen.'

'One of the footmen, George, was telling a joke in the servants' hall while we had our breakfast – he had us all in stitches, milady.'

I sensed that she was settling in at Copeley Park, and I'd noticed her mention this footman, George, a couple of times. The thought of denting her good mood made my task even more difficult.

She put the tray on the bed, and propped up an extra pillow behind me. Dear Gwen always seemed to know what I needed. On the tray was a rack of toast with small bowls of butter and marmalade, along with a pot of tea with jug of milk and bowl of sugar.

'The head gardener, Mr Hicks, will be waiting for you in his shed in the kitchen garden at ten o'clock, milady.'

'Excellent. Thank you for arranging that, Gwen.' I poured tea through the strainer into my cup, adding milk and sugar. 'Now, I need to talk to you about an important matter.'

Her face dropped, and I expected my tone of voice told her that I wasn't about to deliver good news. I interlocked my fingers. 'Winston's mother, the duchess, has requested that I employ a French lady's maid.'

Gwen gasped, and put a hand over her mouth.

'But what will become of me, milady?'

Dismissing an exemplary employee was unfair, and my heart went out to her.

'Well... let me tell you that I did ask Winston to talk her out of it, but he took her side.'

'Thank you for doing your best, milady.'

I'd hardly done my best, and it struck me that perhaps I could have refused. But it would have been a losing battle.

'The duchess is an interfering old bat, I'm afraid.'

Gwen's eyes were filled with sadness. Why had I brought her here to this place? Of course they wouldn't see a Welsh girl with barely any experience as being worthy of dressing a countess. I blamed myself for putting Gwen in this position. She'd been working for me for just over a year. Mama had thought it appropriate that I have a lady's maid, and she'd asked Gwen, our housekeeper's niece who helped out in the kitchen sometimes. Mama would say that you could employ a servant with years of experience but that didn't mean they were suitable for a role. She liked to bring them in when they were young and mould them to do a job how she wanted them to do it. They'd often be so grateful for the opportunity that they'd work hard and be loyal to the family. This had been her way of thinking with Gwen. She was only a year younger than me, and so Mama had thought she'd make a good companion as well as a lady's maid. And she'd been right.

Perhaps, rather than ask Mrs Parsons to find Gwen another role, I should send her back to Wales with enough money to keep her going until she secured a new position. But then there wouldn't be one person I trusted in this place, and it was tempting to be selfish and put my own needs before hers. Maybe I'd find another confidante, but who?

'I don't know what to say... would your parents find me a position at Rodene Hall?'

This was a feasible suggestion. One of my younger sisters

could employ Gwen. Mary would be turning eighteen soon. But I could not bear the thought of losing her completely.

'If you agree, I shall ask Mrs Parsons to find you a role elsewhere in the house. I'm sure she will come up with something suitable.'

Any position that Gwen was given was bound to be more junior than this one, but I refrained from telling her this. Besides, she would work it out for herself, if she hadn't already.

'But I only want to work for you, milady.'

'I know... and I am sorry. My hands are tied, sadly. In this house, I do not seem to wield any power at all.'

'Needless to say, I'm knocked for six, but I do understand your position.'

'I shall ensure that Mrs Parsons looks after you, Gwen, don't worry about that.' I would urge the housekeeper to do this, at least. 'And I hope that you might still come up and see me every now and again?'

'Of course, if Mrs Parsons doesn't mind.' She approached the wardrobe. 'What will you be wearing for your meeting with Mr Hicks?'

'A pair of slacks, a shirt, boots.'

'All right,' she said, her voice wavering. 'Would you mind terribly if I come back after you've finished your breakfast?'

It was clear that she needed a minute or two to compose herself.

'Yes of course. Take as long as you need, Gwen, within reason, obviously. I still need to meet Mr Hicks at ten o'clock.'

I didn't like the way I sounded, after only days as a countess. If I wasn't careful, being Winston's wife would change my character irrevocably. I couldn't bear to think of myself becoming like the duchess – so cold and mean.

Her lip trembled as if she were about to burst into tears.

'I shall return in twenty minutes, if that's all right?' She swallowed. 'You will still have two hours before your meeting.'

'Yes, of course, Gwen. Do go and have a sit-down.'

'Thank you, milady. You are too kind.'

She left the room, and I found myself alone in bed with the view of the lake. My interaction with Gwen had not gone well at all, and I couldn't help worrying about whether she'd be all right. I spread butter and marmalade onto my toast and poured myself another cup of tea from the pot. As it was already proving to be a challenging day, I dropped an extra sugar lump into my tea and gave it a thorough stir, my spoon tinkling against the cup. What would Mrs Parsons give Gwen to do? Would I have any influence over the decision? I felt just awful, but the matter was out of my hands. And for as long as the duchess was alive and well, I'd no doubt remain powerless at Copeley Park. Producing a son and heir for Winston would give me some kudos, to be sure, but still, it probably wouldn't make much difference.

When Gwen returned, having composed herself, she helped me to dress in a pair of khaki trousers, white shirt and knee-high boots. I left the house, and headed for the red-brick wall. When I entered the kitchen garden, I was greeted by birds singing in the trees that rose up from behind the walls. If I stood still, I could hear the swish and gurgle of the river nearby. I approached the shed and saw through the window that Albert was sitting at a desk, pen in hand, as he studied some papers. I tapped on the door, and the sound of his chair scraping the floor was followed by heavy footsteps.

He opened the door and smiled.

'Good morning, milady.'

'Good morning, Albert.'

There was an awkward silence as we looked at each other. He had no idea about my dream, but I was so very aware of it, of how romantic it had been.

Pushing my shoulders back, I said, 'Well, aren't you going to find me some work to do around here?'

'Yes, certainly.'

He walked in the direction of the beds, his boots crunching on the gravel path.

'You could do more weeding, if you so wished, or...'

'Yes, I'll do that. I find it quite satisfying.'

'Oh, all right. Perhaps, if you wanted to another time, you could plant bulbs and sow seeds in the greenhouse.'

'That sounds like fun, but weeding will suit me just fine for now, thank you, Albert.'

He stopped in front of a bed, containing a row of cabbages.

'You can start here then?'

'Of course.'

He took a small gardening fork out of his pocket and handed it to me, our fingers brushing.

'I'll leave you to it, then, milady.'

'And perhaps, Albert, when you have a spare moment, you could give me a tour of the estate?'

His eyes widened.

'I'd be delighted, milady. I'm sure we can arrange a suitable time.'

He went back to the shed, and I watched him go, wondering if we'd get to know each other better while I was working in the garden. How I hoped that we would. I was expecting to be so lonely at Copeley Park, and he seemed like someone who would be good company – especially with his knowledge of plants and flowers and trees. And Gwen had told me that he'd travelled to South America. I wanted to hear all of his stories – and most of all, I wanted to spend time with him.

CHAPTER 11

KATE

When I woke up the next morning – on my thirtieth birthday – there was a message on my phone from Ben, sent half an hour earlier.

> *Dropped your car at the garage and they need to order a new tyre. Should be ready this afternoon. Come over late afternoon?*
> *Ben*

It had just gone eight o'clock, so he must have got up fairly early in order to make the trip to Guildford, a fifteen-minute drive from Copeley. That was good of him to fit it in before starting his working day. I replied saying thank you, and that I'd go over to his place at around five. The thought of returning to his cottage made me smile to myself. Would he hand over my car key at his front door, and send me on my way? There would be no reason to invite me in this time, after all.

I pushed my arms through the sleeves of my dressing gown and knotted the belt. The heating hadn't kicked in yet, and the air in the flat was chilly. I went to make a cup of tea. After filling the kettle, I dropped a teabag into a mug, and went to open the slats on the Venetian blinds. Down below, cars were lined up in a traffic jam, as they usually were at this time of day. Commuters rushed along the pavement towards the tube station. Sophie had already left for the office as she liked to get in early, but I spotted an envelope on the table with my name on it. I lifted the flap, and inside was a birthday card from her and Charlie, and a voucher for a manicure and blow-dry at Pure Beauty in Wimbledon. What a lovely thought. I had a little admin to sort out, but no calls booked all day. I wondered if there would be any availability. Seizing the moment, I keyed the number into my phone, and managed to make one appointment after the other later that morning. Having a birthday on a Monday, when there was less demand, had been helpful in some way at least. What a boost – now my big birthday had some structure to it. I could take a book to my favourite café, Billy's Bakes, and get a coffee and pastry before my appointments. Afterwards, I'd look round the shops, before going back home to change. Then I would pick up the car from Ben's cottage.

I sat on the sofa drinking my cup of tea, and thought back to my conversation with Sophie the night before. I needed to move out, and soon. With Christmas coming, the pressure was real. Where would I go? I could insist on hanging around until I found somewhere, but I didn't fancy sharing with Sophie's brother and his pregnant girlfriend. What were my options? Moving back to Copeley Park was the obvious one, and Dad surely wouldn't mind. He still sent emails every now and again, asking me to try to understand his need to be with someone after Mum. He wasn't built to be alone, he'd say, but would never love any woman more than my mother. And he told me Mum had encouraged him to find someone else when she was on her deathbed – she'd wanted that for him. It would have been like her to say this, but still, that didn't make it any less difficult for me. I really did want to understand, but it was hard, especially as Emilie was so much younger than Dad. If she was closer to his age, it might be slightly easier to accept.

The house at Copeley Park had plenty of space, but it hadn't felt like my home for a few years. Emilie was nice enough, but she wasn't my mum, and being around her and Dad would be difficult. I'd be working some of the time and I could set up a desk in my bedroom if needed. And I could have one of the drawing rooms to myself in the evenings. But although it would be lovely to have the luxury of space to myself, I'd much rather have my own place. What if moving back to Copeley Park meant I was able to get to know Ben? That would be a bonus. Would he want to know me more? Or was he just being nice until the tyre was fixed as he felt responsible for the puncture?

I got up and made a cafetière of coffee and toast with strawberry jam and took it all into my bedroom to have while I was getting ready for my Wimbledon outing. I sat on my bed to scroll on my phone before getting in the shower, and was horrified to see Emilie's latest post on Instagram. She was a beauty product influencer with half a million followers. There it was – a photo of Emilie and Dad. Her hand rested on her stomach, the enormous diamond engagement ring catching the light.

> We're delighted to announce that we will be having a baby in the spring! 🤰

I groaned, suddenly feeling sick. This news was so far from what I wanted to hear. Why had Dad and Emilie not had the courtesy to tell me directly? Not only was she posting this on my thirtieth birthday, but also Dad knew how I'd struggled to conceive with Spencer. How was it fair that Dad was getting to have another child, and so easily – when he already had me, all grown up? He was sixty years old, for goodness' sake, and he was acting as though he was one of the Rolling Stones. So, on top of everything else, now there was a new baby – well, a half-brother or half-sister young enough to be my actual child – to contend with.

Everything felt totally overwhelming and later I'd need to write it all down in the notebook I kept by my bed and try to find a way through. I always organised my thoughts this way before sleeping every night – well, ever since splitting up with Spencer. Keeping diaries helped me to cope when I was struggling with anything difficult life was throwing at me. And I would print some of my favourite photos on my mini printer and stick them in too.

But still, I did need to carry on with my plans for the day. Yes, my life was falling apart more and more by the minute, but surely I deserved to have a nice birthday? I went downstairs, and when I passed the pigeonhole for the flat there was a card for me in there. I took it out and saw that the address was scrawled in Dad's handwriting. I opened the envelope. The card had a vase of flowers on the front, and inside it said:

Dear Kate,

Wishing you a very Happy 30th Birthday!

Do come and see me soon. It's been too long, and I have some news.

Love Dad and Emilie x

Oh, so he had planned to tell me about the baby in person – perhaps Emilie had posted on Instagram before he'd had chance to stop her. Still, I needed some time to process this bombshell. It did grate that the card was from Emilie too – who said she could be included on a birthday card from my father? I put the card back in the pigeonhole – I didn't need to be carrying *that* around all day.

Leaving the building, I took the tube to Wimbledon, where I ordered a cappuccino and almond croissant at Billy's Bakes. And there I sat at my favourite table in the corner, with the book I was reading, until my appointment at the salon. I'd been sent a proof by a publisher of a client's novel about life in London in the nineties.

I had my nails painted in a pastel-pink colour, and asked to have my hair blow-dried in a wavy style. It wasn't long since I'd had my blonde highlights done, and so it looked pretty good by the time the stylist had finished. While having my hair dried, I remembered the vineyard in Verona Granny wanted me to visit, and googled it on my phone: Vineria di San Martino. The photos were stunning. Maybe I *should* visit. I might be able to find out more about the mysterious 'B' that way, as well as take a much-needed break from everything.

After leaving the salon, I had a quick look round Ely's, where I treated myself to a blue cardigan – off the sale rack because one of the buttons was coming loose. I could soon fix that. Then I headed back to the flat and took a long bath. Afterwards, I sewed the button onto my new cardigan, intent on making myself look as good as possible for my trip to Ben's cottage. After the awkwardness of our first meeting, I wanted to arrive all bright and cheery, so he could see the best side of me. I wasn't sure why, but I felt some need to impress him. I wanted him to like me. Did I want him to find me attractive? I wasn't sure, but subconsciously it seemed I did because I was making a lot of effort with my appearance for the first time in quite a while.

CHAPTER 12

LADY CHARLOTTE

I started to spend most mornings in the kitchen garden, and I enjoyed being there immensely. Sometimes, Albert would bring me a cup of tea from Rosemary Cottage, where he lived, on the other side of the far wall. Once he brought me a slice of ginger cake. Although we didn't converse much, I felt that he was beginning to feel more comfortable in my presence, and for that I was grateful. How I wanted him to ask me inside the cottage, so I could sit with him by the fire and drink my tea there. Would it be appropriate for me to invite myself into his home? I could try to come up with a reason to visit, although I had no idea what it could be.

One morning, Albert offered to take me on a tour of the gardens. He showed me the temple of Bacchus – the Roman god of wine – the Gothic tower, the crystal grotto. And then he led me round a corner, where the path steepened and twisted as it wound through the trees. Clusters of snowdrops grew beneath them and I breathed in the scent of wild garlic. At the top of the hill stood a quaint hut with a thatched roof.

'Oh, how very charming,' I said.

'This is the hermitage. The story goes that the third Duke of

Dorking paid a hermit to live here in the late 1700s, as one sometimes did in those days. He attempted to write poetry about the landscape, but legend has it that he became bored within a matter of days and was seen drinking at the Dog and Duck by villagers.'

I laughed. 'One can hardly blame him. I expect he was incredibly lonely out here, especially at night.' I shuddered at the thought of being stuck there in the dark, all alone.

Albert looked at me. 'I'm sure he was, milady. I could probably manage a night or two, but would much rather be in my cottage myself.'

We turned round and followed the path back downhill. Albert pointed at a shrub with glossy green leaves.

'This is laurel, one of many poisonous plants to be found here at Copeley Park,' he said.

A mischievous thought came into my mind. How I'd like to slip a few leaves into Winston's tea when he was looking the other way. Of course I wouldn't resort to doing such a thing, but the thought made me smile to myself.

'Imagine what one could do with them, rather like in an Agatha Christie novel.'

'Indeed,' he said with a chuckle.

He started to walk again until we came to the lake. We passed rhododendron bushes in full bloom, their clusters of large pink flowers a joy to see. A duck waddled past us with a few ducklings in tow – so delightful. The estate at Copeley Park was indeed beautiful, and I counted myself lucky to have the grounds at my disposal – for they softened the blow of having to be married to a man I despised.

Albert stopped walking, and pointed to a slope leading down to the lake.

'You see this slope here?'

I nodded.

'Well, the third Duke of Dorking planted a vineyard there –

he took his head gardener of the day to France, and they brought back vine cuttings. They produced sparkling wine to rival champagne, apparently, and it was popular with local aristocrats.'

'How wonderful,' I said.

'But then when he died, his son had no interest in wine, and the vineyard was left to decay.'

'Oh, what an awful shame. Imagine if we revived the vineyard, Albert. Wouldn't that be fun?'

He laughed.

'Hmm, I suppose it would be... the slope is south-facing, and the lake would help protect vines from frost... but I'm not sure his lordship would be interested in producing wine.'

'Well, I know he happens to like drinking it,' I said.

A smile passed his lips. Clearly, he knew my husband was a drunk, as everyone did.

Then I thought about my cousin, Agnes, who'd married an Italian. She was living on a vineyard near Verona. Imagine if I went to see her – maybe Albert would come with me, and then we could bring back vine cuttings like the third Duke of Dorking had. I made this suggestion to him.

He fiddled with his earlobe.

'That sounds like a wonderful idea, milady,' he said, but I wasn't sure whether he meant it. I supposed that he didn't think Winston would be enthusiastic. Well, I would just have to ask him when the opportunity arose.

Winston spent more or less all of his time in London, although word below stairs had it – Gwen informed me – that he was also travelling to Germany, supposedly in secret, to mix with his vile Nazi friends. I wasn't sure whether to believe this or not. I didn't want to, at all, and, seeing as there was nothing I could do, I tried my best to imagine Gwen hadn't told me anything.

When in London, he would sit in the House of Lords, and he had a house in Mayfair. He would dine at exclusive restaurants and go to gentlemen's clubs with his friends. He didn't seem to be much interested in knowing me, and I could not have been lonelier stuck at Copeley Park with only the servants as company. On occasion, the duchess would take it upon herself to grace me with her presence. She'd try to give me advice on some matter or other. The French lady's maid she'd selected, Madame Dupont, had apparently given notice to her current employer, and she'd arrive at Copeley Park in due course. Mrs Parsons was still deciding what Gwen could do instead and I tried not to dwell on it too much.

Gwen also told me that some of the servants would move between Copeley Park and Winston's house in Mayfair. Apparently, when Winston was in London he had a series of mistresses that he'd entertain there. He would take them to the theatre, and to restaurants. This revelation, if it were indeed true, horrified me. I was merely the potential bearer of his offspring. For as long as I didn't produce an heir, I had little status. I considered whether to raise the matter with Winston. He could be abrasive most of the time, and I did not wish to get into an argument. But at least this revelation didn't make me feel quite so guilty about my developing friendship with Albert. Although perhaps I should find out if there was any truth in this rumour before jumping to conclusions.

When writing in my diary at night, I considered leaving my husband. The chauffeur could drive me to the station. I would take a suitcase, and inform everyone that I was going to stay with my family for a few days. But where would I really go? Papa would be devastated if I left Winston, and it was most unlikely that I'd be welcomed with open arms at Rodene Hall. Leaving did not seem to be a viable option. I found that the only way to cope was to carry on gardening every day – this at least settled the thoughts going through my mind. Problems always seemed to weigh down on me less when I was outside, breathing in the fresh air with my hands in the soil. That was all I could do while remaining optimistic that matters would somehow improve in time.

The house at Copeley Park had so many rooms that, when Winston did come back from London, we were able to go about our daily business without encountering each other at all. When he wasn't carrying out country pursuits, riding or checking on his newly acquired racehorses at stables nearby, he spent most of his time in the red drawing room. And so, I took up residence in the blue drawing room or the library. We ate separately, and at different times. His luncheon was arranged around whatever he was doing each day. Mine was arranged around my time in the garden. I maintained my secret life by taking tea in the library after breakfast where I'd read or write letters. Once I knew for certain that Winston had left the house for the morning, I'd go upstairs and change into the clothes selected for me by Gwen especially for gardening.

One weekend when Winston returned, he brought a handful of guests, including Jasper and Penelope. On Saturday they went to Sandown Park in Esher to watch one of his new horses race, and they all returned inebriated after spending the day in a box. We had dinner and then I retired upstairs, complaining of a headache.

On the Sunday morning, when I thought that Winston had gone out, I went up the main staircase to my bedroom to change for gardening. He was on the landing, walking from his bedroom to the top of the stairs. Now that he'd seen me there was no escape, and I continued to walk up the stairs, bracing myself for our encounter. We hadn't been alone together since that awful dinner party. I'd done all I could to avoid being in a room with him since. He was wobbling as he walked, and he gripped the top of the banister to steady himself. I'd become used to seeing him like this. He would drink from the moment he woke up until he fell into bed at night. It was only eleven o'clock in the morning and he had the remainder of the day to get through. No doubt he would take a series of naps in his chair by the fire in the red drawing room. This certainly wouldn't be the right time to ask him about reviving the vineyard.

'Good morning, Charlotte,' he said.

'Good morning, Winston.'

I reached the landing and found myself standing beside him. He glared at me with those beady brown eyes – I detested the way they assessed me – and I inhaled, quietly. For if he knew that I found him intimidating he was bound to use it to his advantage. I feared that he almost enjoyed seeing me at my most vulnerable. I forced a smile, hoping he'd descend the stairs and leave me alone. But he remained standing there. I moved past him, and he turned round to face me, his back to the stairs. He was so close, I could smell the brandy on his breath.

'I wish you a good day, Winston.'

He looked me up and down.

'Why didn't you come to my room last night, Charlotte?'

'I told you that I had a headache.'

'Codswallop.'

'That's simply not true.'

'I do not wish to be wondering where you might be.'

It was no use disagreeing with him.

'You are absolutely right, of course.'

As he looked down at me, I couldn't have found him more repulsive, with his reddening face and bulging belly. I longed for him to leave me alone.

'Well, I wish you a good day,' I said, again.

'You keep wishing me a good day. But how can it be a good day, when there is no sign of an heir?'

I bit my lip.

'Answer me, will you?' he said.

'I... I don't know what to say, Winston.'

'You know why we married, and you are not keeping your side of the bargain.'

I felt like pointing out that he'd taken a huge sum of money from my father, to pay off all his debts, and he was now living very comfortably. And he had a wife who was almost twenty years his junior. He had done rather well out of the arrangement. I wouldn't dare say any of this.

'I apologise for not coming to your room last night but rest assured that I shall visit you soon.'

'Very good. Tonight, then.'

I nodded, reluctantly. But still, he didn't move. What was I supposed to do? I couldn't be the one to end our conversation – it had to be him. And so I waited, hoping he'd descend the stairs.

'You know what will happen if you don't give me a son, don't you?' he said.

I blinked.

'What will happen exactly, Winston?'

'It will not be good for you. Let us say that, shall we?'

What on earth was he implying? My gut churned. Sometimes I found myself thinking about how both of his former wives had died so young, supposedly one from diphtheria and the other in childbirth. What if... he'd somehow been involved in their deaths after they gave him daughters rather than sons? My imagination was running away with me, and I told myself to stop being so absurd.

'I'm sure that before long I shall become with child, and that child will be your son,' I said, not believing this at all. But what else could I say? The man was drunk and standing over me, and I needed to say what he wanted to hear, so he'd leave me alone and go away.

He smiled to himself as if a thought had struck him all of a sudden.

'Why don't we go to my room now? I'm rather in the mood for love-making.'

The thought of having to take my clothes off and go to bed with Winston while he was so inebriated horrified me. There was no way I would do it.

'I would rather not, if you don't mind.'

He laughed. 'Do you have somewhere to be?' While I struggled to find an answer, he added, 'Because actually, my dear, I do mind. As my wife, you are at my disposal at all times, and if I wish to take you to bed, then you shall do as I say.'

'But—' I said.

'Charlotte, I command you to start walking in the direction of my room.' He started to undo his belt, and I felt sick to the stomach. 'And make haste, I'm having tea with the vicar at eleven thirty.'

There was no way I'd give in to him.

'Why are you not moving?'

'I won't do it.'

'Yes, you will.'

I considered running away from him, back down the stairs. Maybe, as he was inebriated, he'd forget we'd had this exchange.

But before I could go anywhere, he lunged towards me, his eyes blazing with fury. I put out a hand to protect myself, and he fell backwards, crying out, 'You damn fool,' as he tumbled down the stairs one after the next until he reached the bottom with a loud crash. My heart pounded so loudly I could almost hear it in my ears. He lay completely still, the brandy glass on the marble floor of the grand hall next to him, smashed into smithereens.

'Nooo, Winston!' I screamed.

My legs turned to jelly, and I clutched the banister to steady myself. What had I done?

CHAPTER 13

LADY CHARLOTTE

In that moment, everything seemed so surreal. I put a hand on my chest to steady my breath. My heart was thumping, and the blood was rushing in my ears. I stood at the top of the stairs looking down at my husband, who lay on the black-and-white tiled floor. His neck was at a funny angle, and he was completely still, and – dare I think it... lifeless – surrounded by broken glass, with a splash of blood on the palm of his hand. Surely, it couldn't be possible that I'd killed him? I hadn't meant to – I was merely protecting myself.

The sound of a door closing interrupted my thoughts, and a wave of fear rushed through me. Who was that and which room had they just entered? Had they seen me accidentally push Winston down the stairs? Or from a distance, would it look as though he'd slipped while drunk? All the servants and guests were supposed to be at St John's for the Sunday morning service, so I had no idea who could be in the house.

Winston had seemed so determined to have a confrontation with me, and I'd done all I could to prevent it from happening. I'd tried so hard to move away from him, but he'd continued to goad me, over and over again. Was he dead, or unconscious?

How I hoped for the latter. Or did I? Deep down, did I wish he were dead? My life would be easier without him in it. Our marriage had been a disappointment from the moment he placed the ring upon my finger at the altar. I'd lain awake at night, trying to fathom how I was going to endure being attached to this repulsive man for the rest of my life. How did women manage to stay with a man they did not like even one bit? How was it fair to expect a woman to stay with a man who was continuously so cruel and unkind for their whole lives? How was it possible to spend one's days worrying about when that husband might next stand over them in an intimidating manner and say vile things that made them feel utterly worthless?

Pushing my shoulders back, I braced myself and descended the grand staircase, passing the portraits of Winston's ancestors, and it felt as though their eyes were following me. I could almost hear them chanting, 'What *have* you done, Charlotte?' When I reached the bottom of the stairs, where he lay so helplessly, I could barely bring myself to look at him. I wasn't a doctor, but it seemed inevitable that his neck was broken. I bent down and carefully lifted his wrist to feel for a pulse. Nothing. I sat on the floor, leant over his body and rested an ear on his chest. There was no thump of a heartbeat to be heard. He was dead, I was sure of it.

How would I explain what had happened to the servants, and to his family? I needed to concoct a story, and in haste. If anyone jumped to the conclusion that I'd intentionally pushed him down the stairs, I would be arrested and sent to prison. And then before long, I could be hanged for murder, unless I was pregnant with his child – and that was highly unlikely. When I'd put my hand out to defend myself, I hadn't intended to kill him. It had been an accident, and I couldn't allow myself to take the blame. Someone else needed to discover his lifeless body, a servant ideally. And then they would take care of everything, and when they came to tell me I would act as though I were utterly shocked and completely devastated by the news. As I played out this scene in my head, I found myself forming the facial expression I would make when they told me. My eyebrows would be raised, and I would blink very fast, put a hand to my chest and cry out, 'Noooo, but how can this be?' A tear would run down my face, and I would say how unfair it was that my husband of only a few months should meet such a terrible fate. We were just beginning our lives together – what would I do without him by my side?

A dizzy feeling consumed me, all of a sudden, as the reality of what had just happened hit me. I gasped, finding myself struggling to breathe. I needed to go outside and get some fresh air. Besides, there was no way I could risk being caught at the scene of what could be considered to be a crime. I needed to make myself scarce, and swiftly too. I ran across the grand hall, the heels of my shoes tip-tapping on the black-and-white tiled marble floor, and then I opened the grand door. It was old and heavy, and I found it a struggle. Stepping outside, I closed the door behind me and inhaled the spring air, desperate to calm my breathing. Beyond, a morning mist hung above the hills, creating an eerie mood to go with my own. But then I heard someone clear their throat. Looking down, I was horrified to see Albert on his knees, his hands immersed in a flowerbed right outside the front door. Oh no! He would have seen me step outside and look around me, all disorientated. He would put two and two together, wouldn't he? When a policeman came to question the servants, Albert would be obliged to tell the truth about what he'd witnessed. He didn't owe me anything, and I couldn't expect him to be loyal to me, could I?

'Good morning, milady,' he said, brightly, looking up at me.

'Good morning, Albert,' I said, my voice wavering. I raised my chin, doing my best to act as a lady of the house should when coming across a servant unexpectedly.

He stood up and brushed mud off his trousers with his hands.

'You look rather pale, milady. Are you quite all right?'

His concern for my welfare was a comfort. Somehow, I found myself wishing he could put his arms around me and pull me to him and tell me not to worry. Perhaps he would take my side and help me, if I asked him nicely? I had no idea how he viewed Winston – had he interacted with him much, and did he find him to be a fair employer? If I told Albert the truth, could I trust him? My gut told me that he was a good egg. Would he understand if I explained to him that I hadn't meant to push Winston down the stairs, that I'd been defending myself? How I'd put out a hand when Winston had lunged towards me? Would it be me lying at the bottom of the stairs in his place if I hadn't reacted in that way? Should I concoct a story to cover myself? I'd been hoping for more time before seeing anyone, to be able to mull over my thoughts and ideas while taking a walk round the gardens. But as soon as a servant discovered Winston's body, the word would be out. And then what would Albert think, having seen me leave the scene of the crime, believing that I was the only person in the house? I still had no idea who might have witnessed what had occurred.

Albert would surely jump to the conclusion that I had done my husband in, intentionally. By telling him the truth now, perhaps I would be able to get him to understand, and then he'd be more likely to believe my side of the story. My lips trembling, I struggled to get the words out.

'Something terrible has happened, Albert, and...'

'What is it, milady?'

'I don't know what to do.'

'Can I be of assistance, at all?'

'Yes, I would be most grateful... the other servants and guests are at church, and I'm in complete shock, as you can probably gather.'

I noticed that my hand was shaking, and I put it behind my back.

'If Mr Skinner were here, I would ask him for help.'

He looked down at me, his eyes filled with concern. I could tell he was a kind man, and that he really wanted to assist me. Trusting him would be a slight risk, but I didn't have to divulge everything.

'Do tell me, milady,' he said, gently.

'Well, Albert...' I said, my voice breaking up, and I could barely string two words together.

'Yes, milady?'

My mouth was dry, and when I opened it no words came out.

'Why don't you start from the beginning?'

'All right... I was on my way to the kitchen garden when I came across my husband's body, sprawled across the floor and... and there was a brandy glass smashed to smithereens beside him. I think... I think he's dead,' I whispered.

As I explained all of this to him, I realised that I wasn't wearing gardening clothes. This was because I'd been on my way up the stairs to get changed. I hoped that Albert wouldn't notice this minor detail.

'So it seems that your husband was inebriated and probably slipped and fell down the stairs, and you think—'

'Yes, I think my husband is in fact dead, Albert.'

As I repeated those words, I couldn't actually believe I was saying them.

His brow furrowed. Albert seemed to be thinking as he studied my face, and I wondered whether he was considering if I was telling the absolute truth.

'I am so sorry, milady. How can I help you?'

In the distance, I could see the servants coming along the path, on their way back from St John's, their voices a distant murmur as they chattered away. Within minutes they would enter the house, and all hell would break loose. I was running out of time.

'What do you suggest I do, Albert?'

'All you can do is wait for the servants to return.' He nodded in their direction. 'Have a word with Mr Skinner as a matter of urgency, and' – he looked me in the eye as if he knew I was hiding something – 'he will take care of everything. Butlers are used to dealing with all kinds of situations, so he will know how to proceed.'

'Thank you, I do appreciate your reassurance.'

'Are you absolutely certain he is dead though? There is a possibility that he might be unconscious. Shall I take a look?'

'I would appreciate that very much.'

I turned around and went up the steps and pushed open the main door. Perhaps it had all been a dream and I'd go back inside to find Winston's body was no longer lying there. Albert followed me into the grand hall, and across the marble floor, leaving a trail of mud from his boots. But now was not the time to care about such insignificant matters. Winston was still lying there – it hadn't been a dream, after all – and we approached his lifeless body together.

Shaking his head, Albert let out a sigh, then he bent down and checked for a pulse, as I had done.

'Yes, he appears to be dead. His neck is sitting at such an unnatural angle, it's bound to be broken, milady. I imagine that he will have died instantly, if that's reassuring at all, to know that he wasn't in any pain.'

'Yes, that's a small consolation, at least.'

Standing up, he said, 'I am very sorry for your loss.'

He ran a hand through his hair, and we exchanged a look, and again I was certain that he sensed there was more to my story. I could almost read the thoughts running through his head. It was as if we were having a conversation without actually having it. With that look, he was telling me that he knew

Winston had been a bad man – whatever had happened, if I'd been somehow involved with his fall, it was not my fault.

How I wanted to ask, 'Do you think everyone will believe that I merely discovered his body?' But of course, I couldn't.

It was then that I saw Mr Skinner come through the door that led from the servants' quarters into the cloakroom off the grand hall. I called out to him.

'Mr Skinner, please come and help us. My husband has had a terrible accident.'

CHAPTER 14

KATE

When I arrived at Copeley station, there weren't any taxis at the rank, so I walked along the high street, past the butcher, greengrocer, bakery, tea shop, and florist with a wonderful selection of flowers on the pavement in bright colours – roses, chrysanthemums, freesias. There was also an adorable gift shop where I'd bought birthday and Christmas presents growing up. Copeley was a charming village with its eighteenth-century, and even Tudor buildings, and people would visit at weekends to go for Sunday lunch at the Dog and Duck, or they'd take a picnic to a table by the river during the summer months. Ramblers would follow the towpath to Gatley, en route to Guildford. And groups of cyclists would descend every now and again, especially on Sunday mornings. They'd congregate in the square with takeaway coffee cups and bags of pastries before getting back on their bikes and moving on to the next village. The tea shop provided cream teas throughout the year and visitors would take photos of themselves outside St John's because it had been used in hit film from the 1990s, *The Day Out*. Copeley had been covered with fake snow and the heroine drove down the high street in a yellow Citroën 2CV, looking all flustered as she tried to find the church for her friend's wedding ceremony.

At the end of the high street, I took a right at St John's, then at the end of Church Lane I went through the pedestrian gates, keying in a special code for staff members to use. I walked past the main house on my right, and then along the narrow lane towards Ben's cottage, taking care to avoid all the potholes and puddles. I'd put on a pair of boots especially.

Ahead, the sky was a burnt orange beyond the trees. I stopped to take it all in, and snapped photos on my phone. Nature could be truly wonderful. I'd missed out on dramatic winter sunsets when staying in the office at Snowflake Press until late. I'd leave for work in the dark and return in the dark. Usually, I didn't even make it outside at lunchtime, meaning I wouldn't see any daylight during the week. Being here in this moment had stopped me in my tracks. I wasn't working in an office any more, and perhaps I should make more effort to get outside and breathe in fresh air – break the bad habits I'd got into. Perhaps I wasn't an urban girl after all.

My childhood had been spent in this place, and I'd forgotten how peaceful it was. I'd left the countryside for the big city because it was exciting at the time – it was a common rite of passage for someone in their twenties. But now, I'd done it. I'd lived in London for several years, and it had been fun. Being close to restaurants, bars and nightclubs had been convenient, but I wasn't bothered about going out in the evenings any more. Most of my friends had moved further out so they could afford flats and houses with husbands or partners. I'd reached an age where I wanted to sit at home in a cosy environment, embrace my inner hygge – to have a living room with a plush rug, an abundance of lamps, candles, throws and cushions. After seeing Ben's real fireplace, I craved having one again. There was something relaxing about 'just being' beside a real fire, and I loved the aroma of burning wood.

As I made my way up the lane, I was taken back to the days when I'd roamed the fields around Copeley Park with schoolfriends, who I'd invite for sleepovers. The fun we used to have! Sometimes in the summer, Dad would set up a camp for us down by the river, near to Granny's cottage, complete with a real fire made from sticks and logs we'd collected in the woods. He'd fry sausages, and then we would have hot dogs followed by marshmallows that we'd hold over the fire, attached to long wooden skewers. I could almost smell their sugary aroma as this memory came back to me – I smiled to myself. Granny would let us use her downstairs bathroom, and sometimes she'd bring out a chair and join us with a glass of wine. We'd sleep in a tent with Mum and Dad in another one nearby, listening to sounds of the wildlife as we lay there in our sleeping bags – owls hooting, and the rustling of animals in the bushes, probably foxes or even deer.

Had I reached a time in my life where I needed to take a step back and contemplate my future? I'd seen with friends how a big birthday could make you re-evaluate your life. Maybe I should take some time off, and make the trip that Granny wanted me to go on – to the vineyard in Verona. What did I have to lose? I needed to mark my big birthday in some significant way.

At the T-junction, I turned left, and before long, Rosemary Cottage came into view. Smoke wafted from the chimney. Would I get to sit in front of that fire again? I wondered if Ben had a girlfriend. Someone as attractive and kind as him was bound to have a woman who was madly in love with him. He was such a catch that he might even have more than one woman in love with him. I couldn't help envying whoever these women might be. But then I told myself to stop being so ridiculous. Firstly, I didn't want to be with anyone so soon after the end of my marriage, and, secondly, we'd only just met. How can you know someone that quickly? After I'd collected the car, there would be no reason for us to have any more contact. He'd probably delete my number from his phone as if we'd never met.

As these thoughts ran through my mind, a torrential downpour came from nowhere, instantly drenching me completely through. My jeans clung to my legs, and my suede jacket had done nothing to protect my top half. Damn, my incredible blow-dry was totally ruined. Why hadn't I worn a waterproof coat and brought an umbrella? So now I was going to arrive at Ben's cottage completely dishevelled, when I'd gone to all that effort to look my best.

A tall, elegant brunette came out of the front door. She was wearing a mac – very sensible. Of course she was sensible – if she was Ben's other half, she would be perfect, naturally. She got into a car, reversed out of the drive, then sped off up the road, the wheels splashing through the puddles.

The sight of my car, parked in front of Ben's Land Rover, brought some relief. So he must have managed to get the tyre, and fit it too. It was now almost dark, and, using my phone torch, I squatted down and pressed the tyre with the palm of my hand – it seemed firm enough to me. Light flashed across the sky, followed by a crack of thunder, making me jump out of my skin. Rain tumbled down even thicker and faster, and I ran through the gate to the porch by the front door.

Through the window, I spotted the chair I'd sat in the previous day, and a log fire was going at full throttle in the hearth. I rapped the knocker and heard footsteps. This might be the last time I saw him. Should I come up with an excuse to see him again? Our first encounter had seemed significant, as if we were supposed to meet each other. Surely this short time together wasn't it? Well, it would be if that woman had been his wife or girlfriend.

The front door opened and there stood Ben, a big smile on his face. He wore a red lumberjack shirt and jeans, and he looked hot. But I wasn't allowed to think that – he clearly had another woman in his life. When I looked down at his left hand, there was no wedding ring on his finger. So it was unlikely that woman was his wife then. She was probably a girlfriend, and she'd just popped out to the shop or something. I was just here to pick up my car and that was it. Then I'd be on my way – even though I was drenched through, and would be shivering all the way home.

'Hello there, Kate,' he said. Then he studied me. 'Oh dear, look at the state of you!'

I'd gone to so much trouble with my appearance, and there had been no point whatsoever. I took off my gloves – my manicured nails at least weren't impacted by the rain.

Rolling my eyes, I said, 'I know.'

He stood there shaking his head. The situation was quite comical really, and I burst into laughter.

His face broke into a huge grin. He stepped backwards and gestured for me to go inside.

'You'd better come in so we can get you dry. And happy birthday! Maybe I can make you a hot chocolate to warm you up.'

'Sounds lovely,' I said.

At least I'd given him a reason to invite me in.

CHAPTER 15

LADY CHARLOTTE

After Winston's 'tragic demise', the house at Copeley Park fell into mourning and Gwen only put out black crepe dresses and bonnets for me to wear. The servants also wore black, out of respect for the late master of the house. The vicar, Mr Bridges, came to the house to discuss the funeral, and I sat in the library with the duchess while we discussed hymns and psalms. We had to wait for the post-mortem examination to be completed before Winston could be buried at St John's, and every day dragged on and on. All I wanted to do was erase the memory of that horrific morning, but the image of Winston falling flashed through my mind several times a day. And I'd wake up in the middle of the night shouting, 'No, Winston, nooo...' as once again I'd had a nightmare where he tumbled down the stairs before my eyes.

Guilt consumed me, naturally, and I wrote down thoughts and feelings in my diary, which I kept locked in the top drawer of my writing table. For I could confide in no one, not even Gwen. I knew she would understand, but couldn't put her in a position where she might find herself lying to the police. The only person who might suspect I wasn't telling the truth was

Albert. He'd seen me run out of the front door, all flustered. By now, he might have realised that I wasn't wearing gardening clothes even though I'd claimed to be on my way to the kitchen garden. This inconsistency in my story didn't necessarily make me a murderer, but surely it would make him question whether I was telling him the absolute truth.

The only consolation was that I knew Winston had been a bad man. And now I was free from his clutches. His younger brother, Jasper, would inherit the title, but he'd remain at his home in Sevenoaks. If I was pregnant with Winston's son, then the title would go to him instead of Jasper, but that was most unlikely. Papa had drawn up a contract with Winston's father, the Duke of Dorking, when we married to ensure the Copeley Park estate would be inherited by me in the event of Winston's death. However, although I was now free from my vile husband, PC Wilson from the local constabulary had visited the house and conducted interviews with the servants. Afterwards, he spoke to me briefly in the library, and seemed satisfied with my answers to his questions. I stuck to my story, and didn't mention that there might have been a witness in the house at the time of Winston's death. PC Wilson concluded that he couldn't see any evidence of foul play, and for that I was most grateful. He said it had been an unfortunate accident and no one was to blame apart from the man himself, who had clearly been inebriated. I gathered from the way he spoke about Winston that he hadn't been popular amongst the local community, and this didn't surprise me at all. But still, I had no idea who had closed that door after Winston went tumbling down the stairs. And this concerned me somewhat. What had they seen? Had they been eavesdropping on our whole conversation? Perhaps one of the servants had been feeling unwell and hadn't attended church. So far, no one had come forward, but what if whoever it was decided to inform the police? There was no evidence, and it would be their word against mine, if they did, I hoped.

The day of the funeral at St John's, where members of the Clarkson family were buried, going back centuries, came and went. Watching Winston's coffin being lowered into the ground while the duchess sobbed so loudly all of Surrey could probably hear brought some closure to the whole episode. Afterwards, I felt immense relief, for it was a huge weight off my shoulders. That period between someone's death and the funeral is like a no-man's-land of time.

One of my tasks as Winston's widow had been to inform relations, friends and acquaintances of his death, and when the funeral was to be held and where. This involved a great deal of letter writing, and there were telephone calls to make and receive. The postman brought piles of letters to Copeley Park, expressing sympathy, and I was tasked with replying to them all. I chose to do this at the writing table in the library. Gwen had to go to the stationer's in the village as I ran out of the Copeley Park headed paper. But I didn't mind spending my days penning letters, and it helped to pass the time while the house was in mourning.

Although I did not miss Winston one bit, my plight as a widow at the age of nineteen was not one to be envied. Would I marry again? Would any man be interested in me? If I were to marry again, it should be for love – to the right man. I could not allow myself to be coerced into a marriage arranged by my father for a second time. Papa had already sent a letter to say that although he was sorry for my loss, and so soon after the wedding, he would keep an eye out for potential suitors to take Winston's place. Mama told me on the telephone that he'd been talking to acquaintances at his London club – there were a few gentlemen who'd jump at the chance to become my husband. I was most concerned that Papa wanted to arrange another marriage to a man I did not know or like. Although I was a widow, at least I had money of my own, and an estate. I actually wielded more power as a widow than as Winston's wife, and the irony of this was not lost on me.

As Winston's wife, I was expected to spend a respectable period of time in mourning. I did not like the colour black for it made me look pallid, but I had no choice in the matter. I could not socialise but that wasn't important to me, and so I spent my time gardening. No one could object to me doing that now. The duchess had no interest in me any more, and there had been no further mention of Madame Dupont becoming my lady's maid. After the funeral, the duchess had quietly left Keeper's Cottage and returned to the grand house she shared with the duke in a village where Surrey bordered Hampshire.

I continued to work in the kitchen garden every day, and Albert and I grew closer. We would have a conversation every now and again – only small talk, about the weather or some plant or flower. His shed overlooked the kitchen garden, and sometimes when I was weeding I'd catch him standing at the window, looking out in my direction. I couldn't help thinking, nay hoping that he found me to be beautiful. This was not something I should be wondering, I knew that, but I couldn't help being drawn to the man. He was blessed with a face that one could study all day long. I liked the way he'd look out from under the brim of his cap at me with those large green eyes – they seemed to bore into me, as if they were reading my every thought. His shoulders were broad, and his chest immense – he had a physique like the marble statues that graced the blue drawing room. On occasion I'd notice chest hair peeking from where the buttons were undone at the top of his shirt – how I wanted to run my hands over it. Just the thought of doing this made me stop and catch my breath. I would often imagine what he looked like without any clothes, not a ladylike thought for me to have at all. But I couldn't help myself. No man had had such an effect on me before. How I wanted him to take me in his arms and press those lips to mine.

Sometimes, on colder days, Albert would invite me into the shed and make me a cup of tea, and I'd sit in a chair facing him as he looked at me from behind his desk. On occasion, he would offer me a biscuit, made by Cook, Mrs Coleman, who seemed to have a soft spot for him – of course she did. We'd exchange pleasantries, and sometimes a moment of silence would fall between us – for with Albert, I did not feel the need to utter words the whole time. Being with him soothed me, and I savoured every second of his company. Back at the house, after a few hours in the garden, he would occupy my mind. I'd have imaginary conversations with him and sometimes I would write about him in my diary. I'd pen letters to him at the desk in my bedroom, saying how I couldn't help falling in love with him. Then I'd scrunch up the letters and cast them into the fire – goodness, the trouble I would find myself in if anyone read the words I'd written! For a widowed countess to be in love with a gardener, and so soon after her husband's demise under tragic circumstances, would horrify everyone I knew... apart from Gwen, perhaps.

CHAPTER 16

LADY CHARLOTTE

A few weeks after the funeral, I received a note from Lady Penelope, the wife of Winston's younger brother Jasper.

Dear Charlotte,

I would like to invite you to lunch on the 25th July, at one o'clock. I've reserved a table at Clementine's on Regent Street.

Yours,

Penelope

Presumably she was being kind, inviting me to lunch, ensuring that I had someone to talk to after Winston's tragic death. Gwen agreed to accompany me into London, and I suggested she wait for me at Lyons Corner House on the Strand nearby. I wore a black dress and bonnet. We took the train to Waterloo station, and a taxi to Regent Street.

In the restaurant, I was directed to a corner table, where Penelope waited. When she stood up to greet me, I couldn't help noticing that she'd gained a little weight – usually she was rather thin, being the kind of woman who picked at her food.

'Thank you for coming, Charlotte. It's good of you to make the journey into London.'

I unfolded my napkin and placed it on my lap.

'It's my pleasure.'

We ordered fish of the day, which was lemon sole, and glasses of Chablis. The waiter brought over a basket of bread and a butter dish.

'How are you coping without Winston?' Penelope said.

I picked up my glass of wine and took a sip.

'It has been a trying time, to be sure.'

'You must be grieving heavily.'

I couldn't be bothered with all this meaningless small talk. What I really wanted to know was why she'd invited me here.

'Indeed I am.'

'It is such a pity that you were unable to bear his child before he left us.'

'Yes, indeed that is a pity,' I said, not meaning a word.

'Which brings me to the reason I invited you here today. I'm sure you are aware that we had relations during your marriage?'

This news came as quite a shock, but then I thought back to that horrendous dinner when she'd been sitting next to him, giggling as she touched his arm. How dare she! I glugged my wine.

'I had absolutely no idea.'

'Well, I am with child, and it's Winston's.'

I blinked at her. 'I beg your pardon? What on earth do you mean?'

'Exactly what I just said.'

'But wait a minute... how do you know the child isn't Jasper's?'

'He was residing in London when the baby was conceived,

and, seeing as Jasper will now inherit the earldom, we shall expect to live at Copeley Park.'

I almost wished that I was carrying Winston's son, so that Jasper could not claim the title of earl and she would not then get to be a countess.

'Are you not aware of the agreement my father made with the duke?'

She narrowed her eyes.

'What agreement are you referring to?'

'They signed a contract to say that in the event of Winston's demise Copeley Park will be inherited by me, whether I have produced an heir or not.'

'But I'm carrying Winston's child – that changes things, does it not? Don't you think he would have liked his son to grow up there?'

'Firstly, I expect Winston would have wanted nothing to do with his illegitimate son. And I don't recall there being a clause in the contract about his sister-in-law carrying his child—'

'Well, that's where you're wrong. Winston would have been delighted to have an heir, something you didn't give him. I'm sure he would have divorced you and married me instead.'

'Don't be ridiculous, Penelope. You are quite deluded!'

She sucked air through her teeth.

'I expect you've been wondering who closed the door after Winston fell down the stairs?'

My heart plummeted into my stomach, and I picked up my wine glass and drank once again. Oh no, had it been Lady Penelope, of all people? There were no words to say – the cat had got my tongue. Her eyes gleamed as she continued with her story.

'I chose not to go to St John's for the Sunday morning service because I was feeling nauseous – this often happens in the early weeks of being with child, you understand – and well... I left the bedroom to go downstairs and sit in the library.

But then I saw you and Winston at the top of the staircase, having *quite* an altercation.'

'Are you attempting to blackmail me?'

She laughed.

'Come now, I wouldn't put it quite like that, Charlotte. You may think you can hide it from everyone else, but I know that you murdered your husband. You should be hanged.'

Thank goodness PC Wilson had only interviewed the servants. By the time he'd got round to coming to the house, Jasper and Penelope had returned to their home in Kent. Would she have divulged this information if he'd questioned her? I had a feeling that she'd been saving what she saw as a golden nugget for my ears only – to use it to her advantage.

'I didn't murder him,' I whispered.

She shrugged. 'I know what I saw.'

'Well, Penelope, I doubt very much that the police will believe your story if you come forward now. The case is closed after they concluded it was an accident and there was no evidence whatsoever of foul play.'

'Cases can always be reopened. And of course they'll believe me. It's not unusual for witnesses to present themselves long after a crime has been committed – once they begin to feel guilty for keeping their mouths shut.'

'But... Penelope, you must know that I was defending myself. Winston was very drunk and he lunged at me. I merely put out a hand to stop him getting any closer to me and he lost his footing, before falling down the stairs.' Lowering my voice, I said, 'I didn't mean to kill him.'

She just shook her head.

'You have one month to give us Copeley Park. Otherwise, I shall tell the police what really happened. In fact, I shall tell anyone who will listen that Lady Charlotte murdered her husband in cold blood.'

'But you can't do that,' I gasped.

She stood up and dropped a handful of notes onto the table. The waiter hadn't even brought our main courses yet, and she hadn't touched her wine.

'My treat. I'm sure that I've given you plenty to think about, Charlotte.'

She picked up her handbag and slowly made her way towards the foyer. The waiter came over to say that the main courses were ready, but he'd seen my dining companion leave. Was everything quite all right? I asked him to bring my lemon sole. I might as well eat and finish off the wine while I recovered from Lady Penelope's startling threat. What on earth was I going to do?

Back at Copeley Park, I wrote voraciously in my diary at the writing table in my bedroom. I could not risk writing personal thoughts and feelings anywhere else in the house. I studied the beautiful view of the gardens and the lake, the Gothic tower rising up in the distance, seeking inspiration. How would I solve the issue of Lady Penelope? She knew enough to get me hanged, and the thought of this possibility made me shudder. How I wished that I had someone to confide in. But it was hopeless. I had no one to talk to. And so all I could do was wait, and hope that Lady Penelope would change her mind. She'd given me a month and perhaps the answer would present itself before my deadline. Although it was a long shot.

I continued to work in the garden every day, Lady Penelope's threat occupying every waking moment. My nightmares about Winston falling now sometimes incorporated her as well, standing there, pointing her finger at me, saying, 'I shall see to it that you are hanged, Lady Charlotte, if it's the last thing I do.'

Every morning, I'd wake up drenched with sweat. Gwen would come into my bedroom with breakfast on a tray, and sit on the end of the bed, asking me if I was all right. And I would tell her about my nightmare, omitting the part about Lady Penelope. Although I knew she'd be on my side if I confided in her, I couldn't put her in the position of having to lie to PC Wilson if he came back. It wouldn't be fair on the girl. At least Winston's death had meant she was able to keep her position, and I was grateful for that.

One morning I was delighted to receive a letter from my dear cousin, Agnes, who sent her condolences. After Albert had shown me the slope that had once been a vineyard that day, I'd intended to write to her and ask whether it might be possible to visit her in Verona. But I hadn't got round to it because Winston had died shortly afterwards. Papa's sister, my Aunt Fanny, had passed on the news, and it had taken some time to reach Agnes in Italy. She had met her husband, Mario, when he was in London visiting his older brother, who owned a restaurant on Jermyn Street. She'd been dining there with a friend, and he'd fallen in love with her at first sight. He'd taken the two of them to a jazz club in Soho, and then he'd invited her out for dinner the following evening. She found him to be handsome, with thick dark hair and big brown eyes. He'd proposed the night before he was due to return to his home in Verona. Her parents were horrified, as they'd had her lined up to marry the Baron of Tyne the following year. But she couldn't imagine what her life would be like if she never saw Mario again. He was the son of a vineyard owner near Verona, called Vineria di San Martino. His brother had helped him to develop relationships with Italian restaurant owners in London so he could supply them with wine from the vineyard. She went to stay in Verona with her governess as chaperone, and accepted his proposal during her stay.

Agnes said in her letter that she was in desperate need of English-speaking company – she wondered if I'd be interested in visiting her, seeing as I'd recently lost my husband. She suggested that a holiday might do me the world of good. I couldn't believe my luck. She said it was easy to travel from London to Verona by train, changing in Paris. The vineyard was an enchanting place that I had to see with my own eyes. As well as all the vines, and rolling hills, there was an ancient olive grove. There were breathtaking views of Verona, and the wine was sumptuous. She was certain that I'd enjoy tasting all the wine her husband produced. Knowing how much I enjoyed gardening, she thought I'd be interested in finding out about how the grapes were grown. And Verona was a wonderful city, with a Roman amphitheatre. And of course, she said, being Italy, the local food was delicious.

How could I not want to visit this place? Here was an opportunity to escape for a short while, to get away from Lady Penelope, who might continue to harass me. And Agnes was someone I could confide in. I had no qualms about telling her everything that had happened. It would be good to get it all off my chest – how I needed to confide in someone, and to ask for their advice.

I'd never been to Italy, but had always wanted to visit. All the beautiful paintings and sculptures and objets d'art brought back from grand tours made me think it must be a wonderful country, with so much culture. And here was an opportunity to see the city that had inspired *Romeo and Juliet* with my own eyes. But I couldn't go abroad alone. If I took the train, as Agnes had suggested, Gwen could accompany me. But it seemed a sensible idea to take a capable man for security. And Albert was so big and strong, no one would win in a fight against him. I would feel safe if he were nearby to protect us. We'd have to take the train to Paris from London, and via the boat from

Dover to Calais. Then we'd cross France and pass through Switzerland to Italy. Verona was in the east of Italy, not far from Venice and the coast. Would Albert agree to accompany me? We had talked about the possibility of replanting vines on the south-facing slope overlooking the lake when he gave me that tour of Copeley Park. Surely he would agree to go with us?

'Albert,' I said, one morning while we were drinking tea in his shed. 'My cousin, Agnes, recently married an Italian man, and she's living on a vineyard near Verona. She's invited me to go and stay, and I wondered if you might like to accompany me? We could bring back some vine cuttings and plant them – I'm sure she wouldn't mind. We'd take the train – it would be a beautiful, scenic journey through France and Switzerland. We could go into the city of Verona – I've heard it's beautiful and has an interesting history. I find the whole idea of travelling there by train rather exciting.'

'Why wouldn't you just get the vine cuttings from France? It's much closer,' Albert said.

'Well... that is true, but my cousin has invited me to visit, and so we could kill two birds with one stone and get them there.'

He shrugged. 'Seems like a long way to go for vine cuttings.'

His lack of enthusiasm was infuriating – could he not sense my desperation to grab this opportunity with both hands? Did he not understand that I needed to get away from Copeley Park after all that had happened?

'Albert, will you come with me or not?'

He furrowed his eyebrows.

'Tensions are high in Europe, as they are here. What if a war starts while we are there?'

He was right, of course. A war could happen before the end of the year. It was all over the news, with Hitler becoming bolder by the second. But Lady Penelope's threat meant that I was more prepared to take a risk than usual. If she so much as opened her mouth down at the police station, I could be hanged. I really didn't feel as though I had anything to lose by going to Italy.

'I very much doubt it will happen in the next month, Albert. Where's your sense of adventure?'

'Are you quite serious, milady?'

'I am indeed. During these trying times, it would do me good to see my dear cousin. Carpe diem, as they say. And I am anxious about going abroad without a strong man to protect me.'

'I'm not sure it would be appropriate for us to travel together.'

'Nonsense. I'd take my lady's maid, Gwen, and I'm sure Winston's former valet, Mr Cooper would be glad to accompany you.'

'I'm not in need of a valet, milady. Besides, Mr Cooper wouldn't want to serve me, one of his peers – I'd even say he's more senior than me in the household.'

Of course he was right. What had I been thinking? And Mr Cooper's loyalties lay with Winston, even though he was now dead. I wasn't sure he could be entirely trusted – he might even report back to the duchess on every detail relating to our trip. I wouldn't want her to be aware of my growing closeness to Albert.

'We could find you another valet, someone younger who'd be grateful for the promotion, perhaps George, the footman.'

He nodded and stroked his beard.

'George is a good egg, and it would be an opportunity for him to spread his wings. But still, I wouldn't want him to serve me – he could just help with carrying luggage and such like. Can I have time to think about it?'

'Very well, I'll give you a week.'

He looked across the desk at me, and his face broke into a smile.

'All right, milady. I'll let you know.'

How I hoped that his answer would be yes. Albert just had to accompany me on this journey of a lifetime – who knew what might happen between us if the opportunity arose to be alone together?

CHAPTER 17

KATE

Ben took my coat and hung it on the stand while I sat on the bench in the hall to remove my muddy boots. When I entered the living room and saw the roaring fire in the hearth, I instantly felt at home. There was something about Rosemary Cottage that made me want to be there – was it the cottage or Ben, or both? But what about that woman I'd just seen – who was she?

'I'll get you a change of clothes, and then how about that hot chocolate?'

'Thank you, that would be nice.'

'My sister, Lily, has been staying here and so I have plenty in the house.'

'Oh, was that your sister I just saw outside?'

He nodded. 'Yes, she's heading back to the Cotswolds tonight, but she's been using this place as a base over the weekend. She was in London yesterday when I met you.'

Oh, what a relief.

'Ah, I see.'

He looked at me, his forehead scrunched up, as if it was occurring to him that I'd thought they were an item.

'Did you think she was my...?'

I chuckled, feeling like an idiot.

'Girlfriend, or even wife... yes I did.'

He laughed. 'That does happen a lot, actually, because she's only a couple of years younger. I have to jump in quite quickly whenever I meet a woman, to let her know Lily is only my sister. She has a boyfriend at home, and they're planning on getting married next year. I'm actually... in between relationships. How about you?'

A moment of silence fell between us, as I realised he was telling me he was single. And he wanted to know what my relationship status was.

While I was trying to work out how to tell him I'd recently split up with Spencer, he said, 'Let me get you that change of clothes.'

He disappeared out of the room. I heard his footsteps on the stairs, and then the creaking of floorboards above me. He came back and handed me a blue towel that had seen better days, with unravelling threads, and a pair of comfy-looking tracksuit bottoms.

'There's a bathroom at the other end of the hall, if you want to get changed in there?'

I found the bathroom and peeled off my soaking wet jeans before drying myself with the towel and putting on the trackie bs. They were way too long, but I rolled them up at the bottom, and it kind of worked.

Back in the living room, Ben threw me a glance and raised his eyebrows.

'Well, those tracksuit bottoms look kind of ridiculous – sorry I don't have any your size.'

'It doesn't help that I'm pint-sized,' I said, smiling.

He scratched his head.

'I'll go and take the milk off the boil. It would be really nice if you could try my home-made sparkling elderflower wine, but of course you're driving.'

'Another time maybe. Don't you mind me hanging around – is there anything you need to be doing?'

'I can't let you drive off in that storm. The last thing you need is to end up in another pothole. I've finished work for the day, so would just be sitting here on my own anyway.'

He went into the kitchen, and I sank into the brown leather armchair and rubbed my hair with the towel. I could have done with a hairdryer, but doubted he'd have one. What must I look like? I dreaded to think, and stood up to check my appearance in the mirror above the fireplace. As expected, I looked a right mess. Ben came back in and put two steaming hot chocolates down on the coffee table, then took the chair opposite.

'That looks like a real treat, thank you.'

'The tyre is all fixed, by the way.'

'Thanks so much for doing that – it looks great. I did stop to have a look.'

'Of course. It's the least I could do, seeing as it was all my fault in the first place. Oh, hold on, I forgot something...'

He leapt up, went back into the kitchen, and reappeared with two pink cupcakes. One of them had a candle in it, the flame flickering.

'Happy birthday, Kate.'

I put my hands over my mouth, touched by how thoughtful he was being.

He handed it to me.

'This is the best cupcake you'll ever have – fresh from the bakery in Copeley.'

'How lovely of you. Thank you so much, Ben... sorry, do you mind me taking a quick photo, for my social media?'

I took out my phone and snapped a photo of the pretty pink cupcake, on the coffee table with a view of the roaring log fire as a backdrop. I'd been wondering what to post on my Instagram story on my birthday, and now I had a decent photo to use. Then I blew out the candle.

'Don't forget to make a wish,' he said.

'Ha, good point,' I said, desperately trying to think of something as I closed my eyes. All I could wish for was more times like this – good times with someone I liked being with in a place as perfect as Rosemary Cottage.

So, you're one of those social media addicts?' he said.

'Not really. It's more that I work in marketing, so it comes naturally – annoyingly, I feel the need to record everything. But I do actually enjoy taking photos. I did a course once.'

'Well, it's good for the soul to have a creative hobby.'

'I agree.'

'What kind of marketing do you do?'

'I promote books.'

'Oh, I bet that's interesting. Have you thought about helping with the marketing for Copeley Park?'

'Why do you ask?'

'Well... I think we could do with someone who knows their stuff. Everyone kind of dips in and out of the Instagram account when they get a mo, but it needs someone who knows what they're doing to focus on it.'

'I can take a look.'

'I'm not sure if your dad has told you, but quite a lot has been going wrong on the vineyard this year.'

I felt bad for not knowing about any of this. Did Dad need my help?

'Really?'

'We've had a lot of vines affected by powdery mildew, and the frost was particularly bad this year. And some fool left the bung off one of the barrels, would you believe it?'

He rolled his eyes, and I could see he was frustrated by these problems, that he cared about the vineyard a great deal.

'I've always said to Dad that there are so many ways this place could make more money. He doesn't want to open the house up to visitors, but that would make him a packet for a start. And there is so much potential for events.'

'I've told him more or less the same thing,' Ben said.

I picked up the cupcake and took a bite – it was delicious. The icing was soft and buttery and a wonderful strawberry flavour. We both sat drinking our hot chocolates and eating our cakes, the thunderstorm raging outside. The curtains were still open, and the sky continued to flash and rumble.

'So, Kate... seeing as you don't have any plans on your birthday, I'm assuming you're in between relationships like me?'

I made a meal of eating my cupcake while working out what to say. Should I tell him? Then I'd be opening up a whole can of worms. But I felt comfortable around him, and found myself wanting him to know.

'I split up with my husband in July.'

He sat up, as if surprised by this revelation.

'You were married, really?'

Nodding, I said, 'Yes, I rushed into it after my mum died. It was a mistake...'

'Ah, I see... Well, they say you should only regret what you don't do, and I expect that if you hadn't married him you wouldn't have been in a position to know it was a mistake.'

'And then I could have always wondered what might have been?'

'Exactly... that's my way of thinking.'

I wanted to know more about his love life, but didn't feel this was the time to ask. It would be easier with a glass of wine in my hand.

'Well, you've made me feel better about the whole thing.'

'I am sorry about your mum, by the way – I did know that she'd died a few years ago, obviously...'

'Yes, of course you did – it was all over the papers, after all.'

'Well, she was Allegra Banks,' he said.

Nodding, I said, 'I know... I'm still not over it, really. It's been hard.' Why was I telling him this?

'I can understand that, totally – it's your mum.'

'Thanks, Ben.'

We looked at each other, and shared a brief moment.

'You look a little like her,' he said. 'Apart from the eyes – those green eyes are quite something.'

I didn't know what to say to this. Was he saying he found me attractive? Of course I wanted him to fancy me, but still, his comment had taken me by surprise.

My face warming, I looked at my watch. 'Well, I ought to be going. Thanks so much for the cake – and for adding the candle. That was a really nice touch.'

'Do you have any plans to celebrate your birthday properly?' he said.

I shook my head.

'Well, if you're not doing anything on Friday night, you could come here and try my home-made sparkling elderflower wine? I'd love to get your opinion on it.'

'That's a really nice idea, thanks. I'll think about it.'

'What is there to think about?'

'It's just that, well... it would take me ages to get back. If I was drinking I'd have to get the train and the tube, and—'

'You could always stay.'

He put a hand over his mouth as if realising he'd blurted this out without thinking.

'What?' I said with a laugh, knowing that my face must be the colour of beetroot by now.

'No, that's not what I meant,' he said, also laughing. 'This is a two-bedroom cottage.'

'Oh, I see...'

'The spare room is still set up from when my sister stayed, so there will be everything you need – there's a brand-new duvet and cover, which I can wash, obviously, if you decided to stay over. The mattress is pocket sprung, don't you know.'

'Oh well if the mattress is pocket sprung...'

'So, you'll come over?'

I nodded, squashing a smile. 'Okay.'

'Well, that's just great. I'll get a pizza or something.'

'That would be nice.'

'Let me get the bottle of wine your granny gave to you. It's in the cellar.'

He went into the hall, and I heard a door open and footsteps down some stairs. A couple of minutes later, he brought back the wooden box and handed it to me. But then it struck me that there was nowhere suitable to store the wine in the flat. It would make more sense to leave it here, surely, in a proper cellar, until I had somewhere cool to put it. And it would be an excuse to stay in touch too.

'Thank you... actually, do you mind keeping it for a bit longer? I'm thinking that my flat is quite warm, and, well, you have a cellar here.'

'Sure, that's no problem at all.'

I handed the box back to him.

'That's good of you, thanks.'

'Will you go to the vineyard where it came from?'

'I'm seriously thinking about it.'

'It would be a wonderful adventure, there's no doubt about that.'

Ben showed me to the door, and I put my coat and boots back on.

'I just need to find a way to juggle my work around it.'

He reached into the pocket of his jeans and handed me my car key, our hands brushing.

'There you go. So, come over on Friday whenever you like. I finish work at four, so any time after that.'

I stepped outside onto the gravel path and threw him a

smile. He stood at the open door while I walked back to my car. The rain had stopped, and I got in and saw that he was still standing there. I started the engine and gave him a wave. And then I drove away and took a right back along the narrow lane where we'd first met, putting my lights on full beam, and being especially careful to avoid the potholes.

When I reached the end of the lane, I saw that the lights were on in the blue drawing room and library at the front of the main house. Both rooms would have roaring fires in the hearth, and Dad's butler, Mr Jenkins, would be on hand to serve alcoholic beverages – how I missed those days. Mum and I would sit together reading and talking, and, once again, it hit me that those times were over. I sighed. Dad probably wouldn't object to me moving back into my own room temporarily, for there was plenty of space. But could I handle living in the house with Emilie there, and carrying his child?

I pulled over and switched off the engine and lights, like a detective on a stakeout. There I sat with tears streaming down my face, parked outside my childhood home, filled with so many special memories. The hardest part of Mum having gone was that we couldn't make any more memories together as a family. An era at Copeley Park was well and truly over. And now the era of Dad and Emilie had begun. I wasn't sure I could face living there again.

CHAPTER 18

LADY CHARLOTTE

When the week had passed, I rushed down to Albert's shed straight after breakfast, for I couldn't wait for his answer. I knocked on the door and went inside. He sat at his desk, studying some paperwork, a cup of tea beside him.

'Will you be coming to Verona then, Albert?'

He looked up and shook his head.

'I'm afraid my answer is no, milady.'

'Oh, why on earth not?'

'I don't think it's appropriate, milady.'

'Why?'

'You have been a widow for a matter of weeks...'

'And?'

'Should I be going abroad with a woman who has just lost her husband?'

'But Gwen and George would be with us.'

'They are more than capable of keeping you company.'

'But I'll need you to protect me from vagabonds and thieves. Who knows who I might encounter en route?'

'George will protect you.'

'He's a mere child, barely seventeen years of age. Whereas

you, Albert, are a grown man – you are older, wiser and stronger. I would feel safer if you were there.'

'Am I really your only option?'

'No one else springs to mind. Besides, I'd like you to bring back some cuttings, remember, like we talked about. When we return, we can revive that vineyard from the eighteenth century on the slope you showed me that leads down to the lake.'

'You really do want a vineyard?'

'Albert, you said yourself that the slope lends itself to vines, being south-facing, and the lake would protect it from frost. I know that duke who planted one there in the eighteenth century had some success until he kicked the bucket. And then his son wasn't interested in carrying it on. But we have an opportunity here, to do something really exciting. It would be a wonderful project for us to undertake together, don't you think?'

'The cuttings might not survive the journey, and, if they do, they might not grow here. The climate in Italy is much warmer than here in England, milady. You'd have more luck bringing back vines from France.'

'Oh, where's the fun in that, Albert? Stop being such a misery guts.'

He shook his head. 'I'm just being a realist. And who knows when war might break out? What if I get called up? All your efforts will have gone to waste.'

'Build a vine house then.'

'Build a vine house? Are you insane?'

'Yes, like the one at Hampton Court where they keep the Capability Brown vine. That way, you can keep some of the cuttings there, just in case, heaven forbid, we do find ourselves fighting a war.'

'You seem to have an answer for everything.'

'I am quite determined, Albert, when I set my mind to something. Let's embrace this challenge together. Agnes said that they grow the pinot gris grape at her vineyard. It originated in France, so I would say the vines stand a good chance of thriving here, actually.'

I left the shed, banging the door shut behind me. It was frustrating having to deal with Albert's pessimism. Looking back through the window, I caught sight of him throwing his arms in the air as if he found me exasperating.

Determined to get my wish, I asked Albert every day for another week. Whenever I put the question to him, during our tea break in his shed, he'd look at me blankly and say firmly, 'My answer is still no, milady.'

One morning, he came to the house to see me – I was taking a day off from gardening due to a headache from too much brandy consumed the night before. Winston's death along with Lady Penelope's threat and the ensuing nightmares had given me insomnia. I lay awake every night, staring at the ceiling, thoughts running through my mind. How would I get through all this? That night I kept refilling the glass on my nightstand until I drifted off to sleep. It was the first day I'd taken off from gardening since Winston's funeral. Perhaps Albert was worried about me – dare I imagine that he missed my company? Had it occurred to him that, if I went away, every day would be like this? It was clear that he enjoyed talking to me, and I'd noticed his gaze linger for longer than was appropriate between a head gardener and his employer. I liked to think he found me to be pretty. And I liked to imagine that he could be in love with me but hadn't admitted it to himself yet.

Mrs Parsons knocked on my bedroom door and came in to say, 'Mr Hicks would like a word, milady... he wouldn't divulge what it's concerning.'

We agreed that she should put him in the library, and then I asked her to send Gwen to help me get dressed. Albert was used to seeing me in gardening attire, but now we were on my territory, and this was an opportunity to look my best. Gwen selected a skirt and blouse with a pussy bow, and shoes with a low heel.

I went down to the library to find him sitting in an armchair, in front of the fire, reading my copy of the *Daily Sketch*. He seemed to have made himself at home already. I took the chair opposite.

'Good morning, Albert.'

He looked up from behind the newspaper to greet me.

'I noticed your absence from the garden this morning,' he said.

'I woke up with a headache, that's all.'

'The peony bulbs are blooming, and their flowers are a beautiful pale-pink colour – you must come and see them while they're at their best,' he said.

Clearly, he'd used the peonies as an excuse to visit, but I was just glad to see him – it made my heart sing to have him there in the library with me. How I wished he could sit there with me every day.

'Did you come here to tell me that?' I asked.

He put the newspaper down on his lap, and then he leant forwards and looked at me, across the coffee table. Our tea had been placed there on a tray by a housemaid, along with a plate of shortbread, baked by Mrs Coleman that morning.

'If the offer is still open, I'd like to accompany you to Verona, milady.'

Well, this was most unexpected. I'd more or less given up on the idea of him accompanying me and had started to make a list of other contenders in my diary the night before. Now I'd got what I wanted, words somehow eluded me.

I picked up the teapot and poured us both a cup.

'Are you absolutely sure, Albert?'

Why was I asking him this question? Now he'd agreed to go with me, I didn't want him to change his mind again, for goodness' sake. For he was absolutely the best man for the job. And the thought of being away from him from weeks on end didn't bear thinking about. In the short time since Winston's death, we'd become closer with every interaction. I didn't like to think of the distance that might develop between us if we spent time apart. I couldn't imagine not knowing him or having him in my life – I wanted to know him forever. In time, perhaps, I could find a way to get him to fall in love with me. I hadn't ever seen myself as a woman who needed anyone to lean on, but I found myself wanting to lean on him, allowing myself to need him.

If I went to Verona without him, he might fall in love with someone else – for there were plenty of pretty female servants at Copeley Park. What girl in their right mind would turn him down? I'd seen the way maids looked at him, and became all flustered in his presence, giggling and blushing as they spoke to him. He seemed to like their attention too. Of course he did. Who didn't enjoy attention from the opposite sex, especially when that person was easy on the eye?

His voice interrupted my thoughts. I'd almost forgotten my question.

'Yes, I am sure, milady. You are still going, aren't you?'

'Of course I am,' I said.

'Oh, well, that's a relief, seeing as, after much consideration, I've made the decision to go and all that.'

'Thank you, Albert. I shall make the necessary arrangements.' I clapped my hands together. 'Golly gosh, I am truly excited about this adventure we are undertaking – our very own grand tour, if you will.'

'Thank you for choosing me, milady.'

'You are the only man for the job,' I said.

He smiled, and then he stood up and made to leave. I wasn't ready for him to go yet – if only he could stay for luncheon, and perhaps a game of dominoes afterwards. We could then go on to have afternoon tea and scones. But what excuse could I use to ask him to stay for longer? He was a servant and I was his mistress, the lady of the house. It wasn't appropriate for him to be sitting there with me, being served by Mr Skinner, his employer, no less. And I sensed that Albert had felt uncomfortable enough about a housemaid bringing him tea.

I put my cup and saucer down on the coffee table and started to get up, but he said, 'Don't worry, milady, I'll see myself out.'

As he walked away, he stopped and turned round.

'Will you be coming back to the gardens tomorrow?'

I'd only been absent for one day, and I liked it that he was asking.

Nodding, I said, 'Yes, of course, provided I don't wake up with a headache again.'

I wouldn't need brandy to help me sleep that night. Now Albert had agreed to go to Verona, I would close my eyes thinking about our journey and all the opportunities that would arise for us to spend time alone together.

Mr Skinner opened the door, and Albert threw me a nod as he left the room. Then I was left all alone with my thoughts, but they were happy ones. I needed to make arrangements, and soon. I was going to Italy, and Albert would be coming with me. Gwen would be so thrilled, and I would speak to George, the footman, and ask if he'd mind being Albert's valet for a few weeks. I would explain that Albert did not expect him to do much – just help out generally with luggage etcetera. George was bound to agree, seeing as it would be a promotion for him as well as an opportunity to travel. And from what Gwen had told me, he was sweet on her. She'd certainly be delighted if he came along too.

CHAPTER 19

LADY CHARLOTTE

We boarded the train at London Victoria station a few days later. As expected, George was delighted to be promoted from footman to valet and excited about the opportunity to travel to Italy. Also, he seemed to be as fond of Gwen as she was of him – I don't think he could believe his luck. It was one of those situations where he happened to be in the right place at the right time. Under normal circumstances he wouldn't be viewed as experienced enough to be a valet, but if he was, he wouldn't want to take orders from Albert. With some guidance, and patience on Albert's part, George was bound to settle into his new role in no time. Now that Winston was no longer alive, there were no more dinner parties at weekends, and so Mr Skinner didn't mind lending George to me for the trip. He told me that George was hard-working and good-natured – he was especially popular below stairs because of his cheerful demeanour. Albert still wasn't entirely comfortable with having a valet, but I informed him that he could view George as more of a male companion if he so wished.

Albert and I were to travel first class, and Gwen and George would travel second class. Our sleeping cars were single-sex, as none of us were married to each other – and so we were all in different carriages. I would have liked Albert to be in closer proximity at night, but there wasn't anything I could do about that. He said that I could knock on his door at any time, or send the porter with a message if I so wished, and that put my mind at rest.

When we arrived at Victoria station, it was a noisy affair with all the trains rumbling along the tracks as they came and went, leaving clouds of steam in their wake. We made our way to the platform where porters took our suitcases and we boarded the train. Once we'd settled into our respective sleeping cars, I put on a navy-blue dress with a thin-white belt and sapphire necklace – I'd made the decision to end my period of mourning for the journey – and went to meet Albert in the dining car. When I saw him – wearing a beautifully pressed grey suit with shirt and tie – I was stopped in my tracks. I'd only ever seen him wearing gardening attire, usually a crumpled shirt with the sleeves rolled up, a waistcoat, and trousers tucked into knee-high boots. He looked incredibly handsome, and butterflies fluttered in my stomach.

As I approached the table, he looked up at me fondly and our eyes met. Perhaps he was surprised to see that I was no longer wearing black.

'Good evening, Albert.'

He nodded. 'Milady. So, the period of mourning is over?'

'Yes,' I said. 'I've done my bit now. It's time to move on.'

I sat down opposite him, and picked up the menu, but could sense he was studying me out of the corner of his eye. Our dinner felt as though it might be more romantic than one between a mistress and her head gardener ought to be. I couldn't help playing with the sapphire pendant I was wearing – a habit of mine when engulfed by nerves.

A waiter came over, and we ordered soup of the day, which happened to be vegetable, followed by steaks, and a bottle of claret. At the beginning of the meal we made small talk about how much we were looking forward to seeing Italy, but after a couple of glasses of wine, my tongue loosening, I felt an urge to confide in him about Lady Penelope. I hadn't told anyone, and her threat was weighing me down.

'My late husband's mistress is carrying his child,' I blurted out.

He lifted his eyebrows.

'Oh?'

'It's rather distressing, I can tell you.'

'I can imagine it would be.'

I told him about the lunch in London, and how she wanted to take Copeley Park away from me and live there with her husband, Jasper.

'But how can she do that?'

'She knows.'

He frowned.

'She knows... about what?'

I picked up my glass and sipped the wine for Dutch courage. Then I leant forwards.

'About what happened on that day Winston fell down the stairs.'

'What do you mean? Wasn't he drunk?'

'Well, yes, but there's more to it than that...'

'I don't understand. Wasn't the assumption that he'd slipped and fallen down the stairs – that there was no foul play?'

Looking around, I checked to see if anyone might be eavesdropping.

'It was my fault,' I mouthed.

Albert sat up in his chair and put his knife and fork down on his plate.

'Are you telling me that you pushed him?'

'Not exactly.'

'Not *exactly*?'

'I was defending myself. He was being aggressive, as he often could be when sozzled. We were having a conversation, or rather an altercation, on the landing—'

'And you...'

As I explained everything to Albert, I found myself reliving it all – I'd been doing my best to shut it out of my mind until now, in spite of the flashbacks and nightmares. My chest tightened, and I began to feel light-headed. Perhaps I should have a lie-down. I looked out of the window at the Kent countryside whizzing past.

'Go on,' he said.

'He lunged towards me, and I put out a hand to protect myself. I thought he was going to strike me. Somehow, he lost his footing and fell backwards.'

Albert wiped his mouth with a napkin.

'Well, I must admit that when you came outside all shaken, I sensed you might not be telling me the whole story.'

'I wasn't sure if you believed everything I was saying, but somehow I trusted that you wouldn't tell anyone.'

'We all knew what Winston could be like, and I believe what you're telling me now. However, this still comes as quite a shock, milady.'

It didn't seem right that he was calling me milady as we sat at a table across from each other, eating together and talking so frankly.

'Albert, I think you should call me Charlotte. We are going to be spending an awful lot of time in each other's company on this journey, aren't we?'

'All right, if you insist... Charlotte.'

I liked the way he said my name in his deep voice.

'Right after it happened—'

'There's more?'

I nodded.

'I heard a door close somewhere on the same floor. I'd

assumed everyone was at St John's for the Sunday morning service. I should have been there too, but I had a headache. I had no idea who was still in the house – it could have been a guest or a servant.'

'So, you think there was a witness?'

'I know there was. Lady Penelope hadn't gone to St John's that morning because she was suffering from nausea, being in the early stages of pregnancy with Winston's child. She claims that she saw me deliberately push him down the stairs when she opened the door to leave her bedroom and go down to the library. The vile woman is threatening to tell the police if I don't hand over Copeley Park to her and Jasper. I could be hanged, Albert – imagine.'

'It's her word against yours.'

'I do hope you're right.' I lowered my voice to a whisper. 'It's blackmail, that's what it is, Albert.'

'Wouldn't she understand that you were defending yourself from what sounds like a violent man?'

'I believe she would, but she's deliberately creating her own version of events.'

He looked across the table at me, shaking his head.

'I am at a loss as to what to do, but in the meantime I thought it might be wise to leave the country for a short while,' I said.

'So, that's what we're doing here, escaping from Lady Penelope?'

'Yes, partly, although I'll admit that it was convenient when my cousin, Agnes, wrote to invite me to stay on the vineyard. And after you showed me the slope that was a vineyard in the eighteenth century... well, I thought we could tell everyone we were going there to bring back vine cuttings. And I would really like to revive the vineyard – imagine what a rewarding project it could be for us to work on together.'

'Yes, well, as I said, it would be easier to get the cuttings from France.'

'I'm aware of that, Albert. But *Romeo and Juliet* does happen to be my favourite Shakespeare play, and I'd like to visit the city. There's a Roman amphitheatre where they used to have gladiator fights.'

'That's all very well, but what will you do about Lady Penelope when you return?'

'I have absolutely no idea whatsoever. Perhaps you might be able to come up with a way to deal with her?'

He drummed his fingers on the table.

'Hmm. You have bought time to come up with a plan, at least. When is the baby due?'

'Well, I'm guessing that if it was conceived shortly before Winston died, sometime in February.'

He made a bridge with his hands, as if in deep thought.

'So, you have around six months. I suggest you forget the matter for now. When we return to Copeley Park, we can find a way to deal with this scheming woman.'

'Your optimism is admirable, Albert.'

His face reddened at the compliment. I'd embarrassed him, without meaning to, but it was touching that I was able to impact on him in this way.

The waiter cleared our plates and brought over dessert menus.

'Oh, what to have?' I said, skimming the selection.

Albert closed his menu and placed it down on the table.

'I'm going to order crème brûlée.'

'I'm not sure I can eat a whole pudding after that steak,' I said.

'Shall we ask the waiter for an extra spoon?'

He was willing to share his dessert with me.

'Are you sure?'

'Of course. You are paying for it, after all,' he said with a chuckle.

'Haha, you make a good point. Very well, let's ask for an extra spoon then. That's kind of you, Albert.'

'It's a pleasure, Charlotte,' he said, looking me directly in the eye. 'And seeing as you've asked me to call you Charlotte, you may call me Bertie, if you wish.'

I was sure that at that moment my heart skipped a beat, or perhaps it was merely the train going clickety-clack on the tracks, bumping us up and down a little.

'Bertie it is,' I said, softly.

His eyes met mine, and I turned to look through the window as the farm land of Kent passed by. Telling Albert about my situation was a weight off my shoulders, and relief swept over me. I was glad to be leaving the country, and hoped he was right – that we'd find a way to deal with Lady Penelope upon our return. Before long, our train would arrive at the coast, and then we'd cross the English Channel – something I'd never done, but always wanted to experience. Within a few days, we'd arrive in Verona. Oh, it was all rather exciting!

CHAPTER 20

KATE

On Friday evening, I drove to Ben's house with a holdall in the boot. I couldn't wait to spend time at Rosemary Cottage again, and to see Ben. As I was staying overnight, I'd be able to try his home-made sparkling elderflower wine without worrying about getting home, and I was looking forward to celebrating my big birthday properly with a few drinks.

When I arrived, he showed me the spare room upstairs. It was charming, with floral wallpaper and the bedding, bedside table and lamp were all pink. There was even a baby-pink towel folded up on the bed, as if I was staying in an Airbnb.

'Sorry it's so kitsch – the wallpaper was already here, and Lily likes pink so she brought all this stuff with her for when she comes to stay,' he said, rolling his eyes.

'It's lovely, and I appreciate you putting me up,' I said.

'My pleasure. I'll leave you to sort yourself out.'

Back downstairs, I went into the living room to find Ben had lit a fire and the flames were already picking up, creating a cosy atmosphere. The lamps were on, and tea lights glowed along the mantelpiece. A giant candle with three wicks flickered on the sideboard, and I breathed in the scent of vanilla. It was all so inviting. I couldn't help being a little in love with Rosemary Cottage – it was almost as if I'd walked into a rom-com.

Ben came in from the kitchen, holding a bottle with a crown cap on it and two flutes.

'So, are you ready to try my home-made sparkling elderflower wine?'

'Absolutely, of course. I'm looking forward to it. Where did you learn how to make this?' I said.

'I've worked on a couple of vineyards, including one in the Champagne region.'

'Oh, that's impressive. And what equipment did you use?'

'Ah, I have a friend who runs a vineyard down the road.'

In that moment, it occurred to me that we didn't produce any sparkling wine on the vineyard. What was the reason for this?

'I wonder why Dad doesn't produce anything sparkling,' I said.

Ben shrugged. 'Well, costs are higher because for a start you need fortified bottles, like this one' – he raised the bottle he was holding – 'here, you can see that the glass is much thicker than a standard wine bottle, that's to stop it from exploding, and also, the bottle needs' – he tipped the bottle slightly to show me the base – 'this indentation, called a punt.'

'I'd never noticed that! Are there any other reasons?'

'Perhaps he wasn't sure if it would sell. There's competition from champagne, of course, which is viewed as the best sparkling wine because of its name. But it's becoming more and more expensive. And then there's prosecco from Italy, which is a lot cheaper and a trusted name too. And there's cava from Spain.'

'Hmm,' I mused. 'I did notice when looking at the website for the vineyard in Verona that they make a sparkling Pinot Grigio there.'

'Ah yes, that's a possibility, seeing as we have pinot gris grapes. I have noticed that more vineyards are making that – there's one in Kent that sells it for quite a high price.'

'Do you think Dad should have a go at making sparkling Pinot Grigio here at Copeley Park?'

'Well... English sparkling wines are being increasingly recognised for their exceptional quality. The chalk hills of the North Downs share the same geology as the Champagne region, so it would stand a huge chance of success.'

'Oh really, do you think so?'

'You could suggest the idea to him. I guess he'd need to have enough pinot gris grapes left over to produce a limited edition – maybe around five hundred bottles – on the side to start with, to see if it sells.'

'That's something to think about... he could run an event to promote it,' I said, becoming excited as ideas began to percolate in my head. I'd always been an ideas person, but lately hadn't had the opportunity to be as creative in my working life as I'd like. Freelancing had left me with smaller budgets to work with when creating marketing campaigns – depending on what an independent publisher or author could afford. It would be so good to get involved with the family vineyard, to be able to use my marketing expertise and come up with ways to help Dad. 'Maybe I'll run the idea past him.'

'There's no harm in doing that,' Ben said.

'So, are we going to try your wine then?' I said.

His face broke into a smile.

'You'll be the first person to try my new batch. I'll go and open it over the sink as it tends to spray everywhere with this crown cap.'

He went into the kitchen, and I heard a pop and a splash, and he came back with two flutes. He half-filled the flutes, bubbles racing to the top, and passed one of them to me.

Clinking glasses, we said 'Cheers,' locking eyes, as was customary, as we took that first crucial sip at the same time.

'And happy birthday to you, Kate, once again,' Ben said.

It was refreshingly fizzy and light too, on the dry side with notes of honey. It tasted of summer days and I could see myself downing a few glasses quite easily.

'This is really fabulous, Ben.'

'You seem surprised.'

'No... well, I just wasn't expecting it to taste so good – this wine could be a viable substitute for champagne, especially on a hot summer's day.'

'I'm so glad you like it. It would certainly be worth your dad thinking about some kind of revamp and your sparkling Pinot Grigio idea is a fantastic one. And I said before that the social media accounts could do with an overhaul.'

I'd looked at Copeley Park's online presence since Ben had mentioned it, and more time and energy should be put into social media, especially Instagram. There needed to be a strategy to gain followers locally and to increase engagement. This would lead to higher visibility and sales.

'Yes, I did scroll through the Instagram posts and it could certainly do with a big sort-out,' I said.

He sipped his wine.

'I keep saying to your dad how important it is to get the local community on board.'

'You make a good point.'

'At the vineyard owned by my friend, they host tasting events and talk about the history of the vineyard. If we did that here, we could talk about how there was one here in the eighteenth century originally, and then it was revived before the war after your great-grandmother's trip to Verona, and then again by your father.'

'That sounds like a really good idea. Dad's been dealing with an impending threat for some time...' Should I be telling him this? I couldn't see it doing any real harm. Ben seemed to want the best for the vineyard. Maybe he could help. 'There's a distant relation called Jack who wants to buy the vineyard to add to his portfolio...'

Ben's face dropped.

'Did you know about him already?'

'Err no, not at all... go on.'

'Jack is my grandpa's cousin, and he's been after Copeley Park for as long as I can remember. Mum and Dad used to have conversations about him all the time, and the fear of him swooping in and buying us out when Dad was at his weakest. Somehow, Dad's always managed to get by and find money to keep the place going, but I'm not sure if he's up to doing that any more.'

'I'm sure he is. But perhaps... it's not really my place to say...'

'Go on,' I said.

'He's been a little distracted lately.'

Ben seemed to be referring to Emilie, and he was right. Dad no longer seemed to care about fending off Jack. It was almost as if he'd accepted that he was going to be defeated this time.

'Let's not talk about his fiancée.'

'I'm sure you don't want to talk about her, but it can't be easy seeing him with someone who isn't your mum.'

It was as if Ben was reading my mind, as if he really could see me.

'No, it isn't. And today I found out she was pregnant from her Instagram account. Dad hadn't even had chance to tell me.' I told Ben about Dad's card saying he had some news.

'I've been there, but I won't bore you with all that,' he said with a laugh.

'You can if you want to.'

He looked away.

'No, it's okay, but thanks anyway.'

We'd moved from discussing the plight of the vineyard to talking about our personal lives, and our families, and it was perhaps too much seeing as we'd only known each other a few days.

Taking the conversation back to the vineyard, I said, 'Jack is descended from an old nemesis of Granny's, and so she's always felt strongly about him not getting his hands on Copeley Park. But now she's getting older, maybe Dad thinks he doesn't need to worry about pleasing her any more.'

'That's possible. But anyway, there are so many ways to make money in this place, and you seem like the ideal person to help with that. Have you tried talking to your dad?'

'I have considered it.'

'You should. Surely you wouldn't want to lose Copeley Park? Don't you want to take it over from your dad one day?'

'I haven't ever thought about it. Do you think I'd be able to do that?'

'You seem to be someone who is capable of anything.'

'Ha, except for changing a tyre.'

'That's true. And of having one that works in your boot.'

I laughed.

'Maybe I'll drop in and see Dad tomorrow after leaving here. He did ask me to stop by in the card he sent.'

'That sounds like a good plan. And if you can't find a way to save the vineyard that way... you do realise that the bottle of Amarone from 1936 could be worth a small fortune, as long as it's been stored properly.'

'Yes, but how would I go about proving that?'

'You could get it valued by an auction house, somewhere like Pimsy's. They'd need provenance, of course.'

I threw him a quizzical look.

'Provenance is a record of ownership, used as a guide to authenticity or quality.'

'How long do you think it would take to get it valued?'

He shrugged.

'It could take several months. If you go to Verona, you could see if they have any evidence of when it was given to your great-grandmother. Photographs, diary entries, a thank-you letter maybe? That would all help with provenance.'

'Selling the wine would be an absolute last resort though. I'd like to think I could save the vineyard without doing that. How do you know all of this?'

'My gran is into antiques. I used to go to auctions with her growing up.'

'Is that where you got some of this lovely furniture from?'

'Yes, she left me all my favourite pieces.'

'You must have had a strong bond.'

He stared into space, wistfully. 'Yes, we did.'

'It's wonderful how older relatives can influence our lives by passing on their belongings and wisdom. I can't decide whether to visit the vineyard where my granny got the Amarone from. She did offer to pay...'

'Well, if she's paying, you really should go. I've heard that Verona is a beautiful city, with lots of history, too.'

'Yes, there's a Roman amphitheatre, and the Romeo and Juliet balcony. She said that the vineyard where she stayed was like paradise. She has this bonkers idea that if I go there I'll find "luck in love", as the Italians say, like she did.'

'Ha, she thinks you might meet someone there?'

'I know, it's a ridiculous idea. It's only three months since I split with my husband, and I'm not exactly looking for anyone right now.'

He looked down at the floor, and then he said, 'Yes, but you seem to be at a point in your life where you're re-evaluating everything.'

Now was my chance to ask about his love life.

'You said that you were in between relationships. What does that mean?'

'Err, well I was with someone when I started working here actually.'

'Oh yes?'

'She's called Fiona, well, I call her Fi. I think she'd rather be with someone who can provide her with more than I ever could.'

'I'm sorry, that must have been difficult.'

'She's the only girl I've ever loved, and I thought she loved me. But she's too good for a head gardener, apparently. Now she's with someone in his forties – he owns a property business. He lives in a mansion in a charming village just outside of Godalming.'

I didn't know what to say. How could Ben not be good enough for someone? I thought he was amazing.

'Well, she's made a big mistake, there's no doubt about that,' I said.

He looked at me but said nothing. We both sipped our wine.

'Anyway, going to Verona could be the break you need,' he said.

'Do you think so?'

He nodded. I wasn't sure if I was brave enough to go off to Italy all on my own.

'I'll mull it over, I guess.'

'You should.'

We got through the bottle of wine quite quickly, and then Ben brought in another one, and threw a pizza in the oven and sliced it up on a big wooden chopping board. He kept the fire going, adding logs before it went out. I loved being there in his cottage, but also I did enjoy his company – it was so undemanding.

Ben looked at his watch, and said, 'Crikey, it's midnight. I must admit, I'm falling asleep – it's been a long old week.'

The evening had flown by.

I yawned. 'Yes, it's probably time to go to bed.'

He got up and blew out the candles, and I helped him take the empty glasses and bottles and chopping board into the kitchen. He locked the front door, and I went round to click off all the lamps. It was so quiet outside – I was used to traffic noise and people walking past, shouting in the street, at night, especially at the weekend.

Ben went upstairs, and I followed. He stopped on the landing and grabbed the handle of his bedroom door. My room was opposite. After an evening where the conversation had flowed, everything suddenly felt awkward. We were both going to our beds, but by the way he was looking at me with those misty-blue eyes of his he seemed to be sending out a signal that he wanted to kiss me.

'Thanks for a lovely evening,' I said. 'It was a lot of fun.'

'Thank you for trying my wine. I liked sharing it with you.'

He leant forward. I wasn't sure if he was aiming for my lips or not, but then he kissed me gently on the cheek, sending a rush of desire right through me.

'Goodnight, Ben,' I said, going into my room.

'Goodnight, Kate.'

Closing the bedroom door behind me, I wondered if he really had been intending to kiss me on the lips and changed his mind last minute. Or had it all been in my head? He had made eye contact though – why do that if he didn't want anything to happen? But then a kiss on the lips would have turned into more – we'd have ended up in his bed, peeling off each other's clothes. And I wasn't ready for any of that. It was too soon to be with anyone else, no matter how attractive I found him. But I did want to get to know Ben better and allow things to play out naturally, in time.

I put on my pyjamas, then picked up my washbag and went to the bathroom. As I brushed my teeth, it occurred to me that Granny had started something that day when she invited me over and gave me the bottle of Amarone. To think that if she hadn't, I wouldn't have met Ben, and then I wouldn't be here now. I couldn't wait to see what might happen if we spent more time together. Maybe Granny's grand plan for us might come to fruition after all.

CHAPTER 21

CHARLOTTE

On the boat, the four of us descended from the train and went up on the deck, the sea air brushing our faces as we leant over the railings, watching the chalky white cliffs of Dover disappear from view. And then we watched the beaches of northern France appear as we approached its shores. After reaching the other side of the English Channel, our train progressed south through France via Paris and then Dijon. The time passed slowly, for my cabin, albeit a first-class one, was rather small. It consisted of a bed, a chair and a compact bathroom, and there was barely room to swing a cat. I wasn't particularly fond of small spaces and, although it was exciting to be travelling through France, I longed to reach our destination. To be continuously moving was an odd sensation, with the rattle of the carriages and the never-ending clickety-clack. I did however enjoy looking out of the window at the French countryside passing by, oh so flat in the north, and becoming hillier as we moved south. And then there were the vineyards and medieval towns and villages with church spires rising into the sky.

When we reached Switzerland, our train rose up into the Alps, and I'd never seen such a vision – mountains, so magnificent rising into the deep-blue sky, with crests of white on their peaks. I'd seen mountains in the Lake District, but although they were beautiful, they did not compare in height or majesty to these ones, which rose so high, their peaks nestled within the clouds.

The train moved through valleys, with thick lush green forests all around. Tunnels plunged us into darkness when we were least expecting it. Villages were tucked into the side of the mountains, and there were wooden chalets dotted around. Cable cars moved up and down, so slowly it was soporific to watch them. How brave someone must be to go inside one. I would be continually wondering if the cable might snap, plunging everyone into the valley below. One did hear of such things.

I wondered what Switzerland would be like covered in snow during the winter months. It must be so beautiful all dressed in white, but also terribly cold. One would struggle to remain warm in the sub-zero temperatures, and I expected the best course of action was to stay indoors in front of the hearth with plenty of firewood to hand.

As the train climbed higher and higher, the views became ever more impressive. I made little sketches in my diary and wrote about what I could see to pass the time.

On the second evening, Albert and I ate dinner together once again, sitting opposite each other by the window, the Swiss scenery passing by. The dining car was busy, and looking around at other passengers – businessmen, married couples, spinsters – I wondered where they all might be going and what they intended to do upon their arrival. Everyone was impeccably dressed, and several languages could be heard, including French, German and Italian, as well as English, of course.

The waiter brought menus, and I suggested we order a bottle of Chablis. I selected haddock and Albert went for coq au vin. The more I got to know Albert, the more I liked him. But he was the head gardener, and I needed to remember that socially, he was inferior to me. What would people say if we were romantically involved? We'd be the talk of Copeley, nay the whole county of Surrey. Everyone would refer to the countess who fell in love with the gardener, and they'd laugh at me. They might refer to him as Lady Chatterley's Lover – but then why should I care?

'Are you glad you came on this journey, Bertie?' I asked.

'Yes, I am enjoying myself, I must admit. Although, it does concern me that people might jump to the wrong conclusion about us.'

It was as if he'd been reading my mind.

'Whatever do you mean?'

He lifted his eyebrows. Was he implying that other passengers would assume we were a couple?

'Although you are my employee, Bertie, I see you more as a colleague, or friend, even. I'm not sure how you view me.'

'I'd like to think I'm more than your employee, Charlotte.'

'Quite.'

'But...' he continued. 'What if you happen to see an acquaintance on this journey, and they jump to the wrong conclusion. What if—'

'Oh, Bertie, do come on, we mustn't worry about all that.'

'Won't people talk?'

I frowned. 'What will they say, exactly?'

It was obvious, but I couldn't help goading him, as I so wanted to see his reaction. His face reddened, and he looked down at the table. He took a roll out of the bread basket and tore it in half, then picked up his knife.

'I feel as though I might have spoken out of turn,' he said, spreading butter onto the roll.

It seemed that I'd struck a chord with my question.

'Are you looking forward to seeing the vineyard?' I said, changing the subject.

'It will be interesting, to be sure.'

'I'm excited to see the city of Verona too, Shakespeare's inspiration for *Romeo and Juliet*. Are you familiar with the play?'

'I know it's a love story.'

'It is partly, but also it's a tragedy.'

'What happens?'

'They both end up dead.'

'I wouldn't exactly call it a love story then.'

'Yes, it's all rather silly. They both die because of a misunderstanding. Shakespeare likes to play around with misunderstandings – it can be incredibly frustrating as a reader or theatre-goer. Near the end of the play, Romeo believes that Juliet is dead, but she'd actually faked her death by taking a sleeping potion.'

He scrunched up his eyes.

'Why would she do that?'

'To avoid having to marry another man, chosen by her father. Romeo doesn't receive the note from a messenger to tell him she's only asleep. So, when he reaches her, he assumes that she's dead and then takes poison in order to kill himself.'

'Why?'

'Because he cannot bear to live without her. She wakes up and sees that he is dead... and then kills herself with his dagger.'

'So, you might say it's a love story because they love each other so much they cannot be apart, whether they're alive or dead. I couldn't imagine loving anyone that much,' he said.

'Me neither. Imagine loving someone so much that you cannot live without them?'

'It didn't seem to apply to you and his lordship.'

'He was an ogre – I'm sure you could see that for yourself, along with the other servants. Every morning when I saw him, he'd have brandy on his breath. He couldn't get through five minutes without an alcoholic beverage to massage his mood.'

'But now you are free to do as you please. Apart from the Lady Penelope problem, but I'm sure we'll find a way to fix it when we return.'

He was talking about her blackmailing me as if it were our problem to resolve together. It warmed my heart to have him on my side.

'Yes, I am now as free as a bird. Well for now, at least... my father is already talking about finding me another husband, one with a title who will give me children with titles. When I return to England, he'll no doubt have a list of eligible men for me to choose from. He'll be working on his project as we speak, mingling with acquaintances at his London club, putting the word out and all that.'

'Ah, I see. And is that what you want?'

I shook my head.

'No, it isn't. If I marry again, it will be for love.'

Our eyes met across the table, and then we passed through a tunnel, and everything went dark, the dim lights in the carriage hardly making a difference. It was impossible to talk as the train tooted its horn, and we had to sit there in silence until we emerged into the daylight.

'And if that man you fall in love with doesn't have a title?'

'I shall lose the title of dowager countess.'

'Does being a countess mean nothing to you?'

'I never asked to be one. Marrying Winston in order to get the title was my father's idea. He worked hard to arrange our marriage, but it was for him, not for me.'

'Why did the Clarkson family agree to it all?'

'Money, of course. Winston was on the verge of bankruptcy.'

He nodded, clearly registering what I was saying.

'They wanted your father's money?'

'My father saved Copeley Park. Winston would have had to sell the estate otherwise.'

'Goodness, it's almost as if you—'

'Were used as a pawn, so my father could tell everyone in his circle that his daughter was a countess? Now he had really made it, and his descendants would be part of the aristocracy he'd always wanted to be a part of himself. Barons and earls would visit at weekends, even the King himself, well two kings actually, and, if you're counting Edward VIII, the now Duke of Windsor, that makes three. But we wouldn't really count him, would we?'

Albert shook his head.

'He found the Duchess of Windsor to be rather vulgar actually, and didn't invite them back.'

'Wallis Simpson, you mean?'

'Yes. To think she almost brought down the monarchy – how astounding that is. Thank goodness for George VI, stepping up like that.'

'He had little choice.'

'Indeed. Poor man, it must be tricky with that stutter of his. He can barely string two words together. And now his daughters have been thrust into the spotlight, and Princess Elizabeth will have to spend part of her life serving the country as Queen – a role he never expected for her.'

'And one she wouldn't have expected to have either. Why would the royal family mix with your father, if you don't mind my asking?'

'All of these people – they're known as the Hatchley Set – would come to Rodene Hall over and over again, eating our food and drinking our wine.' I explained how Papa had worked his way up from nothing to own a railway company in Cheshire. 'The King himself took a keen interest in the railways.'

'How admirable that your father has achieved so much, against all odds.'

'Indeed, but Papa would never be one of them with his Lancashire accent – which sometimes they mocked quite openly. He'd often make some kind of social faux pas without realising, such as wearing the wrong item of clothing for a shoot. They'd pounce on any opportunity to make an example of him. He was good-humoured about it, laughing along with them. But deep down, I know their mockery made my father feel that he wasn't ever going to be one of them.'

As I told Albert all this, I realised how hard it must have been for Papa to have been so successful in the world of business, but still unable to buy himself what he wanted most of all: class. So, he'd done the next best thing, bought class for his daughter and her descendants instead. I pitied him for being so foolish but, whatever happened, I could not allow him to talk me into another arranged marriage. Next time, I would have to gather all my strength and flatly refuse.

'That must have been challenging for him.'

'He'd worked so hard to make himself what one calls "a better man" and has made a fortune through the railway company he inherited from his uncle. But they will never see him as one of them, however much money he makes.'

'My father is a cobbler from Hastings, and thankfully he is happy with his lot.'

'And so he should be. You're from Hastings?'

'I am indeed. Grew up by the sea – I do miss it.'

'I imagine you would.'

His eyes glazed over, and I sensed that he was thinking about home. Then he looked at me.

'It must have been a trying time for you, Charlotte, over these past few months?'

I rested my chin on my palms. 'Yes, it has been. First I was plucked from my home in Cheshire and placed at Copeley Park – like a fish out of water. And then of course there was Winston's sudden death. And now, the aftermath, whatever that involves. It's been rather a lot to endure.'

'In time, I'm sure everything will settle down.'

'I do hope so, Albert. Do you know what I crave more than anything else?'

'What's that?'

'Peace.'

'Peace?'

'Yes, to wake up each day and feel at peace with one's world – to be satisfied with one's lot. That's what I would like more than anything else.'

Albert did something then that surprised me. We'd consumed the bottle of Chablis between us – well he'd had most of it. But alcohol didn't seem to have the same effect on him as it did on Winston. He seemed to be friendlier, and more talkative – thank goodness drinking didn't make him aggressive towards me. He reached across the table, took my hand and squeezed it gently. And I allowed him to, even though his action was most inappropriate. Our eyes locked for a split second, and then he carefully pulled his hand away.

'I'm sorry, how inappropriate of me to do that. I do apologise, Charlotte, I—'

'Bertie, please don't apologise for doing something so human. We are not at Copeley Park now. We are on a train, making our way to Italy, where I understand people touch each other a great deal more in everyday life. We English are so stuffy, aren't we?'

He laughed.

'Actually, Bertie,' I said, softly. 'I think perhaps you should do it again, but this time leave your hand there for a little longer...'

'Really, are you sure?'

I nodded.

And so, Albert reached across the table again and took my hand and squeezed it, more firmly this time, and I squeezed his hand in return. And we remained there, our hands touching for some time as we descended the Alps and the Italian countryside began to pass by – buildings with terracotta rooftops, and fields with rows of vines, and olive groves, and towns perched on top of hills with towers and church spires, oh so many of them. We had arrived in Italy, 'the country of love', or amore, as they called it. And I wouldn't wish to have anyone else holding my hand at that very moment.

CHAPTER 22

LADY CHARLOTTE

AUGUST 1939

The air was hot and thick when we stepped onto the platform at Verona railway station. People bustled around us, speaking Italian – it was such a beautiful language, the words rounded and voluptuous. The sky was a flawless deep blue, and the sun shone so brightly I was glad to be wearing a hat with a brim wide enough to shield my eyes. We were in Verona at last, and I couldn't quite believe we'd made it. The train journey had been wonderfully scenic, and an experience to remember, but I was glad to be standing on terra firma. And I looked forward to sleeping in a room that had to be larger than the cabin I'd occupied – where it had been necessary to step sideways to get in and out of the bathroom. I certainly wouldn't miss the rattle of the carriages and the continuous clickety-clack and the tooting of the horn as we sped through tunnels at unexpected moments. Now, I hoped to find peace and quiet in the countryside of the Veneto region.

We took two taxis, in convoy, from the railway station – one for Gwen and me, and the other for Albert and George. Our luggage was attached to the roofs in such a haphazard manner that I wondered if it might slide off into the street. This was especially because the drivers edged their way speedily around the vast number of mopeds and bicycles, taking us along narrow streets, rumbling over the cobblestones. The buildings were painted in lemon yellow and terracotta, their walls more often crumbling than not. Tall windows were flanked by shutters in green and brown, and sheets billowed in the breeze from washing lines above. Our taxi passed cafés and restaurants, where people sat at tables on the pavement, cigarettes resting between their fingers. People walked along the shady side of the street, and who could blame them for it was incredibly hot in the sun. Our driver informed us, as he puffed on a cigarette, that it was almost ninety degrees Fahrenheit. He waved his hand and said, 'Che caldo,' shaking his head in despair. It was much warmer than at home, the air incredibly sticky, and I used a handkerchief to mop the sweat from my brow.

We progressed alongside the River Adige – the driver informed us of the name as he pointed at it with a bony finger – over a bridge, and past the Castelvecchio – a castle built in the fourteenth century, he explained. And then we left the city, and the road took us uphill, twisting and winding round, through a village where a grand church stood majestically at a crossroads. A few minutes later, we reached the sign for Vineria di San Martino. Our taxis turned on to a narrow lane, and climbed up a steep hill until we reached a yellow building. It was covered in Virginia creeper, so raucously red and vibrant, and the windows had brown shutters. It was a sight to behold. The drivers removed our luggage from the roofs of the taxis while we stood in the shade, under the awning outside the building where there was a cluster of tables and chairs. Albert paid the drivers, and I was glad he'd agreed to take responsibility for the money. Lira was a bizarre currency, and I had no idea how much any of the different notes were worth. Thankfully, Albert had a head for maths, and for that I was grateful. I asked him to tip the drivers generously, as would no doubt be expected.

Our driver gave an appreciative nod and said, 'Grazie, signore,' before speeding back down the hill. And there we were, deposited at a vineyard outside Verona. We were actually in the Italian countryside, a stone's throw from the city of Romeo and Juliet. It was rather romantic. Albert and George picked up our suitcases and we all made our way towards the entrance to the pretty building – there was a sign: VILLA ROMEO.

'Oh, how apt,' I said to Gwen. She smiled, knowing how fond I was of the play.

Being the leader of our small group, I took charge and knocked on the door. Right away, I could hear footsteps tip-tapping, and then the door opened, and there she was, Agnes, dressed in a long and flowing white cotton dress and brown leather sandals. Living in Italy suited her immensely.

'Dear cousin,' she said, leaning forward to kiss me on both cheeks, which I understood was customary in Italy.

'Hello, Agnes.'

I went on to introduce Albert, Gwen and George, and they all shook hands.

'Welcome, all of you,' she said, throwing her arms in the air. She'd certainly adopted the Italian way of using hand and arm gestures. 'Do come in. Leave your suitcases outside, and Tomasso will take them to your rooms.'

I stepped over the threshold into a hall, and the others followed, our shoes creating an echo as we walked on the terracotta tiles. The walls were painted white, and they were filled with paintings. Agnes called over a young girl, wearing a black dress with a white apron tied round her waist, and addressed her in Italian. I was impressed to see my cousin speaking another language, and so fluently too. She could have been Italian, the way the words rolled off her tongue.

Turning to me, she said, 'Francesca will show you to your quarters – I've put you all in Villa Giulietta.'

'Giulietta, like Juliet?'

'Yes, exactly.'

I smiled. 'Thank you, Agnes.'

'It's a short walk to the villa, but I know you will find it charming. Come on, let me show you where it is. Then you can wash and change before returning later for drinks and supper. I'm sure you are fatigued after your journey. Your servants will sleep on the first floor of your villa – you are on the ground floor, Charlotte, with a terrace – and they can eat with mine here at Villa Romeo.'

Now I could see a problem, as I didn't want Albert to be treated as a servant. I hadn't thought to advise Agnes of this in advance. I wanted him to have a better room, and to join me at mealtimes, and so I took Agnes to one side and informed her of this.

She looked across at Albert, and then back at me, and smiled.

'Of course, that will not be a problem. We shall treat him as your friend.'

And then she raised her eyebrows. Dear Agnes had always been adept at reading a situation. 'Aspetta...' She spoke to Francesca in Italian, and then said to me, 'Albert will now be on the ground floor of Villa Giulietta, in the Rosa room. You will be next to him in Mimosa, Charlotte.'

I thanked her, and she gestured for us to follow her out of the front door.

'Andiamo,' she said, 'You must excuse me as, these days, I tend to speak in a mix of Italian and English, but it will be helpful for you to learn a few words, Charlotte.'

Outside, she led us uphill, along a narrow lane flanked by tall green trees – they were beautiful, almost regal in the way they rose up into the deep-blue sky.

'These trees are very common in Italy – they're called cypress trees,' she said.

'They are so majestic,' I said.

I glanced over my shoulder to see that Albert was looking around him in wonder, and Gwen and George were deep in conversation. Francesca walked alongside them, looking at the ground, her hands clasped behind her back. As we made our way along the lane, there was an olive grove on our left.

'We have many olive trees, and they are hundreds of years old,' Agnes said. 'We press our own olive oil here. It's delicious, and very good for you – you absolutely must try it.'

When we reached the top of the hill, we were blessed with one of the most stupendous views I'd ever seen, with a valley below and rows and rows of vines as far as the eye could see. I had never seen a real vineyard before, and it was exciting to visit a place where grapes were cultivated and wine was produced. In the distance, there was the city of Verona. I could even see the River Adige threading through the city, the bridges crossing from one side to the other, along with all the towers and spires.

'Although we benefit from cleaner air and it's quieter here in the countryside, we are still blessed with a view of the magnificent city,' Agnes said.

She led us through a gate and on the other side was a cluster of buildings, like Villa Romeo yellow with brown shutters, and again covered in Virginia creeper.

'On the left there is our vineria – the winery, where we make the wine. We press the olives in the building next door. There are cellars below where we store the wine in eighteenth-century oak barrels. We also have a farm with sheep, goats and chickens, and we grow our own fruit and vegetables. I recall you are rather fond of gardening, Charlotte – you won't believe what we can grow here as the climate is so much warmer than in England. There are lemon and orange trees and melons with sweet orange flesh, and the peaches are enormous and deliciously sweet.'

Agnes continued to walk and then stopped in front of one of the buildings and took a key out of the pocket of her dress. On the outside of the building was a sign: VILLA GIULIETTA.

'This is where you will all be staying. I hope you like it. We've had the villa redecorated recently so guests can be comfortable.'

She unlocked the door, and I stepped into a hall with a black-and-white-tiled floor. The walls were painted white, and crammed with paintings of countryside scenes and still lifes of bowls of fruit and bottles of wine. Agnes spoke in Italian to Francesca, who then gestured for George and Gwen to follow her up another flight of stairs.

'Francesca will show them to their rooms on the top floor. Albert, you are in the room over there at the end of the hall, marked Rosa.'

'Thank you, Agnes,' he said, making his way along the hall.

Then she opened the door to a room, marked MIMOSA, and ushered me inside.

'I have saved the best room for you, Charlotte, naturally.'

Inside, there were vast windows looking over the valley and beyond to Verona, and French doors led to a terrace that had a table and chairs. The furniture in the room was made from a dark wood and there was a double bed, wardrobe, nightstands, a dressing table with stool and mirror, and a chest of drawers with marble top and animal feet. Two comfortable-looking leather armchairs faced the window, and I couldn't wait to sit in one of them with a book. I'd brought my copy of *Romeo and Juliet* to read again.

Agnes opened a door. 'Here you have your own bathroom as well. One of the servants will bring you water, as and when you need it.'

I stepped inside to see a bath and sink, both made from marble, and there was a water closet. I felt rather spoilt.

'What an impressive room. Thank you, Agnes.'

'I knew you'd appreciate it, especially with that view. Now I shall leave you to settle in. Tomasso will bring your luggage soon in the truck. Just ring the bell if you need anything and one of the servants will bring you tea or whatever else you need. I shall send someone to fetch you for drinks later. And then you can meet my husband, Mario.'

Agnes opened the door, and gave me a wave goodbye, and there I was, all alone, unable to believe my luck. I opened the French doors and went out onto the terrace. To my left stood Albert, outside his room.

'What a place you've brought me to, Charlotte,' he said.

'Are you glad you came with me now?'

He turned to look at me. 'Indeed, I am, Charlotte. There's no doubt about that.'

CHAPTER 23

KATE

When I woke up the next morning, I couldn't believe how quiet it was, apart from a wood pigeon cooing down the chimney. What a refreshing change from the sound of passing cars. I got out of bed and opened the curtains to see a pretty garden with trees and flowerbeds, and a potting shed painted in pastel blue. I picked up my phone from the bedside table, and climbed back into bed. Through the window I could see the Surrey Hills and trees in all their autumn glory, in red and gold. In the distance was Manor Farm, and sheep dotted the surrounding fields.

I logged into Instagram and decided to have a proper look at the Copeley Park account. No one had posted for a couple of weeks. There was a carousel post with photos of the harvest, and a photo of Dad holding a bottle of Copeley wine produced that year. I clicked on the link in the bio, which took me to the website. On the events page, there was nothing apart from a wine tasting that had taken place in the summer. Dad could be doing so much more. And soon the vineyard would close to visitors until the spring, meaning no income would be made from the public during the winter months. He could be organising tours and tastings throughout the autumn and winter instead of stopping like he usually did. And with Christmas coming, he could host events with special deals on cases of six bottles.

A knock came at the bedroom door. I was still in my pyjamas with no make-up on, and I hadn't even had chance to brush my teeth. I wasn't sure if I wanted Ben to see me like this, and besides I needed a cup of tea before communicating with anyone in the mornings. I got out of bed and went to open it. He was standing there, a mug in his hand.

'Morning,' he said. 'Thought you might like a cup of tea?'

'Oh thank you, Ben,' I said, taking the mug from him. 'That's so thoughtful of you.'

'There are croissants keeping warm under the grill, so help yourself when you're ready.'

'Why, are you off somewhere?' I said, trying to hide the disappointment in my voice. I'd been hoping we might have breakfast together, and talk some more, by the fire. I wasn't ready to leave him yet.

'Yes, annoyingly, I've just had a text to say that the alarms are going off in the Gothic tower.'

'Oh... and that's your responsibility?'

'One of the conditions of me getting to live in this cottage is that I need to be on standby at weekends and in the evenings for things like this.'

'Well of course, if it's your job,' I said.

'Hopefully it won't take too long. I need to drive up there in the Land Rover. The alarms have been faulty for a while and we need to get them fixed, well, your...'

'My dad needs to get them fixed?' I said, with a laugh.

'Yes, exactly.'

'Well thank you for last night, and for the tea and croissants.'

'I'll probably be half an hour, maybe a bit more. Will you be here when I get back?'

Shaking my head reluctantly, I said, 'I ought to get going, and drop in on Dad before I talk myself out of it.'

'Okay, well I hope to see you again soon. I'll message you.'

I looked up at him, and our eyes met.

'I'd like that.'

He started to walk away, then he stopped and turned round.

'Good luck talking to your dad.'

Smiling, I said, 'Thanks.'

I closed the door, and sipped my tea. It was the perfect strength – not too strong and not too weak – and it hit the spot. Right, I needed to get dressed and visit my father before I changed my mind.

When I was dressed, I sat at the kitchen table and ate the croissant. It was crispy and absolutely delicious. That had been nice of Ben to heat it up for me. He knew how to look after his guests. Then I put my holdall in the boot and got into the car. When I started the engine the radio came on, playing 'Hello' by Lionel Richie. It fitted the way I was feeling perfectly. The evening with Ben had put me in a fantastic mood. How I wanted to spend more time with him at his charming cottage. This didn't mean that I expected anything to happen between us – I was happy to be his friend for now. Being around him made me feel calm, as if nothing mattered, although I couldn't explain why. Perhaps it was his relaxed demeanour – nothing seemed to bother him much. Even being called out on a Saturday morning to deal with some annoying alarm. Whatever it was, he made me feel good about myself. I liked the version of me that I was in his presence – relaxed, cheerful, dare I say it, fun? And content with life.

I drove along the narrow lane, taking care to avoid the potholes, and, when I reached the one that I'd swerved into when meeting Ben, I decided to tell Dad about it. What if someone else drove into it and they didn't have Ben there to rescue them? As I approached the house, I considered chickening out, and carrying on back to Southfields. But Dad had sent that card for my birthday, suggesting I drop in. Although it was signed from him and Emilie. Did he not realise how it would make me feel to receive a birthday card from his fiancée too? But also, I could talk to him about the vineyard, and the ideas that had been percolating since my conversation with Ben. And I wanted to ask if he knew who the mysterious 'B' could be in the note with the box of wine. I didn't want to upset Granny by bringing it up again, and perhaps it would be easier if I could do some digging and find out on my own. Dad must know who this person was, surely? And it had to be a man, by the affectionate way the note was written. Was it Granny's secret boyfriend? Whoever it was, she had been upset when I discovered the note, as if this person had meant a great deal to her.

As I passed the turning to the house, I slowed down. I could still come back another time. Would Dad even be home? It was still early, and he didn't usually go anywhere before lunch on a Saturday. He liked his lazy weekends and would probably take his two Labradors, Bonnie and Pepper, for a walk at some stage, maybe stopping off at a pub for a pint of bitter and a bag of crisps. Pulling myself together, I turned into the driveway and drove up to the front of the house, where I parked. Grabbing my handbag, I got out of the car. As I approached the front door, it opened and Jenkins appeared, dressed in a suit. I went up the steps.

'Good morning, Miss Clarkson. How delightful to see you,' he said.

'Good morning, Mr Jenkins. Is Dad home?'

'He is indeed. Do come in.'

I went through the door, and he closed it behind me.

'Your father is in his study,' he said.

'Thank you.'

I crossed the grand hall with its black-and-white-tiled floor and passed through the library to the room at the other end. This was where Dad did all his admin. And there he was, sitting at the desk, surrounded by piles of papers, his eyes fixed on a computer screen. Classical music came from the speakers in the corner. He looked up, and our eyes met, which gave me a warm feeling. I had to admit, it was good to see him. Regret at not coming back since Christmas consumed me – how childish I'd been. This was my father, and I needed to grow up – accept this new woman in his life. Mum had been gone for five years and it was time for all of us to move on.

'Oh, hello there, Kate. What a lovely surprise.'

'Hi, Dad.'

He stood up and came out from behind the desk and gave me a hug.

'Let's go into the library and have coffee, shall we?'

'Sure, that would be nice.'

Now was my chance to run a few ideas past him, and, most importantly, to find out who the mysterious 'B' was.

CHAPTER 24

LADY CHARLOTTE

That evening, Tomasso picked us up from Villa Giulietta and drove us down to Villa Romeo, the car roof rolled back. The sun was low in the sky, the clouds tinged with orange and purple. Birds sang in the trees around us as he sped along the narrow country lane, bumping up and down on the uneven surface. An orchestra of cicadas chirruped in the long grass on the verges, butterflies fluttered, and bees buzzed around a lavender bush as we passed. If paradise existed, I imagined that it would be like this place. A week didn't seem long enough to spend here, but, having agreed that would be the length of our stay, I didn't want to impose on Agnes and Mario by asking to stay for longer. Still, I would try to savour every single moment.

We reached Villa Romeo, and a maid showed us into a vast drawing room. When we entered, Agnes was sitting there with a wine glass in her hand. Beside her was a man who I presumed to be her husband, Mario. He had thick dark hair, and he was exceptionally handsome. Now I understood why Agnes had defied her father's wishes that she marry the Baron of Tyne. Not only was she living in this stunning location, but she was married to this attractive man too – my dear cousin had landed on her feet.

They both stood up.

'Welcome,' Agnes said. 'Dear Charlotte, may I introduce my husband, Mario, who I have told you about in my letters.'

'How do you do,' I said. 'This is my friend, Albert.'

Mario leant forward and kissed me on both cheeks – this seemed to be customary even between men and women who weren't acquainted – and then he shook hands with Albert.

'Piacere,' he said.

Albert nodded and attempted to repeat the Italian greeting, rather poorly, and Mario laughed, but not unkindly. He said the word again, more slowly, and this time Albert repeated it almost perfectly.

'Bravo,' Mario said, patting him on the back.

'Would you like to try a glass of prosecco from our vineyard?' Agnes said.

'Oh, yes please,' I said.

Within minutes, a footman had brought in a tray of glasses half-filled with prosecco, bubbles fizzing to the top.

We all took one, and Agnes said, 'Cin cin.' The word 'Cin' was pronounced 'Chin', and we slowly repeated what she said with her encouragement.

'I am absolutely determined for you to learn a few Italian words while you are here, Charlotte.'

I laughed.

When dinner was ready, we were shown into a dining room, and sat down. The table was covered with a red-and-white-chequered cloth, and there were many tall white candles, their flames flickering from the breeze coming through doors that opened onto a vast terrace. And there were jam jars of yellow sweet peas at the centre of the table. Each place setting had a number of knives, forks and spoons as well as four wine glasses in different shapes and sizes.

A butler entered the room with a bottle of white wine and half-filled a glass for each of us.

'This white wine is produced here on our vineyard from pinot gris grapes. It has notes of citrus, apple and pear. I hope you enjoy it,' Agnes said.

We all picked up our glasses and tasted the wine. It was refreshing and crisp, and I liked it very much.

'This is very good,' I said.

My eyes met with Albert's across the table, and he nodded.

'So you are here for a week,' Agnes said. 'You'll have to make the most of every minute – the time will soon pass. Would you like me to take you into the city tomorrow, Charlotte?'

'I'd be delighted to accompany you into Verona, of course. Thank you, Agnes.'

'I shall look forward to showing you around – it's filled with historical and cultural gems at every corner.'

'Albert was hoping to spend some time on the vineyard, to explore and maybe work with the grapes. Is there anyone who could show him what to do?'

'Certo, Agnes said you were hoping to take pinot gris cuttings back to England?' Mario said. 'We have some in the greenhouse, taken when the vines were dormant in the winter.'

'Yes, we'd like that very much,' I said. 'We're planning to start our very own vineyard at Copeley Park.' I explained how there had been one there in the eighteenth century that I wanted to revive.

'Well, Albert, you can work alongside me and the other labourers,' Mario said. 'And later I shall take you on a personal tour, and we can do some wine tasting after.' He winked.

'Thank you,' Albert said.

'I hope you both don't end up getting drunk,' I said, with a laugh.

'Drunk, on a vineyard? What on earth are you implying?'

Mario said, picking up his wine glass. 'We shall swirl it around in our mouths and spit it out, shan't we, Albert?'

'Absolutely, of course,' Albert said, with a smile.

I liked the way that Agnes and Mario were treating Albert as my friend, rather than as my servant. It was so different to see him being treated as my equal in a social situation. And why shouldn't he be? I enjoyed his company immensely and treasured time spent with him.

'I don't need to take my lady's maid, Gwen, into Verona. Is there anything she can assist you with here? And there is also Albert's valet, George, who could do with a task to keep him occupied.'

'They can both work in the vineyard, or, if your maid would prefer, we can find her work in one of the villas.'

'Thank you,' I said.

Footmen brought in our starters. One of them spoke to Agnes in Italian.

'This is a salad made with goats' cheese, produced here on our farm, and these crispy toasts are called crostini,' Agnes said. 'They are topped with a pâté made from wild mushrooms – we call them funghi and we forage for them on the land.'

We tucked in. The flavours weren't what I was used to, but the crostini were delightfully crunchy and scrumptious too. I enjoyed trying a dish that was completely new to me.

Footmen cleared our plates and filled another one of our wine glasses with a red wine.

'This is Valpolicella, produced here. We shall drink red wine to go with the meat we are about to consume,' Mario said.

We were presented with wide bowls filled with pasta covered in a tomato sauce. A salad was placed in the centre of the table. I hadn't eaten pasta before, and found it to be delicious, although also filling. When those bowls were cleared, more were brought out.

'These are polpette, otherwise known as meatballs, with a

sauce made from tomatoes and basil, a herb we use frequently in Italian cuisine. And help yourself to the salad of rocket leaves, grown here – you'll find that they have a peppery flavour,' Agnes said.

The meatballs were exceptionally tasty – they had clearly been cooked slowly as the meat melted in the mouth.

After we'd finished eating, we were presented with another glass of red wine.

'This is Amarone, still a Valpolicella, but aged for at least three years in our oak barrels here in our cellars. You will find that it's richer than the other Valpolicella we tried. And the alcohol content is much higher, meaning it is more potent,' Mario said. 'I sell many bottles of this to my brother's restaurant in Jermyn Street.'

'It has notes of cherry and chocolate,' Agnes said.

When I tasted the Amarone, I was swept away by its warmth and richness. I could quite easily have drunk the whole bottle.

The footmen brought in bowls of ice cream and placed them in front of us.

'This ice cream is also made from the goats' milk produced here on the farm. In this region of Italy we drizzle it with local honey and scatter walnuts over the top,' Agnes said.

The ice cream was delicious, and the flavour was different from when it was made with cow's milk – once again, I found it interesting to try something new.

At the end of the meal, the footmen cleared the plates and brought in coffee served in tiny cups. I added a spoonful of sugar to sweeten, and it cut through all the alcohol I'd consumed during the meal.

Mario got up and left the room briefly, and returned with a bottle of a yellow drink. He filled four tiny glasses with the liquid.

'This is limoncello, a liqueur made from lemons,' he said.

He handed the glasses round, and I took a sip. The limoncello was extremely potent, but tangy and sweet, and it did indeed taste of lemons. I'd never tried anything quite like it.

After dinner, we declined Agnes and Mario's offer for Tomasso to drive us back to the villa, for it was a warm summer evening, and we were in Italy – Albert and I made the decision to walk instead.

'Thank you, both of you, for the wonderful dinner,' I said.

'You're welcome. I shall look forward to taking you to Verona tomorrow,' Agnes said.

I couldn't wait.

Albert and I stepped out into the warm night air. The cicadas still chirruped around us. Albert used a torch to light our way – he was always prepared, and I was glad to have him by my side. The lights of Verona twinkled in the distance as if they were calling us to them. I couldn't wait to explore the city the following day.

'Which was your favourite wine, Albert?'

'I really liked the Amarone.'

'Ah.' I smiled to myself. 'The strongest.'

He laughed, and then he stopped and looked up at the night sky.

'The sky is so clear tonight. I can make out so many constellations – can you see the Plough?'

Looking up, yes, I could.

'I can indeed.'

We both stood still for a moment. A dog yapped in the distance, and a motorcar hummed as it passed by on the main road below.

'I'm already fond of this place,' Albert said.

'Me too, it's rather like how I'd imagine paradise to be.'

'Indeed, you are right, Charlotte. I'm looking forward to discovering more about the vineyard tomorrow,' he said.

When we reached Villa Giulietta, Albert unlocked the front

door – for he was in charge of carrying the key on our behalf. We stepped into the hall and then there was an awkward moment as we found ourselves outside my bedroom. I rested my hand on the doorknob. How I wanted to invite him inside, merely to talk for longer – to sit in the comfortable-looking chairs with the French doors open and the twinkling lights of Verona before us. A glass of brandy would be a welcome end to the evening too. But it wouldn't be appropriate to invite Albert into my bedroom, and besides, I did not have any brandy. Perhaps Agnes could find me a bottle for another evening.

'Goodnight, Charlotte,' he said, moving in the direction of his room, at the end of the hall.

'Goodnight, Bertie.'

He gave me a nod before disappearing out of sight, but I could still hear his shoes tapping on the tiled floor, sending an echo down the corridor. I went into my room, closing the door behind me. And then I leant on the door, closed my eyes, and took a deep breath. I longed to know Albert better. But even if we happened to kiss here in Verona, there would be no more kissing after we departed. For there was no way we could be together at Copeley Park. When we returned, Papa would be ready with his list of potential suitors for my next marriage – a letter addressed to me had probably already arrived. If I kissed Albert here, in this place, and there was no chance of it happening again, my heart was bound to be very much broken.

CHAPTER 25

LADY CHARLOTTE

The next morning, a maid brought me breakfast in bed, and then Gwen came to help me get ready for my trip into Verona. We chose a pale-blue tea dress with a white belt and a hat and shoes to match. It was a stylish outfit, for sure. Tomasso drove us into the centre of Verona, dropping us at Piazza Bra, a vast cobblestoned square. We were instantly blessed with a view of the most incredible Roman amphitheatre – still mostly intact, after all the years it had been standing there for. I had never seen anything quite like it. We got out of the car, and I stood there on the spot and looked up at it, picturing Verona during the Roman era with men in gladiator outfits and togas walking around. I thought about all that had happened there at the amphitheatre over the centuries.

'This amphitheatre, the Arena di Verona, has been there since 30 CE. Incredible, don't you think?' Agnes said. 'Can you imagine how horrific the gladiator fights must have been?'

'It doesn't bear thinking about,' I said. 'And what do they use it for now?'

'Opera, mostly. It is the largest open-air opera house in the entire world. There's a festival there every summer.' Her eyes lit up. 'It's on now, until the end of August. And it has taken place every year since 1913, apart from during the Great War.'

'And I expect it will stop again if there is another war.'

'You're right, everything will stop once again. I live in hope that there will not be another war, but it seems we are close to one happening. We have bought our gas masks,' she said, shaking her head.

I wondered what our fate would be if a war started while we were still in Italy. Would that make it difficult to get back to England? I doubted it would be easy. All I could do was hope that Italy wouldn't go to war until we'd safely crossed the border into Switzerland, and ideally returned to England.

'Do you worry about Mario being sent to fight?' I asked.

Agnes looked at me and blinked.

'It is my greatest fear. I love him so much and couldn't bear to live without him.' Her voice cracked and she cleared her throat.

'If he leaves, that will indeed be very difficult for you.'

'And then who will run the vineyard?' She raised her arms in the air, in the manner of an Italian. 'All the male labourers will leave, and it will be up to us women to manage it all.'

She led me down a street where there were shops and cafés with tables outside. They were filled with men and women drinking coffee and smoking cigarettes.

'So, what is the arrangement between you and Albert then?' Agnes said.

'What are you implying?'

Agnes threw me a look. We'd spent a lot of time together during our childhood, and my cousin knew me well. It was nigh on impossible to hide anything from her.

'You know very well what I'm implying,' she said.

'I merely asked him to accompany me so he could help take back the vine cuttings. Did I tell you that a vineyard was planted at Copeley Park in the eighteenth century, and left to decline and—'

'Codswallop. You do know it's unlikely that grapes grown here will survive back in England?'

'I believe the pinot gris grape might, seeing as it originated in France.'

'It's a good excuse to bring him along though. Well done, Charlotte.'

'What are you talking about?'

'Come on, it's obvious you're in love with him. And that he's in love with you.'

'Do you really think so?'

She put a hand on my arm.

'Which part are you asking me about?'

'That he's in love with me?'

Agnes stopped walking, and smiled at me. 'So, you are in love with him then. I knew it.'

'Do you think it's too soon after losing Winston?'

'Did you love Winston?'

'Not one jot. You know the marriage was arranged, and he wasn't a good man.'

I'd decided not to tell Agnes about how Winston met his end – now I'd confided in Albert on the train, I'd got it off my chest. But she of all people should understand how it could be difficult to love a man your father picked out for you. Somehow, she'd managed to get her own way by marrying Mario rather than the Baron of Tyne. We started walking again.

'Papa will have another suitor lined up for when I return, of course.'

'But Charlotte, you can't put yourself through that again. You need to stand your ground this time.'

'Do you think I'd be strong enough to do that?'

'Of course, you must talk to him. Don't allow yourself to be pressured into another marriage that you do not want. Next time it might be for the rest of your life.'

'But you do know that Albert is my head gardener, a servant?'

'Of course I do. But I can see how much you love each other. He looks at you with the occhi d'amore.'

'Meaning?'

'He looks at you with the eyes of love. And you look at him with the eyes of love too. You are supposed to be together for the rest of your lives. You need to find a way to be with him.'

'You know that marrying him would mean losing my title?'

'Yes, but that doesn't concern you, does it?'

'No, but Papa would be devastated if I were no longer a countess.'

'I think you should write a letter.'

'To Albert?'

She shook her head.

'No, silly.'

'To Papa?'

She shook her head. The road we were following opened out into a large rectangular square.

'This is Piazza Erbe. It was once a Roman forum, and now it's used as a marketplace,' Agnes said. 'Over there is the Madonna Verona fountain.'

She turned right, and then took a left, and we were standing in a tiny square with a balcony.

'This building is called Casa Giulietta, the house of Juliet. I think you should write a letter to her.'

'Who?'

'Juliet.'

'I don't understand.'

'Recently in Verona, people have been leaving love letters at Juliet's tomb in the church of San Francesco al Corso. Word has it that the guardian of the tomb, a man named Ettore Solimani, replies to these letters with sympathy or advice when required, in order to bring luck in love to those who really need it.'

'And you think I should do that?'

'Don't you happen to have a love dilemma?'

'I suppose I do.'

'Well, there you are then.'

'I don't see how writing to a strange Italian man posing as a fictional character from a Shakespeare play will help me.'

'Don't be such a pessimist, Charlotte. If nothing else, it might do you good to write the letter anyway, in order to organise your thoughts.'

'That's an interesting idea, Agnes, and I'll consider it carefully, for sure.'

'All right. Are you hungry, shall we get lunch?'

'That sounds like a marvellous plan.'

'Let me take you to my favourite restaurant. They do the best tortellini di Valeggio, which is pasta twisted into the shape of love knots – rather apt, don't you think – and filled with braised meat. We need to pass the Madonna Verona fountain, and take the street at the other end of Piazza Erbe.'

She started to walk and we left the tiny square, coming out onto a street with shops and cafés.

'Why do you really think I should write this letter to Juliet, Agnes?'

'Because that's what I did.'

'You did?'

'I came to Verona to visit Mario – he invited me to see the vineyard, and so I brought my governess as chaperone. We stayed in a boarding house in the city.'

'And?'

'And Mario and I swiftly fell in love. Well, he told me he fell in love with me instantly when he saw me at his brother's restaurant in Jermyn Street. It was a colpo di fulmine, he said – meaning a thunderbolt, or in other words, 'love at first sight'.

The Italians are very romantic, and they talk about the thunderbolt all the time. The lady who owned the boarding house, Signora Bianchi, told me about these letters that women were writing to Juliet. And so I thought, why shouldn't I write one myself? My father wanted me to marry that baron from Northumberland, but I wanted to be with Mario.'

'And then you wrote it?'

'Yes, I did, and I went with my governess to leave it by the tomb.'

'And you received a reply?'

'A few days later, a letter arrived at the boarding house – I'd given that address, asking Signora Bianchi to forward any post to me. I wasn't expecting a reply to arrive before returning to England.'

'What did it say?'

'It said, simply, "Follow your heart rather than your head, Agnes."'

'And that's what you did.'

'That's what I did.'

'And I don't need to ask, as I already know the answer, but it was absolutely the right decision?'

'Oh yes, Charlotte, I've never been happier in my entire life.'

And so, it was decided. When I returned to the vineyard, I would write my own letter to Juliet. I wasn't sure how to get it to the tomb Agnes had mentioned. But I would deal with that afterwards. Perhaps Agnes could arrange for it to be taken there for me. In the meantime, I needed to put my thoughts into words, to work out what I really wanted, and find a way to get it.

CHAPTER 26

KATE

Dad led me into the library.

'I'll ask Jenkins to bring us some coffee.' He disappeared into the grand hall for a moment, then came back.

'So, how have you been?'

'Good,' I said. 'Although I could have done with finding out your news from you rather than Emilie's Instagram post.'

'Ah yes, I am really sorry about that. I did ask her to wait, but she was so excited to tell everyone once she'd had the scan – and we didn't know if and when you might visit. I did want to tell you face to face rather than over the phone.'

I sighed.

'Well, it's done now.'

'Yes. I am sorry though, Kate. It must be strange news for you to receive.'

'I don't know what to think, to be honest, Dad. I want to be happy for you, obviously, but yes, it is strange – the thought of having a new sibling the same age as my child would be, if I could have one.'

Dad gritted his teeth. This was always something he did

when trying to find the right words. He put a hand on my shoulder and gave it a squeeze.

'Maybe you'll meet someone else and have a child with them?'

I shrugged, and he gestured for us to sit down on the sofas in front of the hearth.

'Did you have a nice birthday?' he said.

'Yes, it was good, thanks.'

'I can't believe you're thirty, the same age as I was when I revived the vineyard.'

To think Dad had taken on such a huge project when he was the same age as me.

'That's amazing.'

He looked into the distance, and his eyes glazed over.

'How that time has flown...'

'I went to see Granny the other day, and she gave me a bottle of wine – Amarone 1936 – from a vineyard in Verona.'

'Oh, did she?'

'She went there just before the war, apparently.'

'I do recall her telling me something about that. She brought back some of the earlier pinot gris vines. One of them was thankfully planted in the walled garden during the war, and I used that to take my cuttings when reviving the vineyard. They're still going strong and produce some of our best wine.'

'That's interesting, Dad. There was a note in the box that came with the wine, written by a person with the initial "B". But when I discovered the note, and read it out to her, she got a little upset. She had no idea of its existence.' I told him that Jane had to take Granny's blood pressure and then she asked me to leave.

'Oh dear. I'm sure she'll be fine now. She does have to take a lot of pills to keep her going, sadly. Someone with the initial "B", you say... Hmm.'

'Do you have any idea who could have written it?'

'All I know is that she went there with her lady's maid, the head gardener of the time and a valet.'

'Do you happen to recall the name of the head gardener?'

'I don't, I'm afraid.'

'Oh, that's a shame.'

'But' – his eyes brightened – 'that information will be somewhere in this room. There's that book a local author wrote in the 1990s, using our archives. Perhaps there's some information in there that can help you.'

'Could we look for it?'

'I can try to find it before you go.'

Jenkins brought in a tray with a cafetière of coffee, cups and saucers, sugar lumps, and a jug of milk, and set it on the trestle table in between us.

'Thanks. And I heard that you've been having problems on the vineyard?'

He sighed. 'Yes, it hasn't been a great year, what with the harvest blighted by frost, and the powdery mildew.'

'It must have been difficult.'

'And other things have been going wrong too – some idiot left the bung off one of the barrels, so it's all turned acidic, sadly.'

I plunged the cafetière, poured coffee for us both and added milk to mine.

'What a waste of wine – who would do that?'

He looked away and ran a hand through his hair.

'I don't know.'

It occurred to me that someone might have done it on purpose, but I hated that thought.

'Dad, do you think Grandpa's cousin, Jack, would plant someone here, a saboteur to ruin the business so it's worth less, and then he could swoop in with an offer?'

He stroked his chin.

'Possibly, although I doubt he'd go to such lengths. I almost feel that I should take Jack's latest offer and get rid of the damn place once and for all.'

The thought of Dad giving in so easily was disheartening. I'd never heard him talk about Copeley Park like this before. But to hand the estate over to a man who was apparently descended from a nemesis of Granny's didn't seem right. What had happened to my dad, who'd always been so driven and determined? I'd always looked up to him because of his positive approach to life. While growing up, I'd drawn inspiration from him. His success had made me believe I could achieve great things if I set my mind to it.

'Wouldn't Granny be devastated if you sold the estate though?'

'Of course she would be, and it would mean she'd have to move out of Keeper's Cottage. So, I'd probably have to wait until...'

'She's not here any more?'

He nodded.

It seemed that Dad was waiting for Granny to die, and then he was going to hand the place over to Jack without a fight. What on earth was wrong with him?

'But Dad, how could you do that? You know Granny would be so upset.'

'That's why I've waited so long. Kate, I've been running this place for thirty years now, and it's my sixtieth birthday coming up soon. Your mother's death took a huge toll on me. And I know it affected you a great deal, too.'

Mum dying had certainly impacted on both of our lives. I often thought about how much it had affected me, but perhaps hadn't considered how hard it must have been for Dad to lose his wife so suddenly like that.

He dropped a sugar lump into his coffee and gave it a stir.

'I don't have as much energy as I used to. With a new fiancée and a baby on the way, my priorities have changed. I'd like to make the most of my twilight years. Besides, the doctor has said I need to lower my cholesterol and find a way to reduce my stress levels.'

It made me sad to think of Dad's health deteriorating, and of him getting older. The thought of losing him as well as Mum didn't bear thinking about. I really needed to get past him being with Emilie so we could see more of each other. I'd missed him. But surely he wasn't going to give up Copeley Park so readily?

'Couldn't you get someone to run this place for you?'

'That's a lovely idea, but who though?'

'I don't know. You could interview a few contenders.'

'It's hard to find someone trustworthy, and with the right experience and approach. I'm not sure I could be bothered with all that.'

I leant forward to pick up my coffee cup and something occurred to me. What if I ran the estate for him? Ben had put this idea in my head, and, the more I thought about it, the more it made sense. Could I run the place on Dad's behalf and give him a cut of the profits to live on? Would he consider me as a successor? I would mull over how to sell the idea to him before mentioning it. He'd be more likely to say yes if I'd done my research.

'When Granny gave me the bottle of wine from the vineyard in Verona, I looked at their website, and they're still going strong. They produce a sparkling Pinot Grigio and sell it at a really good price. Have you ever thought about doing that, Dad?'

'It has crossed my mind, but I decided not to take the risk. I'd need to buy more expensive bottles, because they need to be fortified, for a start. And I'd need someone who knew how to make it. And then how could it compete with champagne, prosecco and cava as well as other English sparkling wines?'

'Ben knows how to make sparkling wine.'

'Does he now?'

I nodded.

'And how do you know that?'

'Err... it's a long story but we met when I drove into a massive pothole after visiting Granny.'

'Oh no, did you? Why didn't you ask me to help you?'

'Ben was there, and he offered to sort it out. He changed the tyre for me.'

'You needed a new tyre?'

'Yes, you really ought to fill in those potholes, Dad.'

'I'll add it to the list... so you've met Ben, huh?'

My face warmed, and I hoped Dad couldn't tell I was blushing. I wouldn't want him to know I'd stayed at Ben's the night before, even though nothing had happened. He'd only tease me about it.

'He is a nice young man. Your granny said she thought the two of you should meet.'

I laughed. 'She told me that too, and I dismissed her idea. Then I ended up meeting him anyway.'

'Well, there's nothing wrong with you being friends.' He sipped his coffee. 'But I'd like to think that you might set your sights a bit higher when choosing your next husband.'

I couldn't believe Dad was saying this.

'What do you mean?'

'Well, he doesn't exactly earn very much, and he's living in one of our cottages, paying hardly any rent.'

'So?'

'So, you should be with a man who can provide you with everything, Kate, especially if you have children.'

'Dad... I think you're getting ahead of yourself. I've only met the man a couple of times. Besides, I'm in no rush to get married again – I'm not sure if I ever will, even if I do meet the right person.'

Dad opened his mouth to speak, but I went on.

'And you know how hard it was for me to have children

with Spencer. I probably won't be having any, so you don't need to worry about that. Or bring it up, in fact. Spencer had a fairly well-paid job, and that didn't do much for us.'

Goodness, I had stood up to my father, for the first time since I could remember. I'd gone easy on him after Mum had died, but enough years had passed, and he was with Emilie now. There was no way he was going to dictate who I had romantic relationships with. Who was he to talk when his fiancée was only five years older than me? All the fury from recent months was rising up inside of me and biting my tongue, I banged my coffee cup down on the table.

He looked at me, clearly shocked that I was standing up for myself. I expected him to keep arguing with me. Instead, he took a breath, and said, 'Let's change the subject, shall we, Kate?'

'Okay, but won't you at least consider asking Ben to produce a limited edition of sparkling Pinot Grigio?' I said, making my pleading face.

'It's a risk I'm not prepared to take, I'm afraid. Besides, we'd need to produce enough grapes in order for there to be surplus. I wouldn't want it to impact production of the Pinot Grigio I make already, which sells very well.'

I'd have to work on persuading Dad to even consider my idea. He was too stubborn for his own good.

'Well,' I said, picking up my handbag and reaching inside for my car key. 'I'd better go.'

'Already?'

'I have to get back home, things to do...'

'Well, all right, it's been nice to see you, apart from your emotional outburst,' he said with a laugh.

His dismissal of my feelings was a little hurtful. I rolled my eyes.

'Why don't you come over again soon, and for longer. We can have lunch?'

I wasn't sure if I'd be rushing back, but I nodded anyway.

'Let's see if I can find that book for you.' Dad stood up and ran a hand along the spines of the books on one of the shelves. 'Ah, here it is.'

He handed me a big hardback entitled, *The History of Copeley Park*. There was a photo of the house on the cover.

'Thanks, Dad, that's great.'

'Hopefully you'll find out who this "B" is. That sounds interesting. Perhaps your great-grandmother had a lover we don't know about. I wouldn't put it past her – she was a beautiful woman in her day.'

'Do you think "B" could have been the head gardener she went to Verona with?'

Dad shrugged.

'Possibly. That's for you to find out.'

The landline rang, and he said, 'Excuse me,' as he picked up the phone. From the conversation he was having, I could tell it was Ben giving him an update on the Gothic tower.

'That was Ben,' he said, putting the phone down with a wink. 'He just went over to check on the tower as the alarms went off – again. We need to get them fixed. Another thing to pay for.' He let out a sigh. If only Dad knew that I'd been at Ben's cottage when he received the message telling him to go over there.

We said goodbye and I drove back to my flat. When I got inside, there was a small package waiting for me on the kitchen worktop. I took a pair of scissors out of the drawer and opened it. Inside was an old red hardback book. It was Granny's copy of *Romeo and Juliet*. Inside there was an inscription, in fountain pen: *Belongs to Charlotte Wells, age fourteen.*

I flicked through the yellowing pages, and some of the words were underlined in pencil. I couldn't believe she was giving something so precious to me. There was also an envelope with my name on it. I slid my thumb under the flap and opened it.

Inside was a letter on headed paper with the address Keeper's Cottage, Copeley Park, and plane tickets for the following weekend from London Gatwick to Verona.

Dearest Kate,

Here's a little something to celebrate your 30th birthday. I know you weren't sure about going to the vineyard in Verona, so I've made the decision for you. You won't regret going, I'm sure of it.

Enclosed are plane tickets and Jane has booked you into the agriturismo at the vineyard – she's requested the Mimosa Suite, where I stayed at Villa Giulietta in the summer of 1939 with my cousin Agnes. Her great-granddaughter, Rosanna, is so excited to meet you. Jane told her about my love for the vineyard, and the trip I made there before the war. Savour every moment!

Much love,

Granny xx

It seemed that I'd be visiting the vineyard, after all. I couldn't wait to tell Ben.

CHAPTER 27

LADY CHARLOTTE

Back in my room at Villa Giulietta, I sat down at the writing table and wrote my letter to Juliet.

Dear Juliet,

My cousin Agnes suggested that I write to you. I don't know if I'll even get this letter to you, but I thought it might be a good idea to write down my thoughts on paper.

Apparently, you're good at dealing with matters relating to love. Well, I'm not sure how that can be true after the way you met your demise – but I'm giving it a try…

When I'd finished, I folded up the letter and placed it in an envelope and wrote 'Juliet' on the front. And then I put the envelope in the drawer of my nightstand, intending to ask Agnes how to get it to the tomb.

The rest of our week in Verona passed quickly and, before we knew it, Albert and I were eating our final dinner with Agnes and Mario. When we'd finished consuming yet another delicious meal of pasta with a rich butter sauce and slices of white truffle, followed by the tenderest of steaks, Mario brought out the limoncello once again, and clinked his glass with a fork. He said how much he'd enjoyed our company, and thanked Albert for all his help on the vineyard. And he hoped that the vine cuttings we were taking back would thrive on our new vineyard at Copeley Park. He could not wait to visit us when the first bottle of wine was ready and to try it. It was all quite charming of him. And then he nodded to the butler, who disappeared, and came back with a wooden box.

'This is our gift to you both, to enjoy together when you return to England. And when you drink it, say "Cin cin", and think of us,' Mario said.

The butler brought the box over to me. On top, the words, Vineria di San Martino were branded in dark-brown letters.

'Open it, Charlotte,' he said.

I undid the latch, and lifted up the lid. Inside was a bottle of Amarone 1936. This was the wine Albert and I had enjoyed the most on that first evening.

'Oh goodness me, this is so generous and thoughtful of you,' I said.

'The least we could do is give you a gift to send you on your way. Then you can remember our vineyard when you are back in England.'

'I don't know what to say... thank you both very much. We have so enjoyed our stay, haven't we, Albert?'

Albert nodded.

'It's very kind of you. This is my favourite of all the wines you have given us to try, and I look forward to drinking it back at Copeley Park... if Charlotte will allow me to...'

I laughed.

'Of course I shall share it with you, Albert. It is for both of us.'

'Perhaps save it for a special occasion, when you have something to celebrate?' Mario said.

Albert and I exchanged a look. It seemed that Mario was implying we might have something to celebrate together in time. How I hoped that he was right.

Tomasso came into the room, holding a camera.

'I would like us to have a photo together to make a special memory,' Mario said.

'Oh, what a splendid idea,' I said.

We all posed while Tomasso photographed us, and then, as it was getting late, Albert and I thanked our hosts for the delightful dinner and thoughtful gift, before saying good night.

Albert and I walked back to Villa Giulietta in the dark, with him using his torch to light our way. I carried the box of wine. When I slipped on a loose piece of rock in the road, he took my hand and stopped me from falling over, and from dropping the bottle of wine – what a disaster that would have been.

'Thank you, Bertie, for saving me,' I said.

'Look, it's the Plough.' He switched off his torch. 'If you look carefully, you will see the brightest star with an orangey-yellow hue – that's Dubhe – and then there is Merak, part of the bowl of the Plough. If you make an imaginary line from Merak to Dubhe, you will see Polaris, the North Star, to be found above the North Pole.'

'How do you know all this?' I asked.

'My father is fascinated by astronomy, and he taught me everything. Ever since I was a little boy, he would take me outside at night and talk me through all the stars that we could see up there. I always found it so magical.'

'It makes you think about life, doesn't it, when you look up at all the stars, and realise how small we all are, here on Earth?' I said.

'Indeed, it puts everything into perspective. All the things we worry about every day are insignificant in the scheme of things.'

'You are always so wise, Bertie.'

He switched his torch back on, and we continued along the narrow lane until we reached Villa Giulietta. He unlocked the door, and we stepped into the hall with the black-and-white-tiled floor.

'So, this is the last time we shall sleep here in this place,' I said.

Albert looked at me. 'Would you like a glass of brandy?'

'You have brandy?'

'Mario gave me a bottle when I mentioned that I can't get to sleep without it.'

'Shall we drink it on the terrace?'

'Your terrace or mine?' he said, stroking his beard.

'Why don't you bring it to my terrace, Bertie,' I said, seizing the moment.

I went into my room, and placed the box of wine on my dressing table. I couldn't help lifting the latch and taking a peek – how very kind of Agnes and Mario to give such a coveted bottle of wine to us. Before long, there was a knock at the door and Albert came inside with a bottle of brandy and two tumblers.

'Let's go and drink it with the stars,' I said, picking up a candle from my nightstand.

I opened the French doors, and we went outside onto the terrazza. The stars twinkled above, and the lights of Verona twinkled along with them. It truly was a magical place, and I would miss it. I struck a match and lit the candle, and we sat at the table. Albert poured us both a generous measure of brandy.

We both raised our glasses and said, 'Cin cin', locked eyes, and took a sip.

'And so, tomorrow, we make our journey home,' he said, softly.

'Indeed.'

'And what do you suppose will happen upon our return?'

'Well, we'll plant the vineyard, and grow some wonderful grapes, and we shall produce our very own bottles of white wine.'

'It is a shame that the climate will not allow for us to produce Amarone,' Albert said.

'Yes, but we now have our very own bottle to share when the right moment arises.'

He swallowed.

'What I actually meant, Charlotte, was what do you think might happen with us now that we know each other better?'

I shrugged and shook my head.

'It's difficult as I know my father will have another man lined up for me to marry.'

'And will you do as your father wishes?'

'I don't want to.'

He looked down at the floor. 'I'll probably be going off to war before long anyway.'

My heart melted. 'Do you really think there will be a war soon then, Bertie?'

'Unfortunately, I do. It's been building up for such a long time now with all the tensions in Europe.'

'If you go to war, Bertie, I can't bear to think about what might... I shall miss you a great deal.'

'And I shall miss you, Charlotte.'

He downed the rest of his brandy, and then he leant forwards, and... what was he doing?

'Charlotte, we might not have the chance again to—'

Nodding, I whispered, 'I know.'

'What would you think if I kissed you?'

'I think...' I downed the rest of my brandy. 'I think that we should make the most of this evening. Who knows when the chance will arise again? On the train, we shall be in different cabins in different carriages. At Copeley Park, there will be so many witnesses to catch us together.'

Bertie leant forwards, and our eyes met in the candlelight. Then he cupped my face, ever so gently, and pressed his lips to mine, and it was the most exquisite kiss I'd ever experienced in my entire life.

CHAPTER 28

KATE

The next morning, I took the book, *The History of Copeley Park*, out of my bag and flicked through it while sitting on the sofa with coffee. There were many photos of the house over the years, and of people connected to it too. The book was divided up by era, and I found the chapter on the 1930s. There was a portrait of my great-grandfather, Winston, the Earl of Waverley, sporting a moustache, the corners curled up at each end. He looked rather stern and serious, and his eyes had a certain coldness about them. I'd seen this portrait on the wall in the blue drawing room. There was a photograph of their wedding day – Granny looked beautiful, like a star from the silver screen. There were also photos of servants who worked in the house: housemaids, cooks, the housekeeper and butler. There was one of the gardeners with the head gardener standing at the centre, a man called Albert Hicks. He was handsome and had a thick beard.

So, if the head gardener was called Albert Hicks, 'B' could not be him. Never mind, I would continue my search. Perhaps Dad might have other books or information in the archives. Or maybe I'd find the answer in Verona. Would they have any record of Granny's visit? Since receiving the letter and tickets from Granny, I'd spent a few days preparing and packing my things. I'd located my travel adaptor plugs and taken out some euros at the bank.

On Friday, I took the afternoon flight to Verona from Gatwick airport. When I came out of the airport at the other end, a taxi driver was standing there with a sign reading CLARKSON. It was dark as he drove me to the vineyard. We passed through the city of Verona, bumping along cobblestone streets. On the flight, I'd found myself thinking about Ben and our 'almost kiss' on the landing. Well, I'd found myself thinking about it many times since Friday night. Would he try to kiss me on the lips the next time we saw each other? I had messaged to say I'd be visiting the vineyard this weekend. He'd said how wonderful it was that I'd be going there after all. I didn't tell him that Granny had made the decision for me by booking and paying for the trip. And now here I was.

I looked out of the car window at restaurants and bars, all lit up, with people inside. I couldn't wait to explore the city of Verona, but first I needed to get settled on the vineyard. After fifteen minutes or so, the driver pulled off the road where a sign said LA VINERIA DI SAN MARTINO, and drove uphill towards a yellow building, covered in Virginia creeper, so vibrantly red. I paid him in euros and got out of the car. He lifted my case out of the boot and I pressed the button to release the handle. The temperature was cold, but the air was crisp and clean. I spotted the twinkling lights of Verona in the distance. Granny was so right – the place really did have a magical feel. Following the sign to reception, I pushed open the door of the main building, named Villa Romeo, and approached the desk.

A man stood there, speaking on the telephone in Italian. Behind the desk was a display of wine bottles and jars of honey and wine vinegar and olive oil. On the crimson walls was a selection of black-and-white photographs. I would take the opportunity to study them when there wasn't anyone around – maybe there might be a photo of Granny amongst them. He put the phone down and smiled as he looked at me.

'Buonasera, how can I help you?' he said.

'Hello, I'm here to check in. My name is Kate Clarkson.'

He tapped on his keyboard for a moment and checked his computer screen.

'Certo. Now, let me give you directions to your villa.'

He put a map of the vineyard on the desk and circled one of the buildings with a pen.

'This is Villa Giulietta. You go out of the door and walk uphill, following the narrow road until you reach the gates. Then you put in this code.' He wrote down a series of numbers.

Goodness, there was a lot to remember. It was dark and cold, and I had a case to lug up there with me. And I was tired out from the journey.

'Through the gates, you will see buildings – the winery is there. On the right, you will find Villa Giulietta. Here is the key.'

He placed a key on the desk, and I slid it into the pocket of my jeans.

'Your room, the Mimosa Suite, is on the ground floor. Here in Italy we have many yellow flowers called mimosa, they are very beautiful and have a wonderful scent.'

I took the key and the map, and said, 'Thank you.'

'And you have a table in the restaurant booked for seven thirty.'

He pointed to an archway, and I could hear the murmur of people talking.

'It's through there.'

The phone rang and he picked up the receiver, and dismissed me with a smile and a wave. There I was, all on my own, being left to find my room. Stepping back outside, I wheeled my suitcase behind me. Apart from the light outside reception, it was pitch black. I switched on my phone torch and made my way along the narrow lane. I just wanted to find my room and have a lie-down and close my eyes for a bit before dinner. Then I'd need to get changed and go to the restaurant.

My case got heavier by the second as I pulled it uphill behind me. I stopped for a moment to have a rest and take in my surroundings. An owl hooted nearby, and some animal rustled in the bushes – I hoped that it wasn't a wild boar. The moon was full, and it shone brightly. The stars were clearly visible, and I could make out the Plough. And then, as I turned a corner, there once again were the twinkling lights of Verona in the distance – almost calling to me. Despite it being a bit of a pain getting to my room this place really was something else. Up ahead, I spotted the gates, with lights on either side. Beyond was a cluster of buildings, but it was all so quiet. Where was everyone? Perhaps they were already in the restaurant, or maybe they'd gone into Verona for the evening.

When I reached the gates, I found the code and tapped it into the keypad. They creaked open, and I passed through to the other side. They closed behind me, and I was met with yet another steep hill. How my legs ached, and I hoped that pulling my case uphill wasn't going to do my back in. Despite the chill hanging in the air, I was all sweaty from travelling, and couldn't wait to shower and change into clean clothes. And I was hungry, and craved a big glass of wine to take the edge off the day – well, I was in the right place! I couldn't wait to try wine produced on the vineyard.

As I passed the building marked VINERIA, the barking of dogs made me jump out of my skin, and I looked up to see two hounds – I couldn't make out what breed they were in the dark – their faces pressed against a gate. And then, at last, I was glad to spot the sign for Villa Giulietta. I took the key out of my pocket and unlocked the door. The hallway had terracotta floor tiles, and a small lounge area with armchairs and bookcases stuffed with musty old hardbacks. And there it was, Suite Mimosa, the room Granny had stayed in. Here I was, following the path she'd taken back in the summer of 1939, when Italy and England were on the brink of war. I went inside to find a vast room with floral everything – curtains, duvet cover and pillowcases and wallpaper. I sat on the bed and logged into the WiFi using the information sheet.

A message flashed up on my phone from Ben.

How is it?

It was so good to hear from him.

Hi, I just arrived. The suite is lovely. I can't wait to see the vineyard in the daylight

Oh good, send pics

I will! Off to dinner in a min

Enjoy. I'm well jel

Smiling to myself at our little exchange, I went into the bathroom – it had a roll-top bath and a separate shower cubicle and there was a pile of fluffy white towels on the rack. Bliss. I took a long hot shower and generously lathered myself with the complimentary lemon-scented gel, the warm water washing off the journey. Then I changed into a clean pair of jeans, top and jumper with turtleneck to keep out the cold on my walk back to the restaurant.

Locking up, I switched on my phone torch and made my way back downhill through the gates and then along the narrow lane. It all seemed easier without my case in tow, and now I had an idea of where to go. It did feel strange being away on my own though, and I wouldn't have minded having a companion. Seeing as Ben was 'well jel', I wondered if he'd want to be here with me, but pushed the thought out of my mind. It was far too soon for any of that – we barely knew each other. At the same time, I liked the idea of having dinner with him – the fun we'd have, trying the wine and Italian food. I couldn't imagine that we'd ever run out of conversation. But this was a solo trip, and I'd have to make the most of it. I had travelled abroad for work, especially to the Frankfurt book fair, but usually I'd meet up with other people in publishing to socialise with. But here I was, staying on a vineyard all alone, and going to eat in a restaurant at a table for one. Eating alone in a business situation was different because it was understandable that you wouldn't have company. But I was in a place where guests were likely to be on holiday with other halves or with families. Sometimes being in a situation like this would make me feel sad that my marriage hadn't worked out. I shut this thought out of my mind though.

When I reached Villa Romeo, I pushed open the door and passed reception, towards the restaurant beyond the arch, past shelves of wine bottles, and the wall filled with black-and-white photographs. I also spotted information about the history of the vineyard, and I looked forward to studying it all carefully during my stay. That evening, I ate polpette, meaning meatballs – there were only three of them but they were huge, and absolutely delicious – slow cooked so they melted in the mouth. On the side, I had a rocket salad with Parmesan shavings and basil leaves – I picked one up and held it to my nose. What a wonderful scent – a sweet and peppery aroma. I'd seen fresh basil in the supermarket, but never thought about buying it. Perhaps I would get a basil plant to keep on my windowsill. Ben would know how to keep it alive. I drank Pinot Grigio, produced by the vineyard. It was light and crisp with notes of citrus, and just what I needed. I sipped it, rather too quickly, while reading the copy of *Romeo and Juliet* given to me by Granny that I'd brought along. She'd underlined some parts in pencil, and when I flicked through the pages my eyes were drawn to 'Did my heart love till now?' Did this resonate with her, for some reason? Was she thinking about the mysterious 'B' when underlining these words?

As expected, I was the only person eating alone in the restaurant, but no one seemed to care. The waitresses were as friendly towards me as they were to everyone else, and this gave me a warm feeling. A woman with dark hair in a bob came over and offered to top up my wine. I nodded, and thanked her.

'Are you Kate, staying in the Mimosa Suite?' she said.

'Yes, that's me.'

'Ciao, I am Rosanna. My great-grandmother, Agnes, was your great-grandmother's cousin, so we are distant relations.'

'Oh wow, yes, Granny said you'd be here. Lovely to meet you,' I said.

'Agnes talked about the time her cousin came here with Albert, shortly before the war, and how wonderful it was to see them. Tomorrow, I shall take you for a tour, if you like?'

I wondered whether she might have some information about who 'B' was, and I would certainly ask her when we had more time. And I wanted to tell her about the bottle of Amarone from 1936 too. It would be interesting to know how much it might be worth, in case we did need to sell it at any stage to save Copeley Park. Although I really hoped it wouldn't come to that, as it wouldn't be what Granny wanted.

'Ah yes please, I'd love to do a tour.'

'And taste some wine?'

'Absolutely, that would be wonderful, thank you.'

'Okay, go to reception tomorrow at eleven o'clock, and I shall meet you there.'

When I'd finished the wine, I signed the bill and walked back to the suite. I changed into pyjamas, brushed my teeth and removed my make-up. Then I checked my phone before plugging it in to charge overnight.

There was a message from Ben on the screen.

Hope dinner was good?

Smiling to myself, I replied.

All very delicious and wonderful wine too

Am even more well jel now. Don't forget to send pics tomorrow. You can find me on WhatsApp. I'm expecting updates

Will do. Goodnight! Sleep well

Night. Sweet dreams

Receiving messages from Ben made me feel less alone, and I climbed into bed thinking it would be nice to have more exchanges during my trip. When was the last time anyone had wished me goodnight? I would look forward to reporting back and to sending him photos. And he'd asked me to send them on WhatsApp – our friendship was moving up to a whole new level. I found myself picturing him: his warm smile and misty-blue eyes looking at me. A lovely vision to drift off to sleep with. And I couldn't wait to wake up in the morning and see the vineyard and the city of Verona in the daylight. And then breakfast – I hoped there would be pastries.

CHAPTER 29

LADY CHARLOTTE

The following morning, I found myself standing on the doorstep of Villa Romeo with Albert. We'd just eaten a delicious breakfast with pastries, freshly baked bread, and cantaloupe melon from the garden – its flesh a brilliant orange, and so sweet and refreshing. The cuttings had been carefully packed and Mario was giving Albert a few final tips on how best to plant them in the vineyard. George and Gwen had walked down to the gate to see where the taxis were. And I expected that, like Albert and me, they were making the most of those last few moments together, because from now on we'd all be separated at night, by class as well as sex, and then when we returned to Copeley Park we'd all be required to follow the rules set out for us as regards to relations with each other.

'Thank you for the most wonderful few days,' I said. 'I can't remember the last time I enjoyed myself so much. This place is a veritable paradise. You are so lucky, Agnes, and have certainly landed on your feet.'

'I have indeed, and I thank the Lord every day,' she said. 'There's a lot to be said for following one's heart over one's head.

Who would have imagined when we were little girls, playing in the gardens at Rodene Hall, that I would end up living here?'

'One never knows what to expect from the future,' I said.

'And who knows what might yet happen for you?'

She nodded in the direction of Albert, and I smiled.

'Oh, before I forget, I did actually write a letter to Juliet. It's in the drawer of my nightstand. Would you mind taking it to the tomb for me?'

'Absolutely, of course. I'm so glad that you took my advice and wrote it.'

'I did find the act of writing it rather cathartic. It helped me to organise my thoughts, if nothing else.'

'I'm sure that it was. Sometimes, writing things down can be helpful.'

'I am grateful to you, Agnes, for your advice. And thank you for the bottle of wine. I shall treasure it.'

'Don't forget to drink it when you have something to celebrate with the person who means the most to you,' she said, squeezing my arm.

I couldn't imagine when that might be. When we returned, Albert would probably be called up to fight in the war that was due to start at any time.

'Yes, well, I hope that there will be something to celebrate, but who knows, with war coming, and everything else?'

'I do fear that Italy will be at war before long. It's a good job that you visited us when you did. The opportunity might not have arisen again for a very long time. Who knows how long this war will last for when it starts? And if we will all survive it?'

My eyes welled with tears as it struck me that I might not see Agnes or Mario again.

'All we can do is pray, Agnes,' I said, my voice breaking.

She raised her arms and leant forwards, pulling me into an embrace.

'Do take care of yourself, dear cousin. I shall miss you.'

'Let's write to each other, while we can.' I doubted letters would get through if we were at war, especially if we were on opposing sides. This was highly likely seeing as the Italian prime minister, Mussolini, worshipped Hitler.

'Yes, let's.'

The sound of car engines was swiftly followed by the appearance of our taxis, with George and Gwen following behind. The drivers got out and attached our luggage to the roofs. We got in and waved to Agnes and Mario, and then we were off, on our way back to Verona railway station.

The journey back from Italy was much the same as on the way, although it was evident this time that war was coming, with Italian soldiers dressed in uniform getting on and off the train at every station. Just the sight of them was unsettling and a stark reminder of what was to come. The night before, Albert had made love to me in my bed in the Mimosa room. I had never known such passion, and to feel those strong and capable hands on me was an experience to be treasured forever.

Afterwards, we'd lain together all night, with his arms wrapped around my body, holding me tightly. When we woke up in the morning, he'd had to go and pack his suitcase and get dressed for breakfast and our subsequent departure. We hadn't had a chance to talk about what had happened, but we'd see each other on the train at mealtimes. I looked forward to sitting opposite him in the dining car again. I'd savour those precious moments together when – after checking for eavesdroppers – we'd be able to speak to each other freely. I had no idea what to expect on our return to Surrey. Did Albert feel as I did? From the way he looked at me, I imagined he might, but perhaps that might be too good to be true. Was it possible to have someone love you as much as you loved them – to love each other mutually?

At Copeley Park, there was no chance that Albert and I

could be together at night. But at the same time, the fear of being stranded in Italy when a war began did not bear thinking about. If Italy was allied with Germany, who knew how we'd be treated? And God forbid, anyone should find out I was half Jewish. Only the previous year, Mussolini had called Jews 'irreconcilable enemies' of fascism and introduced discriminatory laws.

War was inevitable for us all, it seemed. Albert and I did our best to avoid the subject, knowing that time was running out for us both. Before he went off to fight, I wanted to make the most of every second of his company.

When we returned from Verona, Albert went back to Rosemary Cottage, and I settled back into the house at Copeley Park. He was once again my employee, and this would make life difficult if we wanted to spend any time together. But still, I could find reasons to go to his cottage. Servants might see me go there, but I would ensure that it was clear we were discussing the gardens or the vine cuttings we wanted to plant before he was called up to go and fight.

A pile of letters had built up in my absence, and on the first morning after returning I sat at the writing table in the library to go through them. One of the letters was from Lady Penelope.

Dear Charlotte,

I heard on the grapevine – a rather apt term I believe – that you have disappeared off to Italy. When you return from your holiday, I suggest you inform me of your decision relating to our discussion at lunch. I shall be waiting with anticipation.

Yours,

Penelope

The nerve of the woman. Did she really think I was going to give up Copeley Park so readily? If she went to the police, as she'd threatened to over that miserable lunch, I could end up being hanged. I shuddered at the thought. The journey to Italy had brought me strength, and I just couldn't let her get the better of me – I would do everything in my power to save Copeley Park from her clutches.

There was also a letter from Papa – I recognised his handwriting – and my gut lurched as I opened it, for I knew the words it would contain.

Dear Charlotte,

Your butler informed me when I telephoned that you have taken a holiday. Upon your return, you will be delighted to know that, after a conversation at my club, the Baron of Tyne has agreed to marry you. This would mean a demotion from countess to baroness, but still, it would enable you and any future offspring to have titles. I look forward to hearing from you in due course.

Yours,

Papa

So, as expected, he'd found a suitor. And it was the baron Agnes had rejected for Mario. Papa must have spoken to my uncle and approached the baron directly. But I did not wish to marry yet another man who was bound to be much older than me – and who knew what other negative attributes he might possess? I had no desire to live in Northumberland, especially as the Surrey Hills had begun to grow on me, more so since

Winston's death. This time, I wouldn't follow Papa's instructions. I would tell him that, if I chose to marry again, I'd select the man myself next time. If I was going to marry anyone, it should be Albert. That would mean losing my title of countess, but this didn't matter to me one bit. I just wanted to be with him for the rest of my life.

After reading both of these letters, my hand began to tremble as fury rose up inside of me. How were these two people controlling my life? I needed to deal with them both. I'd mull over how to deal with Papa, but I wanted to seek Albert's advice about Lady Penelope. I left the house and passed through the kitchen garden to Rosemary Cottage and knocked on the door. Albert opened it.

'Do you have a moment, Bertie? There's something I'd like to discuss with you.'

'Certainly, Charlotte.'

He led me into his drawing room, where I sat down. He took the chair opposite.

'What can I help you with?'

I handed him Lady Penelope's letter, and he removed it from the envelope and read it carefully. As he did so, I studied him. How I longed to run my hands over his face. Oh, to lean in and kiss him on the lips, and to have him wrap his arms around me. But someone might see through the window. The thought of him not being here, in this cottage, after leaving for war, was horrifying. How would I live without him? Not only did I love him with all my heart, but to have a man like him in my corner made me feel safe. Knowing that he'd protect me was a comfort. All I could hope for was that after doing his bit he would come back to me. Then, once I'd dealt with Papa, we could be together for the remainder of our days.

He sighed as he put the letter back into its envelope and handed it to me, our fingers brushing.

'What do you think I should do?' I said.

He stroked his beard.

'I have been mulling over the issue of Lady Penelope since you first told me about her attempt at blackmail, and I did come up with one idea.'

'What is it?' I said, excited to hear what he had to say.

'Invite her here to your house, for tea.'

'Really? And then what?'

'We turn the whole situation around.'

'What do you mean?'

'It would be as if you're holding up a mirror and reflecting her threat back onto her. Your word is as good as hers, and, seeing as she is carrying Winston's child, you actually have a stronger case.'

'Tell me more.'

'Who's to say that she didn't push Winston down the stairs deliberately after she told him about the illegitimate child? Perhaps she suggested he divorce you and marry her instead, and he said no. Devastated, she lost her temper and pushed him deliberately down the stairs, sending him to his inevitable death.'

'But where was I during all this?'

'It was *you* who did not attend church that morning because you were feeling unwell. You had a headache from drinking too much brandy the night before – as often happens,' he said, looking at me with a smile. 'And it was Lady Penelope who heard you closing the door.'

'But then, as you say, it's my word against hers.'

'Or is it?'

'What do you mean?'

'If you invite her here, I can join you and speak to her.'

'I don't understand...'

'Just issue the invitation, and I'll deal with the rest. It will be all right, Charlotte. Please don't worry.'

'Very well, I shall write to her this afternoon. Thank you, Bertie.'

Albert seemed so sure that he could fix the situation, and all I could do was trust him. What other choice did I have?

CHAPTER 30

KATE

The next morning, I unlocked the French doors and pushed open the shutters. There before me was a vast terrace with the most incredible view. I stepped outside, dressed in my red tartan pyjamas, and looked up at the clusters of tall, dark-green cypress trees – they were so beautiful and gave the place a majestic feel. On the terrace was a table and chairs, and an unspoilt view of vines planted in neat rows as far as the eye could see. A mist hung over the valley and in the distance were the buildings of Verona, from where lights had twinkled the night before. The sky was a flawless blue, and I breathed in the crisp air. It wasn't difficult to understand why Granny had been seduced by this place. I thought about 'B' and how he must have been her lover. What a place to fall in love with someone. This thought made me remember my promise to Ben the night before. I took photos of the beautiful scenery and sent them to him using WhatsApp as he'd suggested.

I showered and dressed and walked down to the restaurant for breakfast. Birds darted between the trees and to my right was an olive grove. In the restaurant, a generous buffet was laid out on tables with white cloths. There were baskets of fresh bread and pastries, boards of local cheeses, a selection of cereals, plates of cold meats, and a fruit bowl with apples, bananas and grapes. Eager to make the most of it, I filled a plate, generously, and ordered a cappuccino from a passing waitress before sitting down at a table by the patio doors. Through the doors I could see the city of Verona, the River Adige twisting and winding through the city with bridges crossing it at intervals. What a perfect view to have with my breakfast.

The room was filled with guests who'd got up earlier than me – couples and families – but the atmosphere was relaxed, and everyone spoke in low voices. I really felt as though I was on holiday. How I'd needed this break. My summer holiday in Corfu had been wonderful – until the last night, when Spencer and I had decided to end our marriage. That evening had spoiled any memories made, and I'd found it difficult to look back on that holiday as I usually would, by scanning through photos on my phone and savouring special moments. I hadn't been able to bring myself to look at any of the photos since the break-up – and I'd taken so many of the stunning Corfu scenery, as well as of the two of us, looking our best, with suntanned skin. I had left the photos on my Instagram grid though, and I couldn't possibly delete them. Maybe one day I'd feel able to study them again. For now, though, they just made me feel sad. My only way to deal with the melancholy feelings they brought was to push those memories out of my mind until I was ready to allow them back in. I'd done a fair amount of decompressing over the past few months. Leaving Spencer had made that easier – but there was still some way to go. Being here in Verona was certainly helping, that was for sure.

Here was a chance to move forward with my life and do some proper thinking. Back home, I'd need to find somewhere else to live. If I ever wanted to make any money as a freelance book marketer, I'd need to go to book events and do some hobnobbing in order to bring in more regular work. I'd need to revive my blog and get out my tripod and ring light to make some video content for posting online. But did I want to do all of that? Admittedly, I'd become quite bored with following the same path for so long with little prospect of anything exciting happening. Although I loved the creative side of my work, it didn't really feel like my calling. Since talking to Dad, I'd been reflecting on how I could make my case strong when suggesting I run Copeley Park on his behalf. I would like to do my bit to save the vineyard. I did know my stuff when it came to marketing – I'd even won a couple of awards for my campaigns on books that went on to become *Sunday Times* bestsellers. If I applied my knowledge and initiative to Copeley Park, I'd stand a good chance of turning it around. Having Ben's support would make that easier too.

We needed to introduce new ideas, look at what our successful competitors were doing, and think outside the box. I knew this myself from working as a freelancer. If I could get Dad to agree to Ben making a limited edition of sparkling Pinot Grigio, that would be a real opportunity to make some money. I'd always loved getting stuck into a new project, and my adrenaline would race at the thrill of making a success of something. Going over to see Granny that day when she gave me the bottle of Amarone, and then meeting Ben, had sparked something inside of me and set me on a new path. After quite a long period of life feeling like it was dragging, I was filled with a newfound hope that things could get better. Suddenly, it seemed so important to put all of my energy into continuing Granny's legacy – to take what she'd started to the next level. I couldn't allow our family business to fail and let it be taken over by Grandpa's cousin, Jack – I just couldn't.

I took my time over breakfast, opting to put my phone in my bag while I read *Romeo and Juliet*. There was something about living in the moment and I'd forgotten how to do this. I needed to stop spending so much time scrolling on my phone, and go back to reading for pleasure again – this was the first book I'd read that wasn't a client's for months. During the IVF nightmare and after the split with Spencer, I'd struggled to focus on books I'd bought myself. Even though this was a Shakespeare play, and not always easy to understand unless I concentrated fully, I was getting through it. I'd studied it at school, and my English teacher had shown us the film with Leonardo DiCaprio – many of the girls in my class, including myself, had fallen madly in love with him. Reading was good for me, and I'd always derived so much pleasure from it in the past. Wasn't it supposed to relieve stress, even if you only read a few pages per day? When I'd finished eating, I put the book back in my bag, and saw a message on my phone screen, from Ben.

Stunning pics!

I replied.

Thanks! Just had a delish breakfast. Going for a tour this morning

Yum. Almost wish I was there with you. Let me know how the tour goes

I loved how Ben was staying in touch with me. It felt as though he was cheering me on from afar, and, seeing as I was here on my own, this was a boost. Did he really mean that he almost wished he was in Verona with me? Maybe he was just saying it. The thought of having a long, slow breakfast here with him sitting across the table from me, and *that* view, was an experience I couldn't help craving.

I left the restaurant, thanking the waitress, and stopped off at reception to pick up leaflets about the vineyard and Verona. Now was my chance to skim the photographs showing the history of the vineyard. And then, there she was. Granny – I recognised her in her youth from her own photos at Keeper's Cottage – and she was sitting at a table next to a man. He had a beard and looked like the head gardener, Albert, from the photo I'd seen in the book *The History of Copeley Park*. On the other side of the table was what appeared to be a couple, as the man had his hand on the woman's. Perhaps they were the owners, meaning the woman could be Granny's cousin, Agnes.

On the walk back to my room, birdsong came from the trees around me, and a moped buzzed past on the road below. The sky was a brilliant deep-blue colour and the air refreshingly cold on my face. Breathing it in, I imagined my cheeks were going ruddy in that way they did on a bracing walk. The vineyard had such a peaceful feel. A sense of calm washed over me. And the scenery was so stunning – how could this place not put you in the best of moods? When I reached the top of the hill, to my left were rows of vines, which I hadn't seen the night before in the dark. I turned into the field and walked slowly along one of the rows, with vines either side of me. The grass was long, and it dampened my socks above the tops of my trainers.

It was uncanny to think that some of the wine we were producing now was being made with a cutting originally taken from these very vines by Albert, the head gardener, on his trip here with Granny. Our vineyard had a special connection with this one, and that seemed somehow significant. I pictured Granny here, walking amongst these vines back in the summer of 1939, shortly before the outbreak of war. How poignant that I was here doing the exact same thing. She was so right – seeing this place was doing me the world of good. All those years the bottle of Amarone had been sitting in the cellar at Keeper's Cottage, and now its discovery had brought me here.

I took some photos for Instagram, and then decided to go back to my room to post them before my tour with Rosanna. I wanted to ask her about the photograph I'd seen on the wall near reception. Did she have any more information about Granny's visit to the vineyard? Might she know who the mysterious 'B' was? And I was hoping to ask her about the sparkling Pinot Grigio. Would she mind telling me how popular it was – did they sell many bottles? I couldn't wait to try it.

More than anything else, I hoped Rosanna would give me some useful nuggets of information to persuade Dad with – I saw producing sparkling Pinot Grigio as our biggest chance to save Copeley Park. Maybe it would finally put our little vineyard on the map.

CHAPTER 31

LADY CHARLOTTE

Lady Penelope came to the house for tea a few days later. I hadn't slept a wink the night before. For who could sleep when the stakes were so high? What if Albert's plan didn't work? I could end up worse off than before. My only option was to trust him, and hope for the best. Lady Penelope's chauffeur delivered her at eleven o'clock, and tea was served in the library. Albert and I had agreed to wait until she was properly established before he entered the room. He wanted her to be caught by the element of surprise as this was bound to work in our favour. When I rang my bell, he'd come in and join us.

I poured us both a cup of tea.

'And how was Italy?' Lady Penelope said.

'It was the most wonderful experience of my life,' I said.

'Oh really?'

'We visited a vineyard, and it was a veritable paradise.'

'And you're starting a vineyard of your own, here at Copeley Park, I heard?'

'Yes. Albert, my head gardener, brought back some vine cuttings, and we're reviving the old eighteenth-century vineyard. It's all rather exciting, as you can imagine.'

'Aren't you getting rather ahead of yourself?' she said.

'What do you mean?'

'Well, considering our conversation last time we met, should you be making plans for Copeley Park?'

I shook my head. She had no idea what was in store for her. Even I didn't know exactly what Albert was keeping up his sleeve, but I had a hunch he might just save me – he seemed so sure that he would. I picked up my handbell, and rang it, and the door opened, and Albert came in. I almost gasped when I saw that he was dressed formally, in a suit with shirt and tie – of course he was! He couldn't really wander into the house in his gardening attire. He scrubbed up so well, and seeing him like this took me back to our dinners on the train and in Verona. Such fond memories they were. But now wasn't the time to appreciate how incredibly handsome he was.

'Lady Penelope, may I introduce my head gardener, Albert Hicks?'

He gave her a nod, and hitched up his trousers as he sat down beside me. Now we were both facing her – two against one.

'Oh, he seems to think he's joining us,' she said with a laugh.

'I asked him to, if you don't mind?'

Her face dropped. 'And why is that, exactly?'

'When we were in Italy, he alerted me to some information I wasn't aware of.'

'And what was that?'

'It relates to the day Winston died.'

Lady Penelope went rather pale. Having to deal with both of us had clearly knocked her confidence. Perhaps it was dawning on her that her grand plan might not come to fruition after all. And she'd been so smug, both at our lunch, and today, upon her arrival.

'What information did Albert alert you to?'

'I shall leave him to tell you that.'

Albert cleared his throat, and I turned to watch him speak, curious to know what he was going to say.

'On the morning that his lordship died, and may he rest in peace...' He leant forwards. 'I happened to be tending to the flowerbeds outside the front of this house.'

'I don't see how that's relevant,' she said, curtly.

'Well, it is, your ladyship, because, you see, there is a window by the flowerbeds.' Lady Penelope pursed her lips. 'When I stood up to fetch my spade, I caught sight of his lordship at the top of the stairs, talking to someone. It was plain to see that they were having a quarrel.'

'That "someone" was Charlotte though, wasn't it?'

'No, ma'am. It was you.'

'It was me? That's impossible.'

'No, I'm sure it was you. Absolutely certain, in fact.'

Lady Penelope swallowed. 'That simply isn't true. It was Charlotte, and they were arguing about her not having been in his bed the night before—'

'I couldn't hear what was being said, as the window was closed. But I did see you push him before he fell, and you seemed to know exactly what you were doing.'

'But that's a blatant lie. Charlotte, set him straight, will you?'

I suppressed a smile as Albert's plan came together so very perfectly, and gladly took over the baton.

'I have no idea what you mean,' I said. 'When I woke up that morning with a headache, I decided not to go to the Sunday service at St John's. But after I'd eaten my breakfast, I opened the door of my bedroom to go downstairs to the library. And do you know what I saw?'

'What did you see?' Lady Penelope said with gritted teeth.

'I saw exactly what Albert just described. You pushed my dear husband – and we'd only been married a matter of weeks – down the stairs deliberately.'

'Who's going to believe this?' she spluttered.

I looked her directly in the eye, ready to deliver the final blow.

'I'm sure the police will believe two people telling the same story over one, especially when it is you carrying the victim's child. An illegitimate child, might I add – and you were clearly revealing this news to him at the time, and making demands.'

'You won't get away with this, Charlotte.'

'Get away with what?'

She stood up. 'You know very well what you're doing, the pair of you. Winston's child deserves to live here, and one day we'll get our hands on this place.'

'Good day, Penelope.'

I rang my handbell, and Skinner came through the door.

'See Lady Penelope out, will you, Skinner?'

She flounced out of the room without so much as a goodbye or thank you for the cup of tea. And that was that. I didn't expect to hear from her again – and I had Albert, the man I loved, to thank for that, the clever, clever man. And he had just shown his love for me more than anyone I'd ever known.

It didn't come as a surprise to any of us when the war began in September 1939, meaning military service was mandatory for Albert – and so he would leave his position at Copeley Park, and, more importantly, me. The other male servants of fighting age were also conscripted, apart from George, who had a heart condition. And so, I'd be left with Mr Skinner and George as the only men in the house.

Even though Albert and I had talked about the inevitability of war, when reality hit I was completely devastated. How would I get through even one day without him? When thinking about marriage, I would often return to the words of Samuel Taylor Coleridge: 'To be happy in Married Life... you must have a Soul-Mate.' I saw

Albert as my soulmate, and hoped that one day, perhaps, if and when he returned from war, we'd get married, and live a happy and fulfilled life together. First, I'd have to manage Papa's expectations, but I'd deal with him when the time came. We had no idea how long the war would last for – the Great War had taken four years – and we didn't know whether we would win either. People talked about what would happen if Hitler managed to invade our shores. We'd all be speaking German, our lives irrevocably changed. I shuddered at this thought. All I could do was remain optimistic and believe in my heart that Albert would come back to me.

When Albert's last day at Copeley Park came, we were ready to make the most of every moment. That morning, we sat in his drawing room at Rosemary Cottage to drink tea during our break from gardening, the fire crackling beside us.

'Should we drink the bottle of wine from Verona tonight?' I asked.

'Let's wait until we have something to celebrate – isn't that what Agnes wanted?' Albert said.

'You think we should wait for the war to be over, and for you to return safely?'

He nodded. 'Yes. Then we can really savour every sip, don't you agree?'

'You are right, of course.'

I'd put the bottle of wine in Albert's cellar at Rosemary Cottage, lying down, as advised by Agnes. For it would be a sad state of affairs if Skinner came across it in the main house, and took it upon himself to uncork our bottle of Amarone 1936 for dinner one evening. This wine meant too much for it to be consumed before the time was right.

'How shall we spend these precious last hours together then?' I said.

'Well, I've been thinking about that,' Albert said.

'And what did you come up with?'

'If you'd do me the honour of meeting me in the bluebell woods, by the old oak tree next to the pond, at one o'clock, I shall tell you then.'

'Shall I bring anything?'

'Just yourself.'

I went back to the kitchen garden for another hour or so before returning to the house to change out of my grubby gardening clothes. Gwen found me a pale-blue dress to match my eyes, and I put it on. We decided that I should wear my hair down, letting it fall to my shoulders, as that was how Albert liked it best.

At half past twelve, I made my way to the woods – it was a good twenty-minute walk, beyond the lake, and then uphill, past the Temple of Bacchus and the hermitage. The leaves on the trees were starting to turn yellow and red and brown with the onset of autumn, but being early September the temperature was still fairly mild. The horse chestnuts and acorns crunched beneath my feet as I walked.

When I arrived, there Albert was, sitting on a tartan blanket by the oak tree. He had a picnic basket beside him.

'Oh, how delightful,' I cried.

'Look at you,' he said, with a smile.

I joined him on the blanket, and we kissed on the lips – as always it sent a small jolt of electricity through me. For now, I would not think about him leaving. Instead, I would savour every last minute of this day.

'You are so beautiful, Charlotte,' he said, stroking my face.

How would I live without him?

Albert reached into the basket and got out a loaf of bread, cheese, boiled eggs, slices of ham, and a bottle of his home-made ginger beer to wash it all down with.

'Mrs Coleman gave me two slices of Victoria sponge for pudding,' he said.

It was all perfect. Who knew when we'd have the chance to do something like this again?

After we ate, Albert suggested we take a swim in the pond.

'But I don't have a costume with me,' I protested.

'Who needs a costume?' he said.

'Are you quite serious?'

'Charlotte, there is no one around. We will be all right here, alone, just the two of us.'

So, we removed our clothes, and Albert took my hand, and we walked into the pond together, completely naked. Brrr, it was freezing cold! But once I'd put my shoulders under the water, it didn't seem quite so bad. Albert ran his hand through my hair, and looked at me directly. How I'd miss looking into those big green eyes – one could so easily get lost in them. And then he leant in to kiss me, and I threw my arms around his neck. After that, we swam for a little while. When we got out of the pond, we lay on the blanket, and he made love to me, slowly and gently, our eyes locked the whole time. How I hoped that it wouldn't be too long before we could do this again. I would pray for Albert to come back to me safely every single day, and I would attend church every Sunday, without fail. If he didn't come back, I would break into a thousand pieces. For we were like Romeo and Juliet, as far as I was concerned. I could not live without him in my life. There was no one else. There never would be anyone else, except for him.

Albert left the following morning, taking my heart with him. I'd asked the chauffeur, Paul, to drive him to Copeley station in the Standard, and I accompanied them. The servants were bound to be talking about Albert and me below stairs by now anyway, and I wasn't prepared to forgo saying a proper goodbye to the man I loved – the man whom I might never see again. Paul parked, and stayed with the car while I accompanied Albert onto the platform. The train would take him to the army barracks at Camberley, after changing en route. The platform was filled with porters and other people doing the same as me: women, and children too, all saying their sad goodbyes to husbands and fathers, and lovers.

I thought back to when Albert and I had stood on this very same platform before our journey to Verona. How I wished we could go back in time, and that we were about to embark on our grand adventure. But those good times were over now, well and truly. Juliet's words, 'Parting is such sweet sorrow,' came to me at that moment, and I didn't know what to do with them. How I hoped that Albert and I would be blessed with the happy ending Romeo and Juliet never had.

Albert kissed me gently on the lips and stepped up onto the train. He went to put his suitcase on a luggage rack, and then he appeared at an open window, and leant out of it. Steam filled the air as the train prepared to leave, and the guard went along the platform, checking that the doors were closed, shouting, 'All aboard, please.'

The train began to move slowly as it pulled out of the station. Albert leant further out of the window, his eyes filled with sadness.

'I love you, Charlotte,' he shouted.

'I love you, Bertie,' I shouted back, waving as the train sped up, and I found myself running along the platform to keep up with the train, until I could keep up with it no more.

And then he was gone.

CHAPTER 32

KATE

At eleven o'clock, I walked down to Villa Romeo to meet Rosanna. When I arrived, she was speaking to someone at reception, and I took the opportunity to have another look at the photographs on the wall. As Rosanna was Agnes's great-granddaughter, she might really have more information about Granny's visit to the vineyard. Perhaps she had more photographs. Maybe she'd know who 'B' was – could it be someone who was living or working on the vineyard at the time?

Rosanna came over.

'Ciao, Kate. Are your ready for your tour?'

'Hi, Rosanna. Yes, I'm really looking forward to it.'

She approached the door and stepped outside, and I followed. We walked uphill towards the rows of vines that I'd been looking at earlier.

'How long are you staying here for?' she said.

'Just the weekend.'

'And you plan to go into Verona?'

'Yes, hopefully tomorrow.'

She nodded. 'So, I understand that you live on a vineyard in England?'

'Yes, vine cuttings were actually taken back from here just before the war started.'

'Ah yes, of course. Jane, your great-grandmother's carer mentioned this on the telephone when booking your room.'

'I saw a photograph of my great-grandmother, Charlotte, on your wall, actually.'

'Oh, really?'

'Yes, I was surprised to see it. And I wondered if you might have any more photos, or any information at all about their visit?'

'Hmm, possibly. There is a drawer of information from the 1930s in the office, behind reception. We can have a look through it on our return if you like?'

'I would love that, thank you.'

We passed the olive grove on our left and then reached the row of vines that I'd walked amongst earlier.

'So, I'm assuming that you know something about growing grapes and making wine, if you grew up on a vineyard?'

'A little, yes. I could know more. I actually work in book marketing.'

She raised her eyebrows.

'You are not involved in the family business?'

'Not at the moment, but lately I've been thinking about asking my dad if I can help manage the estate, now he's getting older.' I explained about my plans to become more involved with the family business.

'I'm sure he'd be delighted.'

I smiled.

'Thanks, I'd like to think so.'

'So here we have some of our oldest vines, producing our best wine. You'll see that each row has a rose at the end, an old tradition to help with the detection of mildew – the rose shows signs of mildew before the vines, giving us chance to protect the grapes before it's too late.'

I recalled Dad talking about this tradition – it was such a clever and simple idea.

'Some of these vines still have grapes on them, shrivelled up and long dead. We leave them there because they were not good enough to pick – damaged by frost or mildew. It would be too expensive to hire anyone to pick and throw them away. Instead, the grapes will be left to decompose in their own time, eventually enriching the soil beneath to help with the growth of future grapes.'

'That's really interesting. I noticed on your website that you produce sparkling Pinot Grigio here.'

'Yes, it does very well. Would you like to try it when we get back to Villa Romeo?'

'That would be lovely. I'm thinking of trying to persuade my dad to produce it on our vineyard.'

'I would say that it's worthwhile. Perhaps he can make a limited edition to start with.'

'That's what I was thinking too.'

We walked amongst the vines in a circle, passing Villa Giulietta and ending up back where we'd begun.

'Shall we go to the restaurant and do some wine tasting now?' Rosanna said.

We walked downhill to Villa Romeo. Rosanna led me inside, through the arch and into the restaurant. There were a few people eating lunch, and she gestured in the direction of a table set up for two in the corner, facing the view of Verona. On it was a selection of wine glasses with each place setting. I was glad to see the knife and fork, as I'd need to eat something if I was tasting wine.

'Why don't you take a seat, and I'll be back in a minute.'

Rosanna reappeared with a bottle of wine, and expertly removed the cork with a popping sound.

'This is the sparkling Pinot Grigio. Here, try it.'

She half-filled two flutes, handed one to me, and sat down.

We clinked glasses, and said, 'Cin cin'.

I took a sip. It was very fizzy, and nicely chilled, with notes of citrus and peach. I found it to be light and refreshing, and couldn't help being excited by the prospect of us producing this wine on our vineyard. I would take a bottle back for Ben to try. On second thoughts, I'd take a bottle for Dad as well, for he needed to try it if I was going to get through to him. I just had to get him to agree to producing this.

'You like?' Rosanna said.

'It's so good.'

'Well, I hope you can persuade your father to produce it. He won't regret it, I'm sure.'

'If I wanted to bring a friend here who works on our vineyard, to look at how you make the sparkling Pinot Grigio, would that be okay?'

'Certo, when were you thinking of coming?'

'I'm not sure...'

'Maybe come in the spring. Aspetta, there is an opportunity you might like. Erica, who does our tours and tastings, will be going on holiday at the beginning of March. If you wanted, you could cover her?'

'What, you mean do the tours?'

'Yes, why not? We need an English speaker as the majority of our visitors use English to communicate – whether they are Scandinavian, American, Australian or English.'

I raised my eyebrows, really surprised by the offer. 'That sounds like an interesting opportunity. Thank you, Rosanna. Can I think about it?'

'Sure, let me know after Christmas. There is no rush. I shall have to do the tours myself if we cannot find anyone, but it takes up my time when it could be used in a better way.'

'Would my friend be able to come here for some of that time?'

'I cannot pay much, but I can give you free accommodation

at that time of year, before we get busy during the Easter holidays – rooms for you and your friend, and we can include meals and wine too.'

The idea of coming here for free and doing tours was exciting. I had to find a way to do it.

'Now...' She stood up. 'Give me a minute. I'll be back.'

Rosanna reappeared with a bread basket, and a board of cheeses, salamis and slices of ham rolled up in cigar shapes. It all looked delicious. And then she brought over a couple more bottles of wine.

'This one is Valpolicella, and the other one is Amarone. Amarone is Valpolicella that has been matured for at least three years, and so it is richer, and the alcohol content is greater too,' she said with a wink.

'So, this is the Amarone my granny has told me so much about.' I told Rosanna about the box of wine from 1936.

'Wow, she still has such an old bottle, and given to her by my great-grandparents too – that's amazing,' Rosanna said.

'She said Amarone is the most sumptuous wine she's ever tasted.'

'It is rather wonderful.'

Rosanna poured the Valpolicella, and then the Amarone, into two different glasses for each of us and I tried them both. They were bold and sumptuous, warm and rich, and I could quite happily have downed several glasses of each one.

'You will probably find that the Valpolicella is lighter,' she said. 'But tell me how you think they compare to each other.'

The Valpolicella was indeed lighter and more fruity. The Amarone was more full-bodied, with notes of chocolate and cherries, and it was easy to tell that it had been aged for longer. So this was what the Amarone from 1936 would taste like, but even richer and more sumptuous, I imagined.

'I can tell that the Amarone has a higher alcohol content – it is stronger-tasting, and am I right in thinking there are notes of chocolate and cherries?'

'Yes, well done. You will find it is more earthy. Also, of cinnamon, figs and plums.'

I picked up the glass and tasted the Amarone again. Rosanna was right. I was really enjoying this experience, especially with the view of Verona as a backdrop. Why weren't we doing tastings with cheese and salami boards at Copeley Park? It would be such an easy way to make money. We could prepare the boards ourselves with baskets of bread – there would be no need to hire a chef.

I could feel the wine starting to make me feel sleepy.

'Goodness, I might need a nap in a minute,' I said.

'Well, why not take a siesta after?' she said with a laugh. Do help yourself to food.'

I took some cheese, salami and ham from the board, and we tucked in.

When we'd finished the tasting, Rosanna said, 'I have a meeting in half an hour, so if you'd like to have a look at that drawer in the office we can do it now? Then you can have your siesta maybe.'

'Okay, that would be great,' I said.

We got up and Rosanna led me into the office behind reception. She sat down at a desk and opened a drawer. It was filled to the top with papers, and looked like it hadn't been touched for a while.

'There you go. Have a sift through it and take out anything you like. You will have to look at everything here – you can't take it out of this office.'

'Absolutely, of course. Thank you, Rosanna.'

'And while you do that, I shall check my emails,' she said, rolling her eyes. 'Always so many...'

I took the papers out of the drawer, and placed them on the spare desk. And then I sat down and began to sift through them.

Piles of letters addressed to the vineyard. Could any of these be from Granny? Perhaps a thank-you letter after she'd visited. Anything that might give me a clue to who 'B' might be. Granny was bound to have mentioned this person in such a letter. I'd certainly recognise her handwriting. I sifted through the envelopes, and then I came across one with simply, 'To Juliet' written on the front. When I turned it over, I saw that the words 'From Charlotte Clarkson c/o Vineria di San Martino, Verona' were written on the back. What was this?

I lifted the tab – it hadn't been glued down – and took out the letter. Was this going to give me my answer? I held my breath as I read her words.

Vineria di San Martino,
Verona
18 August 1939

Dear Juliet,

My cousin Agnes suggested that I write to you. I don't know if I'll even get this letter to you, but I thought it might be a good idea to write down my thoughts on paper. Apparently, you're good at dealing with matters relating to love. Well, I'm not sure how that can be true after the way you met your demise – but I'm giving it a try...

The problem I have is that I am madly in love with a man who happens to be a servant in my household – Bertie, the head gardener. And I am the lady of said household. As if that isn't enough of a problem, my father wants me to marry a man with a title – this will be the second instance where he has become involved with arranging this kind of marriage for me. My first husband died recently – don't worry, Juliet, he wasn't a good man, and the world is better off without him in it.

And so, I don't know what to do. Should I tell this man

how I feel about him? Seeing as I outrank him in terms of status, I don't think he would ever tell me if he did love me because he would see this as an inappropriate course of action. And if I do tell him, and he does indeed love me in return, should I pursue a union with him? Do you think it would work? Would the other servants in my house give him the respect that he deserves?

So, you see, Juliet, I really have more than one problem here, but perhaps in time the right course of action will present itself to me. I do worry about telling my father that I cannot marry another man he's chosen for me. What if he tries to take my money away? I can't see him doing that. But also, I can't see him wanting to know me any more. He might disown me, and then not leave me any money when he dies, which wouldn't be the end of the world, as I probably have more than enough to keep me going for now.

Agnes told me how your letter to her was immensely helpful, and she managed to resolve her own love dilemma. And so I hope that at least, by writing this, I've set wheels in motion for finding a solution to the matter that gnaws at my insides.

As Romeo said to you, Juliet, 'Did my heart love till now?' Mine certainly did not.

Yours,

Charlotte Clarkson

I carefully folded the letter back in half, letting Granny's words wash over me. Wow! This letter gave me so much to think about. Why had it been written to Juliet? Perhaps Rosanna would know. But most importantly, 'B' was Bertie, short for Albert – of course it was. How could I have missed that? So, Granny had been in love with him – and it seemed their romance had begun here, on this very vineyard. I'd have to check the dates, but I would have liked to think this was after her husband and my great-grandfather, Winston, had died. What had she meant by him not being a good man? And what had happened to Albert? Why hadn't they stayed together? At least this all explained why she'd been so upset when I found the note with the bottle of Amarone from 1936. It must have been devastating for her to find out it had been there all that time without her knowing of its existence. I desperately needed to know more. Granny was the only person who could give me the answers, and I'd go and see her as soon as I got back to Copeley Park. What a mystery to unravel.

CHAPTER 33

LADY CHARLOTTE

After Albert left, all I could think was that surely he would come back to me? At last I'd found my one true love, and the thought of losing him was too much to bear. Every Sunday, I went to the morning service at St John's, and each night I knelt beside my bed with my hands pressed together in prayer before sleeping. I wrote a letter to Albert every morning and posted it in the village. His replies were short and erratic, but still I was pleased to hear from him at all. I guessed he wasn't allowed to tell me very much about what he was actually doing or where he was. Reading the words 'I love you, dear Charlotte' warmed my heart each time I read them, over and over again.

I wrote to Papa to tell him that I didn't want to marry the Baron of Tyne. The war wasn't good for any of us, but it did deliver me one small blessing – the baron was conscripted, and so the matter of my second marriage was put on ice. I was immensely grateful. For I hoped that, if and when Bertie returned, we could get married. By then some time would have passed, and Papa would be more likely to accept my decision.

In order to keep going, I'd put on my shirt and breeches every morning and head for the walled garden. I would do weeding or pruning for an hour or two before taking luncheon in the library. Afterwards, I read by the fire until mid-afternoon. Then I wrote letters. Sometimes, I sketched pictures of flora in my notebook – this undemanding activity brought me a great deal of joy. I'd take a walk around the gardens before dark, often with Gwen as company, and then I would have a drink in the library before eating dinner alone.

Sometimes, I spent the morning in the vineyard, and I did all I could to maintain the vines that Bertie had planted. It was a way of staying close to him somehow. I was glad that he'd planted one of them in the walled garden – the special place where we had our first encounter that morning when he found me amongst his broad beans.

Before long, the Canadian army commandeered some of the land at Copeley Park for training. They'd done this with a few country houses in the area, and I had no choice in the matter. Besides, it was only right to allow them to practise their skills so that they were at their very best when they went into combat. I wanted to do my bit to help with the war effort, and this was a way for me to contribute. It was very noisy, though with gunshots being fired all day long in the fields and woodland leading up to Manor Farm nearby. We were not permitted to venture outside the main gardens. I counted myself lucky because I was still able to take walks around the lake and up to the hermitage that Albert had shown me that day on our tour.

For a short while, I carried on tending to the vineyard, but it was too much to manage all alone. George would help me when he could. Mr Skinner, who was too old to go and fight, spent his spare time volunteering as an Air Raid Precautions warden, and so he wasn't able to help. One morning, I decided to stop trying to maintain the vineyard. Even if I could find labourers to help with the harvest, who would make the wine? It would be better to just leave the grapes on the vines and hope that before long the war would end. Then the Canadian army would leave Copeley Park, and hopefully Albert would return, and we could revive the vineyard together.

It didn't take long for the gardens to look rather unkempt, and I took it upon myself to do all I could to maintain them. I spent many hours weeding and pruning but it was impossible to keep up with it all on my own. I had got my wish of being able to spend all of my time gardening, and that at least was a consolation. Seeing the autumn colours, the beech trees with leaves like gold coins and the beautiful carpet underneath was an antidote to the horrors of war. I would read the newspaper every morning and listen to the wireless in the evenings. Hearing the news brought me down, but one needed to stay abreast of what was happening around the world.

After a few weeks, I began to find that gardening was making me rather fatigued, and I struggled to do more than a couple of hours in the mornings. After luncheon I read in the library, and often found myself dozing off, waking with a start when Mr Skinner brought in afternoon tea. I put this newfound tiredness down to the mental strain that the war was having on us all and nothing more.

One morning, I was in the kitchen garden harvesting onions. This required some strength, and I needed to stand with my knees bent, and grab the tops of the onions in order to pull them out of the ground. There hadn't been any rain for a couple of weeks and the soil was especially hard. I placed each onion into a wooden crate, and thought about asking Mrs Parsons if she could make French onion soup that evening. But then, as I stood up, I began to feel dizzy, and my vision blurred. I was seeing stars before my eyes – what on earth was wrong?

I opened my eyes to see that Gwen and a few other servants were standing in a circle over me. I was lying on the ground, amongst the onions, and a housemaid was squatting down as she pressed a damp cloth to my forehead.

'What happened?' I whispered.

'You fainted, milady,' Mrs Parsons said.

Gwen took one of my arms, and the housemaid took the other, and between them they gently lifted me to my feet.

'Let's take you inside and get you a brandy,' Mrs Parsons said.

We went up the steps leading to the front door, and Mr Skinner opened it, and we entered the grand hall. Damn this house. I looked at the staircase where Winston had fallen that day and broken his neck. And then I relived it all in my mind right up until I was running outside to find Bertie tending to the flowerbed.

Mrs Parsons established me in my bedroom with a generous glass of brandy, as promised, and went to call Doctor Marshall who came within the hour. He checked my pulse and listened to my heartbeat with his stethoscope. Then he said that I looked rather pale, and pressed the palm of his hand to my forehead and started to ask me questions. Had I been feeling sick at all? Was I more fatigued than usual lately? When I thought about it, yes, I had lost my appetite recently, and, despite an afternoon nap, I'd still been tired in the evenings. And thinking about it, my bedtime tipple of brandy had been tasting different from usual. Then he asked a rather personal question, and I asked him to pass me my diary from my writing table. My courses – as he referred to them – hadn't been since Albert had left five weeks ago. I was usually regular as clockwork.

'Well, your ladyship, I am almost certain that you are with child.'

I put a hand to my mouth and gasped.

'Doctor, are you quite serious?'

'I can't be entirely sure, but yes there is a strong possibility that you're carrying your late husband's child.'

'But... Winston and I struggled to conceive during the time —' I stopped myself from saying any more. The child must be Albert's, conceived either on the vineyard or perhaps on his last day before leaving, at the pond when we made love on the picnic blanket. Goodness, was I actually carrying his child? 'I am astounded, Doctor.'

'Give it a few more weeks and we'll be certain. If your courses do not come, and if you start to put on weight around your centre, then you will know for sure. The nausea is likely to ease with time.'

He packed up his things and placed his hat on his head.

'I wish you well, your ladyship. What happened to your husband was a tragedy, but at least now you will have his child for company.'

'Thank you, Doctor.'

'Now, make sure you get some rest over the next few days.'

He left the room, and Gwen came in and sat on the end of the bed, and I told her what he'd said. Her face broke into a smile.

'This is such good news, milady.'

She took my hand in hers and squeezed it.

'Thank you, Gwen.' I hesitated. 'But I am a little concerned about my situation. For I shall have to pretend the child is Winston's, otherwise it will be illegitimate, and that would be scandalous.'

'We'll all help you through it, milady.'

'For now, I shall move into Rosemary Cottage to be close to Albert. I hope you understand, and don't mind staying there with me until further notice.'

'Of course not, milady. I shall pack our belongings and take them over there this very afternoon.'

'Thank you, dear Gwen, I'm not sure what I would do without you in my life.'

. . .

Albert and I had planted dahlia bulbs in the flowerbed outside the front of the house, and one morning in September I was delighted to see that they were beginning to flower. They were a deep-pink colour, and I decided to sketch them in my diary later that day. Then I would copy the sketch in my next letter to Albert. He'd be so thrilled to know our dahlias were thriving. I took the flowering of these beautiful dahlias as a sign that our love was as strong as it would ever be, and this brought me a great deal of comfort. I was squatting down, pulling out the stray weeds around them, when I heard footsteps on the path down the side of the house, coming from the servants' quarters. I looked up to see Gwen come round the corner. This was a perfectly usual occurrence, for her to seek me out and discuss when she might be needed that day, and whether I had any special requests. But as she approached I could see she had a glum look on her face. Standing up, I registered that she was holding a letter.

'This came for you just now, milady.'

'What is it, Gwen?'

She handed me the letter, postmarked Hastings, and I took it out of its envelope. I knew what it was, and I couldn't bring myself to read it. But I had to, just in case there was a small chance I was mistaken.

I swallowed, a sick feeling rising through me.

Dear Lady Charlotte,

We regret to inform you that we have received a telegram to say that our son, and your head gardener, Mr Albert Clive Hicks, has been killed in action. We are understandably devastated by this tragic news, and thought that it was our duty to inform you, his employer.

Yours sincerely,

Angus and Margaret Hicks

I put a hand to my mouth to muffle the scream that came from within. How could this be? And how odd that I was receiving this news at the very spot where we'd been brought together after Winston fell down the stairs. Was I supposed to find this out while tending to our dahlias?

My knees buckled, and Gwen took me into her arms and squeezed me to her as I sobbed.

'It's all right, milady,' she said, softly. 'There, there. I'm so sorry. We were all so fond of him. He was such a lovely man, he was. We'll take care of you and your baby, don't you worry.'

How could I lose the love of my life like this, so very swiftly? He'd been gone for a matter of weeks. Why was I being given his child when all I wanted was him? I would have been satisfied with merely his company forever – just the two of us. How on earth would I get through this? I'd have to grieve while building a child inside of me. How could I be sure not to transfer the sadness I felt to this child? I should be grateful that the Lord had gifted me with a part of Albert. Would the child look like him? Would it be a boy or a girl? Would it be painful to look at my child's face and see the man I'd lost? How I hoped that I wouldn't resent this child for taking Albert's place in my life.

CHAPTER 34

KATE

When I'd finished reading the letter I looked across at Rosanna. She was glued to her computer screen as she tapped away on a keyboard. Did she have any idea what I'd just found in her drawer? How long had this letter been sitting there? Granny wouldn't have put it in the drawer herself, surely?

'Rosanna?'

She clicked her mouse, and swivelled round in her chair to face me.

'Yes?'

'I've found something really interesting.'

'Really, already?'

I showed her the letter and explained that my great-grandmother Charlotte had written it.

'What an incredible find,' she said. 'So, it seems she and the head gardener were in love, and they realised that here on this very vineyard?'

'It seems so. I'm not sure if she was still married to my great-grandfather then, I'd have to find out.' I didn't like the idea of this – that Granny might have been having an affair while married to my great-grandfather. She wasn't that kind of person, was she?

'Ah, I see.'

'Do you have any idea how this letter would have got in the drawer, and why it would be addressed to Juliet?' I asked.

'I can certainly tell you why she's written it to Juliet. Otherwise' – she shook her head and threw her arms up in the air – 'the rest is a mystery.'

'Oh, that's a shame. Never mind, I'm glad to have found it. So, tell me what you know.'

'There is a tradition here in Verona of going to see the Juliet balcony in a small square in the city. Since the 1960s there has been a Juliet statue as well, where, if you touch her right breast, it will bring you luck in love,' she said.

How could touching a statue bring you luck in love?

As if reading my mind, Rosanna added, 'We Italians like traditions, and we can be superstitious, and this is the country of amore, after all.'

'Yes, I suppose it is. But why would my great-grandmother have written to Juliet though?'

'Nowadays, there is a letter box where you can post a letter to Juliet about your love dilemmas. A group of women from the Juliet Club will reply with advice.'

'So, my granny was actually expecting someone to reply?'

'In those days, I don't think the letter box was there, but still I think women would write to Juliet. I'm not sure where they left the letters in the 1930s or if the Juliet Club existed then.'

'It's a shame Agnes isn't around to tell us more,' I said. Surely, it would have been her suggestion that Granny write to Juliet – but then why was the letter in this drawer? Perhaps Agnes had promised to pass the letter on to whoever was replying to Juliet's letters at the time but had forgotten about it.

'Yes, if only my great-grandmother were still alive,' Rosanna said, wistfully.

She frowned and then tucked her hair behind one ear as if in deep thought.

'Aspetta, wait...' Her eyes lit up. 'I wonder if the answer might be in Agnes's diaries. We still have them.'

'You do?'

'Yes, they are in the library here at Villa Romeo.'

Well, this was an exciting development.

'If you're able to find diary entries from when my granny stayed here, that would be so helpful.'

'When she first came to Italy with her husband, Mario, Agnes felt compelled to keep a record of everything around her. She was so inspired by the scenery and the new life she was embarking on. And then there was the war of course, and she found the diary helped her to keep going during all she had to endure when Italy was occupied by the Germans.'

'I can't begin to imagine what it would have been like living through the war.'

'Me neither. After the war ended, she continued to keep diaries for the rest of her life. At one stage my sister, Claudia, started typing them up – she wanted to try and get them published. They were a real insight into the war in Italy, a bit like the diaries of Iris Origo from Val d'Orcia, if you have heard of her?'

'I haven't, but they sound very interesting.'

'But then Claudia became distracted when she had a baby, and never finished the project.'

'I would so love to see them.'

'I tell you what. After my meeting, I shall go to the library and try to find the entries from around the date the letter was written – when is it?'

I looked at the letter. 'The eighteenth of August 1939.'

She scribbled on a Post-it note.

'Give me a few hours and I'll let you know, okay?'

'Thank you, Rosanna. That is very kind.'

'Prego, you are welcome.'

I got up and pushed the chair under the desk.

'Do you mind if I take a photo of this letter before I go?'

'Certo.'

I took a photo with my phone. I couldn't wait to share it with Ben when I got back to my room. I had so much to tell him.

'Bye, Rosanna. Thanks again.'

Back in my room, I sat on the bed. I found the photo of the letter on my phone and read it again. Unbelievable. I opened WhatsApp and sent the photo to Ben.

Look what I found! Written by Granny…

I went on to explain briefly about her reason for writing the letter to Juliet. And that Bertie was actually Albert, the head gardener, who'd lived at Rosemary Cottage. All of a sudden, it struck me that Granny had had a liaison with one of Ben's predecessors. Had they continued their romance at the cottage when they returned to England? Had they sat together there in front of the fire, looking into each other's eyes as Ben and I had done?

Albert seemed to have disappeared off the face of the earth after Verona. I'd have to ask Granny where he'd gone to. Perhaps because he was her servant, there had been a big scandal culminating in him leaving Copeley Park. And then it dawned upon me – he'd gone to war, of course he had. Had he been killed? If he'd died, no wonder Granny had been so upset when I found that note from him, saying to drink the wine if he didn't come back. Now it made total sense. Poor Granny – I'd have to tread very carefully when speaking to her about this.

How I wanted Ben to reply straight away, but the two ticks remained grey. He must be busy at work. Hopefully he'd see my message soon and get back to me. I just felt a need to share everything with him, always keen to know his thoughts. And also, I was becoming addicted to the adrenaline rush that receiving a message from him gave me.

All the wine tasting had made me sleepy, and I climbed into bed fully clothed and closed my eyes, ready for a nap.

I was woken up by the room phone ringing. Goodness, it was so loud. For a moment, I was all disorientated, having slept so deeply. The phone kept on ringing.

I reached over and picked up the handset.

'Hello?' I said, my voice groggy.

'Kate? It's Rosanna.'

'Oh hi,' I said

'I have news. I found the diary. Why don't you come to reception before dinner, at around seven, and I'll show it to you?'

'Thank you so much, I can't wait to see it.'

Putting the receiver down, I looked at my phone to see that it was almost five o'clock. Being in this place was making me more relaxed than I'd been in a long time. Still, I needed to make the most of being here, and so I would take a walk. Getting out of bed, I went to the bathroom and removed the mascara that had run while I was asleep.

While I was doing up the laces on my trainers, a message flashed up from Ben.

That sounds really exciting. Keep me posted

Receiving his reply brought the adrenaline rush I'd been looking for. I loved being in contact with him, giving him little updates, and him showing interest in return. It made me feel less alone, but also it was as if we were in this together. Sharing my discovery with him made it even more exciting.

I grabbed my jacket and went outside. I needed to explore before getting ready for dinner. I took a long walk around the vineyard, breathing in the cool, crisp November air, and mulling over everything – my life and what I wanted from it. Being here had given me the breather I'd needed, and I was so glad that Granny had sent me on this adventure. When I returned to England, I would go back stronger and bolder, and ready to embrace my future. It was time to really think about what I wanted from my life, and do all I could to get it.

At seven o'clock, I walked down to Villa Romeo. I was so excited to see what Rosanna had found in the library, and couldn't wait to read Agnes's diary entries. She was waiting for me at reception, and she led me through the arch and along a corridor until we reached a room at the end. She opened the door and inside was a magnificent library with tall windows and walls filled with books. There was a desk with piles of books on it and framed photographs, and a sofa and armchairs in front of the fireplace.

'What a lovely place to read in,' I said.

'Yes, this is my favourite room here at Villa Romeo. I come here often to relax.'

She went over to one of the desks and picked up a book.

'Let's go and sit on the sofa.'

We sat down, and Rosanna opened the book at a page she'd saved with a bookmark. She handed it to me. 'Here you are, Kate.'

16 August 1939

Today I took Charlotte into Verona, and I suggested that she wrote a letter to Juliet. She seemed horrified by the idea, but I think she might do it. I have seen the way she and Albert look at each other with the eyes of love – Mario has noticed it too. I feel that they should be together, and I told her so.

Further entries described Granny's stay on the vineyard, talking about dinners, and there was a description of Agnes and

Mario giving her the bottle of Amarone on the last night. She'd told Granny to drink it when she had something to celebrate with someone who meant something to her, and suggested that person should be Albert. She described Granny departing and how sad this made her. How Europe was on the brink of war. No one knew how long it might all go on for. Mario and Albert would certainly be called up to fight for their countries. Would any of them survive what was to come? I could read the fear in Agnes's words, and it was heartbreaking to read. Granny had probably felt that very same fear – was this how Albert had met his fate? Perhaps that's why she'd never mentioned him to us.

19 August 1939

Charlotte and Albert left the vineyard today. I was immensely sad to see them depart. Charlotte told me she'd written a letter to Juliet and left it in the drawer of her nightstand. I asked our maid, Francesca, to bring it to me and I have put it in the drawer in the office. I shall take the letter to Verona the next time I visit and leave it at Juliet's tomb in the church of San Francesco al Corso. Word has it that the guardian of the tomb, a man named Ettore Solimani, replies to these letters with sympathy or advice when required, in order to bring luck in love to those who really need it. When he replies, I shall forward his letter to Charlotte in England.

Agnes must have forgotten to take the letter to the tomb.

'Thank you so much for finding this, Rosanna. Do you mind if I take photos?'

'Prego, go ahead.'

As I photographed the relevant pages, I couldn't wait to send them to Ben, eager to receive his reply.

CHAPTER 35

LADY CHARLOTTE

After receiving the tragic news about dear Bertie, I lay in bed for days, for life did not seem worth living. Now I really understood how Juliet had felt when she discovered that Romeo was dead. For Bertie had been my Romeo, and I could not envisage my future without him by my side. How I wanted to live my time with him again, starting from when he'd first discovered me weeding in the kitchen garden, my hands deep in the dirt. No man could be worthy of taking his place.

One evening, Gwen brought me food on a tray. But I was not hungry.

'You must eat, for the baby, if not for yourself,' she said, propping up the pillows behind me, encouraging me to sit up. The dear girl was so patient and kind. She sat there on the edge of my bed and spooned soup into my mouth.

'Mrs Coleman made this out of broccoli picked this morning from the kitchen garden. You and Albert grew that together – he's here with you now, helping you to get through this, milady.'

The thought of consuming something that had been nurtured by Bertie gave me a little strength, and I ate all of the soup in that bowl. The next day, Gwen brought soup made from onions, again taken from the garden, and I ate it all.

But still, I found it impossible to see a way forward. I would never meet another man like Bertie, for he had been one of a kind, and he'd understood me as no one else ever had. He'd had such a gentle nature, and he protected me when I needed help. Who would protect me now? And how would I raise a child without their father?

I thought of all the poisonous plants on the estate. Bertie had mentioned them to me that day on our tour of the gardens. This had made me think about how I'd like to slip the leaves into Winston's tea when he wasn't looking. I especially recalled Bertie showing me the laurel plant down by the hermitage, and one morning I went to find it, and picked a few leaves, looking around before surreptitiously pushing them into the pocket of my dress.

Back at the house, I asked a housemaid to bring me a bowl and spoon from the kitchen. When I returned to my room, I mixed up the leaves in the bowl with a little water and poured the liquid into a glass. I wasn't in my right mind, of course, but at this point, it seemed to be my only option, and a way to be with Bertie again – oh how I missed him.

I was about to lift the glass to my lips when Gwen entered the room.

'What is that you're drinking, milady?'

I looked at her but didn't utter a word – for my tongue was tied – and she carefully took the glass out of my hand, before picking up the bowl I'd used to make my poisonous potion. And then I burst into tears, and they ran hot and thick down my face. Gwen came and sat next to me on the bed and put her arm around me. We sat there for who knew how long while I sobbed, and she passed me a handkerchief.

'What a relief that I caught you in time. When Mrs

Coleman said you asked a housemaid to bring you a bowl from the kitchen, I wondered what it was all about.'

I dabbed my eyes.

'I'm sorry, Gwen... I don't know what I was thinking.'

'It's understandable that you'd feel like this, of course it is. But please don't try this again. You have Albert's child to think about now. You need to be strong for the baby.'

'But how will I do that, Gwen?' I said, sniffling.

'You are tougher than you think, milady. Everything will work out, you'll see.'

'I do hope you're right, dear Gwen.'

She put her hand on mine and gave it a squeeze.

'Just promise me you won't try anything like this again?'

I nodded.

'I promise.'

Gwen saved my life that day, and I vowed to always take care of her. For she had been a good friend to me, and I would be forever grateful.

Angus was born at Rosemary Cottage in January the following year. Officially, he was Winston's son, of course, for how could anyone know that my child was illegitimate? And therefore, this meant that he should inherit the earldom. I wasn't sure how to break this news to Lady Penelope though. She would naturally be devastated to discover that Jasper was no longer the heir. I wrote to inform them both, hoping that she would not kick up too much of a fuss – now I didn't have Albert to protect me from her scheming ways. Jasper had been called up, and so the matter was bound to be delayed until the end of the war. Angus inheriting the earldom wasn't important to me – it was just that I needed everyone to think that Winston was his father. Gwen and George knew the truth, of course, but I trusted them implicitly. Possibly, a few of the other servants had gathered that

Angus was Albert's son, but no one said a word. I treated my servants well, and so none of them had any reason to betray me.

I wrote to Winston's mother, the duchess, to inform her of the birth of her supposed grandson. How could I not? If I was to carry on the charade of Angus being Winston's son, I would need to tell her. She sent her congratulations, and asked to visit – of course she did. I made the necessary arrangements, and left her with Angus and the nanny while I went to the walled garden until she'd gone home. The duchess insisted on seeing him once a month, and I reluctantly agreed – for I had no real choice in the matter, and I didn't want to arouse her suspicions by refusing to let her see Angus. All I could do was console myself with the fact that she was spending that time with the son of a gardener – and this thought would make me chuckle to myself. She would be horrified if she knew the truth! And on top of all that, Jasper and Penelope's son, Jack – born only weeks before Angus (I'd heard on the grapevine) – was actually Winston's child. The whole situation was completely absurd.

Gwen and I moved into Keeper's Cottage as it had four bedrooms, meaning I could make one room into a nursery and the other spare bedroom could be used by a nanny. It had been a difficult pregnancy, as I'd been grieving for my beloved Bertie while his son grew inside of me. Bertie had come to me in my dreams every single night, and he would hold my hand and tell me that everything was going to be all right, that we would have a boy. He told me to call the baby Angus, after his father. I'd continued to work in the garden until my size made it impossible to bend down. But even then, I'd sit on a stool in the greenhouse, and plant seeds in pots, and nurture the plants that were growing there. Nature was a comfort, and it was a time when I needed to garden more than ever before. It had got me through those early days at Copeley Park, after marrying Winston, and now it was getting me through my husband's death and being pregnant with a child I wasn't sure I wanted. I would go to the vineyard and walk amongst the vines. The grapes were now completely dead, but still there, a reminder of Bertie's death and also of the war going on around us. We'd never been given the chance to produce even one bottle of wine from the cuttings brought from Verona. I lived in hope that, one day, I might have the strength to bring the vineyard back to life again – that one day we would produce wine at Copeley Park and fulfil the dream I'd started with Bertie.

One morning, Gwen came running into my bedroom, her eyes shining.
'Would you mind terribly if George and I got married, milady?' she said.
I was of course delighted for both of them, although it would mean losing Gwen to him. How would I survive without her?
'That's wonderful news, Gwen.'
'We were thinking about tying the knot soon at the register office in Dorking – this war makes you want to do everything as soon as you can, as you don't know how long you've got,' she said, with a laugh.
'Of course you must get married. It's clear you love each other very much, and he is a charming young man.'
I thought for a moment. What if they moved into Rosemary Cottage? Then, Gwen would still be there for me, and George could continue to work at the house.
'I shall ask Mr Skinner and Mrs Parsons to throw a party for you both and the servants to celebrate,' I said.
'Why, thank you, milady. That is so kind.'
'And I shall give you both Rosemary Cottage for as long as you need it.'
'Oh, milady, I don't know what to say. George will be so thrilled. Thank you.'

How could I not look after Gwen, who had cared for me so well? She had saved my life and I would look after her in return.

After they were married, they moved into Rosemary Cottage, and Gwen found the bottle of Amarone 1936 in the cellar. She brought it over to Keeper's Cottage and, one evening, I sat by the fire with it on the trestle table next to me. Why couldn't Bertie have come back to me? Weren't we supposed to have drunk this wine together as Agnes had suggested? What would I do with this bottle of wine now? I went down into the cellar. In the corner were pieces of old furniture – a chair, a trestle table, a few paintings and a dresser. I didn't want to take the Amarone out of its special box. I opened the drawer of the dresser and put the box inside – it would be safe there until I'd decided what to do with it. Now was not the time to make that decision. One day, perhaps it might be useful for something, but for now I could not bring myself to even look at it.

Time passed and I occupied myself with gardening. The small garden at Keeper's Cottage was manageable, and I made it look pretty. George helped plant a magnolia tree and a cedar and I filled the beds with bulbs that brought bright flowers – tulips, daffodils, dahlias, lupins – and planted lavender bushes. I added a herb garden with paving stones and all of this gladdened my heart.

I left the upbringing of Angus mostly to the nanny and the maids, and a governess, and when he was thirteen years old I sent him to Eton. However much I tried, I struggled to be the mother that he needed. And this made me feel terribly guilty. But I was grieving for his father, and I wasn't thinking clearly. When Angus was fifteen, I started to make an effort to spend more time with him in the school holidays, and we would walk around the estate, and talk. I would regale him with stories about my childhood at Rodene Hall, and he told me about his schoolfriends. We grew closer after that, and I was grateful that I'd been able to save our relationship before it was too late.

Angus went to Oxford University to study English literature and shortly after graduating, he married a woman called Deborah. They moved into the house at Copeley Park, and he managed the estate. I hadn't set foot in the house since finding out Bertie had died, for I felt that Winston had played some part in me losing him. I'd convinced myself that it was his way of getting revenge from the afterlife. Although it had been an accident, I had killed someone. I had committed a sin, and I'd paid my debt, for sure.

Angus and his wife had a son, Hugo, and he looked exactly like Bertie, with the very same big green eyes – it was uncanny. This brought me so much joy. I hadn't been the best mother to Angus, and so I endeavoured to be the best possible grandmother to Hugo. He would come and stay with me at Keeper's Cottage, and we'd go into the garden together, and I showed him how to plant bulbs, and grow things from seed. It reminded me of how my grandmother had shown me how to garden. I would take him to see the vine in the walled garden and tell him how it had come from a vineyard in Verona. Angus had never been interested in learning about gardening, but Hugo had the same love for nature as Bertie had. It was Hugo who brought me back to life after many years of being dormant like a volcano. I was able to enjoy living again. For all those years before Hugo's birth, my emotions had been numbed, and he had thawed me out. He'd returned a small part of Bertie to me in some way.

Hugo was sent to Eton like his father, and he went on to Oxford to study law, and then he became a barrister, and a very successful one too. Although I adored my dear grandson, Hugo, he became a bit of a playboy – probably because his father was generous, and he earned plenty of money as well, and so he fell into the London scene in the 1980s. The paparazzi followed him everywhere and they always wanted to know who his latest catch was. I must admit that I worried about him. I read every single article I could get my hands on – my secretary kept an eye out for any mention of him in the press, and I would study every detail. And then I would invite him to the cottage and try to talk to him, to make him see sense. He needed to find a good woman to marry and have children with. Hugo was charming and always knew what to say to me. 'Don't worry about me, Granny,' he'd say. 'I won't let you down.' And then he'd get back into his sports car and whizz off down the drive and out of the gates, back up the A3 to his swish apartment in London. I would shake my head and smile and hope he would keep his word.

One Sunday I invited him for lunch, and he asked if he could bring someone with him, a woman who he wanted me to meet. Had he at last found someone? I hoped he had, as he was on the cusp of turning thirty and needed to stop going out so much and settle down and start a family. 'Of course,' I said. And so, that day, he brought Allegra to meet me. She was a model from the East End of London. Her father was a builder, and her mother a cleaner and her working-class roots, like my own, meant she was more grounded than the other women he'd spent time with. Allegra was incredibly beautiful with big blue eyes and blonde hair falling to her shoulders. She was charming too, and I instantly adored her. Hugo hadn't been able to believe his luck when she showed an interest in him. They had a great deal in common – she liked to go for long walks in the countryside, and she kept horses at a farm nearby, where she often went riding. They'd met through mutual friends at an event one evening, and, when she told him she liked to go hacking near Copeley Park, they arranged to go together in the Surrey Hills. And that was how their romance started. When he came to visit me they'd only been together for a few months, but he told me that they planned to get married, and he'd be so happy if I approved of their match – this meant a lot to him. Of course I approved. She was lovely and down to earth and good for him.

Despite the glamorous world she'd been inhabiting for a few years, she appreciated the simple things in life.

Hugo and Allegra married at St John's in the village, and we held the wedding reception at Copeley Park. Angus and Deborah decided that they wanted to move out of the main house at Copeley Park, and so Hugo and Allegra moved in. I was delighted to have them as my neighbours. Hugo was tired of being a barrister and of living in London, and he asked if I would mind him reviving the vineyard and trying to make a living out of it. We'd always talked about taking cuttings from the vine in the walled garden one day, ever since he was a little boy.

Hugo had some money set aside, for he'd been earning well. We'd talked about bringing the vineyard back to life so many times over the years. I'd told him about Vineria di San Martino – how we'd planted our own vines when we returned just before the war. I explained how the head gardener had died before we could produce even one bottle of wine, and how I'd allowed the grapes to die on the vines – I couldn't bring myself to pick them, or ask anyone else to do it either. The vineyard was never able to reach its full glorious potential. But now was our chance to bring it back, to fulfil the dream that I'd started with Albert.

'Yes,' I said. 'You must revive the vineyard, and I'll do all I can to help you. Let me know what you need. Let's produce some good-quality wine to sell. It would bring me so much joy if we're able to finish the project started before the war, and make a real success of it.'

Hugo put his hand on mine, and said, 'Don't worry, Granny. I'm going to do everything I can to make this the greatest vineyard in all of England. There aren't many to compete with. I'm sure we can do it.'

I was so proud of my grandson. He had real initiative, unlike his father. Hugo really wanted to make something of himself, and I was reminded of Papa, and how he'd risen up from humble beginnings to being a hugely successful man. But also, Hugo was like Bertie in many ways. Not only did he look like him, but he had the same gentle nature, and a quiet determination. I couldn't wait to see what he was going to do with his life, and, by choosing Allegra over one of those aristocratic girls who pursued him around London, he was doing the right thing. I was sure of it. With Allegra by his side, he could achieve anything he wanted.

CHAPTER 36

KATE

The next morning after breakfast, I left the vineyard and took a taxi into Verona. The driver dropped me in a big square in the centre – Rosanna had advised that I ask him to take me to Piazza Bra. It bustled with mopeds and cars and pedestrians, and it was impossible not to notice the Roman amphitheatre right there in front of me. Wow, it was jaw-droppingly impressive – an enormous round building with arches, and still mostly intact. All I could do was stand there and look up at it in wonder, attempting to imagine what it would have been like to see all those gladiator fights back in Roman times. I'd read online that it was still used for concerts and operas. How I'd love to go there on a hot summer night.

A moped whizzed past, scarily close to me, and I crossed the road to the safety of the pavement on the other side, passing a cluster of cafés and restaurants where, despite it being winter, people sat at the outside tables with heaters above them. I took a few photos of the amphitheatre, and then, using Google Maps, headed for a bustling street, Via Mazzini, filled with shops. I recognised many designer names and I looked through the windows at beautiful leather handbags in all colours, and shoes, drooling at the beauty of them. My destination though was Casa Giulietta, Juliet's house, which Rosanna had told me about. It was off Via Cappello, near the Piazza Erbe, at the other end of Via Mazzini. I followed the brown signs to Casa Giulietta until I reached Piazza Erbe. Then I headed along Via Cappello until I reached a tiny street leading to a small square. And there it was, the balcony. I stood in a quiet corner and looked up it, doing my best to appreciate the experience despite all the people swarming around me. Quite a few tourists were queuing for the Juliet statue – Rosanna had mentioned that, if you touched her right breast, you would find luck in love. Was this something I needed to do? Or even wanted to do?

Most tourists, when they reached the front of the queue, posed for photos rather than touching Juliet's breast. I managed to capture a snap of my own when there was no one standing next to her for a split second. Later I'd post it on my Instagram story. And then I spotted the red letter box Rosanna had told me about, on a wall outside a shop filled with Juliet-themed souvenirs. I saw that there was an email address for the Juliet Club on the front. So, they really did reply. While searching online after my conversation with Rosanna, I'd discovered that the Juliet Club was founded in the 1990s.

For some reason, it suddenly struck me that I should write a letter to Juliet too. If nothing else, this might help me process my thoughts on how I felt about love, and whether I was ready to let someone new into my life. I felt a need to write about Ben – should I pursue anything with him? Was it too soon? I didn't want him to be a rebound guy – he was too good for that. I wondered if anyone from the Juliet Club would actually reply. I was curious to write a letter just to see if this was the case. I'd seen quite a few lovely-looking cafés in Piazza Erbe. This was the perfect opportunity to go and get a coffee and something to eat while I wrote my letter. I had a notebook and pen in my bag.

I left the tiny square, and found myself back on the main

street leading to Piazza Erbe, where I looked for a café that would be nice to sit in. I found one with tables outside, and heaters which meant I could keep warm, but still absorb the atmosphere of the square. A waiter showed me to one and handed me a menu. I ordered an espresso, and a tomato and mozzarella panino. He brought them over, and I gathered my thoughts before putting pen to paper. Then I wrote the first words that came into my head.

Dear Juliet,

Why am I writing to you? Because I'm going through a transition in my life. I recently turned thirty, a milestone and a time for re-evaluating everything. Society expects us to be married with children already or at least on the way. And if you haven't found your person, you're in dire straits because you're running out of time – the biological clock is ticking. I have been married, only for two years, and we split up a few months ago. We weren't right for each other, and I won't bore you with ALL the details, but we rushed into it. I tried to get pregnant, and it didn't happen for us. I might not ever be able to have children – it's highly unlikely – but there's a slim possibility if I find a man who is compatible with me.

So, Juliet, I'm sure you're wondering why I am writing to you. Firstly, because I love the idea of writing a letter to a group of wise women while staying in Verona – I'm staying on a beautiful vineyard, and I just love this city too. I wanted to know really if it's possible still for someone like me to find luck in love. My mother died a few years ago, and if she were alive I guess that I'd be asking her for advice. Since she's been gone, I've never known who to turn to when I needed help. I don't like to bother my friends too much, as they have their own stuff going on. Besides, my mother was so wise. She always knew what to say and would guide me along the right path without really telling me what to do. I don't think that I would have married Spencer if she'd still been alive.

And so, I need to tell you about someone. I've only met him a few times, but there's something about him that makes me feel so calm and still, and I can talk to him so easily, and he always knows what to say. He soothes me. But also, he is so handsome, and I can't help being attracted to him. We almost kissed before I came here, and I wonder if it might actually happen when I go back to England. He's been messaging me the whole time I've been away – and I've been sending him little updates with photos too.

I guess the question is, Juliet, should I go ahead and pursue anything with this man, so soon after leaving my husband? It was only three months ago, but I know it is DEFINITELY over, and that we shall never get back together (in the words of Taylor Swift... 'like ever'). If I enter into a relationship with this new man, what if I get my heart broken? I'm not sure that I can cope with that right now. I've already had a lot of things go wrong in my life recently, and this man breaking my heart might actually tip me over the edge! I don't know what to do, apart from go with the flow, and see what happens. Leave it to him perhaps? I am being presumptuous assuming he'd want anything to do with me anyway. Men are so good at pretending they're in love with you until you've slept together, and then they can cast you aside as if you never existed. If this man did that to me, my world would be shattered. I do feel that I can trust him, but still letting him properly into my life would be a BIG step.

Any thoughts would be greatly appreciated.

Yours,

Kate Clarkson

catherineclarkson@authorsocials.com

When I'd finished writing, I read back through my words. Some force inside of me was driving me to do this, but I wasn't sure where it was coming from. I'd felt a real urge to write it, and now I had to follow through with my plan and go and actually put it in the letter box – before I changed my mind. I tore the page out of my notebook, and folded it into four parts, and then I left some euro notes on the table to cover the bill and tip. I stood up, pushed my chair under the table, and made my way back to Casa Giulietta where I posted my letter in the special red letter box. There, it was done! And the whole act of writing it had made me feel so good – it was so cathartic. Would the Juliet Club reply? And if they did, when would it be, and what would they say? I was so curious to find out.

CHAPTER 37

KATE

On the drive back from Gatwick airport, I thought about all the things I needed to do. Apart from finding somewhere to live, I should go and see Granny, Ben and Dad. There was so much to think about – so much to say. But it could all wait until tomorrow. I would start with Granny, as I wanted to ask her about Bertie – but I needed to be careful, because I didn't want her to have another funny turn. How should I approach this? Should I speak to her carer, Jane, first? When I got home it was late, and I was tired. I went straight to bed, and, as I drifted off to sleep, I thought about Ben, and how desperately I wanted to see him again. I couldn't wait to find out what he thought of the bottle of sparkling Pinot Grigio I'd brought back for him, and hoped we'd drink it together.

The following afternoon, I went to see Granny. I'd called ahead and spoken to Jane, who said I could go round for a cup of tea. Afterwards, I hoped to drop in on Ben. As I drove along the narrow lane, I thought back to when Granny had given me the bottle of Amarone 1936. That day, she'd set wheels in motion that had brought about a huge change in my life in a matter of weeks – just with that one curious item. Bumping into

Ben after leaving her cottage had been only the beginning. Oh, how I'd enjoyed getting to know him during those long, slow evenings by his fire with glasses of wine. And then when I'd checked the Vineria di San Martino website, to see if I could find out more about the vineyard and the bottle of Amarone 1936, I'd come across the information about the sparkling Pinot Grigio, and that had given me an idea for our vineyard. And when Ben told me about the problems Copeley Park was having, I'd mulled over the idea of approaching Dad with my marketing ideas. On top of all that was my discovery of a romance between Granny and Bertie. But what had happened to him? I wanted to know everything, and hoped she'd be able to tell me without getting upset again. Would she even be willing to divulge the full story? I couldn't rest properly until I knew everything.

I pulled up outside Keeper's Cottage, got out and rapped the door knocker. Jane answered and let me inside.

'How is she today?' I asked.

'She's fine,' Jane said.

'I'm hoping to talk to her about something, and I hope that she doesn't find it too upsetting.'

'Go slowly and see how she is. If she seems to be getting upset, then I would stop,' Jane said.

She showed me into the drawing room. Granny sat in a chair by the fire, wearing a lemon-yellow dress and a cream cardigan, accessorised with a sapphire pendant.

'Kate,' she said, brightly.

'Hello, Granny.'

I bent down and kissed her on the cheek. She patted my arm.

'How was Verona?' she said.

'It was so perfect,' I said. 'I can see why you loved the vineyard so much.'

'Why don't you sit down. Jane will bring us some tea.'

I took the chair opposite, and Jane brought in a tray and put it on the coffee table between us.

'You pour, dear,' Granny said.

I did as she instructed, filling the pretty cups with pink and white flower patterns on them.

'So, I found out something interesting in Verona.'

'Oh, did you?'

'Now you must tell me if any of this is upsetting for you, and of course, I shall stop…'

She hesitated, but then said, 'I'm feeling much better today than last time, so let's see how you go.'

'I discovered who "B" is from the note that came with the bottle of Amarone you gave to me that day.'

Her eyes widened. 'So… you know about Bertie?'

I nodded and she drew in a sharp breath.

'Ah, how I loved him,' she said, her voice breaking.

'What happened to him?' I asked, surprised she'd told me that so easily.

Her eyes welled with tears.

'He died.'

'When, how?'

'During the war, only weeks after he left.'

'Oh, I'm so sorry, Granny.'

'Bertie was the only man I ever truly loved, and it was a love one dreams of. So pure, so simple. It's difficult to explain. When we were together, I felt that I was the version of myself I wanted to be. No one else had ever made me feel like that before.'

Poor Granny, losing him like that. She must have been through such an ordeal. I couldn't imagine how hard those years must have been for her. The way she talked about Bertie was how I felt about Ben. Maybe I should tell him about my feelings, or at least try to drop some hints? I considered myself lucky that he was actually still here and didn't have to go off and fight in a war.

'So, you and Bertie were together after my great-grandfather, Winston, died?'

She nodded.

'Yes. He was kind to me after Winston's tragic demise. It was a shock for all of us when he fell down the stairs, as you might imagine.'

I knew how Winston had met his end from the book that Dad had given to me. No one had ever mentioned it before – we just knew he'd died before my grandpa, Angus, was born.

She looked at me over her glasses. 'And tell me, did you find love in Verona, Kate?'

I laughed. 'What do you mean?'

'Well, that's where Bertie and I fell in love. And it's the city of Romeo and Juliet, after all. I hoped it might inspire you, and bring the right kind of love into your life like it did for me. Have you been reading my copy of the play?'

'Yes, I took it with me, in fact.'

'Good girl.'

'I also discovered something else, Granny. When I was at the vineyard I came across your letter to Juliet.'

'Really? So, Agnes didn't take it to the tomb then, as promised?'

I shook my head.

'Unfortunately not. She did say in her diary that she intended to do that though.'

'Apparently a man – I can't recall his name – would reply to any letters written to Juliet and left by a tomb in a church.'

'Oh, I see.' I shrugged. 'Agnes put the letter in a drawer in her office at Villa Romeo to keep it safe. Then I guess she forgot all about it.'

'My letter to Juliet has been in that drawer all of that time?'

'Yes, isn't that unbelievable? Granny... why didn't you tell us about Bertie before?'

She looked away, unable to meet my eye. 'I didn't feel the need to.'

I wanted to know so much more about their romance, and I sensed that Granny was leaving something out – why had she never told us about him? Perhaps if I visited again soon, she might tell me more.

'He lived at Rosemary Cottage, you know.'

It was quite strange that Ben was living there too. I was falling in love with the head gardener just as Granny had done. History was actually repeating itself. Although I did hope that Ben wouldn't go off and get himself killed in a war as Bertie had done.

'Oh, did he really?'

'I understand from your father that you have met Ben?' she said, as if reading my thoughts.

'Yes.' My cheeks warmed, and I hoped that it wasn't obvious. I told her how he'd helped change my tyre when I drove into a pothole after leaving her cottage last time. I left out the part about how I'd ended up in the pothole, as I didn't want to get him into any trouble.

'Well, as I said before, I do think that he's a nice young man, and if nothing else he would make a good friend for you.'

'Thanks, Granny. We have actually spent a bit of time together.'

She clapped her hands, her eyes shining. Granny was such a sneaky matchmaker. 'Well, isn't that just lovely. And your father told me you went to see him too?'

'I did.'

'So, we'll be spending Christmas Day as a family then, with Emilie as well, at the house?'

Nodding, I said, 'Yes, as long as he'll have me.'

'He'll be thrilled to have you there – I am certain of that. And I'm proud of you for swallowing your pride and going to see your father. Well done, Kate.'

It made me so happy that Granny was proud of me – her approval meant so much.

'Thanks, Granny. I'm glad I went. I just need to find a way to accept Emilie now, and the new baby.'

'Oh yes, the baby. That must have been difficult news for you to receive. I'm glad he's told you – I know he was worried about it.'

So Granny had known then. I guessed that was understandable – perhaps Dad had asked for her advice on how he should go about telling me, seeing as they were quite close. Maybe she'd sent me to Verona because she was trying to set me on my own path, so that Dad and Emilie's news didn't impact me too much. I wasn't going to bother her with the minor detail of how I'd found out via Emilie's Instagram post. But it was comforting to know that Dad had actually cared about my reaction to his news.

'I'm sure that I'll find a way to get my head round it,' I said.

'You must, for your own good. It's never a good idea to hold on to negative emotions – I should know. Try to forgive your father and accept this new life he's embarking on.'

Nodding, I said, 'I know, you're so right.'

Jane came into the room. 'How is everything?'

'Good,' I said.

'We've had a lovely chat,' Granny said.

'It's time to check your blood pressure now,' Jane said. 'You're welcome to stay for longer, Kate, if you want to...'

'I'd better get going anyway, I do actually need to be somewhere,' I said.

I got up and kissed Granny on the cheek, and she said, 'Thank you for coming, Kate. And for telling me what you found – it's so nice to speak about Bertie again, no matter how painful.'

We said our goodbyes, and I saw from the time on my phone that Ben would have probably finished work for the day. I'd put the bottle of sparkling Pinot Grigio in the boot, in case I felt like swinging by Rosemary Cottage after seeing Granny. And yes, I was feeling brave enough to drop in unannounced – for I was so excited to see him again, especially after all our message exchanges in Verona. Perhaps he'd invite me inside and I could tell him about my conversation with Granny. I couldn't wait to see him and loved the thought of being in his cosy cottage and sitting beside his fireplace and talking again.

When I pulled into his drive, there was another car parked beside his Land Rover. Ah, his sister, Lily, must be visiting again. So, I'd just drop off the wine and go. Maybe I could come back and talk to him tomorrow. I parked, walked up to the front door and knocked.

Footsteps came, and he opened it and there he was. He was wearing his Copeley Park fleece and khaki trousers, and he was just as handsome as I remembered him to be. His stubble was just the right length, and when those misty-blue eyes met mine, I almost crumbled. But the serious look on his face said it all. He wasn't as pleased to see me as I was him.

'Hi, Ben... I see your sister's car is here, so I wanted to give you something while I was in the area. I just went to see my—'

He scratched his nose.

'That isn't my sister's car,' he said.

It had been dark when his sister had visited before, and I hadn't noticed whether it was the same car. I'd just assumed it was hers. What a stupid assumption to make. I slid my hands into the back pockets of my jeans, not knowing what to say.

'You should have messaged,' Ben said.

'Oh, I'm sorry. I just thought I'd drop in after visiting Granny with something I brought back from Verona for you.'

I handed him the bottle of sparkling Pinot Grigio, and he took it, without looking at the label. Did he know what this was? The wine I'd brought back from Verona especially for him. Didn't he even care?

I opened my mouth to explain what it was, but was interrupted by a female voice coming from inside the cottage.

'Ben, who is it?'

Oh. I bit my lip.

'I'd better go.,' I turned round and walked back down the garden path.

'Wait! Kate,' he called after me.

How could I have been such a fool?

CHAPTER 38

KATE

As Ben shouted after me, I stopped walking and turned around. He was coming down the path towards me, his boots crunching on the gravel.

'Sorry, Kate. It's just I wasn't expecting you to turn up out of the blue like this. She's my—'

'Girlfriend? It's fine, Ben. You are allowed to have a girlfriend.'

'She's my ex, Fi. I think I mentioned her once.'

'Ah yes, didn't you say she was the only girl you'd ever loved and could imagine seeing a future with?'

But hadn't Fiona left him for a much older man with money who ran his own property company and lived in a mansion in a charming village just outside of Godalming? Hadn't she thought she was too good to be with a head gardener? I saw him doing something he enjoyed for a living while earning enough money to live on as a real achievement. Wasn't that what everyone wanted, deep down?

He inhaled and scratched his head.

'While you were in Verona, she messaged and asked to come over to talk – she's recently split up with her boyfriend.

We had a drink the other night, and she came back – she really likes the cottage...'

Of course she did, who wouldn't?

I forced a smile, and, goodness me, it was hard, but this had to be done, for my own pride more than anything else. What had I been thinking, getting all carried away like that in Verona? Writing a letter to Juliet, a woman who hadn't ever existed – who was only a fictional character from a play who ended up dead in the end – it wasn't even a real love story. It was a tragedy. And I'd asked this non-existent Juliet about Ben, for goodness' sake! How could I have been so naive? I guessed that because he'd paid me some attention, and was nice to be with, as well as rather good-looking, and I loved his cottage, I'd been taken in by all of it. But now reality was rising up and hitting me right in the face. Ben and I had no future, that was very clear to me as I stood there on his garden path in the dark. This wasn't history repeating itself after all, it was just me being a hopeless romantic...

'Well, that's great. I'm happy for you.'

The garden was so dimly lit, and it was difficult to have a proper conversation like this. Although what else was there to say?

Ben looked down at me.

'Thanks for the wine. That was really nice of you to think of me like that.'

'It's the sparkling Pinot Grigio from the vineyard in Verona. I only got it for selfish reasons,' I lied. 'Because I wanted you to try it and see what you thought... ask if you'd be interested in helping me persuade Dad to produce it here. I'm hoping to pull together a plan before Christmas Day, when I might catch him in a good mood and get him to agree to it.'

Now I was covering myself by pretending it was all about the business side of things, not that I might have been in love with him. He swallowed, his face all serious. What had happened to the previous version of Ben? It was as if he'd never existed.

'Of course. I shall let you know,' he said, quietly.

'Good. Thanks,' I said, curtly.

I turned my back on him, approached my car and got inside. Starting the engine, I watched him walk back up the path. He reached the porch, then he stopped and turned round to look over at me. And then he went inside.

Damn. I backed out of the drive. If I hadn't gone to Verona, Fiona wouldn't have had her window. How could I have allowed this to happen? Never mind. The most important thing was that he liked the wine and would agree to help me persuade Dad to produce it. That was really all that should matter. Although I couldn't bear the thought of him drinking it with Fiona – I'd hoped that *we* would try it together.

When I got back to the flat, I was tired out. Sophie was still at work, and I was glad to have the place to myself. We hadn't seen each other since I'd returned from Verona, and I couldn't be bothered to make small talk. Our friendship wasn't at its best since she'd asked me to move out. I still needed to find somewhere and would have to deal with that soon. Once I would have wanted to talk to her about Ben, and tell her every last detail from Verona – finding out about Bertie, Granny's letter to Juliet and Agnes's diary entries. My excitement about making the sparkling Pinot Grigio. But I wasn't sure she was that bothered about my life any more.

I went into my room and changed into trackie bs and a sweatshirt, then made a cup of tea and grabbed a couple of chocolate digestives from the biscuit tin before sinking into the sofa. I pointed the remote at the TV, selected *Friends* – always trusted companions, and my comfort show – and put it on mute so they could keep me company while I scrolled my phone, looking at my photos from Verona. They were lovely and were getting lots of likes and comments.

A message flashed up from Ben and my heart raced.

Sorry about earlier. I didn't expect you to turn up like that. I'll let you know about the PG.

Okay, thanks 😊

What else was there to say? The formality of his message, along with the full stop, after all the friendly exchanges we'd had while I was in Verona, said it all. I didn't want to get into another discussion about Fiona. He'd made his choice.

But then WhatsApp showed he was typing something else, and I waited for a minute or two while he was probably working out what to say. And then another message came:

Nothing is going on with Fi btw. She just needs a friend right now

I wasn't sure whether to believe him or not. Wasn't this what he'd say if he was seeing her again? All I could think about was that look on his face when he opened the door and saw me standing there. I'd been so excited about seeing him again, and spending more time at his cottage. But he'd left me feeling deflated and sad. I didn't reply, as I wasn't sure what to say.

Ben and I stopped messaging each other after that dreadful day. I could only assume he'd started seeing Fiona again. If they were together, he probably didn't feel able to invite me over, seeing as we'd almost kissed that night when I stayed. He was being loyal to his girlfriend, and that was fair enough. But how I missed him and how I missed his cottage. It was odd that Granny had fallen in love with a man who was employed in the same position decades earlier, and he'd been living at that cottage too. Had she spent a cosy evening there by the fire with a glass of wine, as I had – while looking across at him in the chair opposite as they talked and talked, never running out of interesting things to say to each other?

The weeks passed and December came, that stressful time in the run-up to Christmas where work requests would come in asking if they could be done before the end of the year. Old friends popped up out of the blue asking to meet for Christmas drinks. Why did this time of year always have to be so intense? I had some client work to do, but also, on the side, I started to draft ideas to run past Dad. On Christmas Day I would take along the bottle of sparkling Pinot Grigio I'd brought back from Verona for him.

This could be my last Christmas with Granny, and I wanted to spend as much time with her as I could. And I needed to try to embrace the idea of Emilie being in our lives, and get to know her. This would be good for all of us. I'd done some serious thinking about Emilie's pregnancy, trying to get my head round the fact that I was going to have a half-brother or half-sister in the spring. It was especially hard, not only to see Dad doing this, and with a woman only five years older than me, but also when I couldn't. And then what if he had a boy? Currently, Dad was an earl, and he'd inherited that title from his father, Angus, who'd inherited it from his father, Winston. There was no male heir. Mum had been advised against having any more children after me as her pregnancy had not gone well, and I'd been born a few weeks early. If Dad had a son, he would eventually inherit Dad's title and the estate. This was because of primogeniture – the title would go to the first male born, not the eldest child. How unfair was that? It was my home, and I wanted to put so much work into it. All I could do was hope that Dad had a girl rather than a boy, but I guessed we'd need to wait until spring to find out.

With everything going on in December, I didn't have chance to find anywhere else to live. Could I face going through the ordeal of flat-hunting again? I'd spent a lot of time doing it in my early twenties, and I felt that I'd grown out of that phase. I wanted to live on my own, but couldn't afford to in London. Perhaps I should ask Dad if I could live at home until I found somewhere. Now we were talking again, living at home didn't seem as big a deal as before. This would buy me some time. I had been mulling over returning to Verona in March to help out with the tours. I would have liked to ask Ben to go with me, but couldn't see how that was going to happen now. Even if he liked the bottle of sparkling Pinot Grigio I'd brought him, he might say that he didn't need to visit the vineyard. He could find out what he needed to know here. Part of me had wanted to use going to Verona as an excuse to spend time together. I would have loved to show him the place that had blown me away, and see it all again through his eyes. I knew he'd love it there too.

I'd forgotten all about my letter sent to Juliet, until one morning when an email popped into my inbox.

> Dear Kate,
>
> Thank you for your letter. I am sorry that you have been going through such a difficult time.
> It is always possible to find luck in love if you want to. You just have to open your heart and let the right person in. It sounds as though you might have found him already. If he is

meant for you, it will happen, I am sure. Just follow your heart rather than your head.

Yours,

Juliet

Little did Juliet know that the man I'd been talking about in my letter was now potentially seeing someone else. Never mind. I moved the email into my trash folder. Writing the letter had been a nice idea, and I'd enjoyed time spent in that lovely café with the coffee and panino. I was grateful to the Juliet Club for taking the time to reply, but Juliet sadly had got it all wrong. Ben and I were never going to be together now, and I needed to forget all about him.

But then one evening, when I was sitting on the sofa eating beans on toast, a message popped up on my phone. *Ben*. It was mid-December and I hadn't heard from him since that night I'd dropped in unannounced.

Hi, how's it going?

Good. How about you?

I was thinking... I haven't opened the sparkling Pinot Grigio yet. Do you fancy coming over and trying it with me on Friday night? I can get pizza

A warm feeling enveloped me. He hadn't opened it yet! This made me so happy. He wanted to share it with me. And he was inviting me back to the cottage that I loved. But was he seeing Fiona? I had to ask, although it was awkward. Drawing in my breath, I typed...

That would be good... but are you seeing Fiona tho?

The three dots danced for what seemed like ages while I waited for his reply.

No. I told you before... she just wanted to talk. I would never have gone back there, especially as I like someone else

Did he mean me?
I smiled to myself.

Okay

Great! Come over any time after six. And feel free to stay again if easier

I sent a smiley face in reply. I'd been slightly standoffish as I should be, but my day was made, and I couldn't wait to see him again.

CHAPTER 39

KATE

The next evening, I drove over to Rosemary Cottage with my holdall in the boot. As well as overnight things, I'd brought a few snacks – posh crisps, olives, cheese and some fancy crackers from Christina's, a deli in Southfields. Ben opened the door, and he was wearing a pale-blue shirt to match his eyes – he looked so gorgeous. He grinned from ear to ear as he stood there, and a flutter occurred somewhere deep inside of me. Damn, it was good to see him.

'Hi Kate. Come on in,' he said.

He led me into the living room, where a fire was already roaring in the hearth. Tea lights glowed along the mantelpiece, their tiny flames flickering, and the room was dimly lit. Ben knew how to create an ambience, and it was all so cosy and rustic. I'd missed this charming cottage almost as much as him. A speaker on the sideboard played Bing Crosby singing, 'White Christmas', and in the corner a tall, bushy Christmas tree was decorated with silver baubles and white fairy lights. I'd walked into a Hallmark movie. All that needed to happen now was for Ben to put on a red-and-white lumberjack shirt and go outside and chop some wood. And then he'd come back inside all sweaty and take the shirt off and wipe his forehead with it – before taking me in his arms. I chuckled to myself at this vision.

'I can't wait to have a drink. It's pruning season and we've been short-staffed. It's back-breaking work and I just had a long hot bath.'

What was he trying to do to me? Now I found myself picturing him naked in a bath, his gorgeous body immersed in bubbles. He had a broad chest, and I imagined his biceps were bulging underneath his shirt. My face warmed as my imagination worked its way down through the rest of him. All that physical work he did probably meant he was exceptionally toned.

'Still, the pruning has to be done. Another month and we'll be almost finished. Do you like the tree?' Ben said.

'Yes, it's really pretty.'

'Your dad said I could help myself to one from the estate, and so I chopped it down myself, with help from a colleague.'

Could he *be* any more masculine?

'I'll plant it in the garden after Christmas and reuse it next year.'

I nodded, impressed that he was thinking of the environment.

'So, your sparkling Pinot Grigio has been chilling in the fridge. Shall I open it?' he said.

'Definitely.'

Ben went to get the bottle. The cork popped as he expertly removed it, and then filled two flutes, the bubbles racing to the top. He handed one of the flutes to me. We said, 'Cheers', clinked our flutes, and locked eyes – oh it was good to see those misty-blue eyes looking into mine again – and drank.

He tipped his head to the side as if in deep thought. 'Hmm, it has notes of peach and citrus, maybe green apple... I like it.'

I beamed.

'Oh phew, what a relief.'

He drank some more and then stroked his chin. 'I like how

zesty it is. It's light, crisp, refreshing. I can see this flying off the shelves if we get it right.'

'Do you think that's possible?'

'Yes, I really do. This could be your answer to saving the vineyard,' he said.

'So, I just have to persuade Dad. I also have a few ideas relating to events and marketing.'

'Are you still planning to speak to him on Christmas Day?'

'Yes, I brought back another bottle for him to try.'

'Sounds like a good plan.'

I so wanted to ask Ben if anything had happened with Fiona, but how could I? All I could do was hope that he was telling me the truth about her. I sipped my drink, and he refilled our glasses. It was going down nicely, taking the edge off the day.

'How will you be spending Christmas Day?' I said.

'Err... with my family. They live in Gatley, a village down the road. Do you know it?'

'Oh yes! Well, I know Gatley Hall. I've got Association of Treasured Properties membership, and sometimes go there for walks,' I said.

'I'll go there for lunch and come back in the afternoon.'

So, he'd be on his own in the evening on Christmas Day, and I'd be staying overnight at the house, only a stone's throw away, so I could drink. Hmm. If I wasn't careful, I might find myself getting plastered and wandering over to his cottage.

'I was thinking...' he said, before taking a sip of the wine. 'Well, I actually wondered what you might be doing on New Year's Eve. I'm sure you've already made plans...'

All my friends were coupled up, and I'd been invited to parties where I would be the only single woman there. I had declined them all. But here was a chance to see in the new year with Ben. How could I say no?

'I'd love to,' I said.

His eyes lit up.

'What, you'd like to spend New Year's Eve with me?'

'Yes, I would like that very much.'

'Great! What should we do?'

'I could come here? Maybe bring a few picky bits with me or something.'

'That sounds great. Okay, if you do that, leave getting the fizz to me.'

'Sounds like a plan.'

'And you can stay of course, if you'd like to.'

I smiled, glad that I now had something to do on New Year's Eve – and hopeful for what it could mean. Sophie and Charlie had planned to have a night in and that would have been awkward if I had to hang out with them. I would write 'Ben' next to 31 December in my diary as soon as I got home, grinning to myself as I did so.

'What happened with Fiona?' I blurted out. Damn. A few sips of alcohol and a New Year's Eve invitation, and there was no stopping me. Although I did need to know the truth before anything could happen between Ben and me.

He cast me a serious look. 'I really did mean it when I said she just needed a friend that night.'

I wanted to believe him, but what if he was just spinning me a story?

'Are you sure?' I couldn't help asking.

'Of course I'm sure. She'd been crying when you showed up – it wouldn't have been fair on her to invite you in.'

Nodding, I said, 'Okay.'

'Anyway, you have nothing to worry about... she got back with her boyfriend, and I understand there's now a wedding proposal on the table.'

This seemed like good news for me as surely there was no way he'd go back to her now. They were totally done. 'And that's what she wants?'

He sighed. 'Yes, she wants to be married to a man who already has everything set up. I'm just a simple guy, no frills. What you see is what you get. Obviously, it would be nice to have a bit of money, but I don't need a big fancy house or expensive clothes. I get a lot of my stuff second hand, and it's better for the environment that way too.'

'That's true.'

'But also, we weren't right for each other. Fi and I never had much to talk about... not like... us.'

My heart fizzed in reaction to the way he said 'us' as he looked over at me and took a sip of his drink. He held my gaze for longer than you would with a friend. There were no words to say – he'd basically just implied that he really did like me in a romantic way.

Ben got up and went into the kitchen, returning with the wine bottle and a bowl of the posh crisps I'd brought. He refilled our glasses.

'How did that visit go with your granny after getting back from Verona?'

I leant forwards to grab a handful of crisps and told him what we'd talked about.

'Crikey, it's amazing to think that your great-grandmother had an affair with the gardener who lived here.'

'I wouldn't call it an affair. They went to Verona together after my great-grandfather died, to visit her cousin and bring back some vine cuttings.'

'But isn't that strange that she was in love with the man who lived here, and now here you are all these years later, sitting with me drinking wine?'

'I know, it is rather strange,' I said, without adding that I might actually be in love with the man who now lived here.

And then – my confidence boosted by the way our conversation had been going – I made a bold move. It was now or never.

'So, now I know you like the sparkling Pinot Grigio, would

you maybe want to come to the vineyard in Verona with me in March? They could show you how they make it, if you wanted? I would so love for you to see the place – it's breathtaking.'

'I like the idea, but would have to get the time off, obviously. Is it expensive to fly out there?'

'I don't think the flights will cost much out of season. And accommodation would be free.'

'Thank you for asking... can I think about it?'

'Sure. I'll probably go back in March myself to do holiday cover for the tours.'

'Have you found anywhere to live yet?' he said.

'I might ask Dad if I can move my stuff back home for now. I'm not sure I can go back to sharing with random strangers like I did in my early twenties. I do feel ready to live on my own, but I'm not sure how I'd afford that.'

'Well, it will give you some breathing space, at least. And you can drop in and see me after work.'

'And we can drink wine and eat crisps.' I laughed.

The evening flew by and, like before, I followed Ben up the stairs when it was time for bed. And we stood on the landing, and once again he gave me that intense look, and as he moved towards me, I wasn't sure if he was going for a kiss on the cheek or on the lips. I didn't want to make a fool of myself, so I turned my face to the side, and he kissed my cheek gently, lingering there for longer than someone usually would. My whole body tingled and ached for him. How I wanted him to take my hand and lead me into his room, to peel off my clothes and lie me down on his bed. But it was too soon for any of that – I didn't want to rush things.

And then he stepped back, and breathed in, looking at me as he touched the handle of his bedroom door. Those misty-blue eyes were saying, 'Come to bed, Kate...' I felt sure they were, but I wasn't ready for that... not quite yet.

'Goodnight, Kate.'

'Goodnight, Ben.'

We went into our separate rooms and, once again, I leant on the door like some heroine in an old black-and-white film. If it was going to happen, it would happen, when the time was right. I was sure of that.

CHAPTER 40

KATE

On Christmas Day I drove over to Copeley Park, with all kinds of feelings brewing up inside of me. I was running a bit late because I'd been dithering over what to wear, in case I was able to drop in on Ben after lunch – in the end, I'd settled on jeans and a fitted cream jumper. It was one of those days of the year that always brought emotions to the surface, and I wasn't looking forward to being around Emilie, despite my good intentions to try harder to accept her into the family. Sophie and Charlie had gone to her parents' house in Shropshire the night before, and so I'd had the flat to myself that morning. It was unusually peaceful and quiet, but also an odd feeling waking up on Christmas morning all alone. An upside of staying at the house that night would be that I could drink as much wine as I wanted. Besides, it would be strange going back to an empty flat and spending the evening on my own too.

Ben and I had been messaging daily ever since the drinks at his cottage a couple of weeks earlier. He would send me little updates about his day, and I did the same. For the first time in a while, I felt as though someone was properly there for me, and this filled me with a warm feeling. We'd both been too busy to meet again until now, but we were booked in to see each other on New Year's Eve. I'd been mulling over whether to dress up – should I wear a sexy dress? That would almost certainly do the trick if I wanted him to kiss me, but it was probably a bit over the top for Rosemary Cottage. The evening was bound to provide the perfect opportunity at midnight when we'd be forced to acknowledge the new year in some way. Was I ready to kiss someone new? Was he? All I did know for certain was that I liked being with Ben in his cosy little cottage, by a roaring fire and with a glass of wine in my hand. I'd brought him a present that I hoped to drop off later, or on Boxing Day on my way back to Southfields – it was a cheeseboard, made from oak that I'd found in a little farm shop just outside of Gatley.

I parked outside the front of the house, and got my holdall, bag of presents and the bottle of sparkling Pinot Grigio for Dad out of the boot. Jenkins opened the front door as soon as I approached the steps, and I went inside. He took my holdall and coat and went to put them in the cloakroom. The huge Christmas tree in the grand hall was so impressive, rising up beside the sweeping staircase. Dad always went to a lot of effort to find the right one. I placed my presents underneath, next to those that were already there. The decorations hanging off the branches had been collected by my family over the years. Studying them, I spotted reminders of my childhood – the bright-red pompom Santa Claus I'd made with Mum using a cardboard disc and wool. And there was the cute little penguin we'd painted together at a pottery studio in Gatley. Taking the penguin in my hand, I blinked back tears, telling myself to be strong. Today would be hard, but I needed to do my best to make it a success, for Granny's sake if nothing else. It could be her last Christmas with us, after all.

I handed the bottle of wine to Jenkins.

'Would you mind sticking this in the fridge for later, Jenkins?'

'Certainly, ma'am.'

He led me into the blue drawing room, and there they all were – Dad, Emilie and Granny, all sitting on the yellow velvet sofas in front of the fireplace, holding crystal flutes, and there was a plate of blinis with crème fraiche and smoked salmon on the coffee table. Dean Martin sang 'Winter Wonderland' from the speakers in the corners of the room. Dad liked his vinyl and still listened to his record player.

'Kate!' Dad said, his eyes lighting up.

'Hello everyone, Merry Christmas,' I said.

He stood up and came over, and kissed me on the cheek, then pulled me into a big hug.

Then Emilie hoisted herself up, slowly because her baby bump was big. The rest of her remained fairly slim though, meaning the baby stuck out in front of her like a football. There was no avoiding the reality of her being pregnant with my father's child now. I swallowed.

'Happy Christmas, Kate,' she said in her French accent.

'Hi Emilie. Congratulations.'

She ran a manicured hand over her bump, proudly, and smiled, then double kissed me French style.

'Don't get up, Granny,' I said, leaning over to kiss her on the cheek.

She squeezed my hand, weakly. 'Hello, dear Kate.' And then she whispered in my ear, 'Thank you for coming.'

We exchanged smiles, and I was glad to have done the right thing, even though I couldn't wait to get the day over with.

Jenkins appeared with a flute fizzing with champagne on a tray, and I thanked him as I took it. Just what I needed. I took a gulp rather than a sip, and the bubbles fizzed up my nose. Then I sat down next to Granny, opposite Dad and Emilie.

'How was Verona, Kate?' Dad said, brightly.

'It was lovely. The vineyard that Granny went to is so enchanting. And the wine they make there is out of this world.'

'Did you find out who "B" from the note was?' he said.

Clearly he'd remembered me mentioning the note when I visited him that time in the library before finding out about Bertie. It wasn't my place to tell him, though. Granny went very pale. Did she not want him to know? I couldn't bear to see her get upset again.

Thankfully, we were both saved by Jenkins, who came into the room and announced, 'Lunch is served, sir.'

'Thank you, Jenkins,' Dad said, gesturing for us all to move.

We got up and made our way to the dining room. I took my glass of champagne and sipped it en route, hoping that the meal would be less tense. The dining room looked lovely, with a Christmas tree in the corner, fairy lights twinkling. There were portraits of our ancestors on the crimson walls all around us, painted by Reynolds, Gainsborough and Raeburn. And I believed that actual kings and queens had sat in this very room. We all took our places – Jenkins had put out name cards directing us where to sit. Dad and Emilie were at the head and foot of the table, and Granny and I sat in between them, opposite each other. I couldn't help resenting Emilie for sitting in Mum's place, but swiftly told myself that five years had passed and it was time for me to grow up.

Jenkins came and filled one of our glasses with wine from the Copeley vineyard. I wanted to mention the sparkling Pinot Grigio I'd brought from Verona, but the moment for drinking anything fizzy had passed. We could always try it on Boxing Day, I guessed.

'I remember...' Granny said, unfolding her napkin. '... a dinner in this very room with fascists –' she spat out the word. 'Oswald Mosley himself sat over there, slightly to your left, Kate. Would you believe that most of the guests were Nazi sympathisers?'

'What? I had no idea,' Dad said.

'Winston did not keep the best company...'

'You've never mentioned that before, Granny,' he said.

'Antisemites they were. When I heard someone utter the words, "Damn Jew", I had to say something – my father was Jewish, you know.'

We did know this – he was the son of an immigrant from Poland, and he'd done very well for himself, owning a successful railway company. But also, he'd lost aunts, uncles and cousins in Poland during the Holocaust, and Granny had mentioned this before.

Jenkins brought in our main courses – plates filled with slices of turkey, roast potatoes, parsnips, carrots, stuffing balls and sausages wrapped in bacon. Yum, I couldn't wait to get stuck in.

I spooned cranberry sauce onto my plate.

'This looks delicious,' I said.

'I hear you've been spending more time with Ben,' Dad said.

'Yes, who told you that?'

'I did,' Granny said, her eyes shining. 'He's a lovely young man.'

'Yes, he is, but I do think Kate could be aiming a bit higher,' Dad said.

I couldn't believe that Dad was bringing this up again.

'Firstly, we're just friends, and secondly, Dad, why do you keep saying this?'

'Speaking as the man who pays his salary, he doesn't earn that much.'

'And?'

'You deserve to be with someone who can support you financially.'

Dad's comments were making me breathless, and he was adding to the pile of negative feelings I was having to deal with already. How could he speak about Ben like this, at the dining-room table, and in front of Emilie? When I looked over, I saw her eyes were glued to her plate as she picked at the food on it with her fork. At least she had the good grace not to stick her oar in.

Changing the subject, I said, 'When I was in Verona, I saw that they make a sparkling Pinot Grigio—'

'Yes, Kate, you mentioned it before,' Dad said, rolling his eyes with a smile.

'And I brought you a bottle to try – Jenkins has put it in the fridge. I really think we could produce it here at Copeley Park, and it's got potential to sell very well. Ben thinks it would fly off the shelves.'

Dad wiped his mouth with his napkin. 'Does he now?'

I didn't want to get Ben into any trouble with Dad – that wasn't my intention, at all.

'He's not trying to interfere. I took a bottle over there and asked his opinion. Please don't say anything to him, Dad.'

He nodded and shrugged. 'Okay.'

The room fell silent as we all ate our Christmas lunch, our knives and forks scraping the plates. Picking up my glass, I drank the wine a little too voraciously, and Jenkins came over and refilled my glass. The only way to get through this lunch would be to drink my way through it.

When we'd all finished, Jenkins cleared our plates and there was a break. Emilie told us about her family, who lived in Bordeaux. She and Dad would be visiting them the day after Boxing Day. They'd usually go to Val-d'Isère after Christmas, but Emilie wasn't able to ski while she was pregnant, so they'd go on to Dad's villa in St Tropez instead.

'Isn't it time to sell that villa?' Granny said.

'What do you mean?' Dad said.

'Well, then you could put the money into Copeley Park, especially with all the problems you seem to be having,' she said.

'I treasure that villa – it's brought me so much happiness over the past few years – I won't live without it,' Dad said.

'Kate thinks there might be a saboteur in our midst,' Granny said.

'Yes, she's mentioned that to me before.' He shook his head. 'I've never heard anything so ridiculous.'

'Well... it's just a theory Ben and I came up with when we were talking about all the things that have been going wrong on the vineyard recently.'

'Ben's name seems to be coming up quite a lot at my Christmas lunch,' Dad said.

'Okay, but as I mentioned before, what if Grandpa's cousin, Jack, had sent someone here to work for you, who was not only spying but trying to jeopardise the business so he can swoop in and buy it?'

'And once again, that's an interesting theory, Kate, but everyone who comes to work for me is vetted very carefully.'

I shrugged. But what if Dad was wrong? Was he really going to let years of hard work slip through his fingers?

Jenkins brought in the Christmas pudding on a trolley and poured brandy over it and made a big show of setting light to it, before serving us portions in bowls. I thought back to when we'd all been eating Christmas pudding the previous year – when Dad told us he'd proposed to Emilie. They still weren't married, and I assumed they'd tie the knot after the baby was born. I didn't really want to be invited, and hoped they'd go away somewhere and do it privately with a couple of witnesses. That would make it easier for everyone.

I picked up the jug of custard and poured some onto my pudding.

'Are you going to put us all out of our misery and reveal who "B" is, Granny?' Dad said. So, he wasn't going to let it go then.

Granny had been knocking back the wine throughout our meal, and I expected Dad had noticed this – now was his chance to find out.

'"B" stands for Bertie, which is short for Albert,' Granny said.

'And he was the head gardener?' Dad said.

She nodded.

'So... what? You had a liaison with him, and went to the vineyard in Verona together, and then he died in the war?'

'Yes,' Granny whispered.

'I'm sorry,' Dad said.

'You do look very much like him, Hugo – both you and Kate have his green eyes. And you have his spirit too.'

A heavy pause fell upon the room, and I gasped.

'What?' Dad sat up straight in his chair. 'Why would I look like him?'

This was a turn-up for the books. What was Granny implying?

'Well, why wouldn't you?' she said, the lines in her forehead deepening. 'He was your grandfather, after all.'

Dad scrunched up his napkin and threw it down on the table.

'Are you serious?'

'Quite serious. Though I didn't mean for you to find out this way.'

'So, I'm not an earl, and Papa wasn't an earl either?'

'No, neither you nor Angus were supposed to be earls. But I had to act as though your father was Winston's son. I didn't want everyone to think Angus was illegitimate. There were a few weeks in it, but somehow nobody noticed – or if they did, they kept quiet about it – and I managed to get away with keeping my secret.'

Dad took a big sip of his wine.

'So, what you're saying is that I'm not related to any of these damn people on the wall?' He pointed to all the portraits of the men who were supposedly our ancestors.

'I'm afraid not, dear,' Granny said quietly, her hand shaking slightly as she rested it on the table.

He stood up, shaking his head. 'I need to go outside and get some fresh air. This is a lot to take in. Somehow, I'm hoping that you've just had too much wine and got a little confused, Granny.'

We all knew that Dad going outside to get fresh air meant he'd be having a cigar on the terrace.

'It is the truth, and I'm sorry,' Granny said.

Dad left the room, and Emilie cast us a nod, unsmiling, as she followed, leaving just me and Granny sitting there with Dean Martin singing from the speakers.

Bowled over by the revelation, I was lost for words. Eventually, I said, 'Goodness me, Granny, that was a bit of a shocker for Christmas lunch.'

'He had to know sometime, and it felt like the right moment to reveal all. I feel like it's all come out for a reason, you finding that note with the wine, and going to the vineyard near Verona. It was time.'

Poor Granny having to keep that secret for all those years. Dad must be devastated to find out he wasn't a real earl after all. But also, he was bound to be sad that Granny had kept such a vital piece of information from him about his lineage. And my grandfather, Angus, had gone to his grave without ever knowing who his real father was.

I got up and went round to the other side of the table, then I put my arms around Granny, squeezing her to me, and kissed her on the cheek. She was so small and slight, and couldn't have seemed more vulnerable.

'How will you be getting back to Keeper's Cottage, Granny? I'd offer to drive you, but I've had too much to drink.'

'Jenkins said he'll drop me home when I'm ready to leave.'

'Shall I arrange that for you?'

'Yes please, dear. I'm feeling rather fatigued after all the excitement.'

As I went to find Jenkins, I hoped Granny would be all right, but then it struck me that this would be a huge weight off her shoulders – a weight she'd been carrying all on her own for decades. This lunch had probably been quite cathartic for her. After Granny had left, with Jenkins promising to take good care of her, I decided to drop in and see Ben. It had gone five o'clock, and hopefully he'd be back from Gatley by now. Jenkins lent me a big, powerful torch, and I put on my boots, and grabbed a waterproof waxed jacket from the cloakroom – we had so many coats collected over the years, and this one had probably belonged to Mum. I held the jacket to my nose, and it still smelt faintly of the floral scent she used to wear. For a moment, I just stood there and allowed myself to be with her – she would be with me in my heart always, I knew that.

I went to get the silver bag containing Ben's present out of the car. Then I made my way along the path, through the cast-iron gate into the walled garden and towards Rosemary Cottage, where smoke wafted from the chimney, as if it were calling to me. Would he mind me dropping in unannounced like this, and on Christmas Day? It hadn't gone so well last time I'd turned up without messaging first. Perhaps I should send a quick text. Looking down at my phone, I saw that there was no signal. Never mind, it would have to be a surprise. What if Fiona had decided to visit again? I'd had quite a lot to drink that day, and I approached his cottage fuelled by Dutch courage, hoping he'd be pleased to see me.

CHAPTER 41

KATE

When I reached Ben's cottage, I knocked on the door, and he opened it.

'Kate, what are you doing here?'

'I didn't like to think of you being on your own on Christmas Day.' I handed him the silver bag. 'And I brought you a present.'

He took it, raising his eyebrows. 'That's very nice of you to check up on me, and to get me a present too.'

'It's nothing, really.'

'I was thinking about you earlier, after what you said about your Christmas lunch last year,' he said.

I liked that he'd been thinking about me. He looked out onto his drive.

'Did you walk over here from the house?'

I nodded, holding up the big torch Jenkins had lent me.

'That's a very impressive torch,' he said. 'I actually have something for you. Come on through. I just opened a bottle of Rioja, by the way...'

He'd got me a present too? My stomach fluttered.

'I will have to get back to the house for supper with Dad and Emilie, but I can stay for one, if that's okay?'

'Sure.'

I smiled and stepped over the threshold, then took off my jacket and hung it on the stand.

We went into his living room, where the lights twinkled on the Christmas tree and a fire crackled and popped in the hearth.

I sank into my favourite brown leather armchair, and he brought me a glass of Rioja. When I took a sip, it was warm and rich, and perfect for a winter evening. He went over to the Christmas tree, picked up something from underneath, and handed it to me.

'Thanks,' I said.

'Go on, open it then!'

I unwrapped my present and was thrilled to find an indoor herb garden in a box. There was a selection of commonly used herbs including basil, mint and oregano.

His gift was so meaningful, and I took a breath.

'You were saying how much you enjoyed eating fresh basil in Italy, and, seeing as you live in a flat, I thought you might like a way to grow your own.'

'That's so thoughtful of you, Ben. Thank you.'

'Although, after I bought it, I realised you're leaving that flat soon, aren't you?'

'Yes, I actually need to speak to Dad. I'm going to ask if I can move my stuff back to the house here while I decide what to do.'

'You'll be all right under the same roof as Emilie?'

'I'll have to be. Perhaps it's time I grew up...'

'It's understandable if you're struggling with seeing your father with someone else,' he said, gently.

It sounded as though he might be talking from experience, but I wasn't sure, and didn't want to press him further. He'd tell me about his life and family when he was ready.

'Are you going to open your present?' I said.

He lifted it out of the silver bag and tore off the wrapping paper to reveal the cheeseboard.

'This is great – we can use it when you come round on New Year's Eve.'

'Well, that's what I was thinking,' I said.

He ran his hand over it.

'It's made from oak – it's really beautiful. Thank you, Kate.'

'I got it in a farm shop down the road. It's handmade, apparently.'

He looked over at me.

'Well, I like it very much. How was lunch today?' he asked.

'It was a bit of a disaster.'

'Oh dear, really?'

I nodded. 'Everything was fine with Dad and Emilie – I'm getting used to the idea of them being together, and the baby now – but my granny just got a bit tipsy, that's all...'

I wasn't ready to tell him about her big revelation just yet. It was all quite personal for Dad, who was his boss after all.

'Well, I'm glad to hear that everything is okay with you and your dad. I hope your granny is okay, though?'

'She'll be fine, I'm sure. How was your lunch?'

'As good as could be expected.'

Clearly, he didn't want to elaborate either, and I didn't want to pry into his family dynamics. There was a pause, and I racked my brain for a safe subject to raise next. He studied me from his chair opposite as he glugged his wine.

'I'd better be going,' I said, putting my glass on the coffee table.

'What, already?'

I stood up, and Ben did the same. We went into the hall.

'I really do have to get back for supper – this will be my big chance to talk to Dad about my ideas for the vineyard.'

'My dad died when I was ten,' Ben said all of a sudden.

'What? Oh, Ben, I'm so sorry.'

'I'm sorry, Kate, to blurt it out like that. I just wanted to tell you because I can see how losing your mother has been so hard for you. I need you to know that I understand.'

'Ah, thank you. It really does help to know someone who gets what I've been through. Although you were only a child. It would have been even harder for you.'

He nodded.

'Yes, well... that's why Christmas Day can be difficult for me too. I don't get on with my stepfather or his sons. I'm very lucky to have my sister, Lily, though.'

'I always wished I had a sibling,' I said. And then I realised that soon, I would have one, well a half-sibling.

'Would you like me to walk you back?'

'No, it's fine, thank you, though. I need the time to mentally prepare for my chat with Dad.'

Ben held out my coat and I pushed my arms through the sleeves – what a gent. He opened the door, and I went outside and turned round.

'So, I guess we'll see each other on New Year's Eve?' he said.

'I'm looking forward to it.'

'So am I. Merry Christmas, Kate, and thanks for coming to see me. And for the cheeseboard – I shall treasure it.'

He threw me a serious look, and then he leant forwards, and kissed me on the lips. It was everything I imagined. I put my arms around his neck, and his hands rested on my waist, and then he pulled me to him. The kiss became more heated, the alcohol I'd been drinking all day making me bolder.

I pulled away, gently, and his face broke into an enormous smile as he said, 'Wow.'

Laughing, I said, 'Same! I'd better go.'

He took my hand and squeezed it, and said, 'Maybe on New Year's Eve we could do more of that.'

'I hope so,' I said, unable to wipe the huge grin off my face.

'Don't forget your herbs,' he said, disappearing into the living room. He reappeared with the box and handed it to me. I switched on Jenkins's torch, ready to make my way back through the kitchen garden to the house.

'Bye, Kate,' he called after me.

I looked over my shoulder and threw him a wave. Poor Ben, losing his father like that at such a young age. Now it made sense that he seemed to get what I'd been through.

When I reached the house, Jenkins let me in through the front door, and I put the herb box and my coat in the cloakroom. Then I found Dad in the library. He was sitting on the sofa, nursing a snifter of brandy.

'Where's Emilie?' I asked.

'She's having a nap. The baby is taking it out of her at the moment.'

'Are you okay, after Granny dropped her bombshell?'

He shook his head. 'It's an awful lot to absorb, but I've had a chance to calm down. It must have been difficult for her, having to keep that information to herself all these years.'

'I know, poor Granny.'

'And she's always been so good to me. How could I possibly fall out with her?'

'You couldn't.'

'Anyway, life goes on... where have you been?' he said.

'Oh, I just had to drop something at Ben's.'

'Really?'

'It was just a very small Christmas present.'

'You're even exchanging gifts? What did you get for him?'

'A cheeseboard.'

'That sounds very cosy. Did he get you anything?'

'A herb box.'

'Well, as I said before, I think you can do better, but deep down I know it's your decision.'

I didn't tell Dad that Ben and I had just made out on his

doorstep, and that I was on cloud nine and couldn't wait to go to my room and lie on my bed and daydream about him – about us being together.

'So, Dad… I wanted to ask how you'd feel about me moving back home for a short while. Sophie is throwing me out, and I don't have anywhere to go. I want to make sure that I find the right place this time rather than rush into making the wrong decision.'

'Of course, Kate. You know that you're always welcome to stay here whenever you want and for as long as you want.'

'Thank you, Dad. That's a relief. Do you think Emilie will mind?'

'Why should she? This is your home, and the house is more than big enough for all of us. The baby will be coming in April though, don't forget – I'm only saying that in case you'll find it difficult to come to terms with.'

'Well, I hope to have found somewhere by then anyway.'

'If you haven't, it isn't a problem.'

'Okay, thanks Dad. And there's one other thing.'

'What's that?'

'Is there any way I could persuade you to produce a very small limited edition of sparkling Pinot Grigio?'

'Oh Kate, how many times do we have to go through this?'

'But Dad, I really think this could be a good way to make money for Copeley Park. And I have so many other ideas too.'

'Like what?'

'Like all the events we could run. I've been looking at websites for other vineyards and there are so many things we could do – run craft-style classes such as basket-weaving, and then throw in a lunch with wine tasting. We could do more interesting tours, and throw in a cheeseboard or two as well. I have so many ideas.'

'But I thought you had plenty of book marketing work?'

'I do, but it takes so much effort to get new clients, and I'm not sure my heart is in it any more. And recently, it dawned on me that I can apply my skills to your business and take the pressure off you. You've been managing it all on your own for years. And I feel more of a connection to the vineyard than ever lately, especially since Granny gave me that bottle of Amarone.'

'I know. Your mother was so supportive – we used to talk through ideas for the vineyard all of the time. She was such a rock, your mum. I do miss her...'

'Oh Dad, so do I. We never talk about her, do we?'

'It's just so painful. I couldn't bear to for so long, but perhaps now some time has passed we should share our memories, maybe look at old photos.'

'I'd really like that, Dad. And on that note... I was thinking that, if we did produce a limited edition of this sparkling Pinot Grigio, we could call it Allegra after Mum?'

'Oh Kate, that's such a lovely idea.'

'Really, do you think so?'

'Yes.'

'And then I thought we could call the vintage version, if we produce one, Charlotte, after Granny?'

'I'm sure she'd be delighted.'

'Rosanna, the lady at the vineyard in Verona, has asked me to do holiday cover for someone who does her tours in March for a week or so, and I was thinking it might be helpful for Ben to come out for a few days to find out more about the sparkling Pinot Grigio that they produce there.'

'Hmm, that's a possibility, I suppose.'

'So, will you pay for his flights? I can get him a complimentary room.'

Dad looked at me and smiled, shaking his head.

'You are being rather persistent, but it's an admirable trait. Okay, you've worn me down, I suppose.'

'Shall I leave it to you to arrange that with him?'

'All right, I'll talk to Ben, and we'll see about putting some of the next batch of Pinot Grigio to one side so we can make a sparkling version – I'm thinking around two hundred bottles?'

'I would love that. And I can help promote it. That was another thing – I'd like to get involved with the social media accounts and start to increase the engagement, especially on Instagram.'

'Okay, I can send you the passwords. We don't update them often as I can't afford to pay someone just to manage social media.'

'Can I manage it then from now on?'

'All right. I'll send you Gina's number – she does general marketing and PR, but only three days a week – and you can liaise with her about various things.'

'Thanks, Dad.'

'I'm glad we had this chat, Kate. It's good to see you've got that fire inside of you again – I'm not sure how you got it back, but well done.'

Dad was right. I had got my fire inside back. And I knew it was all down to Verona, and Ben, and all that had started with Granny giving me the bottle of Amarone.

'I'm so excited about it all, Dad. I feel like I've found my purpose.'

'Good, well I need to go outside and get some fresh air.'

We both knew that meant he was off to have another cigar.

I got up and went into the grand hall, where the lights on the Christmas tree reminded me of the twinkling lights in Verona. So now I had the next few months of my life planned out. I would move my stuff in as soon as possible, and then in March I'd go back to Verona and hopefully Ben would come with me and find out more about making the sparkling Pinot Grigio. Things were looking up, at last.

CHAPTER 42

KATE

On New Year's Eve, I walked over to Ben's. We hadn't seen each other since *that kiss* on Christmas Day, and I wasn't sure if it had happened because we were both a little drunk, or because he wanted it to. Maybe he'd been aiming for my cheek, and somehow met my lips by mistake? It was all a blur, and I didn't know what to expect this evening. We'd exchanged a few messages, with me telling him that I was definitely moving to Copeley Park and couldn't wait for us to be neighbours. And I'd told him that Dad had finally agreed to produce a limited edition of sparkling Pinot Grigio. And he'd thought it a good idea for Ben to come to Verona with me and find out more about how the wine was produced there. I advised Ben to book the flights before Dad changed his mind.

I'd moved my stuff out of Sophie's flat during the dull no-man's-land period between Christmas and New Year, and now I was back in my childhood bedroom at Copeley Park. I counted myself very lucky – it was at the back of the house and looked out onto the lake.

When I arrived at Ben's cottage, he invited me inside, and instantly opened a bottle of chilled champagne.

'Only the very best on New Year's Eve,' he said.

'I did like your sparkling elderflower though,' I replied.

'Did you? I thought you were just being polite.'

'Not at all, I really did.'

'Soon you'll get to try my sparkling Pinot Grigio – well, in eighteen months or so.'

'It's all so exciting.'

'And thanks for getting your dad to pay for my flights to Verona. I feel fortunate to be going on such a trip.'

'I can't wait to show you this place – it's so special, you'll love it.'

The evening flew by as we knocked back the champagne quite speedily. Ben brought out a selection of cheeses – Brie, Roquefort, Cheddar, Manchego – on the board I'd given to him. I was touched that he was actually using it. He opened another bottle of champagne shortly before midnight.

'I was thinking that we could take our glasses into the walled garden. We should be able to see the fireworks from there.'

'I'd like that,' I said.

We put on our coats, and went outside and through the gate leading to the walled garden. We sat on a bench, and he put his arm around me, and pulled me to him. Right there in that moment, I couldn't have felt more happy with life – just being with him made everything okay. Nothing else seemed to matter when we were together – all my worries would just slip away. And then there was the first pop, fizz and bang and the sky was lit up by sparkles in green, pink, white, blue. The display was all very pretty, a perfect way for us to celebrate. Ben took my hand and gave it a squeeze.

'Happy New Year, Kate.'

'Happy New Year to you.'

He leant in and pressed his lips to mine, and the kiss was even better than the one on his doorstep. The fireworks carried on, and we kissed for most of that time, pausing for breathers, and then they stopped, but we carried on for a little longer, until Ben pulled away and cupped my face.

'Shall we get back in the warm?' he said.

I nodded, and he took my hand, and we went back to his cottage. Inside, he hung up his coat and went into the kitchen and, while I was sitting on the bench in the hall, taking off my boots, I noticed a package underneath. Curious, I picked it up – it was something in a brown padded envelope, and on the back it had the sender's address: a Mrs Deidre Clarkson at an address in Gatley, Surrey. Clarkson was a fairly common name, so I thought nothing of it, and put the package back underneath the bench. Then I went to fetch a glass of water from the kitchen. Ben was tidying up, putting glasses and plates next to the sink. I filled my glass from the tap, and glugged it down in an attempt to dilute some of the champagne we'd been drinking. Ben put his arms around me and pulled me to him and kissed me. The time felt right for us to go upstairs and be together at last. I'd waited long enough, and I was ready to be with him. But then it struck me. Deidre Clarkson. Wasn't she Jack's wife?

I pulled away from Ben, and said, 'How do you know Deidre Clarkson?'

'Err, she's my aunt, why?'

'And your surname is Grant?'

He nodded, eyes narrowing.

'She's my mum's sister. Where has all this come from?'

'I saw a package in the hall with Deidre Clarkson's name and address on it, and I wondered what she'd been sending to you.'

He looked at me.

'Ah yes, that's a book she sent me for Christmas. I was going to take it back because I have it already.'

'But... isn't she married to Jack Clarkson, my grandpa's cousin – the man who's been trying to get his hands on Copeley

Park for years? And before that, his mother, Lady Penelope, tried to do the same.'

'It's not what you think though, Kate.'

'And what do I think?'

'I don't know... I'm assuming that you're thinking there's a connection between me and Jack, and that I'm some kind of spy or saboteur on his behalf...'

'Are you?'

'Am I what?'

I looked at him, but said nothing.

He sighed, and pinched the bridge of his nose. 'He's just my uncle, well step-uncle actually, seeing as he's Aunt Deidre's second husband.'

'What?' I exclaimed. 'All those conversations we've had about him wanting to get his hands on this place, and about a potential saboteur. And he's your uncle?'

'Step-uncle.'

'What's the difference?'

'I don't get on with him. I applied for the job here to get away from working for him at Mendies vineyard.'

Shaking my head, I said, 'Ben, I just don't know what to believe. I mean, you've been lying to me the whole time.'

'How have I been lying to you?'

'Omitting the truth is lying, isn't it?'

'Okay, yes, but you have to understand why I didn't mention it. I couldn't see how it would be important, and just knew you'd jump to conclusions like this. I guess I was right.'

'Well done, you,' I said, snippily.

'Kate, listen. I think I know who the real saboteur is.'

'I have to go...' I walked towards the front door, and sat back on the bench to put on my boots and tie the laces.

'Where are you going, Kate?'

'Home.'

'What, why? But it's dark and cold out there...'

'I don't want to stay here tonight any more.'

I took my coat off the stand and put it on, doing up the zip to the top. Then I took my hat out of the pocket and pulled it onto my head.

'All right, well at least let me walk you back. Oh, you look so cute in that hat. Why do you have to go? I have a torch – it's not as big as the one Jenkins lent you, but it will do.'

'I don't need you to walk me back.'

'Please, let me come with you – so we can talk some more.'

'There's nothing more to say.'

'Oh come on...'

'You really don't have to,' I huffed.

But when I stepped outside, he came out too with his torch, and lit my way as we walked together in silence, through the kitchen garden, towards the house.

When we reached the front door, I said, 'Goodbye, Ben.'

'Wait, so that's it? When will I see you again?'

I sighed. 'Let's have a break from each other. I... need some space to think.'

'I'll message you,' he said.

I shrugged, and went up the steps. Jenkins opened the front door and let me inside. I went straight upstairs to my room, and climbed into bed fully clothed and burst into tears. And there I sobbed for ages, hot thick tears running down my face until eventually I got up to go and wipe my face. Standing there as I looked in the bathroom mirror, I couldn't have felt more devastated. Only half an hour earlier, Ben and I had been having the best time as we saw in the new year together, with fireworks for goodness' sake. Now everything was ruined – to think I'd believed I was actually in love with the man.

The next morning, when I picked up my phone, there was a message from Ben.

I'm not a spy or saboteur. Please don't tell your dad – he'll sack me. I think I know who the saboteur is, but I'm gathering evidence. When I've finished I'll show you. You have to trust me – I couldn't bear to not know you any more

I thought for a little while before replying, but there wasn't much to say, so I just settled on:

Ok.

Should I trust him? I was a believer in going with my gut – that was what Mum had always told me. And I'd always had good feelings about Ben as a person. Should I give him the benefit of the doubt? It wouldn't be fair or indeed my place to tell Dad what I'd found out. I would wait for Ben to gather his so-called evidence, and after that I'd make my decision about him. Besides, I needed him on side to make the sparkling Pinot Grigio now I'd persuaded Dad to give it a chance. In the meantime, I didn't want to have any contact with Ben. It was all too much. We needed time away from each other until I knew whether I could trust him or not.

All I could do was look forward to returning to Verona in March. I craved the calmness and clarity it had brought me back in November. How I hoped that being there would do me good just like it had last time... although I wasn't sure if I wanted Ben to be there too.

CHAPTER 43

KATE

In March, I flew back to Verona, and took a taxi to the Vineria di San Martino. Rosanna had arranged for me to have the Mimosa Suite in Villa Giulietta again. The air was warmer than in November. When I arrived, Rosanna showed me around all the areas that the tour groups would want to see and gave me some information sheets to use. I read them and memorised the information about the vineyard and the wine produced there. Groups came from all around the world – America, Australia, Scandinavia – and it was helpful to Rosanna that my first language was English. I would take them to see the vines Rosanna had shown me that day, and then on to the winery, and the cellars, where wine was stored in barrels made from French oak dating back to the eighteenth century. Afterwards, I'd take the tour group back to the restaurant, where they would sit at tables and taste the wine, as I had that day with Rosanna, and eat cheese and cold meats, served on a wooden board along with baskets of bread. There they'd get to see the view of Verona below – the River Adige twisting and winding and with bridges crossing from one side to the other.

Ben and I hadn't been in touch, not since he'd sent me that

message on New Year's Day, once again pleading with me to trust him, and saying that he would show me evidence. Well, I hadn't seen any evidence yet, and I found myself disappointed by what had almost been between us. Despite all of this, I still thought about him a great deal – there was no doubt I had been a little in love with him. This made our separation hurt even more. I'd been living at Copeley Park for the past couple of months, but we hadn't seen each other – and his cottage had only been at the other side of the kitchen garden. It seemed like such a waste – how lovely it would have been to spend that time together, if only we hadn't fallen out. I had no idea if he was still coming to Verona – perhaps he'd cancelled his flights. If he did turn up, I wasn't sure what I would say to him.

When I got back from a tour one day, I saw that the door to the Rosa Suite was open and there was a suitcase in the hallway. I held up my key to unlock my door, and then, there he was: Ben, standing in the hall, looking at me.

'Hello, Kate.'

'Ben... I wasn't sure if you were still coming.'

'Well, I'd booked the flights, so...'

I looked at him, but didn't know what to say.

'Do you feel like going for a walk? I only just got here, and can't wait to look around. It really is a beautiful spot.'

I wasn't ready to spend time with him yet.

'I'm really tired from doing tours all day, and was planning to have a rest before dinner.'

'Oh, well okay. What time are you going down for dinner?'

'Err, I hadn't thought about it.'

'Would you like to eat together?'

Maybe that would give me enough time to mentally prepare myself so I felt able to talk to him.

'Okay. Seven thirty?'

'See you then.'

I unlocked the door to my room and went inside and lay on the bed. Having tasted some of the wine along with people on the tour that afternoon, I needed a nap in order to deal with Ben that evening. I closed my eyes and drifted off to sleep.

That evening, I walked down to the restaurant early, giving myself half an hour to get a drink before seeing Ben. I went to the bar and ordered a vodka and tonic, and then the waitress showed me to our table as it was ready.

Ben appeared, on time at seven thirty prompt, and sat down opposite me. A waitress brought over two flutes and filled them with sparkling Pinot Grigio.

'I took the liberty of ordering us an aperitif, or I believe they say aperitivo here in Italy,' Ben said.

Picking up my flute, I raised it into the air, and said, 'Cin cin.'

Ben did the same.

'I knocked on your door, but as there was no answer assumed you'd walked down here without me.'

'I just wanted to have a vodka in the bar.'

'Why, because you needed a stiff drink before seeing me?'

Squashing a smile, I said, 'To be honest, yes.'

'Because...?'

'Because we went from kissing on your doorstep after exchanging cute Christmas gifts to arranging to spend New Year's Eve together, and sitting in the garden watching fireworks at midnight, to kissing again. And then I found out you're not who you say you are.'

'But I am, Kate.'

I looked across the table at him, unfolding my napkin and putting it on my lap.

The waitress came over. We both ordered crostini to share

as a starter, followed by spaghetti ragù and a salad to share. And a bottle of Amarone, why not.

'I've found out who the saboteur is,' Ben said.

Taken aback, I blinked. 'Really?'

He nodded.

'So, where's the evidence then?'

'On my phone.'

'Are you going to show it to me?'

He took his phone out of his pocket, slid his fingers across the screen and handed it to me.

'Press play.'

I did as he suggested, and watched the video. It started with Dad removing the bung from a barrel in the cellar, looking around, and slipping it into his pocket. Then there was footage of him putting together a mixture for the tractor that was used to distribute fungicide. He was adding in what appeared to be weed killer. I stopped the video, unable to believe what I was seeing. Why would Dad sabotage our vineyard?

'How did you get this?'

'I planted a few hidden cameras, bought online – they weren't expensive.'

'But it doesn't prove anything, does it?'

'Doesn't it? That barrel of wine turned to vinegar because the bung was left off, supposedly accidentally. He seems to be intentionally removing it. That's the second time it's happened now, meaning we've lost a lot of bottles of wine.'

'And the weed killer?'

'That footage is the day before your father claimed that "some damn fool" had sprayed a few rows of vines with weed killer instead of fungicide.'

'But why would my dad sabotage his own business?'

'Because he wants to get rid of it.'

'Don't be ridiculous.'

'If you think about it, it makes sense. He's got a new baby on the way and is almost sixty years old. He's tired and wants to enjoy his final years.'

Dad had told me this that day in the library.

'But why not just sell the estate then?'

'I don't know the answer to that. What do you think?'

I scratched my head. 'I... I'd have to think about it.'

He smiled, softly. 'How about we enjoy the rest of our dinner and forget it for now?'

'Good idea,' I said, sipping my drink. I really didn't want to think about Dad being a saboteur right now, and was still determined to enjoy my time on the vineyard.

After dinner, we walked back to our suites. By now it was dark, and the stars were visible – the sky was so clear. When we got back to Villa Giulietta, there was an awkward moment while I rummaged in my bag for my key. I didn't think it would be a good idea to kiss him. Yes, dinner had been nice, but I still didn't know what to think about the whole sabotage business. He was accusing my father of something quite huge. I'd seen the 'evidence', but was it actually evidence though?

'Goodnight, Kate,' Ben said, walking down the hall.

I went into my room and lay on my bed, looking up at the ceiling. Why would Dad do these things? I couldn't think of a reason at all. I'd have to mull it over, or hope that my subconscious would come up with the answer while I was asleep. There was something to be said for sleeping on a question.

The next morning when I woke up, I opened the French doors and went out onto the terrace in pyjamas and bare feet. The sun was warm on my face. Bliss! After that morning's tour I planned to go into Verona and wander around on my own for a couple of hours. I found myself wanting to go back to see the Juliet balcony, the place where I'd posted that letter about my feelings for Ben.

After the tour, I took a taxi straight to the Juliet balcony. And I stood there and looked up at it. Were Ben and I meant to be together? Now everything had changed again, and I wondered whether to place my trust in him and follow my heart as the Juliet Club had suggested in their reply to my letter. I couldn't help still being in love with him. And we were together in such a beautiful place – should we make the most of our time here together? Somehow, deep down, I found myself believing the evidence he'd shown me. It all made total sense that Dad would do something like that after everything he'd been through. He'd had enough of running Copeley Park, and who could blame him? Sabotage wasn't the best idea, but maybe he saw it as a way of getting out – although I didn't quite understand how. I needed to put myself forward as someone who was a safe pair of hands, so that he could step back and live his life.

A queue of tourists lined up to photograph the Juliet statue, and I moved out of their way. I felt so much stronger than when I'd visited this very spot before Christmas. Dad had been right at least when he said I did have fire inside of me again. I needed to give Ben a chance. He was a good man, and I did love him. I joined the queue of tourists, and made my decision – to touch Juliet's right breast to supposedly bring me luck in love. What did I have to lose?

That evening when I got back from Verona I met Ben for dinner again. We ate and then walked back to our suites. It was my last night on the vineyard. He'd be staying for another day.

This time when I got my key out of my bag to unlock my door, I said, 'Do you want to come in for a drink?'

Ben nodded, and we went inside. I opened the door to the minibar.

'What do you fancy?'

'You?'

I turned round, surprised. Before I knew what I was doing, I was in Ben's arms, and we were falling onto the bed together. He ran his hand up my sides and over my breasts. I sat up so that he could pull my top over my head – I'd been waiting so long for this moment. And now here I was with the man I'd fancied ever since I set eyes on him when he was peering through my car window in the pouring rain. After we took off each other's clothes, we paused for a moment, running our eyes over each other.

'I'm so glad we're doing this, at last,' Ben said.

He leant in to kiss me and pulled me to him.

Ben and I were lying in bed, the morning after the night before. I was resting my head on his perfect broad chest, and he had an arm round me.

'Well, I'm glad that finally happened,' he said.

'So am I.'

He leant on his side and looked at me, ran a hand through my hair.

'You have the most beautiful green eyes,' he said.

And then he leant in to kiss me.

I couldn't believe that we were finally together – last night had been passionate and tender, and I loved him.

As if reading my mind, he said, 'I love you, Kate. Well, I loved you from the moment I first saw you. You were a little grumpy, but it was understandable, of course.'

I squeezed his arm and rolled my eyes. 'Of course I was grumpy after your reckless driving.'

He kissed my head.

Thinking back, our first meeting couldn't have been more romantic. In fact, most of our liaisons had been incredibly romantic, and here we were now, consummating our love on a beautiful Italian vineyard.

'I love you too.'

'I'm glad about that. So when we get home, are we going to see each other?'

'What, you mean go out together, like boyfriend and girlfriend?'

He nodded.

'That's what I meant, yes.'

'You really want me to be your girlfriend?'

'I do, very much.'

He leant in to kiss me once again, and pulled me to him. I couldn't remember the last time I'd felt so happy.

But then we were interrupted by my phone buzzing, over and over again. Someone was trying to call me. Reluctantly, I pulled away to pick it up. No one ever called me, so it must be important. There was a message on the screen. It was a voicemail from Dad.

'It's my dad, he's been trying to call...' I listened to it.

Kate, it's Granny. She's deteriorated a great deal over the past few days, and is so thin and frail, she's a shadow of her former self. It's so sad to see her like this. Jane has brought in a nurse to help care for her. The doctor doesn't think she has long left now. I know you're flying back today anyway, so I wouldn't change anything, but it would be good if you're able to drop in and see her as soon as you can.

Oh no. This had been coming for a while, but I'd been in denial. I would go and see Granny on my way back from the airport. I wasn't looking forward to seeing her on her deathbed, but this wasn't about me. I had to do it for her – to hold her hand during her last moments and be there for her.

'It's Granny,' I told Ben.

'She's unwell?'

I nodded, and blinked back tears.

'I'm sorry.'
'Thanks, I'm going to have a shower and get dressed.'
'Okay.'
'And then I need to pack, and get ready to go home and see her.'

CHAPTER 44

LADY CHARLOTTE

I lay in bed at Keeper's Cottage. The curtains were pulled open, and I could see into the garden – it was showing signs of spring, and the daffodils had come out in the past week, their bright yellow heads pointing in all directions. Jane had opened the window, and I could hear the birds singing – such delightful company as I waited for the end. For I knew it was my time. I was done, and I'd lived a longer life than most.

I thought back to when I first came to Copeley Park – the awful wedding ceremony, and then Winston's tragic death. A memory I often returned to was meeting Bertie in the kitchen garden that morning he came across me weeding, amongst his broad beans – the look of horror on his face when he didn't know who I was! That was the moment when I first saw those green eyes, studying me from under the brim of his cap. We grew to know each other more as I went back to that garden every single day, and I slowly fell in love with him, although I didn't quite know it at the time. And then he saved me when I ran out of the front door after Winston fell down the stairs. He didn't utter a word to anyone about any suspicions he might have had about my involvement in my husband's tragic death.

And he saved me again from Lady Penelope when she tried to get her hands on Copeley Park – how clever he'd been coming up with the idea to turn it all onto her. But most importantly of all, Bertie came to the Italian vineyard with me. We fell madly in love in that wonderful setting – what a place to fall in love. And there in that vineyard, our son Angus was almost certainly conceived. And after him, along came Hugo and then followed dear Kate. Jane had told me that Kate had returned to the vineyard in Verona, and I was glad.

Bertie and I never did get to drink that bottle of Amarone together, but, when Jane found it that day in the drawer of the dresser, I was able to pass part of him on to our great-granddaughter. She'd been so lost for such a long time. Giving her the bottle of Amarone had been absolutely the right thing to do. Somehow, it had launched her into a new beginning – and that was what I'd been hoping for. Things hadn't been going well for her since her mother died. And then she foolishly married that Spencer – he wasn't right for her at all. I hoped that she would choose to spend more time with Ben from next door. He was the kind of man she should be with – he would care for her and be interesting company as well. He was her Bertie. And perhaps he would draw her back to Copeley Park, where she truly belonged.

KATE

When my plane landed at Gatwick airport, I drove straight to Keeper's Cottage. When I arrived, Jane let me inside and I went upstairs to find Granny in bed, in her room at the back of the house facing onto the garden. She was sitting up, supported by pillows. I went over and kissed her on the cheek, a lump in my throat. She was in her nineties, but still, I wasn't ready for her to die yet.

'Hello, dear Kate,' Granny said. 'How was Verona?'

I swallowed, and forced a smile. I didn't want her to see how I was feeling. I needed to be upbeat and good company during her final moments.

'It was good, but I was sad to hear you haven't been feeling well.'

'I don't have long left, dear, so I'm glad to see you.'

I pulled up a chair and placed it next to the bed and sat down.

'I would like you to do something for me,' she said.

'What's that? Anything.'

'Well, two things, actually. I would like you to scatter my ashes at the vineyard in Verona.'

Nodding, and blinking back tears, I said, 'Of course.'

She looked at me. 'Don't be sad. I've done very well to live this long.'

'I know.'

'And the other thing is that I'd like you to have this cottage.'

I gasped. 'What, really? Are you quite sure, Granny?'

'Your father was telling me that you've moved back into the main house. I know that will be difficult for you with Emilie there, and the baby arriving soon. I think you'll be very happy here, and you'll be near your friend Ben.'

'Granny, I don't know what to say.'

'Who else am I going to leave it to? It's yours, my dear, to enjoy. And take my advice, don't let that Ben get away. I just know you are perfect for each other. Just like Bertie and I were.'

'Thank you.' I leant over and kissed her on the forehead.

'I'd be delighted if you drank the bottle of Amarone meant for Bertie and me when you have something to celebrate. Promise me you'll do that?'

I nodded. 'Are you sure?'

'I'm absolutely certain.'

'Well, I would be honoured to do that. I love you, Granny.'

She put her hand on mine, and left it there, and gave me a weak smile. And we sat there for a while together until she slowly closed her eyes. I stayed with her a while longer, unable to move, but eventually I kissed her again, one last time, closing my eyes as I did so. Then I stood up, my heart heavy, and went to get Jane.

Jane felt for Granny's pulse for a moment, and then sighed.

'I'm so sorry, Kate.'

I burst into tears, and Jane handed me a tissue.

'She was wonderful to work for. I shall really miss her,' she said.

'Me too,' I said through my sobs. 'I loved her so much.'

Dear Granny – what would I do without her in my life? I would just have to be strong – that's what she'd want, and I would do it for her.

In the two weeks that followed, we were dealing with Granny's death. Dad had to make all the funeral arrangements, and it was immensely sad for us both. It certainly wasn't the time to talk to him about what Ben had told me. The funeral came and Granny was cremated. She had indeed said in her will that she'd like me to take her ashes to Verona, and also that Keeper's Cottage was mine.

After a couple more weeks had passed, I decided to talk to Dad about the whole saboteur business. It was time. But was Ben right? I had seen his video evidence, but what if it had been manipulated in some way? Why would Ben bother to do that though? It must have been difficult for him to tell me, knowing that he was coming between me and my father. What was I supposed to do about any of it? If I confronted Dad and he confessed to being the saboteur, then what? Should I be understanding? I still couldn't fathom the reason why he would do such a thing to his own business.

One morning I was sitting in the kitchen, on a stool at the island, scrolling my phone. The radio played in the background. Dad came in.

'Morning, darling.'

I was so worried about bringing up what Ben had told me. But I had to, I knew that. It was the only way I'd know the truth. Was now the time? He seemed to be in a reasonable mood.

'Dad, can I talk to you about something?'

'Yes, of course.'

He spooned coffee granules into a cafetière and added hot water from the kettle.

'Would you like some coffee?'

'Yes please.'

He waited a minute and then plunged the cafetière and brought it over to the kitchen island with two mugs and milk from the fridge.

'What is it, Kate?'

It was then that I realised I couldn't tell him that I'd seen Ben's footage – Dad might then be furious and sack him. I didn't want Ben to lose his job – I knew how much he needed it and Rosemary Cottage.

'I was just wondering about all the things that have been going wrong on the vineyard, and you know my theory that someone could have been doing those things on purpose?'

'Hmm.'

Dad filled our mugs with coffee and put one of them on my side of the island.

'Is there anything you want to tell me?' I asked, carefully.

Dad sipped his coffee and looked across at me.

'What do you mean?'

I raised my eyebrows.

'Kate…'

'I know, Dad.'

'Know what?'

'Do I really need to spell it out?'

He tapped his fingers on the island, then swallowed.

'I'm sixty years old next month, and I have a new baby due any minute. I've worked really hard for most of my life, and I am tired.'

'So...?'

'So, I'm ready to sell.'

'To Grandpa's cousin, Jack?'

'Yes.'

'But why devalue the business first?'

'Because your granny wouldn't have accepted it otherwise. I needed to be able to tell her that I had no choice about selling.'

'Couldn't you have waited?'

'For what?'

'For her to die?'

'Yes, well, obviously that's happened now... and I'm very sad about it. You know I was fond of her, and how she'd doted on me since I was a little boy. I didn't want to disappoint her by selling so willingly.'

'Okay,' I said, thinking furiously. I just couldn't let this happen. 'So how about you let me run the business for you?'

'Are you serious?'

'I have some great ideas. And we just can't let it go, Dad. Not now we know it was the product of Granny's great love. She and Bertie dreamt of this vineyard together – it's part of our family history. We just can't give it up.'

'I know you are more than capable of doing it, Kate, but I wasn't sure you'd want to. But you're right, it should stay in our family.'

'You have a fantastic team of staff, including Ben. I'd start by promoting him.'

'That's fair. He's good at what he does.'

'Would you consider moving out of this house?'

'To be honest... I really want to go and live in the villa in St

Tropez with Emilie and the new baby. I wasn't sure whether to mention it – I worry about leaving you here all alone.'

'Dad, it doesn't take long to fly to Nice... besides, I'll be all right. I'm a big strong girl now.'

'Are you sure?'

I nodded. 'Granny is leaving me Keeper's Cottage, so we can open up the house for tours. I think there's so much potential – and you can always visit, any time.'

'Why don't you let me have a think about it?'

'Okay.'

Was Dad really going to come round to what I was asking for, at last? How I hoped he'd make the right decision and let me take over Copeley Park. I just knew I could do it, especially with Ben by my side, cheering me on.

CHAPTER 45

KATE

That evening, I sat in the blue drawing room to watch television. I picked up the remote control, ready to watch something mindless – a reality show or something similarly undemanding, anything to get lost in for an hour or so before going to bed. Although I was tired out, I needed to wind down in order to fall asleep. Lifting my wine glass, I took a sip, but it didn't taste very nice at all. Was it off? I tried it again, but couldn't work out what the problem was – the wine didn't seem acidic, but it wasn't going down well at all. Maybe I was just too tired after the past few days – it had been an emotionally draining time, after all.

I put the glass down on the coffee table and selected an episode of *Friends* on Netflix. It was the one where Rachel was pregnant, and she was working out how to tell Ross. I paused the television and went into the kitchen and tipped the wine down the sink. Then I filled the kettle and put it on. I'd have a cup of tea instead.

Back in the living room, I unpaused the television and watched Ross react to Rachel telling him she was pregnant with his baby. He seemed so surprised that condoms didn't always work. I thought back to Verona, when I'd slept with Ben on that last night in the Mimosa Suite – it had been *the* perfect night until the condom split. I had to explain about my problems conceiving with Spencer, and the whole IVF experience. I hadn't told him up until that point, as I wasn't ready to share my baggage with him. And what if he didn't want to be with someone who might not be able to have children? I'd been getting ahead of myself by thinking such thoughts. Then he told me that, even if somehow we'd conceived that night, it would be okay, as we loved each other, and we'd find a way forward together.

We'd gone into the lounge area of our room and I'd made us both a cup of tea. He gave me a big hug, and told me how sorry he was that I'd had to go through all that – why hadn't I told him sooner? He would have been supportive and talked through it all with me. But it hadn't occurred to me that he'd want to. Spencer never wanted to talk about anything beyond surface-level conversation – he wasn't the deepest person – and this was all a novelty to me. I found it refreshing, to be with a man who seemed so emotionally mature. And who didn't appear to have a manipulative bone in his body.

When my cup of tea was cool enough to drink, I took a sip – and then it struck me. It had been the best sex I'd ever experienced, and that wasn't just because I was attracted to Ben. It was also because I had the deepest emotional connection I'd ever had with a man.

I was sure that although Ben said how much he loved me and had never met anyone like me before... love was really shown through actions. If he really loved me, he would show me when the time came. Wasn't that what men did in rom-com films when they really loved a woman? I was being old-fashioned, and I knew this, but I did love a good old rom-com, like *When Harry Met Sally* or *You've Got Mail*, and especially *The Holiday*, my favourite of all, especially as it had been partly filmed in Godalming and Shere, just down the road from Copeley Park. And didn't we all want to be in Cameron Diaz's position when Jude Law turned up at her cottage late that night after the pub. The best meet-cute ever!

Pulling up the calendar on my phone, I checked when my last period had been. A few days before our encounter. Damn. I looked up at the television as Ross continued to react to Rachel's news. So there was a small possibility that I might be pregnant too. But I couldn't let myself believe it – never mind work out how I felt about the idea. I would just have to get a test and find out.

The next day after work, when I got back from the chemist, I sat on my bed and took the small box out of its paper bag and turned it over in my hands. I couldn't bear to think how much money I'd spent on these tests when I was with Spencer. All those times I'd peed on a stick and waited and waited for the line to appear – it always seemed to take forever. And then there would be a negative reading and I'd put my head in my hands and have a good old sob. This continual testing and subsequent disappointment had gone on and on until I couldn't take it any more.

I'd suggested to Spencer that we consider adoption or try a sperm donor. But he had no interest in bringing up the child of another man, even if it was carried by me. Besides, our marriage was in tatters after the whole IVF experience. I'd started to ask myself why we were together – did we actually have anything in common apart from our place of work?

Sighing, I took the stick out of the box, went into the bathroom and did what I needed to do, and left it on the side of the bath. Then I went downstairs into the kitchen and made myself a strong coffee and sat down and stared into space. What would I do if it was positive? I hadn't expected this to ever happen for me, and wasn't mentally prepared at all. All those times I'd wanted it to be positive, and now there was a possibility that it could be and I wasn't sure if I wanted it to be. What would Ben say if and when I told him? Of course, I'd have to tell him. Would this be what he wanted? I knew that he loved me – that we were made for each other – but did he want a child? Did he want to be with me for the rest of his life?

I went back into the bathroom, picked up the stick, and there it was. Positive. I was actually pregnant. This was unbelievable. After all those times trying with Spencer, and paying a small fortune for IVF, I'd conceived with Ben on our first night together. I smiled to myself – I'd been desperate for this to happen for such a long time, and now it had happened with the man I wanted to spend the rest of my life with. Although there were another six weeks until I was through the most dangerous part – where losing the baby was a stronger possibility – I was halfway there. I needed to tell Ben, and couldn't wait to see his reaction – he would be happy, wouldn't he? But not over the phone. I should go to Rosemary Cottage and tell him right now.

I slipped the test into my handbag and pulled it onto my shoulder. It was a perfect spring evening, and I could smell the blossom on the apple trees as I passed through the kitchen garden. As I walked, my stomach filled with butterflies – I was so excited but also so nervous about telling Ben this huge news. What would he say? When I reached his cottage, I rapped the knocker and went straight inside. I could hear the clattering of pots and pans in the kitchen.

'Hello,' I called out.

Ben came into the living room, smiling, a tea towel in one hand and a plate in the other. He put them down.

'Oh, hello, Kate.'

He leant forwards, and we kissed on the lips.

'Have you had a good day?' I asked.

He shrugged. 'It's been all right.'

'I have something to tell you.'

He cast me a puzzled look. 'What's that then? You seem to be very excited about something by that look in your eyes.'

'I think you should sit down.'

'What, really? It must be important then.'

He took the armchair in front of the fire, and I sat opposite. Then I opened my handbag and took out the test and handed it to him.

'What's this? Oh...' He looked down at the test and then threw me a quizzical look. 'Is this what I think it is?'

'Yes.'

He inhaled. 'But what about... after all that IVF and everything, you didn't think...'

'I know. I never expected to get pregnant. The doctor did say it might happen with someone else – but I'm sorry, if it's not what you want. I—'

'Kate...'

'What?'

His face broke out into a huge smile. 'It's wonderful news.'

'Really, you think so?'

'Yes!'

'You want to have a baby with me?'

'Of course I do. I love you more than I've ever loved anyone in my whole life. How pregnant are you?'

Did he really just say that? My heart warmed.

'I think around six weeks, but I would have to work it all out properly.'

He stood up and came over to me and took my hands, and pulled me gently out of the chair, and put his arms around me and squeezed me to him tightly.

'I really do love you, Kate, so very much.'

'I love you so very much too.'

He kissed me, and looked into my eyes.

'I'd ask if you wanted to get married, but know you aren't divorced yet.'

I laughed.

'Is that a proposal?'

'I believe it is. But only if you wanted it to be. I'm just trying to say the right thing here. What do *you* want?'

'Well, as you say, I'm nowhere near getting divorced from Spencer. We haven't even filed any paperwork yet. But still, I'm not sure if you and I need to be married to be together. It didn't exactly work for me last time. Let's wait and see, and if it feels right that's what we'll do.'

He grinned at me, 'That sounds like a good plan to me. I love you so much. But at the same time, if you wanted—'

'Let's just be happy about the baby. I know you're trying to do the right thing, and that's lovely of you.' I leant in and kissed him on the lips. 'We can talk it all through.'

'Okay.' He smiled, and cupped my face. 'We'll work it all out in time, when we've had a chance to absorb this news. I'm so excited, though.'

'So am I. I just can't wait to have a baby with you,' I said.

EPILOGUE

KATE

THE VINEYARD NEAR VERONA, MARCH 2017

Ben took a right and drove uphill to the main reception at Vineria di San Martino. We were there to fulfil Granny's request to scatter her ashes at the vineyard near Verona. Afterwards, we planned to drive to a villa in Lake Garda and spend a few days together as a family. We'd brought our daughter, Melissa with us. Ben parked, and I got out and opened the back door, and lifted her out of the car seat. She was such a cute little pudding of a baby, with a thick head of blond hair and big blue eyes – the same colour as Granny's. I'd chosen my favourite dress for her, with pink and purple flowers. It had a matching pink cardie to go with it. I loved her so much, and I'd been so overjoyed to be given a daughter by the man I loved. Although Melissa was only a few months old, we already had such a unique and special bond. I felt as though I'd been given a mother–daughter relationship again – something I'd missed very much – and I was so grateful.

Now, it would be about Melissa and me – I had all my lovely memories of Mum to look back on, and at last I felt strong enough to do that. But she'd been gone for almost seven years, and it was time for me to move on, and think about the next generation. With my new little family of Ben and Melissa, I felt complete, and couldn't wish for anything more – well, perhaps one more baby if we were lucky enough to have one. My divorce from Spencer was going through and would be finalised soon. Ben and I still hadn't decided whether we'd get married. We would talk about it, and I knew we'd come to a decision that suited us best. All that mattered was that we were together.

When we got back, Copeley Park would be ours to manage. Dad had recently moved to his villa in St Tropez with Emilie and their new daughter, Celine. I was living at Rosemary Cottage with Ben, and we were renting Keeper's Cottage out to holidaymakers and ramblers. Perhaps we might end up living there if we had another child, and then we'd rent out Rosemary Cottage instead. Celine was an adorable little girl. I'd chosen to embrace my role as her half-sister, taking her pretty clothes and fun toys and books. Ben, Melissa and I would go and stay in St Tropez in the summer. There were only a few months between Celine and Melissa, and it would be lovely for them to grow up together.

The first bottles of sparkling Pinot Grigio would be ready in another few months, in time for Christmas, and I couldn't wait to try it. I'd added so many events to the Copeley Park website, and they were getting booked up already. The house would open for tours in the autumn, and I'd arranged a series of classes – painting, basket-weaving, flower arranging – that could be combined with wine tasting and a light lunch. It was all so exciting, and I was glad that Dad was giving me this opportunity to spread my wings.

And none of this would probably have happened if Granny hadn't given me that bottle of Amarone for my thirtieth birthday and booked the tickets for me to go to the vineyard near Verona. Who knew what path I would have taken instead? Perhaps I would still have met Ben, as Granny had been so determined for us to know each other. But I'd loved the way we met on that rainy autumn afternoon – I often thought back to that moment when he'd peered at me through my car window. And Rosemary Cottage had played its part in bringing us together too – could we have had a more romantic setting in which to get to know each other? Unravelling the truth about Granny and Bertie had brought new meaning and importance to ensuring we kept Copeley Park in the family, and the future was exciting.

Ben, Melissa and I were going to stay in the Mimosa Suite on the Italian vineyard – it was where Melissa had been conceived on that special night together. That evening, we planned to open the bottle of Amarone from 1936 at last, to celebrate our love for each other, and the arrival of our beautiful daughter. And we'd raise a glass to dear Granny and Bertie. The following morning after breakfast, we would scatter Granny's ashes, and I'd take a moment to think about her, and all she'd done for me. She'd lived such a big life – none of us had even known she'd been grieving the loss of her one true love all these years. I could only feel lucky that we had the chance to let that story into our lives before she died – those last moments with my granny would stay in my heart forever.

A LETTER FROM ANITA

Dear reader,

I want to say a big thank you for choosing to read *The Italian Vineyard*. If you enjoyed it, and want to keep up to date with all my latest releases, just sign up at the following link. Your email address will never be shared and you can unsubscribe at any time.

www.bookouture.com/anita-chapman

I hope you enjoyed *The Italian Vineyard* and, if you did, I would be very grateful if you're able to write a review. I'd love to hear what you think, and it makes such a difference helping new readers to discover one of my books for the first time.

And I love hearing from my readers – you can get in touch via my website, and follow me on X, Facebook, Instagram and TikTok to see updates about my books and everyday life as a writer.

Thanks, and best wishes,

Anita Chapman

KEEP IN TOUCH WITH ANITA

www.anitachapman.com

- facebook.com/anitachapmanauthor
- x.com/neetschapman
- instagram.com/neetschapman
- tiktok.com/@neetschapman

ACKNOWLEDGEMENTS

Thank you so much for helping to make this book happen:

To my editor, Lucy Frederick, for the initial conversations about this book, and for doing such a thorough job on the structural and line edits – I really felt they took this book to a whole new level.

To the rest of the Bookouture team, always so dedicated, efficient and friendly, and senders of beautifully written emails. To see who has worked on this book, see the information in the following pages.

Special thanks to cover designer, Debbie Clement who has once again designed the most incredible cover! I was absolutely blown away when my editor, Lucy sent it to me. Also thank you to copy-editor, Jacqui Lewis, who has done an absolutely thorough job – I am so grateful for all the things she picks up. And to proofreader, Anne O'Brien who also found lots of important things.

To the reviewers who read advance copies via NetGalley and for the blog tour. I really appreciate you taking the time to read *The Italian Vineyard* and write reviews before publication day. It's so wonderful to have your support, and it always gives me such a warm feeling to see your social media posts and reviews go up during launch week. Special thanks to Barbara Wilkie, Anne Williams, Karen Hilton, Linda McFall and Lizanne Lloyd who have reviewed all of my books. A special thanks here to my lovely publicist, Jess Readett, who has once again organised a wonderful blog tour.

To Nancy and Oliver at Greyfriars Vineyard in Surrey for talking to me about the vineyard and the wine produced there. I'd already put sparkling Pinot Grigio in the book when I went to visit, so couldn't believe it when they told me that they were producing a limited edition this summer! I've tried it and have bought a bottle to drink on publication day. Also thank you to Simon Akeroyd, Head of Estates and Historic Landscape at Painshill Park for speaking to me about eighteenth-century gardens, winemaking and the vineyard there which was started in the eighteenth century, left to decay and replanted in the 1990s.

To the Vineria San Mattia in Verona for the most wonderful few days which included a fascinating tour of the vineyard. I really enjoyed the wine tasting afterwards too where I got to try Valpolicella and Amarone.

To my social media followers, especially all those who continue to cheer me on and share news about my books.

To my family and friends.

To everyone who bought, read, spread the word about and wrote reviews for my other novels, *The Venice Secret, The Florence Letter* and *The Tuscan Diary*. Thank you for encouraging me to write more books with your lovely words.

PUBLISHING TEAM

Turning a manuscript into a book requires the efforts of many people. The publishing team at Bookouture would like to acknowledge everyone who contributed to this publication.

Commercial
Lauren Morrissette
Hannah Richmond
Imogen Allport

Cover design
Debbie Clement

Data and analysis
Mark Alder
Mohamed Bussuri

Editorial
Lucy Frederick
Melissa Tran

Copyeditor
Jacqui Lewis

Proofreader
Anne O'Brien

Marketing
Alex Crow
Melanie Price
Occy Carr
Cíara Rosney
Martyna Młynarska

Operations and distribution
Marina Valles
Stephanie Straub
Joe Morris

Production
Hannah Snetsinger
Mandy Kullar
Nadia Michael
Ria Clare

Publicity
Kim Nash
Noelle Holten
Jess Readett
Sarah Hardy

Rights and contracts
Peta Nightingale
Richard King
Saidah Graham

RAISING READERS
Books Build Bright Futures

Dear Reader,

We'd love your attention for one more page to tell you about the crisis in children's reading, and what we can all do.

Studies have shown that reading for fun is the **single biggest predictor of a child's future success** – more than family circumstance, parents' educational background or income. It improves academic results, mental health, wealth, communication skills, and ambition.

The number of children reading for fun is in rapid decline. Young people have a lot of competition for their time, and a worryingly high number do not have a single book at home.

Our business works extensively with schools, libraries and literacy charities, but here are some ways we can all raise more readers:

- Reading to children for just 10 minutes a day makes a difference
- Don't give up if children aren't regular readers – there will be books for them!
- Visit bookshops and libraries to get recommendations
- Encourage them to listen to audiobooks

- Support school libraries
- Give books as gifts

Thank you for reading: there's a lot more information about how to encourage children to read on our website.

www.JoinRaisingReaders.com

Printed in Dunstable, United Kingdom